THE
GIRL
ON
WILDFIRE
RIDGE

BOOKS BY LESLIE WOLFE

DETECTIVE KAY SHARP SERIES

The Girl From Silent Lake

Beneath Blackwater River

The Angel Creek Girls

The Girl on Wildfire Ridge

TESS WINNETT SERIES

Dawn Girl

The Watson Girl

Glimpse of Death

Taker of Lives

Not Really Dead

Girl With A Rose

Mile High Death

BAXTER & HOLT SERIES

Las Vegas Girl

Casino Girl

Las Vegas Crime

STANDALONE TITLES

Stories Untold

Love, Lies and Murder

ALEX HOFFMANN SERIES

LESLIE WOLFE

THE
GIRL
ON
WILDFIRE
RIDGE

Published by Bookouture in 2022

An imprint of Storyfire Ltd.
Carmelite House
50 Victoria Embankment
London EC4Y 0DZ

www.bookouture.com

ISBN: 978-1-80314-705-5
eBook ISBN: 978-1-80314-704-8

ONE
THE FALL

It was finally over.

Shaking and whimpering, she could hear their voices, merciless and gutting in their indifference, sprinkled with bursts of laughter as they departed from the ridge. They climbed down hastily, probably to catch the thinning remainders of daylight before heading into the woods.

The chill of the evening air rattled her aching body. Even summer nights were cold on Wildfire Ridge, although snow melted every spring and didn't fall until late September. Slowly rolling onto her side, she hugged her knees as tears started falling again. Silent tears, of humiliation and defeat, of unspeakable shame. In the distance, the waning bouts of laughter felt like slaps across her tear-stained face.

She was alone.

No one had heard her screams. No one could help her.

The words they had said still resonated in her mind. The names they called her. The unspeakable things they did to her. All she wanted to think of was home, her mother's loving arms and healing touch. Feeling safe again. Hiding what had happened to her from her father because she couldn't imagine looking him in the eye if he ever found out. Only her mom would understand. She would keep her secret safe.

But home was far away, a three-hour mountain hike in the dark, by herself, coming down from the peak on rocky terrain and through thick woods, then fifteen miles or so on the road from the southwestern versant of Mount Chester to the small California town that bore its name. Might as well have been a hundred miles. The thought of crossing the woods in the dark gripped her heart with merciless, frozen fingers. Every forest sound she used to find soothing when the sun was shining, now spoke menacing whispers in rustling leaves and evergreen cones.

The night was falling hard on Wildfire Ridge, the last hues of orange, crimson, and red that had earned the peak its name fading quickly with the setting sun. The deep, menacing red vanished last, a blood-smeared reminder of the day that had ended, an unspoken threat of the day to come.

Still dizzy and growing weaker with each passing minute, she tried to sit up. Her body, aching and bleeding, put up a fight, and her willpower was quickly defeated. Setting her throbbing head down on the coarse moss-covered boulder, she resigned herself to face the cold darkness alone on the mountain.

The sound of a snapped twig sent her heart racing, thumping against her rib cage. Was it a bear?

"Hello."

The voice, a low, throaty whisper, startled her back to a state of disoriented alertness. The night chill had seeded icicles in her blood. Numb, shaky, and frozen, she found the strength to sit up.

Maybe there was hope. Soon she'd be home again, warm and safe. Confusion engulfed her brain like a persistent fog, clinging to every corner of her mind, fueling her fears. With a fleeting thought, she realized she'd been drugged. She had to have been, or she would've been on her way home already. Seeing the dark silhouette against the moonlight, she desperately wanted to run but knew she couldn't.

What was the stranger doing there? It was too late in the day for anyone to wander on Wildfire Ridge just by accident.

Her breath caught in her chest, and she took the hand offered, noticing in passing the warmth of the skin that touched hers. She stood and struggled for a bit to find her footing, then let go of the stranger's hand. Dizziness made the mountain crest spin and dance against the star-filled August sky. Out of balance, she grabbed a thick hemlock branch and steadied herself.

Her eyes followed the stranger's cold, analytical gaze, failing to understand why she saw hatred in those eyes, hoping she was reading it wrong. Her clothes were a mess, torn and bloodied. With trembling fingers, she tried to cover herself as best she could, fresh tears of shame burning her eyes and blurring everything around her.

"Will you help me?" she whimpered.

A short cackle tore through the silence of the mountain night. "Help you? Dear girl, what happened to you today was entirely your doing and nothing short of what you deserve. You're nothing but a cocktease."

The words dropped onto her like tombstones, heavy, menacing, deadly.

Fear gripped her chest, paralyzing her. Her chin trembled, threatening sobs she didn't welcome. "Please... I'm not... I haven't done anything—"

The blow came unexpectedly, shattering her breath. Jenna heard it splitting the air before she felt it burning her face, bursting her lip, sending stars in a whirlwind dance inside her brain.

This wasn't happening. It had to be a nightmare. Something that couldn't exist in the light of day, only in the deep, troubled shadows of Wildfire Ridge. Yet the metallic taste of blood on her lips proved differently.

Afraid of another blow, Jenna took a step back, then another. With each step, she tried to put more distance between her and the assailant, but that distance was narrowing down instead. Slipping on a pebble, she lost her footing for a moment. She yelped, then continued feeling her way, stepping backward without looking, unable to take her eyes off the threatening, vengeful gaze inching closer to her.

Her faltering steps loosened a few pebbles and sent them over the edge of the cliff, rattling and bouncing against sharp rock edges until she couldn't hear them anymore. She was closer to the abyss than she'd realized. Afraid she'd fall, she stopped, willing herself to move away from the edge of the cliff and fight her way back to safety if she had to.

The stranger smiled and took one more step, eyes glinting like ice picks against the weak rays of the crescent moon.

She screamed as she fell, grasping desperately as the merciless hand pushed her firmly over the edge of the ridge. Then the scream stopped abruptly, inviting the silence of the night to take over once the echoes died.

TWO
RENEWAL

One more day, maybe three, and the kitchen would be done.

Detective Kay Sharp had been telling herself that for the past few days, when she pushed herself to leave the warmth of her bed before first light, to work on spackling the kitchen walls before the start of her day.

Rubbing her eyes and fighting pointlessly against a yawn, she stretched and walked into the small bathroom. Cold water dissolved whatever remnants of sleep still clung to her eyelids. When she looked at herself in the mirror, she smiled tentatively, shyly, as if she were planning to flirt shamelessly with a heart-throb at some fancy ball, not run sandpaper over dried spackling to smooth it over.

It was the age of renewal, of healing.

It was time.

Back in her bedroom, Kay slid on a pair of paint-stained denim shorts and an old Metallica T-shirt. A couple of years ago, she'd reluctantly condemned that T-shirt to be worn for chores after an incident with a spilled glass of red wine. Several faint purple blotches still stained the fabric, underlining the name of her once-favorite rock band.

Like the T-shirt, the kitchen walls had stories to tell, one for every scuff, scratch, dent, or hole. Unlike the fading wine stain, those stories were mostly painful, forever etched into her memory with the sound of her mother's cries and sobs. The smell of drunken sweat coming from her father. The taste of tears on her lips. The fear in her brother's round eyes as he crouched behind the couch.

Scars memorialized in weathered drywall; a testimony of the years Kay desperately wanted to forget.

Maybe a layer of light-yellow wall paint and smoothness that would make a professional contractor choke with envy could erase some of those flickers of nightmare still embedded into her memory.

Tiptoeing into the kitchen, she filled the coffee maker quietly, careful not to wake Jacob. Moments after she'd pressed the button, the aroma of French Vanilla filled the kitchen with the promise of an excellent day. Those two hours she took in the mornings to fix the walls were hers. Hers alone. She was still looking for healing, processing her trauma, reliving every moment, hopefully for the last time. There was no reason to drag her brother into this; he seemed to have put the past behind him in typical male uncomplicated style. His role had been limited to signing off on the paint color, his protests drowned by Kay's voice, seconded by his girlfriend's, in an instant alliance of female dominance in all matters pertaining to the way a home should look.

She took the lid off the can of spackling and started covering up some holes with the pink paste that turned white as it dried. It smelled fresh, of new walls and cleanliness. Sanding yesterday's patchwork was second on the agenda for when Jacob would wake up. Sanding walls, even by hand, was noisy.

She'd worked counterclockwise through the kitchen, starting from the window above the sink. Yesterday, she'd noticed the back door structure needed a little more work, its frame loosened by years of being slammed angrily by her father's hand. Jacob had reserved a pleasant surprise for her. The frame was stabilized, and the walls that held it were ready to be worked on.

Finishing up a long scratch where the leg of a chair had landed after being thrown across the room during one of her father's drunken outbursts, Kay realized she'd been holding her breath for a while. She forced air into her lungs slowly, then held it in for a couple of seconds before releasing it. If she closed her eyes for a brief moment, she could hear the shouting, the chair flying over the table, then slamming against the wall with a thud before falling to the ground.

Her hand froze in midair after she loaded the spackling knife with more pink paste. Then it started shaking and turned heavy. Kay dropped the knife into the can, her eyes burning with tears as she stared intently at a small hole in the wall. Since the renovation project started a few days earlier, she'd been avoiding that spot. She'd been veering her eyes away from it for sixteen years.

Her shaky index finger touched the edges of the small hole, where the drywall had cracked and crumbled when she'd removed the bullet from it with the tip of a steak knife. The bullet that nearly killed her brother. The bullet she'd fired with her father's gun.

A sob shattered her breath and stopped on her lips as she covered her mouth with her hand. "Oh, God," she whispered as tears flooded her eyes.

"Hush now, sis," Jacob whispered, wrapping his strong arms around her. Lost in her past, she didn't hear him come into the kitchen. "Soon, you won't even know where this hole was," he added, a tinge of humor in his voice. He rocked her back and forth slightly as she sobbed, her face buried at his chest. "Everything will be, um, lemon meringue yellow. That the color we're painting these walls?"

"Uh-huh," she mumbled, wiping her eyes with the back of her hand. She pulled herself away a little but couldn't look her brother in the eye. Not yet.

"Who gives shades of paint these stupid names? Can you imagine having that job? Making up stupid, crazy shit all day and calling it work?"

She glanced at Jacob quickly, then looked away. Her eyes found the window, where the rising sun was chasing away the lingering gloom of night. A few yards away, two massive willows were casting long shadows tinged in dawn shades of orange and gold.

Jacob turned her head away from the willows with two fingers gently pushing her chin. "Don't do this to yourself, sis."

"I could've killed you that day. It's a miracle I didn't." Kay finally looked up at him and held his gaze for a brief, loaded moment, then stared at the stained floor.

"You didn't, and it's over. It has been over for years." He lifted her chin up until Kay's eyes met his. "I do hope they taught you how to shoot at Quantico."

She couldn't help the smile that scared away the last of her tears. "You'd think, yes."

"Or was your crappy marksmanship the reason why you quit the FBI and resigned yourself to be a small-town cop instead? Profilers are more like paper pushers, aren't they?"

She gasped. Was he serious? She was about to remind him why she'd returned to their hometown, but the well-guarded secret was written in his eyes. Unspoken truths weighed heavily between them, some unbearable. Kay's guilt had been a painful burden all those years, but Jacob had always been there to help her carry it. That guilt still persisted, although she knew what she'd done sixteen years ago was right. Justified. Necessary. And still, she'd never managed to rid herself of that guilt, of the nightmares that came with it, fueled by the relentless anguish of her mind. By the secret they were both protecting.

A wave of unspeakable sadness washed over her. No matter how many coats of lemon meringue yellow she applied to those walls, it wouldn't change what she'd done. Nothing ever would. And if the truth ever came out, her life would be finished. Jacob's too.

A shudder ran through her body. Jacob looked at her intently, his brow furrowed.

Without a word, he rolled up his blue-striped pajama sleeves and grabbed the can of spackling paste from the counter, loading the knife with a fresh pink dollop. Then he applied it to the wall, covering the bullet hole with one swift, expertly choreographed move. Once done, he looked at her with a silent question in his eyes.

Kay nodded and smiled weakly, admiring his work, then lifted her gaze to meet his. There was strength in those eyes, vulnerability too, and love. One by one, the scars of the past were fading away, even if some were still agonizing.

"Why stop now?" she asked, gesturing toward a deep scuff in the wall that needed leveling.

Jacob shook his head in disbelief. "I never wanted to repaint the house, you know," he replied, loading more paste onto the knife and getting the work done quickly.

"Did you say 'house'?" Kay grinned. He was coming to his senses.

He sighed. "I'm not an idiot, sis. I know you won't stop with the kitchen."

"You are wise indeed, little brother," she quipped, but the fake cheerfulness didn't touch her eyes nor color her voice. *Fake it till you make it*, she thought, willing herself to smile for her brother's sake.

"The main bedroom would probably come next," Jacob said, patching up the holes quickly. "Then the bathrooms, then the rest of the house, just because."

"Yup," she admitted, pouring coffee in Jacob's mug and setting it on the counter close to him.

He paused his energetic work pace and took a sip, then set the mug down on the counter. "Ugh, it's hot." He studied a big hole by the fridge he'd rolled to the center of the room, and grumbled an oath. "This will need some bridging material."

Her father's fist had gone through the drywall and stopped against the two-by-four on the other side. Kay still remembered that day, that fight, the sound of the forceful punch cracking the wall. He was aiming for her mother's head, too drunk to land the blow that would've been deadly. She shuddered as she willed the nightmarish vision away.

"Or we could move," Jacob said, staring at her. "Sell this place, take our chances, and go. Disappear." He stared at the floor for a moment, then gestured at the walls. "Leave all this shit behind. All the bad memories."

They looked at each other without a word, then Kay's eyes veered to the window, where the willows stood tall, the rays of the sun piercing through their foliage.

They could never move.

Jacob shrugged and resumed his work. "Well, at least the place is paid for. I'll help you make it nice."

She squeezed his hand gently. "Let's tile this kitchen and replace the cabinets."

"Whoa, there, now wait a minute." But she was facing him with her hands propped on her hips, her jaw thrust forward, and an expression on her face she usually reserved for suspect interrogations.

His arms fell in a gesture of defeat. Kay smiled. An easy victory.

"It's the least I can do since I'm not paying any rent."

"Rent? It's your house too."

She nodded. "Okay, but you'll take the main bedroom as soon as it's done. We'll do that next. Lynn will love it."

A moment of silence, heavy, unwanted, like a dark storm cloud chasing away the sunshine.

"It was his room," Jacob whispered. "I won't sleep in there. You take it if you want it."

There was a stern finality in his statement.

She couldn't see herself sleeping in her parents' room either. Too many memories, seeding endless nightmares.

She managed a weak smile.

"Why don't we discuss this again after it's redone and unrecognizable? Your girlfriend might have the final say in this, you know." She winked. He didn't smile, didn't look up from the scuffed linoleum. "The walls aren't to blame, Jacob," she whispered, squeezing his arm. "It's our house now. Our future is what we make of it."

The loud chime of the phone startled them both. She had a new message.

Kay read it after a quick glance at the display told her it was almost seven.

A Mrs. Jerrell was waiting for her at the precinct to file a missing person report.

Her teenage daughter had vanished.

THREE

ROUTINE

He'd brought a few things with him from the Lone Star State. Some wide-brimmed cowboy hats. A small collection of belt buckles, large enough to fry eggs for breakfast in them without soiling the stove. And a six-year-old brown buckskin American Quarter Horse with a white blaze running all the way from its forehead to its sensitive nose.

Elliot's mornings started the same way. Fresh hay in the bucket for his horse, greeted by the animal with an enthusiastic snort. Then a ride toward the base of the mountain, across fields and by the woods, saving a mile or two for a high-speed gallop. A brisk walk on the way back home, punctuated by happy snorts and foggy blows through flaring nostrils in the early morning chill.

He always left the stable doors open after putting the horse inside the fenced pasture to graze at will. Almost every morning, he rewarded the animal with a crisp apple or two. Their foreheads touched for a brief goodbye as he gently patted the horse's neck, then scratched it with long moves, up and down, before hitting the shower.

That was his routine.

Wednesday morning was no different, not on the surface, anyway. His mind was preoccupied, escaping into the past whenever he tried to think of the future. At the center of his thoughts was his partner, Kay Sharp.

Dr. Kay Sharp, no less, as if their worlds weren't far apart already.

She was a shrink and a darn good one. She could read his mind just by looking at him for half a second. He'd seen her with suspects and witnesses. He'd watched her chat casually with killers and rapists and hardened criminals, twisting their minds into a knot without breaking a sweat.

The woman could charge hell with a bucket of water and put it out for good.

And yet, there was something that drove him to want to shield her from all that was dark in the world as if she was a frail, fearful, and lost little girl. It made no sense whatsoever, but his mind could argue with a wooden statue over the issue of Kay Sharp, the detective, the shrink, the beautiful hazel-eyed blonde who had stolen his heart without even knowing she had.

It was at that point in his thoughts' gallop when the past came rushing in. Nine years ago, he was an Austin, Texas, cop, his head filled with ambitions and dreams. Almost two years later, just as he'd finished building a stable for his new horse, a yearling with lots of attitude and a kind heart, he'd met his new partner. Laurie Ann Sealy was a fiery brunette and a rookie, fresh out of school. He made the mistake of falling for her, of getting romantically involved with a colleague, another cop. His partner.

His recklessness had brought consequences.

Six months later, he was leaving the state of Texas with his entire life packed in the back of his truck, and a young, impatient horse in a trailer hooked up behind the blue, rust-bit Chevy.

Whatever Kay Sharp was doing to him every time she

looked at him, he wasn't going to repeat history. He'd learned his lesson.

Or had he? He had his doubts, given that every morning, about the time he trotted back around the river bend, he needed to recite that mantra to himself only to steel his willpower.

By the time he crossed the river through cold water splashed up high by galloping hooves, he let himself think, one last time, what if? What would happen if he let it happen, if he told Kay how he felt? Then he'd remember once more what a terrible idea that could be.

Still immersed in thoughts, he drudged through the morning routine. Showered. Shaved. Got dressed in white-washed, tight jeans and a navy-blue T-shirt. Gave it a moment's thought but then chose the black hat, just like yesterday and the day before. Then locked the door and hopped behind the wheel of his black, unmarked Ford Interceptor wearing a lopsided grin on his face.

He loved his job. He was good at what he did and couldn't see himself doing anything else.

And part of that job was Kay.

The first stop on his drive was Katse Coffee Shop, at the top of the hill. Two fingers touching the brim of his hat was all he needed to do to get the standing order started. He chatted with the blushing barista for a couple of minutes, savoring the heady smell of freshly roasted java until the two large coffees were brewed and Kay's butter croissant was warmed up to crispy perfection. He paid for everything and dropped the change into the tip jar before leaving.

By the time he reached the precinct, it wasn't even seven thirty yet, but Kay's SUV was already parked in front of the white, single-story building. A brief frown touched his brow as he grabbed the coffee cups and the small brown bag exuding the mouthwatering aroma of warm pastries, then closed the door of his SUV with a quick nudge from his elbow.

Something was going on.

As soon as he stepped through the glass door, he saw Kay rushing toward the interview room. She seemed tense, holding a notepad and pen close to her chest in a tight, white-knuckled grip.

"Hey," he said, raising the croissant bag in the air to draw her attention.

She turned and smiled briefly when she saw him, then hurried toward him. "Missing person case, a teenager. Wanna sit in?" She grabbed the bag and expertly exposed the croissant without touching it with her bare fingers, enough to take a bite.

"Sure. I didn't get the message," he replied. A speck of something white at the corner of Kay's mouth drew his attention. He reached to wipe it off, but his fingers froze in midair before touching her skin.

Her inquisitive eyes followed his move. "What?" she asked, chewing quickly. The tension he'd noticed earlier was creasing her brow and making her voice sound cold, distant.

"You have something, um, there." His finger drew closer, pointing, but still hovered a few inches away as if afraid to touch her skin. Swallowing an oath, he forced an innocent smile. He was behaving like an idiot.

Kay chuckled lightly as she took another bite, then gestured with both hands. One was holding the croissant, the other the pen and pad. "I won't bite," she said as soon as she swallowed, then drew closer to him in an unspoken invitation. "Want some?" she offered. "Make it quick. The woman's waiting."

He bit into the remaining pastry, leaving a good chunk for her. Then, holding his breath, he rubbed the white substance off her face with the tip of his finger. Their eyes locked for a heated moment before Kay looked away and took a step back. Whatever spark he thought he saw in her eyes as he touched her skin must've been in his imagination.

The speck of white was solid but crumbled easily between his fingers, turning into a fine powder. He studied it curiously.

"Spackling," Kay said, crumpling the empty pastry bag into a ball and throwing it into the kitchenette wastebasket. "Long story. Let's go."

She led the way to the interview room with a spring in her step and a straight back. Rushing through the hallway that led to the interview room, she looked over her shoulder as if to see whether he was still behind her.

Where else would he be?

FOUR
TRIP

"Seriously, man, you're starting to piss me off." Pete wiped his sweaty brow with his sleeve. "Who knew you could be such a trailer?" He trotted ahead, his guitar still balancing casually on his right shoulder as if to show how easy the hike was, then turned around and walked backward, just to give Bryan his middle finger.

The three young men could've been brothers. Wearing what they'd agreed was appropriate attire for the hike, they'd planned ahead with a shopping spree at the Metreon as if they needed more ripped jeans and buffalo plaid shirts in red and black, with some gray mixed in there in Bryan's case. They were going for the lumberjack look, the entire trip the outcome of a sports bet Pete had won against his two best buds.

Pete had been born with the hyperactivity gene, per his mother's own words. In Zack's opinion, the man had ADHD, with a spotlight shining brightly on the H. At twenty-one, he had incredible stamina and the drive to constantly move, to exceed his own limits. Unfortunately for the more common Zack and Bryan, Pete was also very lucky and rarely placed a bet unless he was certain he would win. His two college pals were yet to figure that part out, and he routinely engaged them in bets they subsequently lost. It was so easy it should've been illegal.

Pete never bet on money because he didn't need any. In a moment of sheer inspiration several decades earlier, his grandfather had sold everything he owned and bought Apple stock. One simple yet legendary action carried rippling consequences that covered generations, the most remarkable being the family wealth that was built based on that single decision. Told at family reunions over and over, the boldness of Pete's grandpa was often referenced as an act of inspired lunacy.

No. Whenever Pete placed a bet, he wanted company on some outdoor activity he had planned, and he needed leverage to reel Zack and Bryan along. He enjoyed spending time with them, but the two had to have been the laziest, sorriest, screen-addicted couch potatoes he'd ever met.

Zack was well-built, his shoulders broader than Pete's from countless hours of weightlifting at the Embarcadero Center gym. Pete believed he secretly wanted to become a movie star, but Zack never admitted to having such dreams. He was nicely ripped. His bare abs were showed off proudly because Zack rarely buttoned his shirt, even if the mountain morning was chilly. Maybe he could lift weights like a pro, but he couldn't hike worth a damn. He lacked conviction.

At least he didn't whine like Bryan did, on his phone all the time, falling behind and running out of breath when he tried to catch up. They'd been climbing for about two hours, and Bryan had already stopped twice for a break. The last time they stopped, he rolled a joint with unexpected dexterity, and they smoked it like it was a secret ritual, with long puffs and smoke held in their lungs for a second or two, to numb the pain, in Bryan's own words.

The three-day outing Pete had planned was nothing an old woman couldn't handle if she put her mind to it. They had driven in the night before from San Francisco, where the three were sophomores at San Francisco State. They had enjoyed a good dinner at the hotel, followed by beers on the patio, while Pete strummed his guitar and sang, oblivious to the tourists that slowly and silently gathered to hear him play.

They stayed up late enough for Pete to struggle to get them out of bed in the morning, but he managed to get the show on the road after all. They were supposed to climb the mountain on the slope under the chairlift, then on the rocky crest he'd learned was called Wildfire Ridge. Seemed the views from up there were spectacular. Then they'd climb down and spend the night at the same hotel, take a boat out on Silent Lake and fish the next day, then drive back home in the evening.

A loud yelp and Bryan landed on his butt, holding his leg. "Oh, shit," he moaned, rubbing his knee with both hands right where the fabric of his denim was torn, and a thin streak of blood appeared.

"Are you okay?" Pete asked, stopping and swallowing a curse. It would've been easier to hike with a toddler.

"Yeah," Bryan replied, looking around him as if he'd lost something. Reaching into the grass-covered boulders to the side of the trail, he fished his phone and carefully checked the screen. "Whew, it's not broken."

Pete rolled his eyes. "There goes my last hope."

Zack chuckled.

"Screw you," Bryan said. "Both of you." He picked himself up and ran his hands over his clothes, brushing off a few blades of grass. "This is not my thing, all right?" He undid another button on his shirt. "Really, what the hell is wrong with air conditioning and some *Call of Duty*, huh?"

Pete wasn't paying attention to him anymore. He'd started climbing, eager to enter the woods and start scaling by the vertical wall of the ridge, one of the few Class Three hikes within driving distance. He cringed as he envisioned what

Bryan would say when he saw that section. Of course, they could also climb the entire way on the soft, grassy slope stretching under the chairlift, but where was the fun in that?

When he reached the edge of the woods, Pete stopped, propping his hands on his hips and taking long, deep breaths. The air was perfectly crisp, the morning sun burning through whatever fog still remained and giving him tan lines at the edge of his sleeves. The California blue sky was perfect, not a cloud in sight.

Seeing how far behind Zack and Bryan had fallen, he looked around for something to sit on and found a moss-covered boulder. Tapping the rhythm with his foot against a log, he started singing Willie Nelson's "On the Road Again." His voice carried over the valley, the happy tune meant to encourage his friends to move faster.

They both gave him the bird with broad gestures and off-key hollers.

Unabated, he kept on singing. By the time they caught up with him, they were both singing along with him, cheering and hollering.

Eager to keep going, he stood, but Bryan laid a heavy hand on his shoulder. "Play us another one, bro. I need a minute to catch my breath."

Of course, he did. Resigned, he thought of another song. Then he vocalized the first few notes from another classic they all loved, "(I've Had) The Time of My Life." They sat and listened quietly, as they always did when he sang that tune and a few others.

A few moments of silence followed after he finished the *Dirty Dancing* anthem. He stood and stomped his feet a couple of times, ready to go. Zack and Bryan followed suit with groans, Bryan's quite loud and sprinkled with oaths.

The wooded part of the trail was dark and ominous, the thick layer of fir needles absorbing every sound they made. At their left, a chasm opened gradually, the blue granite wall almost vertical, several thousand feet high.

Leading the way, he looked over his shoulder for Zack and Bryan. They needed to stay closer together for this stretch. Zack was only a few yards behind, but Bryan was almost at the starting point, walking slowly, looking at his phone. By the rapid swiping movements he made with his fingers on the screen, he was playing some stupid game.

Pete rushed back toward him and extended his hand. "Give it," he demanded. "You have to pay attention, or else you could break your neck out here."

Bryan laughed dismissively. "Nah, I'll be fine."

Zack approached. "No, he's right. Stop with the stupid phone already, man. Let's get the hell up there and back, okay?"

Bryan wasn't going to budge. He hid his phone behind his back and tried to run past Pete, but his foot slid on fir needles. He landed hard on his side with a groan and a loud thump. His phone slipped from his hand and rolled into the ravine, bouncing and rattling, quickly disappearing from view.

"Oh, shit," he shouted, taking Zack's hand to get up. "Now what?"

"Now you go down there and get your phone," Pete said, grinning wickedly. The ravine was deep, the slope had a steep incline, and the terrain was treacherous, with rocks and loose boulders covered with moss and dry needles. "Or you could leave it there; either way, that's fine by me."

Bryan looked at him with frustration in his eyes. The time for giggles had passed. Pete had expected Bryan to ask him to go after the phone in his stead, and he would've gladly done so, only Bryan had suddenly turned stubborn and proud just as much as he was offended. As if Pete had thrown his phone into the ravine.

Bryan started his descent, purposely ignoring every bit of advice Pete was trying to give. A beginner in all things hiking, he did everything wrong; he let himself climb down too fast, holding on to thin branches for balance, too thin to hold his weight. Eventually, one of those branches gave, and Bryan fell. He slid forward on his butt for a while, bouncing like a rag doll, yelping and groaning whenever he hit something. In about ten yards or so, he came to a stop at the bottom of the ravine and screamed, desperately squirming to get away, his voice sending echoes bouncing against the rock face.

Then he screamed again, a bloodcurdling shriek of pure terror.

FIVE
MISSING

Before entering the interview room, Kay stopped briefly by the observation window and looked inside.

The woman seated at the dented and scratched metallic table was dressed in powder blue hospital garb and looked tired. Black circles under her eyes glistened with tears. Restless, she was wringing her hands incessantly, staring worriedly at the wall above the two-way mirror, where a clock showed the time.

Kay opened the door and stepped inside. Elliot followed.

The air within the cramped room was stale and smelled badly, of sweat and fear, of human misery. The fluorescent light on the ceiling flickered, one of the tubes yellowed out, and about to die, lending the walls the look and feel of a decrepit basement.

"Mrs. Jerrell?" The woman sprung to her feet, the legs of her metallic chair screeching in protest against the stained floor.

"Y—yes." She nodded vigorously. Her eyes were red and swollen. "I'm Brenda Jerrell."

Kay gestured toward the chair. "Please, sit down. You needed to report a missing person?"

The woman swallowed hard and licked her dry lips. "My

daughter, Jenna. She didn't come home last night. Her name is Jenna," she repeated. Her voice was breaking despite her visible efforts to hold back her tears. Her hands gripped the edge of the table, her knuckles white as if she was about to fall into an abyss and that table was the only thing keeping her alive.

"When did you last see Jenna?"

"I—yesterday morning, but, um, that's not relevant," she stuttered. "I pull double shifts these days, and I'm never home. My husband last saw her yesterday afternoon, at about four. She came back from school, changed, and rushed out, saying she was meeting with friends."

"Do you know whom she was meeting with?" Elliot asked. He was still standing, leaning against the scratched wall.

Mrs. Jerrell wiped the corner of her eye with her fingers. "We—he didn't ask." She lowered her gaze to the floor. "You see, it was one of the few times she was going out since April. We were thrilled for her."

A slight frown creased Kay's brow for a moment. A teenager who doesn't go out? "How old is she?"

"She turned seventeen this summer." She let go of the table's edge and clasped her hands together tightly as if in silent prayer. "In June."

"At seventeen, she doesn't go out with friends? That's unusual," Kay commented, careful not to instill more anxiety into the woman's heart.

Mrs. Jerrell nodded a couple of times, then lifted her gaze from the floor and looked at Kay with a silent plea. "She used to before she..." her voice trailed off on a shattered breath. "We think something happened to Jenna last spring." Her hands grabbed the edge of the table again, and she leaned forward, closer to Kay. "We think she must've been bullied, or worse."

"Tell me what happened?" Kay asked, pushing a box of tissues across the table. "What did Jenna say?"

Mrs. Jerrell shook her head. "She didn't; that's the problem.

Our daughter didn't trust us to tell us what was going on. She just... stopped living. She didn't go out anymore. She spent all afternoons in her bedroom with her door closed. Sometimes, when I worked days, I would hear her crying herself to sleep."

"Did you ask her what was going on?"

She pressed her lips together and gave Kay a grim look. "She wouldn't say, no matter how hard we pressed, her father and me. But I'll show you." She grabbed her purse from the back of the chair then extracted a zippered wallet. She opened it and laid it flat on the table, turning it around so that Kay could see the two photos slid under the transparent plastic side.

One showed a beautiful, smiling girl with long brown hair and confident brown eyes, dressed in a buttoned blue shirt and wearing a thin gold necklace. She exuded happiness and poise, the kind that foretells when someone's future is about to blossom.

The second image told a different story. The girl's eyes were haunted, the expression one of intense despair, of despondence. Her face was drawn and pale. All the earlier self-confidence was gone without a trace. Her hair was now shorter and unkempt, her blouse black and wrinkled.

Kay looked at Mrs. Jerrell inquisitively.

"This photo was taken last March for her college application. She's going to Cal State, you know," she added, a tinge of maternal pride coloring her voice. "This one was taken in June, on her birthday, only three months ago. We had to drag her out of her bedroom for cake."

Kay studied the two photos in silence for a moment. The change was consistent with someone going through intense hardship. And still, she hadn't said a word to her parents. It couldn't've been a medical problem; her mother was a nurse. She would've seen symptoms, would've recognized a disease. Couldn't've been a pregnancy; it would've started to show. Or maybe she'd miscarried without her mother learning about it.

Elliot reached for the wallet. "May I?" Mrs. Jerrell nodded. "We'll need copies of these photos." He took the pictures and stepped outside.

"Walk me through what happened with Jenna since last March. Anything worth mentioning might give us a clue where to find her."

Mrs. Jerrell nodded without taking her eyes off Kay. "It happened gradually, and I don't think I noticed anything until the end of April. She stopped hanging out with friends that much, but slowly. Then she and her boyfriend broke up, and for a while, I thought that's why she was crying all the time. Then, one night after a day shift, I found her asleep with lipstick on her face, smeared on purpose as if she'd put it on and immediately ran her hand over her mouth, smudging it all over. When I woke her up, she didn't explain; she just sat on the side of her bed, staring into nothing." The woman's gaze darted toward the floor, then landed on her clasped hands. "I noticed she'd cut her hair that night and did a botched job of it, on purpose I believe. I—I tested her urine for drugs that night. It was clean." A long, pained breath left her lungs. "I was so relieved it wasn't drugs; I wrote it off as teenage hormones and boyfriend trouble. It wasn't. Jenna was loathing herself, and I missed it."

Silence filled the room when Mrs. Jerrell stopped talking. In the distance, two deputies were arguing over a baseball game, their voices climbing, laughter mixed with expletives and name-calling. Then the chatter died abruptly. A moment later, Elliot returned with Jenna's photos.

"Thank you," he said, placing them gently on the table.

Mrs. Jerrell nodded. A fresh tear stained her scrub top. Sniffling, she patted her eyes dry with a Kleenex. "That's what happened, and we—we didn't know how to address it."

"Did you speak with anyone at the school about it?" Kay asked.

"Yes, we did, more than once. I was suspicious of them for a while. No one knew anything or admitted to anything. Her grades had slumped somewhat, but—"

"Tell me about the past twenty-four hours before she disappeared." Kay spoke softly, patiently, although she wanted the interview to be over as quickly as possible. Every minute was critical. "Did you or your husband argue with her? Was she more upset yesterday than she'd been in the recent past?"

A spark of panic lit up Mrs. Jerrell's eyes. "Are you saying she left? She ran away?" High-pitched panic tinged her voice.

"It's a possibility we have to consider. Last year, more than ninety percent of all missing teenagers were, in fact, runaways."

Tears streamed down Mrs. Jerrell's face. She stood up and walked around the table. Kay stood, too; she was painfully aware Mrs. Jerrell couldn't handle any more questions.

Her chest heaving, the mother clasped Kay's hands. "Please, please don't give up on her. She would've never left us. I know this in my heart. I do, I swear." She broke down in uncontrollable wails. "Please, find my baby."

Kay helped her to the chair and crouched in front of her, still holding her hand. "We'll do everything we can to find Jenna. I promise you that." She sought the woman's gaze and repeated her commitment, looking her in the eye. "I promise you we won't give up until we have answers."

Elliot disappeared and returned promptly with a water bottle and a plastic cup. He unscrewed the cap and filled the cup for her. Mrs. Jerrell took a sip, her eyes squeezed shut, brimming with tears. Then she set the cup on the table and said, "Tell me what to do."

"Breathe," Kay replied gently. "First of all, breathe. You know the drill. You have to take care of yourself first, to be strong for your daughter." The woman nodded. "Before we get started, one more question, if I may. I'm not exactly clear on how you didn't know Jenna was gone the entire night."

Her lower lip quivered for a moment. "I work double shifts

these days. There's never enough money, and Jenna's going to college next year. I worked the afternoon and night shifts yesterday and got home at about seven this morning. Her bed was made, and she never does it herself; I make it for her."

"How about your husband? Wasn't he at home?"

A sad smile flickered on the corner of her lip. "Bill is always home. He's a Marine veteran, a wheelchair user since Afghanistan. He's in severe pain and takes medication. By seven in the evening, he's out like a light."

"Do you think Jenna could've returned last night without Mr. Jerrell knowing about it?"

Mrs. Jerrell took a moment to consider the idea but then shook her head. "There was no trace of her being in the house after she left yesterday afternoon. She didn't sit on the bed or eat or do anything that I would notice."

Kay looked over her shoulder at the clock on the wall. Jenna had been missing sixteen hours already. And if Kay had to venture a guess, her disappearance was in some manner tied to what had been happening to her since spring.

Mrs. Jerrell followed her glance and clasped her hands together, wringing them nervously. "I watch TV on my breaks, and I read when night shifts are lighter. The first twenty-four hours are... I mean, my baby's still alive, right?"

Kay's phone chimed before she could answer. She ignored it, but within a second, Elliot's phone rang too. His eyebrows locked in a frown as he held the screen in front of Kay's eyes.

"Is she, Detective?" Reaching across the table, Mrs. Jerrell grasped Kay's hand. "Please tell me she's going to be okay."

Kay's blood turned to ice as she looked at the screen. The dispatched message read:

Young girl's body found by Wildfire Ridge. ME on the way.

SIX

SCENE

It wasn't noon yet, but it was hot as hell out there and worse inside the Interceptor. Three hours of direct sunlight had baked the black SUV to the point where Elliot couldn't touch the steering wheel without muttering an oath. The scorching air was an unusual occurrence for Mount Chester, where temperatures borrowed the coolness of the nearby mountain's alpine climate during summers. But he welcomed the heat as a reminder of his native state, with a faint smile and a touch of melancholy. He didn't miss the dust settling on his face or the horseflies, but there was something about those endless Texas prairies that still clung to his heart.

Kay climbed into the SUV without saying a word. Since they'd been dispatched to the crime scene, she'd turned silent and grim. She was staring straight ahead at the road, her jaw clenched and her breaths shallow as if she'd just been hit in the gut.

"Do you think it's Jenna?" he asked. The Interceptor's wheels crushed loose shoulder gravel as he took the turn off the highway at high speed, heading toward the ski resort. From there, a couple of more miles to the Winter Lodge, then another

mile to the Wildfire Ridge trailhead parking. Soon they would
know.

She didn't reply at first. Her lips were pressed into a fine
line, tense and rigid. "I'm hoping it's not Jenna," she eventually
said. "But whomever she is, she's still someone's daughter." She
looked at him briefly, and he thought he saw the glistening of
tears in his partner's eyes. "And we'll have to let another mother
know her child is never coming home." She breathed deeply as
if to steel her frayed nerves. "Sometimes, this job gets to me,
that's all."

She didn't usually show it. Not in the faintest. During the
emotionally charged interview with Mrs. Jerrell, his partner had
displayed   impeccable   self-control   and   amazing   skill   at
comforting the anguished parent. It seemed as if none of that
touched her. Kay's eyes had remained dry while he'd struggled;
grief, like most intense human emotions, is contagious.

Resisting the urge to pull over on the side of the road to
sweep her in his arms and seal those lips under a fiery kiss, he
pushed the gas pedal all the way down, the SUV swerving and
bouncing on the uneven, curvy mountain road. Kay's unexpected vulnerability did things to him he didn't want to
acknowledge.

The road curved for miles, flanked by tall evergreens on
both sides that filtered sunlight and hid the stunning view of the
mountain at times, less and less as they approached. He drove
around the Winter Lodge, and soon, the flashing red-and-blue
lights of two marked deputy vehicles came into sight at the base
of the slopes near the chairlift terminal.

Elliot stole another glance at Kay. The earlier moment of
weakness was gone as if it had never been there. Her eyes were
dry and focused, her demeanor alert.

"Yes, I believe it's Jenna," she said. Her voice was calm,
steady, professional. "Chances are this is not coincidental."

Elliot reduced speed as the asphalt ended, replaced with a

mix of loose gravel on a two-rutted earth road leading to the trailhead parking, nothing more than a cleared piece of meadow marked with two posted signs and surrounded by tall firs.

Traditionally filled with at least a dozen vehicles belonging to tourists, most of them California tagged, the trailhead parking was almost deserted today. The two deputy vehicles with flashing lights and the coroner's van likely deterred any visiting hikers.

Elliot slowed to a stop near one of the marked SUVs. Deputy Hobbs was busy unloading four-wheelers off a platform hooked to his vehicle. He was down to the last two of the six all-terrain vehicles the Franklin County Sheriff's Office used for rugged terrain interventions.

"Hey," Elliot called through the open window, touching his hat briefly with two fingers. "How far is it?"

"Hey, Detective," Hobbs replied, smiling widely. He was young and a bit on the chubby side, enough to make his uniform shirt buttons be stretched within a thread of their lives. Usually pale, the young man was red in the face from the hot sun, or perhaps from the effort he was visibly not used to. Beads of sweat marked his forehead, although a stain on his right sleeve proved he'd been wiping them off every so often. "About a mile or so past the chairlift terminal." He swiped his brow with his sleeve in a quick move accompanied by a loud breath. "Farrell is up there with a couple of ATVs."

"All right," Elliot replied, looking quickly at Kay to see how she wanted to proceed. She nodded slightly. Behind them, red flashing lights and a familiar siren warned them a fire truck was approaching. "Where's the fire?"

Hobbs chuckled. "No fire, D. Just a deep ravine. They can't get the body out, from what I'm hearing." A wide grin displayed two uneven rows of tobacco-stained teeth. "I heard the perps were collared already, so no rush."

"You got it, boss," Elliot replied sarcastically. Everyone

thought they had all the answers, but few bothered to ask questions. He gave the SUV enough gas to make it lurch ahead, throwing loose gravel against its steeled underbelly. "That would be the day when we get to crime scenes and the perps are collared already," he muttered. "I'd be as useful that day as the second buggy in a one-horse town, but slick as a whistle ain't coming my way today." He grinned sheepishly. "Or yours, for that matter."

But Kay wasn't paying any mind to his childish blabbering. She was carefully taking in the setting: the hiking path as it narrowed down gradually as they drove uphill, the SUV's wheels riding low in deep ruts, the nearby fir branches low and heavy, scratching against the sides. She'd rolled down the window halfway and her nostrils were flaring in the wind like a predator's out for prey.

"You have five senses, six if you're lucky," she'd once told him when they were working their first crime scene together. "Use them all."

He inhaled the air and noted the smell of fresh fir and sap, the dryness of the air, the tinge of heated dust he picked up driving only a minute or two behind another vehicle. Bone dry, the path was covered with fine dust lifted up high in the air in a reddish-brown cloud that took a while to settle after each passing vehicle.

Another turn and they reached the end of the drivable path. A widening in the road allowed several vehicles to be parked between the trees lining up the trail. Deputy Denise Farrell signaled them with broad gestures of her hand, then pointed at a space between two old firs where Elliot's Interceptor could fit.

Approaching as he slowed down, Farrell nodded a quick greeting. She wore her hair in a ponytail that day, not just entirely up to regs. "I can take it from here if you'd like. An ATV is waiting for you."

"How far to the scene?" Kay asked. She climbed out of the

SUV with the nimbleness of a teenager. She'd make a fine horse rider one day.

"About four miles. It's at the base of Wildfire Ridge." As Kay approached Farrell, the deputy lowered her voice. "I hear it's a bad one." Kay nodded, and the two women locked glances for a split moment. Then Farrell pointed at the ATV parked on the side of the road past the sheriff's vehicle. "That's a two-seater, or I can give you two four-wheelers if you prefer."

Elliot searched Kay's eyes. "That's okay, we'll take this." He dropped the keys to his Interceptor in Farrell's hand and climbed onto the ATV.

The road was bumpy and turned more treacherous by the minute, with loose boulders and a narrowing profile adding to the challenges of an increasingly steep grade. After several minutes, that seemed more like hours, they reached the scene.

The three young men were dressed almost identically in the type of hipster, overpriced imitation of mountain logger attire one could only find in San Francisco's posh malls. They sat on a large, moss-covered boulder under the vigilant gaze of Deputy Leach from traffic. Sheriff Logan had pulled everyone to the crime scene, including the thin, mousy-looking deputy who irritated Elliot like mustard on a raw burn.

One of the suspects had fared much worse than the other two. His exposed shaved chest was scratched, bruised, and bleeding. The unbuttoned plaid shirt in red, gray, and black was stained with vomit and blood and torn in several places.

"He found the body?" Elliot asked, gesturing with his head.

"Found it?" Leach scoffed and gave Elliot an all-knowing, slightly arrogant look. "He's the one who put that poor girl down there."

"Is that so?" Kay said quietly, studying the three. "Who was first on scene?"

"Novack," Leach replied, sucking his teeth.

Thank goodness for small miracles, Elliot thought. Leach

couldn't hit the floor if he fell out of bed; there was a reason why the man had been working traffic for his entire career. But Novack had a brain and knew how to use it.

Kay seemed to agree; her face lit up slightly as she walked toward the senior deputy.

"Detective," he greeted her with a stern voice. His eyes were hidden behind mirrored sunglasses. "We've been waiting for you."

Novack had a brain but needed to learn some manners. Elliot would've loved to teach him some.

Unfazed, Kay ignored the offhand comment. "Walk me through the scene."

Novack flipped open his notepad. "Call came in at nine seventeen this morning," he mumbled, following the scribbled notes with his finger. "I was here at ten fifteen. I found those two jokers on the edge of the ravine, trying to pull the third one out using a tree branch."

SEVEN
DETAILS

Kay walked to the edge of the ravine and looked down. The body was barely visible at the bottom, shielded from view by several firs and shrubs. Blue harebells rose above the grasses, swaying slightly in the summer breeze. Something moved at the base of the ravine, barely visible through all the greenery, only specks of white between the wind-rustled leaves.

"The ME's down there," Novack said as if reading her mind. "He wouldn't wait for the fire truck. We lowered him with the boss's ATV winch." He shot the three cuffed young-sters a glance and curled his lip. "Doc said that one fucked up the scene badly. Peed and barfed on that body, emptied himself real good. Bet he had a blast down there, with that girl." He placed his notebook into his pocket and propped his hands on his hips, sliding his thumbs under his belt.

Perhaps Novack would be less obnoxious if he'd bothered to ask himself one question: if the perp has peed on the victim as part of his homicidal ritual, why did he do that with his pants on, all zipped up? The stain marking the young man's jeans told a different story. He'd peed himself out of fear or shock.

Kay didn't vocally disagree with Novack, still examining the body from the edge of the ravine. "What's their story?"

"They said the tall one, Bryan Danko, was trying to recover his phone when he slipped, fell into the ravine, and discovered the body. Then they called nine-one-one." He pushed his sunglasses higher up his nose with a finger. "I think they panicked when the Danko kid couldn't climb back out of the ravine, and that's why they called. I read them their rights." He grinned with an air of superiority. "You're welcome, Detectives."

Elliot's lips stretched into a quick smile, probably anticipating Kay's reaction to the deputy's decision to call the case solved.

But Kay's mind went in a different direction. "Do you have a positive ID on the victim?"

"Not yet," he replied, shifting his weight from one foot to the other, visibly annoyed.

"Time of death?"

"N—no. Doc's still down there."

"Are these men local?"

"Nope, they're on a three-day slide from San Fran with Daddy's money." His voice was loaded with unfiltered disdain, the kind that poisons someone's mind leaving it rusted and darkened as if it had been wrought in fire, unable to see past the hate.

Kay walked toward the three young men, and Elliot followed. The tallest one seemed the oldest, but not by much. He was calm, composed, patiently waiting for the situation to resolve. Kay could tell that man wasn't afraid; just slightly worried, and that was probably because he hadn't done anything wrong. His jeans were clean; there wasn't a bloodstain anywhere on his clothes or hands, and the same went for the third man. Those two had never set foot in the ravine.

"Uncuff them," Kay told the deputy, looking at him intently. Hesitating for a moment, he decided to comply without argument. *Smart man*, Kay thought, grateful she didn't have to get into an argument with the deputy.

As their wrists were freed, the three stood and took to massaging them vigorously. One of them reached for the guitar that was leaning against a tree trunk and inspected it carefully. Then he approached Kay. "May we go now?"

"In a moment, after you leave your contact info with the deputy." She turned to Bryan Danko. "Tell me what happened."

Still rattled, the young man struggled to find his words as his gaze darted all over the place. He was rubbing his reddened wrists over and over, obsessively.

"We, um, I just found her, that's all. I dropped my phone, and it went down there. I had to try to get it. My entire life is on that phone."

That much Kay believed. "Did you recover your phone?"

He nodded vigorously but couldn't find the words.

"Did you touch the body or do anything to it?"

"N—no, ma'am," he replied quickly. "I just fell on top of it." A bout of nausea flared his nostrils and crinkled his nose. He'd probably unloaded his breakfast near the body.

Kay's lips pressed together in a thin, disapproving line. By accident or intentionally, the crime scene was compromised. "Hang out here for a little while longer, okay?" She turned to Elliot with a determined look on her face. "I'm going down there."

She didn't wait for his reply. He probably didn't expect her to. A few minutes later, dressed head to toe in white protective coveralls, Elliot descended first into the ravine, using the winch hook to hold on to and slow his descent. Once at the bottom, he signaled Leach, and the winch cable started pulling up.

Moments later, Kay joined him, still angry with him for having been the first down. He absolutely had to play the protective male. While charming and heartwarming, she felt that took from her professionally.

Once at the bottom, she tread around the bushes until they reached the body. The county medical examiner was an old acquaintance of Kay's; the two shared a friendship that spoke of years together on the force.

Doc Whitmore greeted them, but Elliot was staring speechlessly at the victim, his jaw visibly clenched.

Her face, defiantly beautiful even in death, rested open-eyed under the azure sky. Her brown, silky hair fanned around her head, bringing out the alabaster pallor of her skin. Her lips, slightly parted as if she was still breathing, as if she still whispered her goodbyes. Her arms, raised along her body, her fists slightly open, in a final defensive stance against an unseen assailant. Her clothes, torn and bloodied, revealed the story of her untimely fate. More telling than anything, were the bruises around her neck and on her arms, the dried streaks of blood on the inside of her thighs, the torn fingernails as she had fought for her life.

It was Jenna.

Kay kneeled by the girl's head to examine the bruising around her neck. The thick layer of fir needles had absorbed most of the blood, but some had congealed on the boulder under her head.

"Cause of death, Doc?" Kay asked.

"Consistent with a fall from a significant height, most likely from up there." Doc pointed a gloved finger at the Wildfire Ridge, four thousand feet above them. "I will rule it a homicide."

Elliot looked at him but didn't ask anything. The medical examiner seemed to have read their minds.

"Even if she fell without being pushed, I see enough

evidence she was the victim of a violent sexual assault. If her death occurred during the perpetration of that assault, the law is clear. Her rapist is also her killer, even if he had intended for a different outcome."

"Time of death?"

"Between seven and ten last night." Doc approached Kay but remained standing. "I'd hoped this was an accident, some hiker who lost her footing, but—" He sighed, the pained breath leaving his lungs ending his lament. "I wonder why the serenity and seclusion of this mountain brings out the worst in some of the people who climb it."

Silence filled the air for a moment.

Doc Whitmore crouched next to his open kit and extracted two plastic bags and some tape. Then he walked over to the body and kneeled by the girl's hand, on the other side from Kay.

"Would you mind, my dear?" He offered Kay a bag; no other instructions were necessary. If Jenna had scratched her assailant during the attack, her fingernails could hold DNA evidence that had to be carefully preserved.

Once the bags were sealed around Jenna's wrists with two layers of tape, Doc stood and beckoned them to his side. He lifted Jenna's arm, exposing a small pink object. Kay took an evidence pouch and captured the object Doc Whitmore collected with two gloved fingers.

It was a plastic hair clip, girlish and cheap, shaped as a wide-winged butterfly. It might've fallen off Jenna's hair. Or it could've been one of the many items Wildfire Ridge hikers found entertaining to throw into the abyss opening up at their feet, completely unrelated to Jenna's demise.

The unzipping of body bags always chilled Kay's blood, and this one was no exception. Two firefighters had joined them at the bottom of the ravine, carrying a basket stretcher. They helped Doc Whitmore load the body into the bag, then onto the stretcher, and secured it with zig-zagging straps. Then the two men disappeared from view with their load while Doc Whitmore still lingered, collecting his gear and organizing the sealed and signed evidence pouches.

"I found this in one of her pockets," he said, holding up an evidence pouch. It was Jenna's phone. "It's broken."

EIGHT
MOTHER AND DAUGHTER

Alexandria stomped her yellow, high-heeled sandal against the floor, scuffing the polished hardwood. Nothing was going her way this morning. Life was blowing raspberries at her.

This morning, when she'd looked closely at her reflection in the mirror, she'd found a gray eyebrow hair.

A. Gray. Eyebrow. Hair.

She was only thirty-six... it wasn't fair. Not when she still looked twenty-five-ish. People thought she was Alana's *sister*, not her mother. She'd just started dating again. Living again.

Well, not exactly dating, she thought, holding herself honest, her eyes glistening at her reflection in the mirror.

She had naturally thin eyebrows, but she didn't hesitate. She wiped her tears with the back of her hands and sniffled, deciding it didn't matter. It wasn't a sign of aging; it couldn't be. It had to be some chemical imbalance. Maybe she needed to stock up on some vitamins and start downing them by the fistful in the mornings, like those health freaks on TV. She picked up the tweezers with a steady hand and plucked the offending hair out, leaving an empty spot. Then she arranged the remaining hairs with a tiny round brush until they lined up perfectly.

There. Disaster averted.

One disaster, anyway.

The other one, her rebellious, defiant daughter Alana, was an ongoing crisis requiring immense patience. Soon to be going to college, the breathtakingly beautiful seventeen-year-old blonde had inherited her mother's good looks, reminding Alexandria constantly that, at her daughter's age, she used to be someone. Precisely eighteen years ago, proudly wearing the Miss Wyoming crown on the head she held up high, she'd made second runner-up in the Miss United States pageant. It was the year America suddenly remembered all the islands it owned and felt obligated to acknowledge them by corrupting the beauty pageants from sea to shining sea. The crown went to Hawaii, the first runner-up to Puerto Rico. It was obvious the competition was rigged. *Everyone* loved blondes more than brunettes.

Gutted by searing disappointment, the brokenhearted blonde didn't see the doors that were opening for her even as a second runner-up. Aimless, she sought solace in the readily available arms of a recently discharged Army ranger from her native Wyoming by the name of Billy Joe.

A week later, she accompanied Billy Joe to see his doctor, desperate to find something to do with her time that would take her mind off the stupid pageant. The following Saturday, she was dining at one of San Francisco's finest restaurants with Billy Joe's orthopedic surgeon, a Dr. Aaron Keaney, originally from Kentucky. As for Billy Joe, she never saw him again.

Four months later, she was pregnant with Aaron's baby. Another three months later, they were married at the St. Ignatius Church in downtown San Francisco, in front of a few of her family and friends and hundreds of Aaron's.

And so, her old life ended abruptly, and her new life began. A life some would call comfortable, a life many could only dream of. For Alexandria, it was a life of solitude and boredom, of watching her beauty wither under the stretching and sagging realities of motherhood. Aaron was constantly busy, working at the hospital, giving speeches, teaching at Stanford Medicine, or appearing on television as an expert in traumatic injuries of the rich and famous, from the likes of Tom Cruise or Keanu Reeves who broke bones performing their own stunts on set, to NBA and NFL players with names even she was familiar with. Meanwhile, she took to college, but college wasn't the least bit fun for an expectant mother. One semester later, she'd put everything on hold until she'd have more time and she'd regain the physical appearance of a college girl.

It didn't happen for years. Eventually, she went back and finished her degree in business with lackluster performance and increasing disinterest. She never worked in her chosen field; in fact, the only time she used any of the knowledge acquired in college was when she negotiated her divorce settlement. It came swiftly after she caught Aaron sexting with a second-year resident, a freckled red-haired stunner with long legs and big, round blue eyes, by the name of Rachelle.

Alexandria had cried herself to sleep for exactly one night after seeing evidence of Aaron's betrayal. The insult of being cheated on faded quickly when she realized she was being offered the opportunity to be free again. Unlike she remembered freedom from her days in beauty pageants as an impoverished girl from Wyoming, she would have money. And that was real freedom.

Alexandria had a lot to be grateful for to Rachelle. The comfortable house in Mount Chester, a sizeable alimony for herself until she remarried and for Alana until she turned twenty-five, and two million dollars in cash were the terms of the divorce settlement. Aaron got to keep the San Francisco apartment and most of his money, and their divorce never turned ugly.

Of course, Alana stayed with her. In the rapidly growing

blonde angel, a cutting streak of her father's stubbornness surfaced on every occasion mother and daughter disagreed. That happened mostly every day, about almost everything.

Then Alana bloomed into a teenager with looks that reminded Alexandria of whom she used to be. But not in a way that made her feel proud; rather, in bouts of painful realization that she was growing old, a used-to-be, while the defiant blonde rebel was slowly replacing her, taking all the limelight.

The future was hers; Alexandria was the past.

It took Alana's entire first year of college for her mother to come to terms with what was going on. Alexandria struggled to find new purpose; she even went to therapy for a few months, but eventually, she did. Zeroing in on her daughter with the precision and inescapability of a laser-guided missile, she decided she was going to give Alana everything she wished she had when she was young. Perfect looks, access to all the right circles, a Stanford education. (Stanford, just because the assholes at Harvard wouldn't know what was good for them if it hit them in the head, and they had rejected Alana's application.)

Alexandria was getting another shot at stardom through her daughter, but still. She was back in the game. With renewed fervor, she orchestrated the perfect life path for her daughter.

Then she'd met The Stud—as she liked to call him—and had rediscovered carnal passion in the arms of a rather self-centered, younger man with gorgeous eyes and a level of skill between the sheets she hadn't dreamed of. Within weeks, she'd become addicted to him, waiting for his messages like a teenager, hoping she'd see him every day. But her new lover was a slippery bastard, keeping Alexandria on tenterhooks, probably part of the heady game he played.

Every day she got dressed, she hoped he'd be the one to undress her. New Fleur du Mal satin bodysuits, Cosabella sleep rompers, and La Perla lace lingerie had recently occupied her dresser drawers, raising Alana's eyebrows occasionally.

This morning was no different. A skin-colored demi bra and panties set from Fleur du Mal with luscious, embroidered accents made her slender body look like a lingerie model walking the runway. A white, low-high maxi skirt in shimmering satin that hugged her long, toned legs and a bright yellow top gave her a buoyant, youthful look, a perfect fit for the serene summer day she had planned for her daughter and herself.

But Alana wasn't ready; she was never ready on time unless she was going out for a date. They were running late for her appointment, and Alexandria was running out of patience. She was taking her daughter to the dentist, the best one north of the Golden Gate, to be re-evaluated after she'd stayed the Invisalign course for a year. Her smile still needed a little work.

"Are you coming already?" Alexandria called, stomping her right heel rhythmically, her hands propped firmly on her hips. Her voice carried over the large, open-concept living room, followed by silence. "Alana?" she called, her voice starting to sound threatening.

"All right, all right, I'm coming," Alana finally replied, rushing across the floor in a white, off-shoulder top, ridiculously short Daisy Dukes, and bedazzled flip-flops. "You'd say the house is on freakin' fire."

"You're not going to the dentist dressed like that," Alexandria said, steeling her voice as much as she could.

"You got that right, 'cause I'm not going to the dentist." She tied her long hair in a ponytail with quick, precise movements. The blue scrunchie she'd chosen was covered in sequins. Long strands of silver beads stemmed from it, clinking gently with every move she made.

"Yes, you are." Alexandria cut into her path. "And you know why?" Her question was a dare Alana should choose to not answer.

"No, why don't you illuminate me, huh?" her daughter

replied, typing something quickly on her phone. "'Cause I can't figure out why would I have to go to the damn dentist again, after wearing plastic in my mouth for a year."

Maybe she was sick of the braces, Alexandria thought. She approached Alana and reached out to caress her cheek, but her daughter withdrew as if her touch would've burned her skin. Teenagers.

Alexandria forced some air into her lungs, counted to three, then exhaled slowly. It was working; she was calmer already. "A perfect smile is just as important for your future as your SATs, Alana, you know that. It can make or break a career. It can open doors for you. Teeth, clothes, hair, gait, posture, everything is important."

The girl shrugged, and the ridiculously flimsy top slid farther down off her left shoulder. "Nick's coming to pick me up at ten. We're going to the beach. Everyone's going."

"Nick again, huh?"

Alana didn't reply; didn't even grant her a side glance, totally absorbed by whatever was going on with her phone.

"Dentist first, then you do whatever you want to do."

"But, Mom," she pleaded, "it's not that often we get a day off from school."

"That is such bull, young lady, and you know it. You just came back from summer vacation, and you did whatever you wanted every single day. Beach, Nick, movies, road trips, you name it. You didn't work, didn't do house chores—"

"Ha! Are you kidding me?" Alana said, approaching her mother defiantly. "You'd have me do chores when we have staff?"

Their conversation was going nowhere fast. But Alexandria was still the mother. At least in theory, mothers always won those kinds of arguments. "We're going to the dentist, then I'll take you to the beach myself." She spoke calmly, but her voice sounded just as threatening as she'd wanted it to, instantly cooling the air between them. "Is that understood?"

"Whatever."

Alexandria checked the time and rolled her eyes, staring at the white ceiling for a moment or two, begging the heavens for patience. "You have exactly two minutes to put on a skirt or a decent pair of shorts and some sandals. You're dressed like a piece of trash, and people will treat you as such." Alana scoffed and grinned with insolence. "Not just the people you don't give a crap about," Alexandria whispered, at the end of her wits. "People you care about will be first in line to judge you. And they'll treat you like a piece of meat."

"Look who's talking about meat," Alana mumbled, her eyes lowered, her voice subdued. "You're the one who treats me like that. Always looking to improve my *packaging*," she said with unexpected bitterness as she flashed her mother a quick glance. "Women are liberated these days, in case you haven't heard. I'm not planning to compete in some stupid pageant just to get out of Casper, Wyoming. I'm not flat broke, and I have a little more going for me than my ass."

Breath rushed into Alexandria's lungs with a loud gasp. It took every shred of willpower to keep her composure. She stared at her daughter squarely and said, "Change. Now."

She followed Alana into her bedroom to make sure she made the right choices for shorts and shoes this time. She watched her slide on a tight stretch denim skirt. A short pang of envy shot through her mind as she looked at her daughter's perfectly slim figure, budding breasts, and tan, luminous skin.

"Whatever you think you have going for yourself, missy, can go *kaboom* in an instant," Alexandria said on the way to the car, gesturing with her hands. "Then all you're going to have left is yourself."

"I'm not you, Mom, all right?" Alana protested, climbing into the passenger seat with a pout on her glossy lips. "I have

Dad, and I have—" She stopped short, crossing her arms over her chest and looking out the window as Alexandria turned into traffic and took the road to the interstate.

"It's always about Nick, isn't it?" Alexandria sighed bitterly. Since Alana had met Nick Papadopoulos, their lives had become quite complicated.

There was no answer from Alana, only disapproving silence.

"What do you think will happen next year, when you'll go to college?" Still no answer, but Alexandria thought she'd heard a muffled groan. "He's going to Harvard, isn't he? Leaving you behind?" she asked, mercilessly twisting the blade, realizing there was something good after all in Harvard's decision to reject her daughter. She'd be better off at Stanford, where the name Keaney meant something, where her father could open some doors for her. She'd be better off without Nick.

Alana shot her a glance of pure, distilled hatred, chilling her blood. "Back off, Mom," she said coldly. "We have one more year, and I intend to make the most of it. I'm not going to let anyone stop me. Not even you."

One more year.

Then she'd be all alone in that big house on the hill, slowly going insane.

NINE
NEXT OF KIN

The climb out of the ravine was challenging, even if Kay held on to the whirring winch for balance. The terrain was slippery, covered in a thick, moist layer of fir needles and moss. Once she reached the edge of the ravine, she was quick to take Elliot's hand and be pulled up over the ledge. Once safely on her feet, she ran her hands quickly over her body, absentminded, forgetting she was wearing crime scene coveralls.

She couldn't get Jenna's image out of her mind. In death, the anguish the girl had been going through had dissipated, leaving behind serenity and calm. That was unsettling; it was simply wrong. A seventeen-year-old shouldn't find her serenity in death.

A disturbing thought ripped through Kay's mind. Had she climbed up on the ridge with the intention to jump to her death? Suicide couldn't be ignored as potential motivation, not for her actual demise, but what would have driven Jenna to leave the house, considering what her mother had shared about the girl's recent state of mind? If she'd wanted to end her life, she would've told her parents a lie, then climbed the mountain by herself. Only up there, on Wildfire, she'd run into a predator.

Or had she been lured expertly by someone with the intent to do her harm? It must've been someone she trusted, someone she believed was a friend. But how does a seventeen-year-old girl who doesn't leave the house make friends?

Online.

"I don't believe you want to keep that as a memento, do you?" Dr. Whitmore asked, holding a large trash bag open. He'd collected everyone's coveralls and was patiently waiting for hers. His smile was kind, but his eyes were sad, the way she'd seen them at certain crime scenes.

She unzipped the coveralls and peeled it off her clothes. Filled with static electricity, it clung and sparked in protest, but eventually, it was off. She crumpled it into a ball and shoved it into the bag.

"Thank you, my dear," the medical examiner said.

Without a word and not really knowing why, she stood on her toes and placed a kiss on Whitmore's cheek. They'd worked together for a few years when she was a San Francisco profiler, and he was the county's medical examiner before he semiretired to Mount Chester, yet she'd never done that before.

Slack-jawed, the medical examiner watched her as she approached the three young men who'd found the body. They sat on the same boulder as before, uncuffed yet guarded by Novack with undiluted suspicion. They'd buttoned their shirts all the way up, although it was getting hot.

As she approached, the three men stood anxiously. "Where were you last night between six and midnight?"

They looked at one another briefly, then Bryan Danko took a step closer. "We drove from the city yesterday. At about six thirty, we checked into the hotel, then we went to dinner."

"We had some beers on the restaurant patio," Pete added.

Kay was losing her patience. "When did you leave the restaurant?"

Bryan's eyes darted toward Zack, then back at Kay. "About one in the morning?"

"You mean to say that three young men like yourselves spent, what, six hours having dinner?" Novack intervened, uninvited.

Kay stifled a frustrated sigh. The deputy always rushed to conclusions; he wanted to make detective one day and was looking for easy collars to impress Sheriff Logan, but was screwing things up. The hotel had cameras everywhere. The boys' alibi was an easy one to check.

Unfazed, Bryan grinned. "Pete had his guitar, and when he plays, people come and listen."

"You're free to go," she said, looking around for Elliot. He was bringing the ATV. "Make sure I can find you if I have more questions." She took one step closer to the three men and lowered her voice. "I better not find any crime scene photos online because I'll know where they're coming from, and I'll hit you with an obstruction charge faster than you can say social media." She looked at each of the men for a second. "Understood?"

"Yes, ma'am," Bryan replied, nodding enthusiastically. "You have my word." The other two followed suit.

Elliot pulled the ATV by her, but she wasn't ready to leave yet. "We need to find the primary crime scene," she told Novack. "I need a K-9 here within the hour; clear it with the sheriff first, all right? And confirm with me once they're inbound."

The deputy acknowledged her silently. His lips were pressed together tightly, with a hint of disapproval etched on his features. The man carried grudges like no other cop she'd worked with.

She climbed onto the ATV and held on to the bars while Elliot drove downhill through the rugged terrain, the vehicle

bouncing on rocks and ruts. A few minutes later, they abandoned the ATV and took Elliot's Ford, heading back into town.

They traveled in silence for a while, Kay looking at the sky
with a frown on her face. Several dark clouds, a rare occurrence
for August, had clumped together over the peak of the mountain. In the distance, toward the ocean, more clouds were gathering. She checked her phone. Rain was forecast for later that
afternoon. With it, their crime scene would go straight to hell.

"I can't wrap my mind around it," Elliot said, stealing a
quick glance at her. "Jenna's clothes, I mean."

"What about them?"

"Would you climb the ridge wearing a skirt?"

"Why not?" She thought for a moment. Maybe he was on to
something. "I, personally, wouldn't. But Jenna—"

"Isn't it uncomfortable?" He cleared his voice quietly. "Not
seeing where you're stepping?"

"Skirts, gathered ones especially, give freedom of movement, and they're comfortable to wear."

"Gathered?"

"Frumpy ones with lots of fabric."

"Ah."

"But you're right. I would've worn that with leggings or
something." A thought ridged her brow. "We might find that at
the primary crime scene."

"Oh," he replied, lowering his gaze for a moment as he
turned into the Jerrell driveway.

Kay took a moment before climbing out of the vehicle. A
couple of hours ago, she'd promised Jenna's mother she would
find her daughter. With every fiber in her being, she had
believed that she would find Jenna alive.

Elliot looked at her without a word, waiting. She opened the
door, climbed out, and then walked over to the door.

TEN
SORROW

The Jerrells lived in a small, single-story bungalow with light-green siding and a nearly flat roof. It seemed dated, although it hadn't fallen into disarray. The lawn was clean of debris and trimmed, albeit showing some bald spots here and there. The peach door was decorated with a wreath made of white wild-flowers. On the porch, two Adirondacks and a small wooden table had been painted in the same shade of pink.

Her hand caught in midair, about to ring the doorbell, when the door swung open. Mrs. Jerrell's eyes, filled with hope, searched Kay's and found the truth she feared more than anything else. Gasping for air, she dropped to her knees, wailing. Her hands clasped Kay's clothes spasmodically.

"No... my baby... no." As Elliot was helping her up, she looked at Kay, pleading. "Tell me it's not true."

Kay knew the words to say on such occasions; she'd delivered next-of-kin notifications more times than she cared to remember. Yet the words didn't come to her that day, not when the memory of Jenna's body lying broken and bloodied at the bottom of that ravine was so fresh in her mind. She didn't trust herself to speak; instead, she clasped Mrs. Jerrell's hand and squeezed it.

A man was sitting in a wheelchair with his mouth agape and hollow eyes, blocking the doorway. He rolled the chair backward, making room for Elliot, then watched powerlessly as Mrs. Jerrell finally settled on the couch, sobbing in Kay's arms. He just looked at Elliot with an unspoken question in his eyes.

Elliot nodded slightly, his eyes lowered, his hat in his hand.

"She was being bullied, you know," Jenna's father said. His voice was hoarse, as if he smoked or had had a recent cold. "Brenda said she mentioned that this morning." The man, whose age was showing in the lines around his eyes and sunken corners of his mouth, spoke softly as if all the fight had left his body. "If I only knew who—"

"We'll find out," Elliot said. "I give you my word we will find out."

"Whoever it was, it's in here somewhere," he said, rolling over to a small table and returning with a laptop on his knees. He gave it to Elliot. "Find them. Make them pay."

"We will," Kay added, gently pulling away from Mrs. Jerrell. "Is there anyone we can call? Family, someone who could be with you?"

"There's no one," Mrs. Jerrell said, her voice barely a whisper. "She was all we had. My sister's... she's in Detroit."

"Since we spoke this morning," Kay said, still holding the woman's hand, "is there anything else you might want to tell us about Jenna?"

She raised her tear-filled eyes and looked at Kay. "How did she... um, did she suffer?"

Kay shook her head slowly. "I promise you; she didn't suffer. It was instantaneous."

"How?" Mr. Jerrell asked, his weak voice breaking. He looked at Kay briefly, his eyes haunted, hollow.

Kay hesitated, but he had a right to know. "She fell off Wildfire Ridge."

Mr. Jerrell lowered his head. A tear dropped on his jeans, bleeding into the denim. "I didn't know she was going hiking. She said she was meeting friends."

"Any idea whom she met with?" Kay hesitated for a moment, then added, "I'm afraid there's more... she was sexually assaulted. I'm so sorry."

Mrs. Jerrell gasped. "My poor baby," she sobbed, covering her open mouth with her hands. Her husband shook his head bitterly. His lower lip quivered. "I should've asked. If I had, she might still be alive. Some father I am."

"Sir, there's no—" Elliot started to say, but the man held his hand firmly in the air, stopping him.

"After Brenda came back from the precinct, she and I remembered Jenna's depression started after she went camping with her school."

"When was that?" Kay asked quickly.

"In April, on the seventeenth."

"It was just a day trip," Mrs. Jerrell added.

Kay nodded and stood, extracting a business card from her pocket and placing it on the coffee table.

"If she'd told me who was giving her trouble, I would've talked some sense into that kid." Mr. Jerrell breathed shakily. "Now it's too late."

He looked straight at Kay, then at Elliot. He rolled his chair next to the couch, and took his wife's hand between his, then raised it to his lips and held it there for a moment, sobbing quietly, whispering, "I'm so sorry, please forgive me," over and over. She caressed his hair, leaning her forehead against his for a long moment. Then he looked at them and said, "I need to be alone now, if you'll excuse me." He turned away and disappeared into the bedroom.

A moment later, he closed the bedroom door behind him. A

pang of anxiety unfurled in Kay's gut; there was an unspoken finality in the man's words, in how he'd said them, in the calmness that shrouded him, freezing the pain on his features as if it was etched in stone.

Maybe she was imagining things; he was understandably distraught. Before she opened her mouth, she had to consider the consequences if she was wrong. After weighing her options, she let the air escape her lungs with a sigh and decided to keep her concerns to herself.

Kay and Elliot were walking over to the door, ready to leave, when Mrs. Jerrell said, "Talk to Mackenzie Trenton and Alana Keaney; they're Jenna's best friends."

Kay's eyebrows shot up. "Oh, so she had close friends after all? Since April, I mean?"

The woman's lips trembled. "I don't know anymore. She used to have. But even those girls... they stopped coming around so much. Maybe they'll tell you why."

The sharp sound of a gunshot ripped through the brief silence.

It came from behind the bedroom's closed door.

ELEVEN
GIRL TALK

The dentist in their rearview mirror, Alexandria drove toward the coast while Alana sulked with her arms crossed, slouched in the passenger seat, staring out the window.

Her daughter had been a complete brat at the dentist. She'd barely said hello to the staff, glaring at everyone over the lenses of her oversized shades. She'd squirmed and whimpered during a perfectly painless procedure, a simple scan of her teeth. Then she'd rolled several f-bombs when she heard the dentist finally agreeing with Alexandria and ordering aligners for three more months of orthodontic treatment.

It took some doing, the new aligners. At first, the dentist was totally defensive, probably thinking Alexandria was trying to get the new aligners for free. Once she cleared the money issue out of the way, he mellowed out, although he'd dared to say a bit of overbite wasn't all that bad.

The gall.

Not all that bad wasn't going to cut it for her daughter. Her incisors had to be absolutely perfect. Everything had to be perfect.

She sometimes fantasized that she was Alana, young and

naïve again, and that someone with means and good intentions had invested the time and resources to make her the best she could be. Maybe if her teeth had been straight and perfectly spaced, Miss Hawaii would've been the runner-up, and she would've taken the crown. Perhaps if she could've afforded better shoes, she would've been a movie star today instead of that Puerto Rican who'd cut ahead of her, clacking on the podium in her red-soled Louboutins.

Alana didn't know these things like she did. That's why it was her job to teach her daughter how to win at the game called life, whatever the cost. Fairly or not.

The silence had lasted long enough. "Come on, it wasn't so bad, was it?" Alexandria said in a cheerful voice, looking at her sulking daughter with a quick encouraging smile.

"Whatever." Alana chewed gum loudly, with her mouth open, and popped bubbles with obstinance, sending droplets of saliva in the air. She knew better, but that was her way to punish her mother, by behaving like a total embarrassment, someone spawned out of a trailer park deep in the Midwest.

It wasn't the first time, and Alexandria had learned not to let herself get aggravated by her daughter's appalling behavior. One time, when she'd dragged Alana away for a doctor's appointment she didn't want, her sweet little daughter took revenge by telling dirty jokes to a bunch of sweaty construction workers who were laying tile in the building. When she came back from the lab, Alexandria could've sworn at least three of them had erections. The lewd smirks on their faces made her sick to the stomach. She wanted to drag Alana out of there by her hair, but she knew better than to humiliate her daughter in front of them.

This time, she was determined to ignore the sulking and pretend nothing was wrong. After all, she deserved a good day, too, not just Miss Congeniality over there.

"I know how you feel," Alexandria said as if they were

having a real conversation. "Some of us aren't blessed with straight teeth, and we have to work for it."

Alana crossed her legs, bouncing her foot rhythmically against the fine leather of the car door. She shot her mother a disapproving glare, then resumed watching the scenery. Cedars and live oaks lined the freeway, their shapes more contorted as they approached the windy shore.

"Take Jenna, for example," Alexandria continued, her voice soft like a knife with a velvet-covered handle. "She was born with perfect teeth. Otherwise, that poor girl... I don't believe her parents could afford braces. If they could, it would have to be the cheap wire ones." She threw her daughter a quick glance. "But she doesn't need braces. Her smile is absolutely perfect, isn't it?"

Alana glared at her mother without a word. She inflated a gum balloon until it covered most of her face. She kept blowing into it until it popped, falling in sticky, disgusting shreds against her nose and chin. With a swift move of her tongue, she collected the remnants and continued chewing with her mouth open.

Alexandria smiled briefly. Her tactic was working.

"She's really sweet, isn't she?"

"Who?" Another pop.

"Jenna. Isn't she your best friend?"

Pop. "Screw Jenna, all right?"

"Ooh... I touched a nerve, didn't I?" She smiled with warmth and squeezed her daughter's knee. "I didn't mean to upset you."

"I'm not upset. We're just not that close anymore."

"What did the poor thing do to earn your wrath?"

A moment of silence. "Nothing. Who said she did anything?"

"Then why aren't you guys friends anymore? I thought you,

Jenna, and Mackenzie were inseparable." She chuckled. "Three peas in a pod, right?"

"Shit... now the sun's gone," Alana muttered, staring at the clouds gathering above the ocean.

"Language," Alexandria said sharply. "I won't tolerate this kind of trash talk."

"Don't be a hypocrite, Mom. You're not exactly a lady either when you're on the phone with your friends." She grabbed a piece of gum with two fingers and extended it out, then chewed it back into her mouth slowly. Strawberry flavor filled the car. "Male and female friends."

Her jaw dropped. "You've been eavesdropping on my calls?"

"You haven't been too discreet about it. Not my fault if you're being loud. Kinda bothers me, but I'm the kid. Nothing I can do, right? Swear away, for all I care."

Ten more miles, and they'd get there. Alexandria realized she was eager to drop her daughter off and enjoy a little peace and quiet by the ocean, without the constant struggle that meant being with her.

"What happened between you and Jenna, huh?" she pressed on.

"Nothing fucking happened, all right?" Alana raised her voice and turned toward her, her face scrunched in anger. "Why can't you let this go?"

"She used to come and visit all the time, now she doesn't."

"She doesn't do anything anymore," Alana replied quickly. "She doesn't get out of the house anymore. We're too good for her or something, I don't know."

Seemed as if her daughter was jealous of her once best friend. "Did Nick sleep with her? Huh? Tell me. Is that what happened?"

Her mouth agape, Alana stared at her in disbelief. "Jeez, Mom, you're insane. We're not a soap opera here. We're normal kids, doing normal kid stuff. If Nick was looking at another girl, I'd take it up with him."

"He's really popular, this Nick, isn't he?" Alexandria drilled on mercilessly. "He doesn't seem too committed to me. Maybe he didn't look, but Jenna could've made a move, right?"

"On her best friend's boyfriend?" Alana scoffed. "No one would speak with her again until graduation. You don't do shit like that; it's our code." A quick, loud, angry pop. "Sisters before misters, remember that?"

"Then what happened between you two, huh?" Alexandria asked gently this time, pinching Alana gently by the chin.

The teenager pulled away and shrugged. "I think she'd been dating someone; I don't know."

"Someone from school?"

She bit her lip and gave Alexandria a scrutinizing look as if to figure out if she could be trusted. "No, Mom. A guy, not a boy. A real man."

"An older man, you mean?" *Damn perverts... they're everywhere, lurking near schoolyards.*

"Yeah... I guess."

"How much older?"

She looked out the window, her only answer a dismissive shrug.

"You'll have to tell me what you know about this, Alana. I'll have to tell Jenna's mother, maybe even the police."

Alana clenched her fists and raised her arms in a gesture of despair. "Argh... Mom, that's why I never tell you anything. Just... let it go already. She'll be eighteen in a few months."

Alexandria slowed and pulled into the parking lot at the beach. Alana shifted in her seat, brimming with excitement, her earlier frustration seemingly vanished at the sight of Nick's red convertible Beemer. Several other cars she recognized from her daughter's last birthday party were parked nearby in a tight cluster.

"Mind if I hang out with you guys for a while?" Alexandria asked serenely.

Alana reacted as if she'd stepped on a snake. "What? No, Mom. No one comes with their mother to these things. I'll be the laughingstock of the entire school. You have to leave. Nick will drive me back."

Impervious to her daughter's plea, she climbed out of the SUV and stretched, taking in the fresh, salty air filled with moisture. She didn't come to the coast nearly as often as she wanted.

Beyond the edge of the parking lot, the beach extended several yards out to where the Pacific surf washed ashore, glimmering in the filtered sunlight. The waves had the most perfect shade of aquamarine she'd ever seen.

Alana grabbed her bag from the trunk and dashed toward the chatty group that was lounging on the sand a few yards away. She ran past her, throwing over her shoulder yet another plea, "Please, Mom, just go away."

Alexandria didn't rush. She leaned against the rusted parking lot railing overlooking the beach, and closed her eyes, taking in whatever sunshine made it through the clouds, feeling the ocean spray on her heated skin.

When she opened her eyes, Alana had reached her friends. Nick pecked her lips, then took her bag and set it on the towel by his side. Was her daughter sleeping with Nick? She probably was.

She closed her eyes again, leaning into the railing with both hands, stretching her shoulders. A strong gust of chilly Pacific breeze lifted her skirt, wrapping it around her legs. The soft fabric fluttered furiously around her thighs. It felt good... youthful, brazen. She didn't make any effort to hold it down, although her lace panties were showing at times. The wind touched her skin like a lover's hand, rushed, trembling, leaving a trail of fire in its wake.

When she opened her eyes again, Nick was standing in front of her, his eyes avoiding hers. Alana was by his side, barefoot in the sand, her arms crossed at her chest. She was wearing that string bikini that barely covered her nipples, although Alexandria had repeatedly told her no. She could've sworn she'd thrown that thing in the trash a couple of weeks ago.

"Hello, Mrs. Keaney," Nick said. "I wanted you to know I'll drive Alana home myself tonight."

"No later than eight," she said calmly, still ignoring what the wind was doing with her white silk skirt. Still enjoying it.

"Mom," Alana cried in protest, but her boyfriend didn't seem to mind, "why do you always have to be so—"

"Understood, Mrs. Keaney," Nick replied. He took Alana's hand, and they both ran toward the ocean, laughing and squealing in the frayed sunshine. Her daughter seemed really happy. It was showing in the way she turned to her boyfriend laughing, throwing her hair over her shoulder and looking sideways. In her fingers intertwined with Nick's, their arms swinging back and forth in sync. Alana was falling in love with him.

Damn that kid, he's nothing but trouble.

TWELVE
HIKE

Self-blame never helped anyone.

Kay kept telling herself that while tears choked her, threatening to break loose. She should've said something. She'd seen the signs, yet she'd doubted herself and decided to clam up. And now a man was dead, partly because of her silence, her cowardice. His widow, in shock, had to be taken to the hospital.

Elliot's hand squeezed hers, startling her back into reality.

"You couldn't've known," he said. His voice was gentle, understanding, yet undertones of sadness told her he was just as troubled by what had happened as she was.

"I *did* know," she replied bitterly. "That's exactly the problem. I knew, and I said nothing."

"I don't think you knew," he replied calmly. "I believe you *suspected*, and there's a difference."

She pressed her lips together and stared at the road ahead without seeing anything. She'd offered the Jerrells her support. Bill hadn't said a single word to confirm her suspicions. If she'd been wrong, she would've had a grieving parent committed to psychiatric care against his will. What kind of person would do that to a disabled parent who'd just lost his child?

It would've been better than this. Anything would've been better than this. Or would it?

Elliot clenched his jaw for a moment, muscles knotting under his skin. "How exactly do you tell a grieving mother that you think her husband is about to blow his brains out?" He shook his head slowly, pulling into the trailhead parking lot. "Can you imagine saying that and being wrong?" He cut the engine. "No, partner. I'm no shrink, but in my book, Jerrell's death is on the same perp as Jenna's. And we're going to get that son of a bitch if it's the last thing we do." He waited for a reaction from her, but she remained silent. "Right?"

She nodded, veering her gaze toward the parking lot. The ATV trailer bearing the insignia of the Franklin County Sheriff's Office was empty. One ATV was waiting for them, a two-seater, and Deputy Farrell was leaning against it, texting.

They climbed out of the SUV, and, just like earlier, Elliot took the driver's seat on the ATV.

"Where's everyone?" Kay asked, aware she'd said they'd be back from the next of kin in an hour or so, and it had been more than three.

Farrell pocketed her phone. "The boss was here." A quick eye roll. "He sent people to canvass the trails. Everyone's up there." She took her radio off her belt and pressed a button. The device spewed some static. "Farrell to Novack. Where are you? Over."

Another burst of static, then the deputy's garbled voice, barely intelligible. "We're past the ravine, about a mile farther up. Nothing so far."

Kay climbed on the ATV and thanked the deputy with a nod. "K-9 here too?"

"Not yet. They had to bring one from Marin County." She looked around cautiously. The parking lot was empty. "One more thing," Farrell said, lowering her voice as if anyone could hear them. "Logan wanted you to call him as soon as you got here. He sounded pissed."

Great. She'd expected to hear from Sheriff Logan sooner or later, ever since she'd noticed that news van trailing them. There was no keeping the reporters away once they'd caught the whiff of blood. In a small place like Mount Chester, the opportunity rarely presented itself and they couldn't waste it.

Groaning, she speed-dialed Logan's phone on speaker. He took the call with a short, "Yeah," against an auditory backdrop of wind gusts and nearby voices.

"It's Kay Sharp, sir, and I have Elliot with me. You wanted to speak with us?"

He mumbled something unintelligible, as if he'd covered the mic with his hand and spoken with someone else. "Mainly you I wanted, Sharp. What the hell happened out there at the Jerrells?"

She drew air sharply into her lungs and was about to blurt out a reply when he continued.

"Did you see it coming?"

"Y—yes, I believe I did," she replied, bracing herself.

"Damn," he muttered. "There was nothing you could've done, was there?"

In the brief silence that followed, she heard the sound of a lighter being flicked. He was probably lighting up one of his famous Cubans, his most dangerous vice as he liked to advertise it.

"My professional code of ethics leaves very little room for interpretation, sir." Her voice was calm, measured, cold as if she was delivering a review of someone else's lacking performance. "I should've reported it."

"And had him locked up?" Logan reacted. "Can you imagine the press after that?"

"Sir, we don't service the press—"

"No, we don't," he cut her off abruptly, then exhaled what

sounded like a lungful of smoke mixed with frustration. "But some of us have to get elected every few years if we want to keep our jobs. You went there as a cop to deliver a death notification, Sharp, not as his therapist."

She was about to start an argument with him when Elliot gestured with his hand that she should take it easy. He was right. Getting into an argument with her boss over the ethical dilemmas of her other profession would've been meaningless, if not damaging. "Then, what can I do for you?"

"I'm almost up at the ridge, and we haven't found anything so far."

"You're here?" she reacted, surprised.

"Yeah, and I ain't got all day. Take the ATV up along the chairlift and leave it at the upper terminal. Then you can cross the meadow and climb the eastern versant."

"Copy that," she replied with a slight frown, looking at her watch. That would save her some time.

"I'll take the ATV down, and K-9 can bring it back up. Daylight's running short, and rain's about to start."

"Understood."

"While you're on your way, figure out how to hold the press at bay. Contain the shitstorm for me, Sharp. Do your best."

The call ended abruptly. Elliot started the ATV and drove it as the crow flies toward the chairlift path. The system was built as a near-surface lift and opened seasonally as soon as a thick layer of snow covered the ground, luring skiers from all over the state.

She was just about to call Barb Foster, her only connection in the local media when she noticed the chairlift was working. Empty chairs moved up and down the mountain, whirring and clanking.

"Head over to the terminal first," she said, looking at the cloudy sky with concern.

Their approach drew the attention of the lift operator, who

came out of the terminal with one hand propped on his hip and another holding shade above his eyes. He wore a knitted hat low on his sweaty brow, although it was one of the hottest summer days the mountain had seen in years.

Elliot flashed his badge, and the man immediately frowned, shoving both his hands into his pockets and taking a step backward. "Detectives Young and Sharp, FCSO."

He nodded. "You here about the girl who died yesterday?"

"Yes. Do you know anything about that?"

"Uh-uh. Just that she ain't the first one to die on this mountain. Ain't gonna be the last one either." He scratched his head through the green hat. His hands were dirty, lined with grease, as one would expect for a lift technician.

Kay pointed at the moving chairs. "I didn't know the lift worked in the summer."

"It doesn't," he replied calmly. "It's scheduled maintenance. Not many people hike the ridge during summer. It's a waste of money to run it."

"So, you didn't take anyone up on the mountain yesterday?" Elliot asked.

"No, sir," he replied with a hint of a smile, taking a small step forward.

He seemed more comfortable engaging with Elliot than with Kay. Still, she asked, "Your name?"

"It's Jimmy. Jim Bugarin. I own this pile of junk," he added, giving the chairlift an annoyed look. "It works, you know, and it's safe if you want to hitch a quick ride up the mountain. Happy to oblige." He grinned, displaying irregular, stained teeth.

Kay glanced at the storm clouds gathering from the coast. It was tempting, but Logan was waiting for the ATV at the top terminal. "Not this time, but thanks."

"Well, call me if you need me," he added, pointing at a phone number painted on the terminal's wall for the sale of seasonal permits. "I'll be tinkering with it for a couple of days at least."

They were almost at the top terminal when they spotted a chair with two passengers: a man in uniform and a police dog seated next to him. The deputy had his arm wrapped around the dog's shoulders, holding him close as one would a child. The dog panted and seemed wary, although the chairlift rode low, close to the ground, and he could've easily jumped and continued the hike on foot.

"I'll be damned," Elliot said, giving the two a long stare. "There's nothing these dogs won't do."

Once at the terminal, the ATV exchanged hands, and Kay had to tell a furious Logan she'd done nothing yet to manage the media situation.

"Call them," Logan urged her from the driver's seat of the ATV. "Today. Now. I want them off my back."

Then he sped downhill, on the smooth path next to the chairlift.

Kay called Barb Foster, hoping she'd pick up. She thought she'd recognized the colors of the local TV station in the logo affixed on the white news van that had been trailing them all over town. Instead of Barb, she got her voicemail.

They continued the hike with the K-9 unit, a Belgian Malinois by the name of Spartan and his handler, Deputy John Deramus from Marin County.

"Someone's got a sense of humor," Kay commented, hearing the dog's name. Spartan was the lead detective in the movie *Demolition Man*, one of Kay's favorite action flicks.

Deramus grinned widely, beaming with pride. He must've named the dog himself.

"I thought you were going to start tracking at the bottom of the trail," Elliot said.

"Wouldn't do us much good," Deramus replied. The dog

was pulling ahead, the leash taut, although they hiked at a fast pace. "She was found in the ravine, wasn't she?"

"Yup." Elliot took a sip of water from a plastic bottle after offering it to Kay.

"He'd lead us to where the smell is strongest, and that's the ravine. We don't want that."

"Right."

"But if we start up here, he'll find the crime scene first, then he'll signal where she went down over the edge."

The deputies were in sight as they climbed over the last portion of the eastern versant. Spartan pulled against his leash, panting, and Kay could barely keep up. She was over the rocky edge of the path and onto the last stretch of the hike when Elliot spotted a candy wrapper near the path. He picked it up with a glove and sealed it inside an evidence pouch. "I'm surprised we didn't find more," he said, continuing at a brisk pace to catch up.

Ahead of them, Novack and Leach searched the bushes for evidence. Spartan led them past the deputies, and they were almost out of sight when Kay, out of breath and trailing behind, noticed Deputy Leach had picked something up from the ground and discreetly shoved it into his pocket.

She turned and walked straight to him. "What did you find?" she asked.

He shook his head, a little nervous. "Nothing." He gestured toward a large plastic bag holding numerous evidence pouches. "Everything we find we collect in there."

She extended her hand. "Give it." The man muttered an oath under his breath and Kay pretended not to hear it.

From a few yards away, Novack watched the scene with a smirk on his face.

"Now," she insisted.

Leach curled his lip and shoved his hands in his pockets. "I don't know what you're talking about."

"What's going on?" Elliot asked. He'd turned back, probably noticing Kay was no longer hiking with them.

"Your left pocket," Kay replied, unfazed. She didn't want to have to call Logan over this or to shove her own hand into the man's pocket.

Elliot looked at Leach with eyes widened in surprise. The deputy lowered his gaze and reached inside his pocket, then extracted a partially smoked joint nested in the palm of his hand.

"You might've compromised the evidence," Kay said, her voice riddled with frustration. "You know better; what the hell?" She held open an evidence pouch, and Leach dropped the joint in. "If we can't get DNA from it, there will—"

"It's mine," Leach replied, looking at her with cold eyes brimming with hatred. "I sometimes come up here and smoke. That's my roach; I know where I sit when I come up here and where I flick 'em. But I swear I didn't touch that girl."

"You're going to get a formal writeup for this," Novack announced, finally taking sides. Kay held her hand up in the air to silence him.

"Then why pocket the roach?" she asked Leach.

He scoffed and looked at her with pure contempt as if she were too dense to figure it out for herself. "You find my DNA up here, you tell me I wouldn't land on the suspect list?"

He had a point. Kay couldn't say she condoned what he'd done, but she could understand where he was coming from. His motivation was a good one unless he was hiding something else.

She pressed her lips together for a moment, then asked, "Where were you last night, between six in the afternoon and midnight?"

Irked as hell and turning red in the face, Leach slapped his hands together once, the sound echoing against the stone versants. "See? What did I tell you? Now I'm a suspect. I was at home, where the hell else would I be? I downed a couple at the Hilltop, then I went home. I had a long day."

"All right, you're done here," Elliot said. "Take the lift down if it's still running, then report back at the station. And stay there until we get back."

"Son of a bitch," Leach muttered, departing quickly.

Kay watched him heading downhill for a moment, then continued to climb up the ridge. Only fifty or sixty yards were left, the most treacherous ones, on a narrow path made of sharp boulders covered in moss.

Spartan's bark tore through the peaceful silence of the mountain. In the distance, Kay could see the K-9 sitting, his tail wagging furiously.

They had found the primary crime scene.

THIRTEEN
PRIMARY SCENE

The ridge widened in that spot and flattened into a small plateau covered in moss. Scattered, crippled old firs—forever bent eastward under the prolonged effects of gusting westerly winds blowing from the Pacific—provided shade for the summer hikers who wanted to spend time up there, taking in the wondrous landscape.

Wildfire Ridge was the second-highest mountain peak, its majestic rock face overlooking the western plains rolling gently toward the ocean. A fallen tree trunk was the preferred seating for hikers who climbed to watch the sunset or take photos of the scenery. On a clear summer day, one could see the gentle Pacific waves glinting in the sunshine.

Not today.

Clouds were gathering quickly, threatening rain, maybe a thunderstorm to go with it. In the distance, lightning flickered at times, the clouds tinted orange and red by the setting sun.

Kay reached Spartan and his handler. The dog still barked at intervals, signaling his find. Under an old fir with low, heavy branches, she found torn black leggings and panties stained with blood.

Putting on a fresh pair of gloves, she collected the clothing as soon as Novack finished photographing it with a yellow marker bearing the number seven on it.

A couple of feet away, she found the place where Jenna had been pinned down and sexually assaulted. White fabric fibers clung to a tree stump. Sharp-edged rocks still bore the stains of her blood. A few drops of blood had fallen on a rock, and a smeared dab of something white was visible next to them. She shone a small black light at the spot, and it luminesced in the dark twilight.

Semen.

The unsub was disorganized and sloppy; he'd left a generous trail of evidence she was happy to follow. Crouching next to the stains with a satisfied grin, Kay took multiple samples. She was still close to the ground when she noticed something colorful under the fir. Two torn condom wrappers found their way into evidence bags, same brand, same color. She searched for the used condoms, but couldn't find them. Maybe Spartan would if the perp hadn't thrown them over the edge into the abyss.

Kay stood and looked at the scene from a few feet away, changing perspectives. A big drop of rain splashed against her head.

"Rain," she yelled. "I want this entire area covered in plastic. Use the large bags, weigh them down with rocks."

The deputies hustled into action, laying plastic bags over certain areas and weighing them down with small boulders. One of them had placed a plastic sheet over a section that Kay had overlooked.

"What's there?" she asked, giving the sky a scornful glare.

"This," Hobbs replied. He was a young and rather chubby deputy, always enthusiastic and eager to learn. He lifted the plastic sheet enough for Kay to see what he was pointing at.

The plastic fluttered in the wind, rustling angrily. "I think it's a fingernail. A fake one."

Kay approached and crouched to take a closer look. She beckoned Novack to bring an evidence marker and take photos, then picked up the fingernail with two fingers. Before dropping it into an evidence pouch, she studied it closely. It was pink and glittery and had been forcefully torn off someone's finger, perhaps Jenna's if they were lucky, and she'd scratched her assailant during the assault.

"Got multiple footprints here," Elliot called. He was covering the section of terrain next to the fallen tree trunk with several overlapping plastic bags.

The rain had stopped falling, but clouds still clumped and swarmed above their heads, heavy, drawing closer to the peaks.

Kay held her hand out, but no fresh raindrops found it. "All right, quickly, let's get this done."

Hobbs brought markers, and Novack snapped photos of several footprints that Kay pointed out with quick gestures. Right in front of the fallen tree trunk, the ground was barren, probably from too many feet stomping it, and ripe with partially faded footprints. Most of the prints were old, almost indiscernible partials, but three distinctive footprints caught Kay's interest.

Two were men's sneakers, a size twelve and a size thirteen, clear, recent. A third one was a smaller, narrower print, a size eight woman's running shoe. A second female shoeprint, most likely from a Converse, was partly visible under one of the male prints but seemed fairly new. It seemed smaller; Kay thought it was a size six. Moving quickly and effectively, Hobbs poured molds of all the relevant prints.

Those prints led nowhere.

Aside from the patch of barren ground in front of the fallen log, and a couple of other spots where thick moss or ground allowed footprints to be discerned, the surface was covered in rocks.

Kay stepped away from the log and looked at the entire area, visualizing the attack.

"First, they sat on the log," Elliot said, appearing by her side. "I don't think they did that after the attack."

"No, you're right," Kay replied, frowning. There was something that kept tugging at her gut. Why two recent male shoeprints? There was only one semen stain, one condom brand, but two torn packets. Still, they'd been torn the exact same way. Soon, they'd know if the fingerprints were the same on both wrappers. "There's no blood by the log," she added, a little absentminded, still working scenarios in her mind.

"Was this date rape, you think?" Elliot took off his hat, ran his fingers through his hair, then put his hat back on. "She must've come up here with someone she knew." He looked at his watch, then around. The sun had set a while ago, and the shadows had grown long and heavy. "Then it got dark, and he knew no one else was coming."

"Maybe," she admitted, still staring at the log, then at the rock by the old fir where she'd found the bloodstains. "Hobbs," she called, "get us some light over here, will you?"

The deputy unzipped a large canvas bag filled with crime scene gear and extracted a foldable, battery-powered LED light on a small tripod. "Where do you want it?"

"Here, by these footprints." She turned to Elliot. "They don't make much sense." She bit the tip of her index finger the way she did when she was preoccupied with an unnerving thought. "Did you happen to notice what shoes Jenna was wearing? The pattern on their soles?"

"Not the pattern, no," Elliot replied. "But I believe she was wearing black canvas shoes with white laces; you know the kind. They're popular with kids."

"Converse," Kay muttered. "Damn."

"Why are you lower than a gopher hole?"

"What?" she asked, surprised as always by his unusual turn of phrase. "Oh, it's these footprints. Trying to understand what happened here." She walked over to the center of the log, stopping short of stepping onto the soil where the prints were still visible, now stained by leftover droplets of blue silicone casting material.

"What about them?"

"I also remember she was wearing Converse," Kay replied. "This is a Converse sole." She pointed at the partially covered shoeprint. "Highly recognizable, with these squares cut in half by continuous lines that run toe to heel. This other print came after the Converse, and it's by far more prominent."

"Maybe Jenna stood first and walked over there, then the guy walked almost in her footsteps, behind her."

"And this?" Kay pointed at the size eight women's running shoe.

"Could've been from earlier," he replied, shrugging. "It looks recent, but there's no way of knowing. I'd be safe betting everyone who hikes this ridge ends up sitting on this log for a rest."

Kay took out her flashlight and searched the entire space for more size eight footprints. There weren't any to be found. Coincidence? Tourist traffic from earlier, like the many other partials lining the barren ground. Like the other male shoeprint. Because no one had climbed the mountain since Jenna's body was found.

Spartan's bark, followed by a long, mournful howl, tore through the silence. Kay saw the K-9 and his handler standing by the side of the edge. Watching her step on sharp-edged rocks and loose boulders, Kay approached quickly.

"Whoa, this thing's dangerous. They should install a railing here. This is where she went over," Deramus said.

"Why is he howling?"

"He's sad he can't take us there. It's his job."

Kay flashed her light over the edge of the rock, carefully approaching. One wrong step, and she could fall to her death, just like Jenna.

A couple of feet from the edge, she found another partial Converse print. Jenna had stood there, her back turned to the abyss.

She placed a marker and asked Novack to take a photo with a gesture of her hand. "Elliot, why would someone stand so close to the edge, facing away from the fall?"

"It could've been dark already, right? She could've been disoriented after the assault. Maybe she didn't know the fall was there."

Or maybe she was pushed.

FOURTEEN
HUSBAND AND WIFE

It was almost ten in the evening when Richard William Gaskell returned home from his best friend Rennie's place. The eighteen-year-old with a tall, well-built stature and medium-length hair combed back in an imitation of Bieber's early days' quiff resented coming home. Less than a year to go until he'd finally leave for Harvard to study law, just like his parents. Yet, he wanted to be nothing like them—with one exception.

Money.

Quite the difference between Rennie's place and his.

His best friend, Renaldo Cristobal, almost a year younger than Richard and a senior as well, had been dealt an entirely different hand at the game of chance called life. Rennie had grown up without a father, raised by a mother who stretched every dollar of her physical therapist paycheck to breaking point. Still, Rennie's small, simple, and sometimes messy abode was more welcoming than the sprawling two-story, ultramodern house Richard was forced to call home.

Some lawyers were like drug dealers, and he wanted to be just like that someday, on the speed dial of the country's richest, most feared and powerful criminals. Richard used to say his home was the best real estate drug money could buy north of San Francisco because his father was a notoriously successful criminal attorney whose client list read like the *Yellow Pages* of Colombian cartels and Yakuza businesspeople. The only thing Richard still admired about his father was his seven-figure income.

His mother, also a criminal attorney, used to specialize in white-collar crime before she decided work wasn't the thing for her anymore and stayed home to ruin his life. She'd had the gall to blame her laziness on him, to say she forfeited her career and a significant portion of the family's income because her son needed hands-on guidance to become more accountable and learn how to make the right decisions in life.

In a few short weeks after that appalling statement, his satisfying life in San Francisco's Nob Hill was uprooted to the Mount Chester cottage. To call the four-thousand-square-foot cubist structure in concrete, steel, and tempered glass a cottage was an insult to mountain cottages everywhere as much as to modern architecture.

Richard didn't care about any of that; he would've happily lived in a tent popped up in Rennie's backyard. He missed his city friends, the girls in miniskirts and high heels wearing expensive makeup and real jewelry, and always looking for a good time. Just when he'd become old enough to go out there and have a real life, he'd been locked up in last century's small town soon to be another San Fran overpriced suburbia. Instead of bustling city life, he could hear the mockingbirds at night. He'd been buried alive, with his overbearing mother playing both Hades and Cerberus.

Since he'd turned eighteen, every passing day brought the same question: should he run away and be done with it? The promise of Harvard and having his tuition and housing covered enthusiastically by his parents was too alluring to ignore. Day after day, gritting his teeth and clenching his fists, he decided to stay. One more year. Harvard was bound to be much more fun with money lining his pockets.

But he didn't have to like it.

Richard sought refuge at Rennie's every chance he got. When he'd started school in that forsaken place two years ago, he discovered Rennie was the choice target of the resident bullies. The sensitive, pale-skinned, and dark-haired boy was shy and somewhat effeminate, taking the beatings and abuse without fighting back much. Thin and not very tall, Rennie was smart enough to intuit that resisting would've only motivated his bullies to strike harder and for longer.

The bullying ended a couple of days after Richard started classes, angry as hell and looking for a release. He'd stumbled upon the three idiotic brutes who were just starting to pummel on Rennie, and wiped the floor with them. He was only one, and maybe just as strong as any of the three, but the countless martial arts movies he'd watched had taught him a few slick moves, and he was enraged to begin with. Crazy beats strong all the time.

When the fight ended with the three bullies on the floor bleeding and writhing in pain, he offered Rennie his hand to get up and sealed the beginning of a lasting friendship. When the school investigated the fight, the matter was swiftly closed; all the students who had witnessed it swore the three bullies had fought among themselves. And so, in only a few days, Richard had become the school's unsung hero.

Natalie Gaskell, Richard's mother, was thrilled with her son's friendship with Rennie. In her own words, Rennie was a sweet boy, a good influence, educated and intelligent and courteous, nothing like the street thugs Richard used to run with in San Francisco. She didn't mind him spending time at Rennie's, and he spent as much time there as he could.

The aged couch in Rennie's small, dark living room, with its worn fabric and lumpy cushions, was more comfortable than the extended white leather sectional at Richard's house. Rennie's mother was rarely home, and when she was, she quietly brought food and cold sodas for the boys who watched TV or played video games, filling the small home with hollering and laughter.

The afternoon had started a bit off. When he arrived, he found Rennie watching the news. A TV announcer was saying the body found at the bottom of the Wildfire Ridge was Jenna Jerrell's. Visibly shocked, Rennie looked at him. "Did you know about this?"

"What the fuck?" Richard asked, drawing closer to the TV and turning the volume up. "Jenna's dead?"

Rennie nodded. "They didn't say anything else."

Richard shrugged. "I wonder what the hell happened." After moment of silence he didn't particularly enjoy, he added, "Let's play *Call of Duty*."

After the game, he spent the rest of the evening educating his shy and unusually nervous friend into the art of bringing a woman to orgasm using visual aids on the internet's most popular adult sites. Then he reluctantly had to leave. It was almost ten, and Rennie's mom had returned from work; he couldn't stay any longer. He jumped into his custom Jeep Wrangler and drove home, his mood sinking with every mile.

When he arrived, he could hear his parents from the driveway, even before he cut the engine. They were going at it again.

His mother, wearing a loosely tied blue silk bathrobe and looking disheveled, was screaming at his father. Still wearing his thousand-dollar charcoal suit, he was taking it cowardly, staring at the floor, not saying much. Richard watched them from the driveway through the large curtainless windows, tempted to turn the Jeep around and leave. But where would he go? And why risk having the banshee scream at him tomorrow for breaking curfew?

Resigned, he entered the house, careful to close the door quietly behind him and planning to seek immediate refuge in his bedroom wearing his Bose headphones to mute the sounds of the fight. But something stopped him in his tracks. This argument wasn't like any other he'd witnessed.

"You did this on purpose, didn't you?" his mother was saying. With every angry gesture of her hand, she took one step forward, getting closer to her husband, Ed. "You pretended to care about Richard's well-being, when in fact you wanted me gone from San Francisco so you could screw—what's her name, again? Bambi?" Her white-knuckled fist punched the air near Ed's face. He withdrew. "Oh, it's Heidi, yes... how could I forget. Is she legal, at least?"

Slack-jawed, Richard froze in the living room arch, staring at his father in disbelief. How could he take that kind of abuse and say nothing? His cowardice made him sick to the stomach. Edward Gaskell, one of the most respected criminal defenders in California, had been rendered speechless by a crazed bitch with a venomous tongue and baseless accusations. She'd turned his father into a pussy, and Richard into a pawn she sacrificed as she saw fit, a pinball bounced back and forth in an argument to score points.

Noticing his arrival, both parents acknowledged his presence with a quick glance, but the fight didn't skip a beat because his shrew of a mother wouldn't let it happen.

"I want you to start working from home. From here," she added, pointing a furious finger at the floor. "Go to the city if and when you have court dates. And fire that Heidi girl before I come down there and drag her out of your office by her phony hair extensions."

His father ran his hands through his thinning hair as if he wanted to pull it out of his head. "Geez, Natalie, you're absurd. Heidi has a law degree. She's a professional."

"A professional what?" she replied with a crooked grin.

"Where did she use to work before she landed in your lap, the Tenderloin? Corner of O'Farrell and Hyde?" she asked, referencing a popular pickup spot for the city's hookers.

Seeming at the end of his wits, Ed slapped his hands against his thighs. "What do you want from me, Natalie?" he asked, after emptying his lungs of air with a frustrated sigh. "I can't work from here more than a day a week, at the most. I have an office, client meetings, depositions. I need to be there."

"Then drive home every night," she said, hands propped firmly on her thighs.

"Here?" Ed took his hand to his forehead, rubbing furiously. "It's a two-hour drive, one way, with speeding! You're being ridiculous. Absurd." He looked at the room, at its walls as if they were a prison cell holding him confined. "Why don't you move back to the city with me? We have the condo. Richard would love it."

Richard's heart skipped a beat. *Yes!*

"And have him chasing women and smoking pot every day, just like his dad?" She didn't even look at Richard when she spoke of him; just flicked her hand in his direction in a gesture of contempt.

"He's just being young, Natalie. It's what boys do. You're reading too much into this. Just let it go, baby—"

"I'm not your fucking baby, all right?" She stomped her foot down angrily against the hardwood with a loud thump. "Heidi or Bambi or whoever is next after them is your baby." She smiled wickedly. "Isn't it, *sweetheart?*" Her voice was dipped in poison as she spat the word.

Ed straightened his back, and a line of stern tension appeared in his jaw. "What do you want, Natalie?"

"I want Bambi gone—"

"You mean Heidi."

She gritted her teeth. "Whatever. I want her gone. Hire male lawyers and paralegals from now on."

"What else?" He was inexplicably calm.

"No client dinners anymore; only lunches."

A hint of sarcasm colored Ed's stunned gaze. "For real? Can you imagine how that would go with my clientele?"

"Don't care. And stop cheating on me!" she yelled, seemingly more irritated by his serenity than she'd been by his anger.

"Why are you saying I'm cheating on you? I swear I haven't—"

"Don't!" She raised her hands to stop him. "Just don't cross that line." She paused for a moment, out of breath. With shaky fingers, she gathered the loose robe around her body and tightened the sash, then collected a strand of hair off her face and tucked it behind her ear. "I know you're cheating, Ed. I found the condoms."

"What?" Ed asked quietly, his eyes round in disbelief. "You're going through my pockets now?"

She nodded. "The pack in your pocket is missing four condoms. The one in your briefcase, two."

"There's no limit with you, is there?" Ed said, his voice barely a whisper.

"Ah, spare me," she replied with a disgusted smirk. "You taught me, remember? You said, 'People are responsible for their own fate if they can't push themselves to find the truth, even if it hurts.' Did I quote you correctly?"

He stared in Richard's direction without making eye contact. "Yes, you did."

"And it hurt to find those Trojans, you know. But I was willing to give you the benefit of the doubt. Maybe they were old... some item you forgot all about because you didn't *need* condoms anymore." Her eyes darted at Richard for a brief moment, then scoffed bitterly. "The expiration date on the purple pack is four years from now. I called the company with the serial number. They confirmed you bought them after last February when this lot was released for distribution in stores."

She mumbled something unintelligible as she counted on her fingers. "In six months, you used six condoms that I know of." She looked to the side, seemingly defeated. "Prosecution rests, Your Honor."

"Natalie, hold on for just a moment. It's not what you think."

"Now you're going to tell me you moonlight as a volunteer for clean sex education, and those Trojans are handouts for young people who can't afford them? Spare me," she said, turning her back to him and staring out the window. "Whatever excuse you could come up with, I thought of already, trying to forgive you." A beat of silence. "I wish you'd have the backbone to admit it like a man, not cower and lie like a yellow-bellied jackal." She wiped a tear with her index finger. "I'm not going to let you ruin this child's life so you can keep your fly zipped up."

Anger rose in Richard's throat. Why bring him into their fight? And how dare she speak to his father like that? Men had needs... it was her fault she decided to move to Mount Chester. What was his father supposed to do? Become a monk? He looked at his father, but he seemed lost, dismayed; his eyes, deeply saddened, stared at the floor.

She had castrated a fearsome man. If Richard didn't pay attention, she would soon castrate him too.

Without a word, he turned around and left, slamming the massive door behind him. With a few rushed strides, he reached his Jeep and jumped over the custom door, sliding into the driver's seat as the key found the ignition and the engine started. As he reversed out of the driveway, he heard his mother shouting again.

"See? Now you're driving our son away. If anything happens to him, I swear..."

The rest faded behind him as he sped through the hilly,

sleeping street, then across town heading for the ski resort. Up there, on the deserted mountain, under the stars, he could find some peace.

FIFTEEN
PRELIMINARY

The sun peeked from behind Wildfire Ridge, sending sharp rays burning through the lingering fog that colored the glens and ravines a misty gray. It was going to be another beautiful summer day.

Kay barely registered that; her mind wallowed in the darkness surrounding Jenna's brutal death. What could've happened to that girl in April to transform her from a confident and easygoing teenager to someone who looked as if she'd lost everything that had any meaning to her? She had to find out. Might've not been related to her actual death, but Kay's gut wouldn't let go. Whatever happened in April had turned Jenna into whom she had been in the last few months of her life, which spoke to victimology. Maybe, under her recent duress of unknown origin, Jenna somehow became vulnerable, and someone knew about it. Someone who wanted her dead.

"Why did you become a cop?" Elliot asked, shattering the silence that had been lingering between them since they left Kay's place. He was driving the Ford to the medical examiner's office on nearly deserted streets; the town still sleeping at that hour. Dr. Whitmore had spent another sleepless night and had summoned them to his office at first light.

Elliot shot her a quick glance from underneath the wide brim of his favorite cowboy hat, a black felt one with a small silver buckle on the hatband and a pronounced front dip. He'd picked Kay up a few minutes earlier. The moment she'd received Doc's text invite, she'd stopped her early morning routine of spackling walls and sanding them ready to be painted, but even so, she barely had time to get dressed and be ready to leave before he arrived. A straggling thought nudged her; had she closed the lid on the spackling paste container? Or would she find it all dried up and clumped in brittle, white, useless bits?

Elliot's question threw her into a whirlwind of emotions and memories. "You mean, now? You know why," she deflected. Elliot was part of the reason she'd decided to stay in her home-town instead of returning to her previous life in San Francisco, but she wasn't about to tell him that.

He flashed a quick smile he rushed to contain. "No, not now. When you joined the FBI."

"Oh." She considered her answer for a moment.

Like many traumatized people, she'd chosen psychology as her major, probably in a clichéd attempt to figure out her own problems. But she'd taken it to the next level when the FBI had offered her a job upon graduation. She'd accepted the offer enthusiastically, forfeiting the fat paychecks that psychologists made either as therapists for Silicon Valley's overworked millionaires or becoming overworked business professionals themselves. She'd never looked back; she wanted her life to have meaning, and to the twenty-three-year-old graduate she used to be eight years ago, that meant preventing other families from going through the hell that hers had. If she could save one family, if she could keep one daughter from having to—

No. She couldn't let herself think about it again.

Since her early days with the FBI, her concept of meaning had changed, had evolved in lockstep with her career, but it was still about saving lives, about giving victims a voice, about finding the truth, and delivering those responsible for crimes to justice.

"Why? Don't you think I have the talent for it?" she replied with not one question, but two, a perfect example of how unwanted queries should be handled.

Elliot's smile reappeared, lingering on his lips for a moment. He was onto her deflective tactics. "You're faster than greased lightning to dodge my question."

Unfazed, Kay calculated how much longer she needed to stall. Two more minutes, tops until he'd pull in front of the medical examiner's office. "I wanted my life to mean something. If I could save a single life..." her words trailed off, realizing she was getting dangerously close to letting Elliot see past her defenses. "That doesn't mean I didn't work my share of white-collar crimes and embezzlement cases." She frowned for a moment, thinking where she was going with that and why what she was saying felt wrong. "Those are important too, and in many cases, lives are saved from poverty and despair, but it's not—"

"How did you graduate from white-collar to serial killers?" Elliot said, turning onto the medical examiner's street with slightly screeching tires.

She smiled widely as she grabbed the door handle for balance. "I went looking for trouble. There was a case in San Francisco; it was my second year—"

Kay stopped as Elliot cut the engine in front of the single-story gray building that housed Dr. Whitmore's office. "Some other time, I'll tell you all about it," she said, glad to focus all attention on Jenna instead of herself.

Quicker than her on the front steps, Elliot held the door open. She turned to say thanks as she entered the building and noticed the grimace of disgust on his face as the chilly morgue air with hints of formaldehyde hit his nostrils. She hid a smile and crossed the deserted lobby, then pushed through the stainless-steel swing doors that led to the autopsy room, passing quickly by the empty reception desk. It was still too early for any of Doc Whitmore's helpers to be present.

The autopsy room was flooded in powerful light coming from several ceiling fixtures and an LED operating-room lamp installed on a mobile flex arm screwed into the ceiling. Only one of the two autopsy tables was occupied, the body resting on it covered with a white sheet.

Doc Whitmore sat on his four-legged lab stool on casters, rolling quietly from the microscope to the centrifuge whirring by the wall, using his hands to push or pull himself against the edges of the table. Next to it, a row of slides held samples treated and ready for his examination.

A trove of equipment was laid neatly on a long, tiled table that took almost the entire length of the left wall under the X-ray lightbox and wall-mounted monitor. His back was hunched, his lab coat wrinkled, and he raised his gloved hand to greet them a little shakily. His eyes still glued to the equipment he was working on, he mumbled, "That was fast."

Kay approached the table quietly. A strand of Jenna's silky brown hair had slipped from underneath the white sheet, hanging over the side of the cold steel table. She fought the irrational urge to tuck it under the sheet; it didn't matter anymore. Nothing mattered anymore for the bodies that landed on Doc Whitmore's table other than the truth they were willing to share, the evidence they could deliver.

Stopping by Doc's side, she gently squeezed his shoulder. He shot her a brief glance though the thick lenses of his black-rimmed glasses.

"You've been in these clothes for more than a dance," she

said, noting the sweat stains on his shirt, where the lab coat was open.

"Ugh, is it that bad?" he asked, apologetic and embarrassed as he gave his armpit a disapproving glance.

"Oh, nothing like that," Kay replied. "Just the wrinkles on your shirt." A beat. "And around your eyes."

"Those ones were years in the making," he said, standing up with difficulty, a hand propped firmly against an offending left hip. A grimace of pain washed over his face as he stood. "I do my best work at night when everyone leaves, and I can focus." He cleared his throat quietly, looking at the thin body on the table. "Some evidence is time-sensitive, as you well know."

"Like what?" Elliot asked, taking a step closer to the table. While in the autopsy room, he always liked to keep his distance, probably counting the seconds until it was all over. Some cops got used to the cold exam room with time, while others ended up retiring without ever managing to stomach a postmortem from start to finish. A healthy dose of professional curiosity was slowly bringing her partner around.

"Like fingerprints on the skin, for example," Doc Whitmore said, grabbing a magnifying glass from a drawer and handing it to Elliot. "Take a look there, above her right elbow. That's the killer's thumbprint." He pulled the sheet lower and exposed Jenna's arm. The sight of her skin touching the steel table made Kay shiver.

"I found a latent print and preserved it with cyanoacrylate fumes." A quick glance at Elliot's confused face, and Doc added, "Superglue. Otherwise, in a few more hours, it would've been gone." He pointed with the blue tip of his gloved finger. "Here, and here. She was held like this," he demonstrated, pretending to hold Kay's arms without touching her. "She was pinned down, most likely. On the underside of her arm, her skin was lacerated in multiple places, most likely by sharp-edged rocks. You see here? On the dorsal side of the arm, you have the bruising from the perp's hands, and on the ventral, the lacerations from the surface she was pinned against forcefully." He pressed his lips together. "But we're skipping ahead."

He picked up a remote from the lab table and clicked it a few times, displaying digital X-rays in rapid succession. Then he stopped on an X-ray of Jenna's skull. The whitish shape showed cracks and dents in various places, especially the back, the left cheekbone and temporal.

"She fell to her death, right, Doc?" Elliot asked, taking yet another step closer to the wall-mounted screen.

"Yes. Cause of death is blunt trauma consistent with the fall from a significant height, consistent with the laser distance finder results of four thousand, fifty-seven feet we measured from up on Wildfire Ridge to the bottom of the fall. Any of these skull fractures could've killed her on the spot." He clicked the remote again, and X-rays of Jenna's spine took the screen. "Her backbone was shattered in several places, also consistent with her landing on rocky terrain at terminal velocity. Broken ribs pierced her heart in several places." Another click to display X-rays of her arms and hands. "This is where the consistencies with a free fall end. Both her humeri show spiral hairline cracks, consistent with her arms being twisted forcefully. Seeing the same here," he tapped the screen where the image of a hand was displayed, "in her third proximal phalange, left hand. A head fracture in her second proximal, right hand." He turned to them and demonstrated with his own hands in the air. "He twisted her hands like this, forcing her on her knees." He looked at the screen for a moment. "Oh, and there's a spiral fracture on her wrist too. This happened when he pinned her hand down, like this." He held his left hand against the table surface with his right. "See the corresponding lacerations on the dorsal side of the hand." He paused for a moment, then added, "I will rule it a fatal sexual assault. This was murder; there's no doubt about it."

In the thick silence, only the distant humming of the cold storage shelves lining the autopsy room's back wall could be heard.

A phrase resonated in Kay's mind. *Broken ribs pierced her heart in several places.* She found herself wondering if Jenna had jumped to her death after the assault so that the pain would end. The psychological pain etched on her beautiful face and the physical pain that had found her up on Wildfire. Or did the unsub finish her off with one swift push? Either way, she'd died quickly. At least there was that. *Broken ribs pierced her heart in several places.* And still, the thought of that brought shivers to Kay's spine.

Her throat had dried up; she swallowed before she spoke. "Did she fall straight down?"

"It's difficult to say. The rib fractures here, corresponding with a deep, elongated laceration on her back," he pointed at Jenna's rib cage without removing the sheet, "indicate that her body hit a rocky protuberance on the vertical wall, on the way down. People don't bounce off rocks; they roll and slide. I don't see any evidence of that, but some rocky edge might've been sticking out and got her in the back. If you'd like, I can take scans of the mountain and determine—"

"It doesn't really matter to the investigation, Doc," she replied quickly. "Either way, it's the same unsub we need to find. Tell me about him, if you can."

A brief smile stretched Dr. Whitmore's lips, not touching his eyes. "That I can, and plenty."

He removed the sheet that covered Jenna's body with a gentle action and folded it quickly, placing it at the side of the table, near her feet. Elliot took a step back and lowered his gaze to the floor.

"There's evidence of sexual assault with oral, vaginal, and anal penetration. Abrasions and bruises on her cheeks, gums,

palate, and lips. There are significant split-type lacerations, radi-
ally oriented at five, six, and seven o'clock, lacerations to the poste-
rior fourchette, and bruising to the labia, which we see in forceful
penetrations. There's more than enough tissue damage to support
the sexual assault finding. Trace evidence of condom lubricant
was found, consistent with the two condom wrappers you recovered from the scene." He pushed his thick-rimmed glasses up his
nose with the back of his forearm. "But this perpetrator is inexpe-
rienced, I would dare assume, because he left smears of semen on
her inner thigh and on her cheek." A flicker of that earlier sad
smile returned. "DNA is running on both samples."

"Good," Kay replied, refraining from rubbing her hands
together. DNA meant she would find this unsub and make her
case watertight beyond any reasonable doubt.

Dr. Whitmore looked at her briefly, then at Elliot. "If you
could turn your attention to this laceration on her face," he said,
pointing alongside a scratch several millimeters wide that ran
from her right cheekbone near her temple to the tip of her nose.
"There was a trace substance in this laceration, so minute I have
it running in the mass spectrometer. It can analyze samples
down to a molecule in size, so, whatever it is, we'll soon find out.
I nearly missed it, being so small, but it had a slight reflectivity.
It glinted against the light."

Kay frowned. "Any idea what that could be?"

"None yet." He peeled off his gloves and sent them flying
into a wastebasket, then shoved his hands into his pockets.

"All right, Doc, this is a good start. I'm guessing there will be
more?" She shifted her weight from one foot to the other, eager
to leave. The mystery of Jenna's recent hardship kept her mind
preoccupied with speculation, and there's nothing worse in an
investigation than speculation instead of fact.

"I'm not done yet," he replied. Noticing Kay's expression,
he took the sheet and unfolded it, then covered Jenna's body.

Kay helped from her side, making sure the sheet covered every inch of her skin.

Something about her young body laid out under the strong circle of lights, bare and vulnerable, tugged at Kay's heart. And Jenna wasn't the first girl whose body Kay had visited in an autopsy room during her eight years in law enforcement, but this one felt different. As if Kay could still ease her pain somehow. As if she could still make things right for her, beyond catching her killer.

"I found two hair fibers, without follicles, unfortunately, that still clung to her clothes." Doc walked over to the lab table and brought an evidence bag, sealed and signed, holding a coiled strand of hair. He held it up against the light, then lowered it next to Jenna's head. "I didn't have time to look at it yet, but it does seem to be a different color than Jenna's, lighter, a bit longer too. I'll study its characteristics a little later and compare with Jenna's to make sure."

Maybe it was the unsub's hair. Many young men wore their hair longer; some even bleached it blond. When they didn't dye it green or blue. "How long would you say it is, Doc?"

"About sixteen inches. If you'd like, I can—"

"No rush, I have an idea what I'm looking for. Hair can wait, but fingerprints can't. Did you find any on those condom wrappers?"

"Ah, yes. I almost forgot," he added, looking sheepish for a moment. "Old age, I guess." He picked up two evidence bags holding the purple wrappers covered in dark fingerprint powder. "Both wrappers have fingerprints on them, belonging to the same person. They were also torn in precisely the same way. One of the condoms had a partial that probably belongs to the same individual, but I'll need the ten card to confirm."

Kay cringed. The assault had been long, repeated. And brutal. He'd stopped, but then he wanted more, and raped her again. She found herself wishing Jenna had been unconscious for it. "Did you run the prints through AFIS?"

"It's still running. Nothing yet." Doc Whitmore took a seat on the stool with a quiet groan, then looked through his notes quickly. "This is preliminary, you know that, right?"

"Yes, sir," Elliot replied. "You'll let us know when you have anything else?"

Doc nodded, still staring at his notebook, following the scribbles on the page with the tip of his finger.

"Stomach contents?" Kay asked. "I need to map the last twenty-four hours of her life, and that would help me."

"It's next on my list," he said, taking his glasses off and rubbing the bridge of his nose between his thumb and index finger. "Tox screen is pending too."

They were almost at the door when Doc Whitmore caught up with them. "I knew I forgot something. I found fingerprints on that pink plastic hair clip we found at the scene. They don't match Jenna's."

SIXTEEN
DRUNK

She didn't get dressed until long after her daughter was picked up for school in Nick's red Beemer. She'd let herself enjoy the soft touch of her fuzzy bathrobe, secretly planning a long, relaxing soak in the Jacuzzi after Alana left and she could finally stop arguing with her. What was it with that kid, looking to contradict every word she had to say, pushing boundaries as far as possible, willing them broken? She missed the daughter Alana had been only until a few years ago, when she'd say, "I love you, Mommy," then stretch up on her toes to get a kiss.

Those days were long gone, never to return once the teenage years had descended upon her, with glares and scowls and oaths at every other word. Alexandria held on tightly every day, committed to investing every ounce of energy and commitment she had into making Alana the girl she couldn't herself be at her age. A winner, a celebrated beauty, the most desirable young woman who would have her choice of men and careers and everything else she wanted. The good thing was, she read in some women's magazine that teenagers aged too and, in their twenties, rediscovered their love for their mothers. All she had to do was wait the teenage years out and not burn any bridges with her rebel child.

She soaked for about an hour, letting her mind wander aimlessly. Then slipped on a black lace Fleur du Mal lingerie set, and picked a midnight-navy Milano silk shirt to go with a pair of stretch jeans that made her bum seem tighter, perkier than it was. A touch of concealer under her eyes, some lip gloss, and blush to add color to her pale skin, and she was ready.

She lingered in the kitchen, trying to decide what to do with the day. She could drive up the coast, to that quaint café overlooking the ocean, where she could take her time basking in the sun with a cappuccino in her hand, making small talk with the young barista who always seemed to check her out. Or she could go shopping in the city; she hadn't driven down there in a while. Westfield Mall had tons of new fashion items every month, Hillsdale too. It would definitely be worth her time.

The doorbell chime interrupted her thoughts. Running her fingers quickly through her carefully styled hair, she shot herself a glance in the mirror as she walked over to the front door and smiled, satisfied with her youthful appearance. A look through the sidelight, and she recognized her lover's car, parked in the driveway.

A flush of heat stormed through her blood as she opened the door. He stood there on the porch, unbuttoning his shirt, his eyes drilling into hers with urgency. She lowered her gaze, following his fingers as they did quick work of the last button, then dawdled with his belt buckle. He was already hard for her, impatient, demanding. Desire swept over her and took control of her mind, vibrating in every fiber of her body, setting her blood on fire, making her insides tremble with need.

She grabbed the front of his loose shirt and dragged him inside, finding his lips as she pushed the door shut. He lifted her up, and she wrapped her legs around his body as he carried her into the bedroom. When she landed on the bed, she grabbed his tousled hair and held him close, unwilling to let the kiss end, but he pulled away and stood above her, studying her with an intense, serious look on his face as if deciding what to do to her. How to take her.

She squirmed and whimpered, eager and needy, but he silenced her with one finger held against her lips. Then he let that finger travel south until it met the luscious fabric of her shirt. Slowly, he undid one button at a time, his eyes dominating her into still submission. Her chest heaved with tormented breaths as he exposed her, peeling off the shirt and throwing it sideways to the floor. Her jeans were next, and then his. She reached for him with both her hands, yearning to touch his skin, but he pinned her wrists above her head and held her still, watching her, waiting.

"Please," she whispered. "You're driving me crazy."

He brought his lips close to her ear. "Please, what?"

She whimpered, lost in a whirlwind of emotions as he made love to her, slowly yet passionately, building desire into her body instead of quenching it. She was his. She lived for his touch, for a moment of caress, for another day like that. There was no escape.

Spent and deliciously tired, she shifted in his embrace, running the tips of her fingers across his chest. "I love chest hairs on you," she whispered. "Don't ever start shaving it."

He reached over and kissed her lips. "I've been considering it. All the movie stars do it these days. Why shouldn't I?"

"Because I like it like that," she said, smiling. "It's a sign of virility, and it turns me on."

He chuckled. "Might not be good enough, I don't know." His eyes were serious, tense. He sat on the side of the bed and reached for his clothes. He was leaving.

He was always leaving.

Yet she had no right to ask him to stay.

A wave of sadness crashed over her, threatening to ruin the

moment. She forced herself to smile and sat up, covering herself with the wrinkled bedsheet. "When will I see you again?"

His lips stretched into a lustful grin. "You want more?"

She'd lost all her dignity the day he'd touched her the first time. "Yes," she replied, her voice trembling, choked with raw emotion. "You know I do."

"Then you'll see me again," he said, walking toward the door while tucking in his shirt and tightening his belt.

She rushed after him, draped in the lilac sheet that smelled like him and his lovemaking. She stopped in the open door, unwilling to step outside looking like that. "Wait," she called when he was almost at his car, "I—"

He turned around and rushed to her. Still hungry for her, he found her lips and kissed her breathless, tilting her head back in a fiery embrace that fused their bodies together. Then he let her go. "Bye, babe. Got to run."

Moments later, long after his car had pulled away from her driveway, she closed the door and locked it. The silence in the empty house was bringing tears to her eyes, tears that weren't supposed to come, tears she despised.

She pushed herself to make the bed and pick up after herself, then she got dressed again, this time in a pair of denim shorts and a T-shirt. She wasn't going shopping anymore, not today.

Finding the sofa, she lay down, giving her trembling muscles a break. She was insane... this relationship wasn't healthy. They weren't dating; they weren't even friends. She knew very little about him, and he probably knew even less about her. But the chemistry between them wasn't anything Alexandria had encountered before. One touch, and she'd catch instant fire, going ablaze for another, needing him more than she'd thought possible.

What future did it all have?

None. No future whatsoever. One day, one of the many she

spent wishing he'd come to visit, getting dressed for him, yearning for him, he'd just stop coming. She'd be left alone, barren, forgotten, unable to reach out and ask why he'd vanished because she already knew.

He belonged to another.

That made Alexandria loathe herself and her secret love affair just as much as she needed him to touch her again. To other men, she used to be the girlfriend, the fiancée, the wife... what was she now, to him?

One day would be the last time they'd made love, and she wouldn't even know it, not for a while. Was that day today?

She whimpered, shuddering at the thought. Chasing the terror away, she stood and walked over to the kitchen, where she found a bottle of wine in the fridge. Struggling a little with the corkscrew, she managed to open it and poured herself a glass, filling it to the brim. Then she took it back to the sofa and started drinking it with small sips until the fear subsided and only the memory of his sensual whispers was left to haunt her.

The second glass was almost empty, abandoned on the small coffee table. She'd dozed off for a minute when Alana came home, the slamming of the front door waking Alexandria up. She tried to stand, but felt weak and resigned to lean back against the cushions.

"Whoa, Mom, it must be five o'clock somewhere, huh?" Alana quipped mercilessly, giving her mother a stern, disapproving look. "Well, don't stop the party on account of me. I'm just here to change. I'm meeting Nick for a movie at six."

An unfamiliar feeling left a bad taste in her mouth.

Envy.

Alexandria envied her own daughter for going to the movies with her boyfriend, for the normal life she was leading. For a moment, she envisioned herself putting on lingerie and a little black dress for her lover, anticipating the date and what followed after the movie, the butterflies in her stomach.

It wasn't going to happen. Not for her. Not with him.

She closed her eyes, but the tears she tried to stop still fell. She topped off the wine in her glass with whatever remained in the bottle, then took the burgundy to her lips and let it soothe her aching heart.

SEVENTEEN
NAME

One of Elliot's best-kept secrets was his contempt for social media. Keeping his opinions to himself unless someone actually asked him, the Texas-born detective strongly believed social media was solely responsible for the psychological damage suffered by youth everywhere.

The darn thing spat out narcissists faster than a well-oiled press, creating hordes of people busy patting themselves on the back, so spoiled salt couldn't save them. Especially the young ones. The older ones, maybe up to his generation, had caught a little of the old-style education when kids still had to pull their weight and prove their worth before earning the right to open their mouths.

Social media had rewritten the way cops investigated crime. Despite his feelings toward the time-sucking, brain-eating, nuts-numbing platforms, he had to pore over thousands of inept postings, photos, and comments, to try to piece together what a victim or a witness might've said, seen, or done.

No one talked to anyone anymore. People didn't call other people; they texted. They had followers they didn't know and online friends they'd never met. In some cases, those so-called friends were stalkers, pedophiles, and murderers waiting for the right opportunity to strike.

In all fairness to said platforms, and although it didn't make him appreciate them any bit more, social media brought a certain advantage. People bared their most intimate thoughts on there, without restraint or censorship, not realizing that everything they put on the internet was no longer private. Of course, the same people also lied on social media, posed as something they were not, and hunted for prey better than lions in a jungle. Some were even born for it, naturally gifted to hide in plain sight and deceive like chameleons.

Elliot accessed Jenna's newsfeed and postings, gaining some insight into what the girl had been up to since April. Kay had been adamant about finding out what had happened to Jenna to cause the change in her behavior her parents had described. Not that his partner had to insist on doing that; it made tons of sense, like everything else she wanted to do.

They split the tasks to conquer them faster and burn as little daylight as possible. With an understandable groan, Kay had taken one, leaving the other to him. She used her own computer to access Jenna's stream while he took the girl's laptop and set it on the side of Kay's desk. And he'd been scrolling for a while.

Nothing had been posted on Jenna's accounts since April. Whatever it was that had uprooted her world, she never talked about it. She stopped talking altogether, not responding or engaging with other people's postings anymore.

Before April, and specifically, April seventeenth, her social media told a different story.

Those kids were whistling up the wind all day long, posting on those sites, and Jenna had been no different back then. Out of curiosity, he took a moment to count, and there were over a hundred posts Jenna had written or interacted with during one day before April. When did these kids find time for any school? For anything, for that matter?

Realizing his thoughts resembled those of a bitter old man, he grumbled some swear words and resumed his endless scroll through the musings of Mount Chester's high school seniors. He was only thirty-five; no need to think like a golden-aged coot. Traditional police work might've become a dying art in favor of video surveillance, social media investigations, and database searches, but every generation of youths managed to surprise, outdo, and impress even the most cynical of critics. Those kids would probably do the same, and end up being all right.

His rumblings earned him a quick glance from Kay before she sunk her eyes into her own pile of digital manure. He followed suit, reading a few exchanges between Jenna and her closest connections.

She used to have a few close friends. There were two girls, Mackenzie Trenton, whose avatar was the movie poster for *Twilight*, and Alana Keaney, whose photos seemed more suited to a centerfold wannabe than a high school student. Alana was obsessed with jewelry of all kinds and always showed skin in lascivious poses, even in photos with her apparent boyfriend, Nick Papadopoulos. That young man was into Beemers and racing and talked about competing in rallies once he went to Harvard. It seemed he'd already been accepted, but he was posting at least once every few days that he's still weighing his options, as if to say, "I'm going to Harvard, bitches, and I'm not letting anyone forget it." What an infatuated jerk.

Jenna also used to have a boyfriend, a young man named Tim Carter. He liked Ferraris and cats, and he skied a lot on Mount Chester; he'd even won a couple of competitions. That had been the case until April. After a brief absence from social media, Tim had reappeared with a new girl, a sophomore named Kendra Flannagan. His last posting about Jenna had been on April fifteenth. His first about him and Kendra, on June twenty-fourth.

Confused by the absence of questions about Jenna, Elliot returned to her last few active days online. Right before April seventeenth, Jenna had posted daily, albeit a bit less in the final few days leading to that date. Then she disappeared from the social network. And no one had bothered to reach out to her, ask about her, or comment on her absence. Mackenzie continued posting news about Kristen Stewart and Robert Pattinson, what they wore, what other parts they played in what movies, and who they were dating. Alana Keaney was all about herself and no one else, taking at least fifteen selfies a day. Every move she made was documented online. What she wore, where and with whom, what she ate, what clothes she bought. And she bought a lot of stuff.

Jenna had stopped interacting with her group of friends, and no one had said a word. Not even out of curiosity, which meant they all knew why she'd vanished. They knew, and they kept it on the down low, never commenting about it. Not one of them, not even by accident.

Damn.

Maybe some good old-fashioned detective work would answer his questions, assuming he or Kay could get those kids to talk.

One final step before closing the lid on Jenna's social media life, and that was going through her messaging app. The same story was reflected in her chats, lots of interactions with the same friends until April, then silence, except for one profile, a man she called DeGraw in her messages.

He was a new friend, this DeGraw, someone Jenna had met online after April, more precisely on May seventh. They'd chatted for a while, and Elliot could see from her messages that she was depressed, didn't want anything, and was chatting with him more to have a shoulder to cry on. Almost an hour into reading countless messages, Elliot was able to notice how their relationship bloomed, becoming more and more engaged, with

Jenna opening up to that man and developing feelings for him. Then the two arranged a meeting face to face.

Last June, on the ninth, in Mount Chester.

DeGraw drove over from San Francisco just to meet Jenna. Based on subsequent messages, their first date was something Jenna remembered fondly. Then they met again and again, at least once every two weeks, when the mystery man would travel to meet the sullen teenager who was slowly falling for him.

He clicked on his name in the messenger to open his profile. There wasn't one, just a blank avatar and no personal information, no photos or interactions with anyone else.

"I got nothing," Kay said, letting out a long sigh loaded with frustration. "I can't believe the amount of crap these kids generate every day. Nothing useful; it's as if she completely vanished after April seventeenth, and no one cared to notice. Not a tweet, not a single email, nothing." She rubbed her nape vigorously as if to dissipate the tension coiled in there. "I'm missing something. Any luck on your end?"

"Yeah," he replied, turning the laptop her way. "We need a warrant. She was seeing someone, a man who was driving over from the city every few weeks to be with her."

A deep frown ridged Kay's forehead as she read through the more recent messages between Jenna and her secret boyfriend.

"This is a grownup, Elliot," she whispered, then bit the tip of her index finger. "An adult. Could be a predator, some pervert who found her online and—" She stopped talking, focused on what she was reading. "This man's a ghost. We have the dates he traveled here and the approximate times. If nothing else works, Golden Gate toll cameras will help us track him down. We need to know who he really is."

"We need a subpoena for the social network to reveal the man's ID."

She crinkled her nose. "I believe I might have a faster route."

Of course, she had a faster route. She always had, as if her time was made of New York minutes. Waiting was a concept unknown to his partner's vocabulary.

"An old buddy of mine from the FBI might be willing to run an unofficial search for us." Kay fished her phone out of her pocket and scrolled through the saved contacts list until she found whom she was looking for. She initiated the call and waited impatiently with the phone at her ear, rapping her fingers against the scratched surface of the desk. "Hey, it's Kay Sharp," she spoke softly into the phone, standing up and putting some distance between them. "Got a minute?" Approaching the window facing the parking lot, she kept her face turned away from him as if what she was about to discuss was private. Personal.

He leaned forward casually, pretending he was still scrolling through Jenna's laptop, but perked up his ears as if he were night hunting for wild hog.

"Need a favor from you," she was saying. "I have a vic who's been dating someone she met online. Screen name is DeGraw, but I'm sure that's fake. You'll find him in my vic's messenger." A pause. "Yes, I can. Her name is Jenna Jerrell, seventeen years old, from Mount Chester. Yes, California, where else?" She laughed, the subdued, warm laughter of people who had shared more than an office. "Sure, I'll wait." She paced back and forth in front of the window, keeping her eyes warily on any movement in the precinct. It was quiet at that time, almost four in the afternoon, and Sheriff Logan hadn't returned yet. "Yeah, I'm still here," she said, after a few minutes of tense waiting. "His name is what?" A beat. "And you're sure about that?"

He could swear he saw consternation shading her face, even from that distance. A little pale, she ended the call and slid the phone into her pocket, then came back to her desk as if nothing had happened.

"So?" he asked casually, lifting his eyes from the computer screen. "Any luck?"

Her glance veered sideways. "Oh, they'll get back to me when they have a name."

She was lying.

He wasn't sure of too many things in his life, but he could bet the farm on this much: his partner had never lied to him before. And now she looked as if she was about to faint.

EIGHTEEN
DEGRAW

Kay drove herself home despite Elliot's protests. She said she felt sick, and that wasn't a lie; she didn't have to fake it as an excuse to leave early. It felt as if the ground was moving, spinning out of control, and there was nothing she could hold on to for balance. She had to pause her argument with him and run to the bathroom to empty her stomach.

She came out of there patting her mouth with a tissue and touching the gray wall to steady herself. He was waiting for her with a worried look in his eyes.

"Let me drive you," he said again. "I don't mind if you throw up in my Interceptor. I've had perps do that before." His attempt to lighten her mood was heartwarming, making her feel even worse for lying to him.

She avoided his gaze and gestured no with her hand, then stopped by her desk to pick up her keys. "I'll be fine, Elliot. Must be something I ate. The sandwich I had for lunch was a little off." One lie always invited more until a swarm of them would buzz in her mind, making everything worse.

"You could doze off on the way home, if—"

"No, Elliot, please." Her voice was stern, colder than she'd wanted. "I'm sorry... I'm just not feeling well."

Visibly confused, he lifted his hat and scratched the roots of his hair, staring after her as she exited the building. There would be some explaining to do at some point, only not right there and then.

She unlocked her SUV and climbed behind the wheel. The intense heat brought back her nausea, but she was finally alone. She could let the mask fall off.

Starting the engine, she allowed the tears that had been choking her to fall freely as she drove away from the precinct. Turning onto the main street, she saw the sheriff's car approaching. She barely had time to put on her sunglasses before the two cars ran past each other, flashing their headlights in lieu of a greeting. A few unbearable minutes later, she was home.

She locked the door behind her and dropped the keys on the kitchen counter, then hobbled into the living room and let herself fall onto the couch. Her tears had dried, leaving room for panicked bewilderment.

DeGraw.

Now she understood why Jenna had nicknamed her secret boyfriend DeGraw.

Because his first name was Gavin. Like the pop singer whose best hits still played on the radio a decade or so after they'd hit the charts, inspiring Jenna's nickname for him. Or maybe he had chosen it for himself.

But that wasn't all of it. Jenna's secret boyfriend's full name was Gavin Sharp.

Just like Kay's father. Exactly like him. Same name, same age.

For a brief, irrational moment, Kay wondered if the man could've been her father. Heart thumping in her chest, she shook her head as if the gesture could've helped her get rid of the stray, unwelcome thought that didn't make any sense.

Her father couldn't've been Jenna's boyfriend because he was dead.

Only Jacob and she knew the truth about where her father was; everyone else thought he'd run away one night after nearly beating his wife to death, and was believed to be somewhere in Arizona.

Only he wasn't.

His body was slowly rotting under the willow trees in Kay's backyard. She lifted her gaze and looked outside. She could see their majestic crowns through the window, slowly moving with the summer breeze, undisturbed.

Still dizzy and nauseous, she stood and faltered into the kitchen. The walls were patched with putty and sanded, almost ready to be painted. Only a small section remained, marred by the scratches and dents accumulated over time from thrown objects and slammed fists during her father's drunken rages. That section near the fridge still showed her mother's blood-stains, although she'd done her best to clean it.

Without realizing it, Kay stood where she'd stood almost eighteen years ago, reliving the nightmare. She was thirteen, still going by Kathy at the time, before her father's revolting lewdness had made the sound of her own name unbearable. Her brother was barely twelve. Their father was pinning their mother against the wall, strangling her with one hand and groping her with another, next to where the fridge used to be.

He'd slammed her head against the wall because there wasn't any wine left in the house for him to drink.

"*Gavin, please, no.*" Her mother's whimpers filled the empty room as if she was still there, falling to the ground under his fists. "*I really don't have anything left.*"

Her words made him instantly angry as if her double rejection had fueled his rage and fanned the fire burning already inside him. He slammed Pearl against the wall, and she fell to the ground, seeming too weak to withstand his attack.

Kathy jumped to her feet and Jacob with her. They both rushed to their mother's side, and Jacob tried to get his father's attention away from his mother.

"If you want, I can go ask the neighbor if he can spare a bottle for you," Jacob offered in a trembling voice.

"Uh-huh, you do that, son," their father replied, staring at Kathy and licking his lips, his eyes bloodshot and lustful. "I bet this young thing won't say no to me," he said, his clumsy fingers struggling to get his belt buckle undone. "Kathy, pretty Kathy, my sweet Kathy, Daddy really loves you," he said in a singsong voice ending in a coughing spell. "Come on over here, Kathy, love your daddy back."

Kathy stared at him with wide eyes, not sure where to run. Pearl moaned but managed to stand again, holding on to Kathy for support, then shielding her daughter with her weakened, aching body.

"It's your own daughter, Gavin, your own flesh and blood," she pleaded. "Don't you touch her."

Gavin unzipped his pants, his mind seemingly made up, and took two steps toward Kathy, but Pearl pushed the girl out of the way and stood in front of him, trembling.

"Here, take me," she offered, undoing the top button of her shirt with hesitant fingers.

He shoved her to the side and reached for his child, mumbling words that Kathy didn't understand. Letting out a short scream, Kathy bolted and found refuge on the other side of the room, by the dresser, where she desperately looked for something to use as a weapon, fear rendering her fingers weak, quivering, useless.

Kathy turned her eyes briefly away from him, going through the drawers as quickly as she could when she heard a commotion. In the corner of her eye, she saw her mother hit her father in the head with a frying pan.

He barely flinched.

He let out a raspy roar of laughter, and then, as if incited by Pearl's actions, he lunged toward the kitchen where she'd taken refuge by the counter and hit her hard, sending her tumbling to the ground. Then he turned and grabbed the largest knife from the block and raised his arm, ready to deliver a fatal blow.

"I will end you, scum of this earth," he bellowed.

"No," Kathy shouted, her hands going through the top drawer in a trembling rush and finding the pistol she knew he kept there.

She fired just as Jacob had charged with his baseball bat, the bullet barely missing her little brother. Horrified, she screamed but then saw Jacob backing away from the line of fire, the bat clattering as it fell from his hands. He was still standing, unharmed.

Her father groaned, the knife still in his hand, coming down forcefully toward Pearl's chest.

She pulled the trigger again.

Reliving the moment, Kay gasped as if the gunshot tore through flesh and bone instead of memory, startling her.

She leaned against the counter, staring at the floor where her father's body had fallen that day. Her mind was playing tricks on her, overlapping memories over reality, the old bloodstains on the linoleum covered in drywall dust and drops of paint primer.

Gavin Sharp was dead.

Yet his name was back to haunt her, to bring back the memory of her drunken, abusive father in the minds of local law enforcement after it had taken them so many years to forget. How would she survive their questions, their legitimate curiosity? How would she keep on lying to Elliot?

The secret she'd been guarding for years was threatening to come out and ruin hers and Jacob's lives, in a wicked twist of fate she couldn't explain.

And somewhere out there lurked a fifty-six-year-old

predator named Gavin Sharp who had met with Jenna days before she was killed.

NINETEEN
ARGUMENT

After spending Wednesday night on the Winter Lodge restaurant patio curled up in a ball on one of the lounge chairs with his teeth clattering, Richard had earned himself a stuffy nose and a cough. With the Jeep's hardtop back at the house, and the seats that didn't recline more than a couple of inches, he didn't have any choice but to seek shelter on the restaurant's covered patio.

His clothes smelled of something acrid mixed in with his sweat. It was strange he'd broken a sweat despite feeling so cold overnight; it must've been the sniffles. He didn't believe spending any amount of time in the cold gave people colds. No. The cold gave them exposure if the temperature was below freezing. He must've come close to someone who was sick in the past few days. That someone and his shitty luck were to blame for the crappy way he was feeling.

At first light, when he was forced to hightail it out of there before the restaurant staff showed up, he was tempted to drive by his house for a hot shower and some fresh clothes. But the thought of running into that bitch and enduring through her screams seemed more than he was willing to put up with after a night spent in the cold and on an empty stomach. He didn't trust himself in her presence. Not anymore.

Instead, he'd parked his butt on an old tree stump at the base of the chairlift, where the early sun touched the ground, and lit up a cigarette, then a second one. The craze with electronic cigarettes and cinnamon-flavored nicotine vaping hadn't taken with him. There was no substitute for the fine smell of tobacco when the lighter's flame hits it for the first time. Vaping was to smoking what masturbation was to sex. It got you there, but not really.

In the weak rays of the early morning sun, he'd debated whether to go to school or take the day off. He'd quickly fall asleep on that grassy meadow, as soon as it got a little warmer. The thought of that was tempting, but he was a rational and controlled person who liked to think before he acted. He'd sleep there, then what? He needed money, food, and a place to lay down his head at night. He wasn't ready to be homeless any more than he was willing to forfeit his future paycheck as a lawyer for California's richest scum just because his father was spineless, and his mother a vindictive bitch.

He'd showed up on time for class, dirty and disheveled, with bits of straw hanging from his clothes and hair. His Jeep needed gas, and his stomach was growling. His wallet was empty, except for a couple of dollar bills that couldn't buy him much. Rennie turned his packed lunch into Richard's breakfast and watched it being gobbled quickly with large gulps when the first-period teacher wasn't looking.

Richard wasn't thirty minutes into the first period when his mother started texting him.

Where are you? she asked, ending her query with an angry face emoji.

School, he replied quickly.

I don't believe you, she texted back.

Muting his ringer for a moment, he waited for the teacher to turn his back and snapped a quick photo to send her, then typed, *Leave me the fuck alone.*

That had silenced her through the rest of the unbearably boring chunk of art history, then through trigonometry and calculus. By the time biology class started, his nose ran like a broken faucet, and he was burning up.

Come right back home after classes, was a new message from his mother. Damn that woman.

"Prokaryotes are the studio apartments of cells," his teacher was saying in his annoying, nasal voice, drawing a figure on the whiteboard with several colors. "What's so special about them? Does anyone know?" He allowed a moment for the classroom to engage, to no avail. No one paid that much attention to him.

In that drawn moment of silence, a new text vibrated Richard's phone, also from his mother. This time, she wrote, *If you're not home for dinner, I'll cut off your phone service.*

"Son of a fucking bitch," he blurted before he could restrain himself.

The teacher turned as if something had bitten him in the ass. Red-faced and agitated, he looked straight at Richard. "Mr. Gaskell, stand up, explain your outburst, and apologize to the class."

Richard clenched his teeth until they hurt but managed to appear humble and regretful in front of the fifty-something students who wore cheap polyester suits and worn-out shoes. "I just hurt myself, that's all. I got a splinter under my fingernail, and it hurts like a—" he paused for dramatic effect, holding his thumb in the air. "I'm really, really sorry. I hope you can forgive me."

The teacher stared at him, seemingly unsure if he was being taken for a ride. He looked straight at Richard, who held his gaze calmly, then added, "They lack nuclei and other membrane-bound organelles. That's why they're the studio apartment. All facilities in one room."

Another beat of silence. "Exactly," the teacher said, returning to his drawing while Richard still fumed. For the remainder of the class, he spaced out, thinking of his future, long-term and immediate, and how his mother's insecurities could be managed to his advantage.

Right before the recess bell, something the teacher said caught his attention, reeling him back into reality.

"—of your classmate's passing. We have psychologists and grief counselors available in person and on the phone if you'd like to speak with someone about Jenna. The police are asking everyone with pertinent information that could lead to an arrest to call the sheriff's office directly."

Richard turned to the guy behind and asked him to lend him ten bucks. The boy obliged quickly, and two fivers changed hands. Then he reached across the aisle to Rennie and handed him the money. "For lunch," he whispered. White as a sheet, Rennie looked at him as if he'd never seen him before. "Snap out of it already," he encouraged Rennie with a wink. "I gotta go home now, but I'll swing by later in the afternoon. What time are you back?"

"Um, seven," Rennie replied. His lips were pale, his eyes wide as if he'd seen a ghost.

"Mr. Gaskell," the teacher said, raising his voice in frustration, "we were about to observe a moment of silence for your classmate. Do you think you can be bothered with that?"

He was just about to reply with more apologies when the bell rang. The timing of the exchange was hilarious, and a few chuckles ended the standoff. In under a minute, he was driving off on his way home, with the gas indicator on his dash blinking orange and Ed Sheeran's "Bad Habits" blaring on the radio.

As he drove away, his mind wandered. He didn't remember seeing one of those piles of flowers, cards, candles, and teddy bears that looked like the dump truck had broken down and was scattering the goods in its wake. What were they called, shrines?

Whatever they were called, he hadn't seen one of those put up for Jenna. Maybe there was one on the other side of the school building where students who took the bus were dropped off, but he hadn't heard anyone raising any money for her or doing the usual crap bored rich girls did on such occasions. He would've expected Alana Keaney to be the first in line to do that and post a million selfies on the subject, with that judgmental bitch in tow, Mackenzie Trenton.

He got home in a few minutes and used the back door to sneak inside the house without passing through the living room where his mother was reading a book. When she looked up from her read, she'd notice his Jeep parked in the driveway, but by then, he'd be in the shower, or better yet, fast asleep.

His plan almost worked, only he wasted a few minutes standing in the fridge's open door, wolfing down some leftovers from last night's dinner. Then he snuck up to his room and slid under the covers. When his mother checked on him, he pretended to be asleep, and she let it slide with a long sigh.

He slept like a rock until about six, then got up and dressed, ready to go to Rennie's. His friend needed company this evening; he seemed worked up by the news of Jenna's death. He was a softie, his new friend, getting all jittery as if he'd killed her.

He was almost ready to leave when his mother stopped him.

"Where do you think you're going?" she asked. She was wearing a pair of blue slacks and a silk blouse, also blue, in matching shades. Her hair was neatly done as if she'd just returned from the salon.

"To Rennie's," he replied, veering his eyes sideways. "Why, you need anything?"

She stepped closer to him. "Yes, for you to look at me."

He obliged, shoving his hands in his pockets and taking one step back. Pressing his lips together, he kept his mouth shut despite the many things he wanted to say to her.

She tentatively reached to caress his hair, but he withdrew, scowling, silent. "What your father and I said last night has nothing to do with you," she said, smiling apologetically. "You know that, right?"

Rage filled his chest, burning him on the inside. "The hell it doesn't, Mom!" He stomped his foot against the hardwood with a loud thump. "What am I doing here? What are *you* doing here, in this damn place, away from the city where we had such a good life?"

Her jaw dropped. For a moment, she just stared at him, speechless. Her hand caught in midair, tentatively between touching him and withdrawing. "It wasn't a good life, Richard. You were starting to—"

"Don't you dare blame any of this shit on me, you hear? I didn't do anything to deserve this! You wanted to stop working and used me to justify it. Now Dad's cheating on you, and it's entirely your fault."

"How dare you?" she whispered, her eyes glinting with rage. Her face was flushed, in anger or shame.

"Tell me it's not true," he snapped. "What's he supposed to do? Let it wither and fall off?"

The blow resounded loudly in the large living room, echoing against the vaulted ceilings. His face burned where she'd slapped him, and unexpected tears stung his eyes. He didn't want to cry; he wasn't a little kid anymore. He stared at her menacingly, willing himself calm, determined to walk away without saying or doing anything else.

Natalie's hand covered her agape mouth. "I—I'm so sorry," she stammered, "I—I didn't mean to—"

"You make me sick." He spat the words as if they were bitter to the taste, then turned to leave. She didn't follow.

In the hallway, by the door, he saw her Chanel purse abandoned on the console table. He unzipped it quickly and rummaged through it until he found her wallet. He took all the cash in there and her American Express Gold card, then slid the wallet back inside the purse. He slammed the door behind him as he left the house, the large windows rattling in protest.

Behind the wheel, he rubbed his face where it was still smarting, mumbling an endless oath. Hopefully, she'd feel guilty enough for what she'd done to leave him be for a few days. And one day, soon, he'd make the bitch pay.

As his Jeep peeled away from the driveway with screeching tires against the asphalt, a smile blossomed on his lips. He had money and he had time. The sky was the limit.

And there was no reason to spend the night alone.

TWENTY
NIGHTMARES

Kay was thankful the moment the night sky started graying out toward the east. She hadn't slept a wink and couldn't bear tossing and turning in bed anymore, alone with the ghosts of her past. All those questions she'd asked herself over the years were haunting her. Could she have done anything differently? Had she hesitated, would her mother have died that day?

She pulled on the rundown T-shirt and shorts and tiptoed barefoot into the kitchen. Turning on the lights, she started the coffee maker and spent a few seconds nearby, inhaling the aroma of the strong, fresh brew. Then she grabbed the putty knife and proceeded to clean yesterday's remnants of dried-out paste off its blade.

She found the lid snapped closed on the putty bucket and sighed in relief. The last thing she wanted was to bang on Ace Hardware's front door at six in the morning for a new one. She opened the lid and loaded the knife with pink paste, then proceeded to where she'd left off the day before. Right where the fridge used to be, where her father's fist had torn a hole in the wall, so large Jacob had to consolidate the repair with a piece of drywall he'd cut to shape and screwed against the two-by-four.

Next to the edge of that hole, the old wall paint still showed, ugly and weathered and sullied with a faded bloodstain. Her mother's blood. With trembling fingers, she touched the edge of the mark, fighting back the tears with a clenched jaw. She wished she could jump back in time and hold her mother in her arms, soothe her pain, tell her everything was going to be all right. A wail climbed up from her chest and erupted from her lips, sending her to her knees, covering her mouth with her hands to mute the sound.

She felt Jacob's strong arms around her and let him hold her, rocking her back and forth like she used to do with him when he was little and hurt himself. Then she stood up, holding on to his arm, and wiped her eyes with the back of her hand. "It's all right," she said, "I'm just grieving."

He'd crossed his arms over his chest and was studying her with a look of disbelief. He wore crinkled pajamas, the top almost entirely unbuttoned. His hair was clumped and sweaty, a natural out-of-bed look that some women paid small fortunes to imitate.

The thought of that brought a shy smile to her lips. Eighteen years, and she still wasn't over that night. Some shrink she was if she couldn't heal herself. "He sure did a number on us, didn't he?"

"Uh-huh," he replied, then walked over to the counter and put the lid on the putty container. "This goes dry real quick, sis," he said. "Why don't you let me finish these walls myself? I'd be faster. I'd have it done in an hour."

She nodded, still sniffling. "I know, and you'd do it better than me." She gave the walls a long stare. "Let me do this room. All of it, please. New floors, new cabinets. It's healing for me. It helps me erase his stain from my memory, one inch at a time."

Her brother scoffed quietly, lowering his gaze to hide his

anger. "Yeah, and you'll forget him, all right, with the other Gavin Sharp on everyone's mind. Really, what are the odds of that?" He walked over and grabbed a coffee mug from the cabinet, then filled it to the brim from the machine. "It kept me up last night. I can't believe this is happening. How are you going to handle it?"

A shattered breath of air left her lungs. "I don't know yet. Thing is, he might be our unsub, Jenna's killer. What was a fifty-six-year-old doing on dates with an underage girl? I can't think of a good reason for that."

Jacob shrugged with a crinkle of disgust on his lip. "I don't know—being a perv, I guess?"

She looked at the willow trees, then away from the window when she saw Jacob's disapproving gaze. "However upsetting this might be to us, I have to follow the leads where they might take me. Just saying his name or reading it on police reports and in databases feels so strange to me. Gives me the creeps."

"Does your cowboy know about this?" Jacob asked, a touch of amusement in his eyes as they veered to the front window as if expecting Elliot to pull into their driveway any minute.

She fake punched him in the shoulder. "He's not *my* cowboy, Jacob. How many times do I have to tell you?"

"He could be," her brother replied, speaking slowly. "He'd hang his hat on that doornail in a heartbeat."

Kay pretended to glare at him for a brief moment, then she turned away to hide a smile. Maybe... if the stars aligned, and Jacob wasn't wrong in his assessment. But that would definitely complicate things. "No, he doesn't know anything. I told him I was sick yesterday... because I was. I threw up when I heard the name spoken to me. It felt as if—"

"Yeah, no need to explain, sis. I felt gut punched when you told me last night." He smiled with sadness. "But that's what alcohol is for, right?"

"Not at six in the morning," she said, raising her coffee mug and meeting his in the air as if they were both drinking wine. "Cheers."

They drank in silence for a moment or two, sipping the hot, bitter liquid slowly, savoring it. Then she set the mug on the table and picked up the putty knife. She had to clean it again.

Turning her attention to the repair Jacob had done, she tore several lengths of adhesive mesh from the roll and started to apply the paste. Soon all the bruises and bloodstains would be gone. "I wonder why Mom didn't report it as self-defense," she said, thinking out loud. She didn't expect an answer to the question that had been at the center of her thoughts for years, every time she had to sweat during a polygraph test. Thankfully, when she'd been polygraphed during her tenure with the FBI, she wasn't asked questions where she would've had to lie; not even the polygraph people had thought of asking her if she'd killed her father. But she'd held her breath every single time she'd been tested. "It was legitimate, you know." Back then, the thirteen-year-old girl had been terrified of what she'd done while at the same time knowing she'd had no choice. Remembering it, though, still sent shivers down her spine.

"I can tell you because I asked Mom," Jacob replied. Kay looked at him and almost didn't recognize him. He'd turned into a responsible adult overnight. Over *that* night, eighteen years ago. He was no longer her little brother, whom she had to rock back and forth in her arms when he scraped a knee; he hadn't been that in a while. He was a strong man, a protector. "She didn't want our names dragged through the media, the internet. And she was afraid you'd be arrested, taken to stand through a trial we didn't have money for." He swallowed and looked away for a moment, his eyes moistened. "She was protecting you, me... us. She wanted us to be free of him." He reached out and squeezed her hand. "What do you say we make her wish come true, sis?"

She nodded while a tear found its way down her cheek. She

wiped it off and smiled just as the noise of pebbles ground under moving tires got their attention.

"Oh, crap," Kay said, recognizing Elliot's Interceptor. It wasn't even seven. What the heck held *him* up all night?

She ran into the bathroom and hopped into the shower. While she patted herself dry, she overheard Elliot and Jacob talking casually, laughing as if nothing was wrong. She had to give it to Jacob; he was a better liar than she'd thought.

Emerging fully dressed a few minutes later, she met Elliot's concerned gaze with a reassuring smile. "Good morning. Did Jacob offer you any coffee?" Not a trace of her earlier tears showed up under her fresh makeup.

"Yes, he did. Served it with a side story of your adventures."

"Oh?" She shot her brother a quick glance, but he was relaxed. "Should I be concerned?"

"Only if you decide to eat from the vending machine again."

"Ah, I see." The vending machine, even if it deserved the bad rap it got with the people it fed with stale sandwiches and overpriced junk food, had come in handy as an excuse. The only downside would be Elliot's raised eyebrow if she ever decided to eat from it again.

She slipped on her shoes and grabbed her car keys. "Come on, partner, we have a killer to catch."

His smile vanished. "That's why I'm here so early. There's another girl missing. I thought you got the message from dispatch."

TWENTY-ONE
BREAKFAST

Alexandria sneezed, then reached for the box of tissues without looking. Her eyes watered, squinting in anticipation of a second sneeze. She pulled three tissues from the box quickly, then clumped them under her nose.

The second sneeze brought tears to her eyes. She hated being sick. She had plans for every moment of every day, and none of those plans included feeling like crap with a stuffy nose and a fever, watching endless soaps on TV, and sweating under a blanket.

Determined to fight it tooth and nail, she gargled some apple cider vinegar, her face scrunching from the sourness after spitting it out, then put some drops in her nose. With her head tilted back, she didn't see Alana coming into the kitchen.

"Gesundheit," Alana said, "well, a belated one anyways. I heard you sneezing from the shower. Hope you didn't bring home some nasty shit."

Alexandria was about to thank her daughter; it rarely happened that she said something nice, even if she packed it with sarcasm, impertinence, and foul language. Her smile died on her lips, and the "Thank you" she said was barely a whisper.

"Where are you going?" Alexandria asked, a light frown creasing her brow. "It's a school day."

"And that's exactly where I'm going," Alana replied, pulling a chair out and taking a seat at the breakfast table without bothering to bring anything.

Alexandria checked the time with a quick move of her eyes from her daughter's face to the digital wall clock and back. It was seven in the morning on a Friday. She had twenty minutes to get her daughter to comply with the school's dress code. "Not dressed like this, you're not."

Alana sprung to her feet with her hands on her hips. The chair, pushed backward violently, fell and hit the wall leaving a dent before landing on the tiled floor with a rattle. "Is that so?" she asked, her voice tense, low, menacing.

Alexandria weighed her options. Maybe Alana was PMS-ing or something; she was in a foul mood, although minutes earlier, she'd seemed fine. But she was wearing a black fishnet top over a white sports bra, along with frayed and illegally short Daisy Dukes and a studded black belt. She'd adorned herself with numerous bangles, long earrings, and several chains and pendants that clinked and jingled with every move. Gray eyeshadow and thick eyeliner completed her makeup, hardly appropriate even for a Friday night party.

"I see you're going for the trashy biker look this morning," Alexandria said calmly, pacing herself. It was going to be a long battle. "It suits you," she added with an angelic smile.

Alana's brow furrowed. A look of suspicion made her stare at her mother for a moment before speaking. "Thank you... I guess."

"Are you doing a fundraiser for Jenna's memorial service?"

The furrow deepened. "I wasn't going to."

"Why, baby? She was your best friend."

Alana's eyes darted away, then back at her mom. "Yeah."

"Do you think that man is to blame? Hm? The grownup you said she was dating?"

Alana shrugged; her jewelry marked the gesture with a jingle. "I don't know." A beat, punctuated by a frustrated, ostensive breath of air. Her hands left her hips and snuck into her pockets. "And I don't care, really."

"Oh, honey," Alexandria said and walked toward her with open arms. "I'm so sorry she's gone. That must be terrible for you and Mackenzie. You guys were so close."

Alana looked out the window like a trapped animal searching for an escape. Her left heel tapped against the floor a few times, nervously. "Well, lately, she didn't go out much. Not with us, anyway."

Alexandria caressed her long blonde hair, tucking a strand behind her ear. "But you still loved her, right?"

Alana lowered her eyes but didn't say anything for a while. "I guess."

Alexandria hugged her again, ignoring her daughter's lack of response. "Then do this for her, baby. It will make you feel so much better." She turned toward the counter and fished out her wallet from her purse. "I'll be the first to chip in." She held two twenty-dollar bills in the air.

Alana glanced at the money like a mouse would eye the cheese baiting a trap. Then she took it and shoved it into her pocket. "Thanks," she muttered reluctantly.

"Do you think we should tell the police about that man?"

Alana's eyes promptly rolled back. "Last thing I need is talking with some damn cops."

"It's important that they know about that man, sweetie." Silence, the heavy and disapproving kind, filled the room for a moment. "Will you let me tell them if you're not up to it?"

Alana pressed her lips together in what seemed like an effort to not curse out loud. "If those stupid cops are worth anything, they'll find that man by themselves."

She had a point. "All right. Let's give them a few days, and if we don't hear anything about that on TV, then we'll call them. Sound good?"

"Whatever," Alana replied, fidgeting with her phone. Her thumbs typed quickly, and muted sound effects marked the sending and receiving of every new message. She was having a conversation with someone.

It was getting late for school. "Why don't you change into something more appropriate since you're running Jenna's fundraiser and all?" She paused for a moment, expecting Alana to explode. "I'm sure Nick won't mind if you wear jeans today and a T-shirt or something."

At the mention of his name, Alana's eyes drilled into hers. "Since when are you an expert on what Nick does or doesn't mind?" Frustrated, she slammed the phone on the table and started pacing around. "Do you even remember what it was like being young?"

Alexandria's breath caught in her chest. She still remembered... she *was* still young. She walked across to the tipped-over chair and picked it up, then slid it under the table with a scraping noise. "I do remember, Alana. I was just like you, ready to fall in love, to show everyone who I was, to go out there and make my mark. But there's time. And you shouldn't try so hard... people laugh at desperate women, regardless of age. Especially men."

Alana stared at her for a while, standing completely still with her mouth slightly agape. Then, slowly, she started to remove her bangles, then her long earrings. "Will you teach me, Mom?" she eventually asked.

"What, sweetie?" It was hard to figure out where her daughter's mind was.

"How to make someone fall in love with me and only me?" she whispered, blushing under the light layer of makeup. "Forever?"

Oh, God... Alexandria thought. *Nick Papadopoulos again. The bane of my existence.* But she smiled encouragingly, trying to instill some confidence into her daughter's heart. "Of course, I will. It's a promise." She kissed Alana's forehead and met no resistance.

In the corner of her eye, Alexandria noticed Nick's red convertible pulling into the driveway. "Your ride's here."

Alana shot a look outside the window and instantly lit up. "Tell him I'll be a minute," she said, rushing into her bedroom to change. "We're going to the movies after school and then to Tim's birthday party."

Alexandria frowned, disturbed by the idea of someone having a birthday party right after one of their friends had passed. "Tim Carter? Isn't he Jenna's boyfriend?"

"Used to be," came Alana's hesitant reply from inside the bedroom. "Not since April or May."

"And you guys are having a party when she's just, um, died?"

Alana came out of the bedroom wearing stretch denim and a black shirt, the top two buttons undone, showing a bit too much cleavage, but still. Much better. She'd removed her makeup, wearing only pink lip gloss. She gestured with her hands in the air, drawing two circles that didn't intersect, but avoided her mother's scrutinizing glance. "Different worlds, Mom." She blushed as she said that. She might've played it cool, but Alexandria could tell her daughter had been affected by her friend's death.

"She hasn't even been buried yet," Alexandria protested weakly.

Alana put on a pair of white, heeled sandals. "Well, how long is enough to wait to have a party after someone dies? And who gets to decide that?" She placed a rushed kiss on her mother's cheek and grabbed the door handle. "She'd be okay with it, anyway. I'll make sure we observe a moment of silence and all that." She was flustered, avoiding her gaze again.

Alexandria would bet her last dime there wasn't going to be any party, just sex with Nick somewhere, at his house most likely. She must've thought of that lie a while ago, before Jenna's death, and simply hadn't realized the lie she'd rehearsed in her mind was no longer fitting. "Don't be too late," she called, but the door had already closed behind her.

Watching through the window, she saw Alana climbing into Nick's red Beemer. Holding her breath and fighting back unwanted tears of frustration, she watched him wrap his arms around Alana's slender body and give her a long kiss.

They'd been gone for a while, but Alexandria still stared at the now empty driveway, a sense of unbearable dread nestled in her stomach. She wished her daughter had never met Nick Papadopoulos, had never fallen for him.

If only she could turn back time.

TWENTY-TWO
ASSIGNMENTS

Elliot could tell Kay wasn't happy about the dispatcher omitting to copy her on the new missing person case. Right after Elliot mentioned it, she checked her phone and found nothing. No email, no text message, no missed calls.

"Maybe because they knew you were out sick," he offered, promptly earning himself a disapproving gaze filled with disbelief. "I'm sure they didn't mean anything by it, Kay."

She just nodded and unlocked her vehicle while Elliot climbed into his. They drove separately to the precinct, which was a rare occurrence. Without any formal agreement between them, he'd started driving her home and picking her up the next morning while her unmarked Ford Interceptor spent the nights in the almost empty parking lot behind the sheriff's office building.

He tried not to think about that, his mind troubled by Jenna's death and now, the disappearance of another teenager. He saw a connection between the two cases, but, really, was there one?

Following Kay's Ford at a small distance, he had to notice his partner hadn't called him on the phone to get the details of the missing girl. Rewinding the film of yesterday's events in his mind, he was sure he hadn't done or said anything to upset her. Instead of fretting about it like a buzzard without roadkill, he'd better gather a can of beans' worth of courage and ask her directly.

Unbelievable how complicated things could get if he had a female partner, especially one he was falling for. Not his first rodeo, and the last one ended with broken hearts and an out-of-state move. There was no point in wondering how this one would end because it hadn't started yet. Would it, ever?

Frustrated, he pressed his lips together, holding an oath captive in his chest. He didn't want to behave as if they were a couple; they weren't one. He didn't even want to think about that, about Kay and him together, because it was all so very wrong, yet he wanted nothing else more. Hot would cool if greedy would let it, they say; all in good time if he could hold his horses, and that meant, in most cases, his mouth. Shut. As in refrain from asking stupid questions. Stop being overprotective; his partner could very well hold her own. Didn't they say, in some magazine or TV show, that overprotecting an independent woman was insulting to her abilities and her intellect? Then why the hell was he wired to do that at all costs?

He pulled into the parking lot right next to her, and met her at the precinct's door. She barely acknowledged him, veering her eyes away from him immediately. She didn't seem upset, nor did she say anything; she just seemed tired, running with one wheel down and the axle dragging.

Damn.

If she'd only tell him what was wrong, he could help.

"Good morning, Sheriff," Kay said coldly, her voice sounding a little bit nasal as if she'd been crying.

In the middle of the hallway, Logan was waiting for them with his hands propped on his hips. His gaze wasn't promising anything good; for some reason, his beef seemed to be with Kay.

"Ah, if it isn't Detective Kay Sharp." He clapped his hands together then rubbed them in mock enthusiasm. "The one and only who promised to keep the press off my back. Then did exactly nothing."

Kay lowered her head for a brief moment. "You're right, boss, and I'm sorry. I left Barb Foster a voicemail, but I should've followed up and I didn't."

"Well, she was on TV Wednesday night with news of Jenna's death that was not coordinated with this office. I'm surprised she bothered to wait for next-of-kin notification."

"Sheriff, I—" Kay started to say, but was immediately cut off.

"She was also on TV last night, prime time no less, stating that our office refused to return her calls. Is that true, Detective?"

Kay frowned. Retrieving her phone from her pocket, she started scrolling through messages quickly, then she pressed her lips into a thin line and looked at the sheriff briefly. "I have nothing. She might've tried my office line, but I wasn't—"

"Yes, I know," Logan interrupted her again. "Hope you're feeling better," he added, giving her a long, insistent look as if to figure out if she was up for whatever he had in mind. "Your first order of business for the day is to find Barb Foster and dance for her until she makes us look like superstars on tonight's news. And I haven't got the foggiest idea how you'll be doing that, because, um, do we have any suspects?" He paused for a moment, rubbing his chin, but Kay hesitated to answer. "Any leads? Anything? Reporting a collar for Jenna Jerrell's murder would be one straightforward way to go about this."

He waited another second, then turned on his heel and headed toward his office. "With me," he said, not looking at them.

They complied. Kay, not her usual talkative and confident self, took a seat on one of the black leather chairs reserved for

Sheriff Logan's visitors and seemed relieved to be off her feet. Elliot remained standing behind Kay, his arms crossed.

Logan opened a blue folder that was waiting for him on his desk, topping a three-inch pile. It bore a white case number label in the upper right corner; it was probably Jenna's. "I'm not seeing a whole lot in here. What's going on?"

"There's more to Jenna's death than we had initially antici-pated," Kay replied, her voice calm and steady. "A thorough review of her social media accounts revealed she was dating a man from San Francisco who occasionally drove to Mount Chester to meet with her. We suspect he is a much older indi-vidual," she added casually. "Efforts are underway to identify this man. I've made some calls."

That statement surprised Elliot a little. He had no idea they were suspecting he was a much older man. Older than Jenna, yes. An adult predator of sorts? Most likely. But much older? What was Kay not saying?

"Did you get a preliminary from Doc Whitmore?" the sheriff asked, his voice a little lower-pitched than before. He seemed less aggravated.

Kay nodded at the same time as Elliot. "She was brutally assaulted. We have fingerprints and DNA samples. No matches in AFIS, but you know CODIS takes longer."

Logan snapped his fingers a couple of times, the way he did when he was figuring out next steps. "I still can't believe this ME used his own money to buy a DNA machine. Helps us a lot, I guess. Doc must be loaded or something."

Kay smiled the way someone does before correcting a child. "He's a passionate professional with financial resources on his side, yes. We're lucky. Otherwise, it would've been six months to see DNA results back."

"When can we expect DNA with the doc's wonder machine?"

"In a couple of days at the most."

"No fingerprint match, you said?"

Kay shook her head. "We'll find him. And when we do, we'll have someone to match the prints against. Less than a third of the country's population is in AFIS; chances are, if he has no criminal record, he's not in there."

"I know the stats, Sharp. I might be an old country cop, but this isn't my first ball game." He closed Jenna's file and picked up another one. "There's a teenager missing, Kendra Flannagan. Last night she had dinner with her family, then vanished. At five o'clock this morning, her parents found her bedroom empty, her bed not slept in. She's sixteen, a junior. I'd like you both to—"

"You were actually right in your first instinct, Sheriff, when you didn't notify me about Kendra. I believe it's best if my partner takes this case while I focus on Jenna's murder investigation."

A deep frown ruffled Logan's brow. "You don't believe these cases are related?"

"I'm not seeing any similarities yet, Sheriff," she replied. "Jenna went out to meet friends, and ended up dead within hours after a violent assault. What do we know about Kendra? She might've run away."

Elliot took the file folder from the sheriff's hand and read through the report quickly. "These girls go to the same school, Ash Creek High."

Kay looked at him briefly over her shoulder. "But of course they do. There's only one high school in this town, Austin." She called him that nickname whenever she wanted to draw his attention to the many differences between small towns and large cities like Austin, Texas, when it came to police work. Until that day, she'd only done so in private and in an endearing way, her voice warm when speaking the name of his hometown, and he loved it. But today was different, her voice cold, impersonal.

Kay was definitely off her game, and determined to keep him at a distance.

"You don't find it suspicious that two different high school girls left their homes one night, one to be killed and one still missing, within a few days of each other?" Elliot insisted, but somewhat reluctantly. If she didn't want him by her side, what was the point of pushing her?

"I have the press to handle," Kay replied. "Chasing Barb Foster with me would be a total waste of your time. I'd suggest, you interview Kendra's family, figure out where her mind was at, check her laptop and her social media, while I manage the newspeople and follow up on the San Francisco man's identity." She waited, looking at him with a polite smile. Then, she turned her gaze to the sheriff, who tapped twice against the desk with his hand. He'd made a decision.

"You're set," Logan replied, standing up. "Get me some answers, both of you."

Elliot followed Kay out of the sheriff's office, then watched her take her seat at her desk. She didn't look at him once, seeming absorbed in her thoughts as if he wasn't there.

"And that's how you kick an old tire to the curb," he muttered, leaving the building and walking briskly toward his Ford. Starting the engine, he wondered if he was reading too much into his partner's behavior, but his gut was telling him to be wary.

He had no idea how to be wary of Kay Sharp. Or why.

TWENTY-THREE

SUSPECT

Stirring the coffee in her cup as if she'd added sugar, Kay followed Elliot's departure discreetly. She wasn't ready to answer any of his questions yet. Painfully aware she couldn't keep Elliot at bay for too much longer, she sat at her cluttered desk, refraining from sweeping everything off the scratched surface with one broad move.

Her partner was the strong, silent type, but he was also smart and an excellent cop. She'd seen his instincts in action over the almost two years they'd been working together. If he hadn't already, he'd soon put things together and figure out she wasn't being entirely honest with him. For that moment and for her own peace of mind, she needed answers.

Stacking paperwork quickly, she cleared a portion of her desk and started her computer. Coffee cup at her side, she gave the phone a long stare, then dialed Barb Foster's number. The call went straight to voicemail. She redialed, then left a message.

"Hey, Barb, it's Detective Kay Sharp with the FCSO. I'm hoping you and I could touch base today. You might be interested in the recent developments in Jenna Jerrell's case. I'm willing to go for an exclusive with you," she said, lowering her voice just enough to bait the trap effectively, "but I can't wait forever. Call me back, please, on my cell." Then she hung up with an amused expression on her face. How long would it take this TV reporter to bite, once the word "exclusive" had been used?

What would she tell Barb, though? As little as possible, at least until she figured out the connection between the Gavin Sharp who was dating Jenna and her father.

What connection?

The other Gavin was not her father; this entire situation was nothing but a weird coincidence. Starting to doubt her sanity, she typed the name into the search field for the CLETS database. The California Law Enforcement Telecommunications System gave her access to state databases, such as the DMV and CORI—Criminal Offender Record Information, and national databases maintained by the FBI, such as the NCIC—National Crime Information Center.

Her father featured prominently in there, with several misdemeanors and two drunk and disorderlies on his record, and an open warrant for the assault with a deadly weapon that had taken place eighteen years ago when he'd stabbed his wife. The statute of limitations had since run out; it was only three years.

Tears stung as Kay's eyes stared at the screen. Such an unspeakable ordeal, and only three years? That wasn't justice, but it stopped mattering eighteen years ago. Forcing some air into her lungs, she chased away the ghosts of her past and focused on the other Gavin Sharp, the suspect in Jenna Jerrell's rape and murder.

There was also a criminal record for the Gavin Sharp of San Francisco. He'd served six months for assault and battery thirty-two years ago, and nothing else since. He'd been walking the straight and narrow on paper; in reality, he'd been preying on underage girls. Other than that, his DMV records showed a clean driver's license and a registration for a blue Hyundai Santa Fe.

She stared at the man's photo, her emotions a whirlwind she could barely contain. He was fifty-six years old, but didn't look a day over forty-five. He seemed attractive in his DMV photo, which explained what Jenna had seen in him beyond a father figure. Shaving his head to hide his baldness and wearing a two-day stubble, the man was tall and slender, boasting a sensual smile. His alluring demeanor was calculated, carefully constructed.

He was charismatic in a weird, familiar way that stirred Kay up, making her feel uneasy, revolted. Frowning at the computer screen and drawing her chair closer to her desk, she put her father's photo next to the suspect's.

The resemblance was uncanny. Her father, about forty years old in the latest photo CLETS had, looked older than his age because of his drinking. The San Francisco Gavin Sharp looked younger than his real age. On the screen, with their images side by side, they could've been brothers. The same pattern in their baldness, only her father had never shaved his head. Same dimple in their chins. Dark hair. Brown eyes. Same build.

The only discrepancy she could find was the age. This man was fifty-six. Her father, had he lived, would've been sixty. Close.

Her FBI contact, an analyst on her former team, had sent her the suspect's social media channels. Browsing his messages, she found his exchanges with Jenna, the dates he'd arranged to meet with her in Mount Chester. Strangely for a hunter like him, there were no other girls he was targeting at the same time, only Jenna.

The girl's growing happiness with the relationship tugged at Kay's heart; she'd been the perfect victim for a sexual predator like Sharp. Vulnerable and depressed, she believed the first person who told her what she needed so badly to hear. And now she was dead.

Coincidence or not, Kay owed it to Jenna to bring her killer to justice, consequences be damned.

Staring at the screen, fascinated and drawn to the edge of a bottomless abyss, Kay continued her research into the second Gavin Sharp's background. Her throat parchment dry, and her heart thumping in her chest like a caged bird, she peeled the layers off the suspect's past.

Unsettled by each discovery, she found even more commonalities between her father and that man. The facts went beyond what coincidence could explain. The two men were born in the same town. Had attended the same schools. Every new commonality she uncovered in their past painted a nightmarish picture with only one possible explanation: one of these men had stolen the other's identity.

She looked at the two photos as if the truth was written on their faces somehow. One had led a life in the open, active on social media, not hiding as far as she could tell, since he'd been released from prison. The San Francisco Gavin Sharp had friends and a social life, went on vacations, posted photos of himself online. Even if he was a sexual predator, on paper and online nothing stood out; no red flags.

The other man, her father, had buried himself in a small town and never cared about interacting with anyone from his past. She couldn't remember a time when his family or friends would've visited or called, before or after that fateful night eighteen years ago.

The conclusion was obvious. Her father had stolen this man's identity, then had laid low, hiding from who knows whom and for what reasons.

"Always steal from criminals," she muttered, quoting her father's own words from many years ago, "because criminals won't call the cops on you." He'd said that one time, to Kay's mother, after swiping a coworker's toolbelt and bragging about it during one of his daily intoxicated rants.

It seemed her father had found the perfect criminal to steal an identity from. It made sense.

But if that was true, then, what had been her father's real identity?

TWENTY-FOUR
KENDRA

The first thing that caught Elliot's attention about the Flannagan place was the smell of wine. Not fresh wine, not spilled, but the kind of smell old casks get after storing wine for ages, a mix of fermented grape and oak. The kind that fills the nostrils the moment one enters a winery's tasting room.

The Flannagans owned a small winery south of Mount Chester, only a few acres of hills covered in neatly aligned rows of vines. Although not much of a wine drinker, Elliot was familiar with their two most popular labels, both Cabernet Sauvignons. Blue Mountain was one, distributed mainly through local stores and a grocery chain or two. Elliot had seen it in a Safeway store in San Francisco a few years back, when he didn't know the wine was made only ten miles from his new home. The second wine, Black Rose, was a boutique label, a small production reserved for local connoisseurs with deep pockets and a personal connection to the family.

The Flannagans were new to the wine business, first-generation winemakers, but passionate about it. Elliot had seen them in passing, at county events, wine tastings, and carnivals, but had never spoken with them. They belonged to different worlds.

He stood in the middle of the wine tasting room, waiting for the cellar tour guide to tell the Flannagans he was there. The winery was unexpectedly busy for eleven in the morning; it seemed wine tasting started early. A colorful tour bus had unloaded a flock of elderly tourists, their lively chatter filling the room with echoes of good cheer.

He was quickly shown into a hallway that led to the main residence, an older farmhouse, renovated and equipped with modern accoutrements, but still showing wide, smoke-stained darkened oak beams supporting the vaulted ceilings. It reminded him of an old, turn-of-the-century tavern. It smelled like one too, maybe without the cigar smoke and the scent of sweaty leather horse tack.

Mr. and Mrs. Flannagan met him at the door. The woman was about forty years old, dressed in black slacks and a black shirt. Her skin was pale, and her lips were quivering as she searched his eyes with a terrified yet hopeful gaze.

"Did you find my daughter?" Mr. Flannagan asked. He was older than his wife, maybe pushing fifty, also dressed in black clothes, jeans and a golf shirt. Judging by the slightly pitted, reddened skin on his cheeks and nose, he seemed to be the one most passionate about wine.

Shaking his head, he flashed his badge, but they didn't break eye contact to look at it. "Detective Elliot Young, Franklin County Sheriff's Office. I have a few questions, if you don't mind."

"You don't look like a detective," Mr. Flannagan commented, giving Elliot a curious look, head to toe. His blood-shot eyes lingered on his hat, then studied his belt buckle for a moment, then stared at his Roper boots.

"I've been told," Elliot replied calmly.

Mrs. Flannagan showed the way into a living room

furnished with aged leather sofas and armchairs. Elliot took a seat across from them, in an armchair that squeaked under his weight.

"Please walk me through yesterday afternoon, moment by moment, until you noticed Kendra was missing," he asked.

Mr. Flannagan uncorked a bottle of wine and filled three glasses. He set them on the coffee table, sat by his wife with his glass in hand, then raised it to his lips and gulped a thirsty swig. "She went out yesterday, after school," he said. He wiped the wine droplets on his lips with his sleeve, then looked at his wife as if asking for help.

"She went out with friends after school," Mrs. Flannagan said, "but she was back by eight, when we sat down for dinner." Her eyes darted around the room as if looking for something that wasn't there. "We always sit down for dinner at eight, then Vern comes back to the tasting room and spends time with the regulars. We close at ten."

The two huddled closer together, holding hands and looking at Elliot as if he held all the answers. Mrs. Flannagan's eyes were brimming with tears, but she was fighting them bravely.

Elliot opened his notebook. "Do you know who she went out with, and where they went? Any detail could prove significant."

Mrs. Flannagan's eyes veered toward her husband for a moment. "Kendra hangs out with a bunch of seniors. Vern isn't too happy about it, but if she's—I mean, if they accept her, why not, right?"

"Do you have some names?" Elliot pressed on.

"Um, yes, sorry. There are two girls she's close with, Mackenzie Trenton and Alana, um, I forgot her name."

Them again. Seemed that Kendra and Jenna had the same friends.

"Keaney," Mr. Flannagan said, without looking up from the

glass abandoned on the table. The burgundy fluid left barely covered the base of the glass.

"Yes, that's it, Keaney," Mrs. Flannagan said. "There are a few boys in the group—"

"Of course, there are," Mr. Flannagan said, his voice dipped in sarcasm. "Where there's honey—"

"Oh, shut up," Mrs. Flannagan replied, withdrawing her hands from her husband's grasp. "She's a beautiful girl, Vern, what do you expect? It's normal. She's sixteen." She stared her husband down until he leaned back against the couch with a resigned sigh. "Couple of those boys are the girls' boyfriends. Nick, I believe is his name, goes out with Alana, right?" Vern mumbled something in agreement. "Then there's a Tim Carter, and a Richard, um, I don't know his last name."

This time, Vern didn't have anything to add.

"Are all these kids seniors?" asked Elliot.

"Yes," Mrs. Flannagan replied quickly. "I'm quite sure they are."

"Do you know where they went?"

The parents exchanged a glance. "I'm not sure where they went last night, but they usually go to the coffee shop or to the Winter Lodge. Not that many places to go around here."

"And Kendra came back home last night, on time for dinner?" Elliot asked, his pen stuck in midair, inches above the notebook.

Both parents nodded. Mr. Flannagan still stared at the almost-empty glass, but his eyes weren't focused; he was spaced out, falling apart faster than a deflated tire. Mrs. Flannagan looked at Elliot with a silent plea in her insisting gaze.

"Did she seem all right to you? Her usual self?"

The two glanced quickly at each other. "Yes," Mrs. Flannagan replied. "After dinner, she said she still had some homework to do. We kissed her good night, and she went to her room."

"You didn't check on her until this morning?"

"Y—yes," Mrs. Flannagan stammered. She clasped her hands together nervously, wringing them as if they were made of clay, not flesh and bone. "I handle the winery's accounting, and it's a lot of work. Vern was with the guests until almost midnight. I was in the winery until eleven, closing the books."

Elliot frowned. "I thought you said the tasting room closes at ten."

She gave her husband a long, disapproving look. "Officially, we do. But some of the late-evening guests are regulars, and we don't exactly kick them out. Vern shows them a good time. They buy a few cases of wine before leaving, and a week later, they're back for more. It's good for business, as long as Vern's liver can take it." She pressed her lips together and lowered her head. A tear fell on her clasped hands. "The light was off in Kendra's room; I just thought she was asleep, and didn't want to wake her." She took her hand to her mouth to stifle a bitter sob. "Oh, God... my poor baby."

Vern wrapped his arm around his wife and held her tight at his chest as she sobbed, all the time staring at Elliot intently. "Please find our little girl. She's all we have."

Elliot nodded, holding his gaze with all the reassurance he could muster. Then he stood and walked toward the door, but then stopped and asked, "May I see Kendra's room, please?"

Their earlier statement said that Kendra had disappeared from her bedroom, and they had found the window open in the morning, no trace of her. A technician had already dusted the windowsill for prints and had reported no signs of forced entry, but another set of eyes couldn't hurt.

Mrs. Flannagan led the way to a bedroom at the far end of the house. It was a rather large room, decorated with pop band posters on the walls and a few dreamcatchers. The window was closed, the sheers were closed. Filtered sunlight shone through the glass stained by fingerprint powder. Elliot looked outside; the window was only three feet above the ground, an easy feat for a teenager sneaking out for a late-night date.

Had she run away? Or had she been lured away from her family home? Had a skilled predator waited for her in the thick brush that extended past the neatly mowed lawn?

He pulled the sheers open and lifted the window. It went up easily; the window frame was new, light, running smoothly. Outside, the soil was covered with grass trimmings from a recent mow, and some foliage from the oaks nearby, the scent of fresh cut grass carried by the gentle breeze. If Kendra had left any footprints, they were long gone.

Closing the window, he gave the room another look. The bed was made with pink sheets, and covered in pillows and stuffed animals, the clutter on it cozy somehow, warm and friendly. Her desk was stacked with schoolbooks and notebooks. In the middle of her desk was a Dell laptop with its lid closed, adorned with several stickers.

"I'll need to take this, if that's okay," Elliot said. Mrs. Flannagan nodded.

He unplugged it from the wall, coiled its cord, and slid it under his arm, then headed for the door. In the hallway, Mr. Flannagan waited, holding a photo of his daughter in his trembling hands.

"This is Kendra," he said, holding out the picture for Elliot. "Take it, so you know what my daughter looks like." He slurred his words a little, and his eyes were watery, red, and swollen. "So you won't forget her."

Elliot took the photo and studied it for a moment. Kendra was a beautiful girl with long brown hair that fell on her shoulders in loose curls. In that picture, her head was tilted a little. She had a mischievous smile that put a sparkle in her large brown eyes. "Mr. Flannagan," he eventually said, sliding the photo in his pocket, "my partner and I will do everything in our power to find your daughter. We won't rest until we bring you answers."

"Thank you," the man whispered, then turned away and found the couch.

Elliot touched the brim of his hat with two fingers and left. The door closed behind him with a thud that echoed through the large hallway, and his heels clacked on the stone tiles as he walked briskly toward the tasting room. Bouts of laughter were coming from there, muted by an arched, rustic oak door with black iron ornaments.

Kendra could've screamed her lungs out the night before; there was no way anyone could've heard her from the tasting room.

Ten minutes later, Elliot dropped Kendra's laptop on Kay's desk, startling her from what she was doing. Then he placed Kendra's photo on top, pinning it in place with his finger.

"I don't care what you think. These cases are related. Back in the day when you used to look me in the eye and tell me the truth, you would've been the first to see that."

Kay leaned back and looked at him silently for a moment. "Yes, you're right. We need to talk."

TWENTY-FIVE
LUNCH

The air in the school cafeteria was a little stuffy. The mashed potatoes reeked of garlic; Alana had to steer clear of those, and hoped Nick would too. Her plans for Friday night didn't include long passionate kisses with the stink of the bulbous flowering plant from hell on their breaths.

Sadly, the salad had onions, another no-no. It was as if the cafeteria was doing it on purpose. She imagined a newspaper headline, SCHOOL USES MALODOROUS VEGETABLES TO CURB TEENAGER LIBIDO, and chuckled. They were probably laughing their hearts out, seeing all the girls hesitating in front of the food tables, trays in hand. The bitchy old hag who filled the plates was definitely enjoying herself every time she asked, "Some mashed with that?" and a girl would say no with regret in her voice.

Instead, Alana looked the hag straight in the eye and said, "I prefer corn, thank you." Then she grabbed an apple from the basket, while the woman deposited a piece of corn on the cob on her plate.

"No salad for you today?" the crone asked with a crooked,

all-knowing smile. Her teeth were irregular and yellow. Her name tag read "Betsy," and it fit her.

"No, ma'am," Alana replied defiantly. Unlike Betsy, she had plans for that night.

She felt Nick's hand on her shoulder. Beaming, she turned to face him.

"Chicken nuggets?" he asked, staring at her nearly empty plate.

"You'll have to take me out tonight," she whispered close to his ear. He brushed his lips against her cheek as she pulled away. Thrilled, she studied the full cafeteria to see if anyone was noticing them.

A few skanks were. A couple were whispering about them, their heads brought close together, their eyes fixed on her and Nick. *Choke on this, bitches*, she thought, smiling and flipping her hair over her shoulder, before heading toward one of the few empty tables.

She set the tray on the table, then sat, with Nick beside her. In an attempt to keep invaders at bay, she put her backpack on one of the empty chairs. Then she turned her attention toward Nick, holding the apple close to her lips, but not biting into it yet. "Where are we going tonight?"

He bit a mouthful of ham-and-cheese sandwich and chewed it quickly, with the typical appetite of a healthy teenager. "Wanna watch a movie later?"

She reached with her foot under the table until her shoe touched his. Lowering her eyelids, she batted her lashes a couple of times, looking to the side. "Whatever you want." Then she looked straight at him as she bit into the apple. He smiled, the metaphor not wasted on him at all.

"May we sit with you?" a girl's voice interrupted her moment of meaningful apple appreciation. Three of them were standing by the table with their loaded trays in their hands, waiting.

Alana glared at the girl who'd spoken, a redhead with a nose piercing missing its ring, but she didn't notice. She was looking straight at Nick, her head tilted, biting her lower lip, shamelessly flirting. And he was falling for it, smiling and probably feeling flattered by the attention, inviting them to join their table with a hand gesture.

Looking around, Alana noticed the cafeteria was full. Some kids were sitting on the stairs, eating with their trays in their laps. She would've gladly told those girls to get lost, but it wasn't the right thing to do. She wasn't going to become possessive, desperate, and mean. She was much better than that.

Her glare morphed into an inviting glance. She grabbed her backpack from the chair next to her. "Sure, you guys, join us."

Two of the girls took the available chairs, while the third went looking for a spare. She didn't return; moments later, Alana saw her seated on the stairs next to a guy in a team jersey.

Nick chatted with the two girls casually, while eating his sandwich. They were talking about movies; what they had watched recently, and if they'd liked it. Any recommendations they would make, anything they'd want to see. It seemed as if he'd completely forgotten about her.

Feeling the threat of tears in her throat, she drank some water and pushed the tray aside, leaving half the nuggets to keep the corn on the cob company on the way to the trash can. She hated how vulnerable Nick made her feel, how she saw a threat in every girl who walked by. But most of all, she hated the attention Nick gave them, when she was right there, by his side, ignored and miserable.

It wasn't the first time that had happened. Probably it would happen again and again. Nick was handsome and intelligent, charming, a veritable chick magnet. His Grecian features were close to what his ancient people had seen in Adonis. Tall and dark-haired, with black eyes that drilled into a woman's soul and a smile that lit her blood on fire, Nick was simply irresistible.

Adding the red convertible he drove and his elegant manners, she understood why competition for her boyfriend would always be fierce.

But she was ready, defending the walls of her castle the best way she could. At least she told herself that, counting the minutes until she had to return to class, minutes wasted by Nick on the chatty sophomores.

She was about to walk away from the table when Nick leaned closer to her and whispered, "What do you say we watch *Iron Man* tonight?"

His breath touched her skin, sending waves of desire throughout her body. "Uh-huh," she replied, smiling and leaning closer to him.

"My place?"

She pulled away a little and glanced at him quickly. She knew exactly what that meant. "Uh-huh," she repeated. His eyes lingered on her full lips.

"My folks are in San Fran for the weekend," he added, drawing closer, still keeping his voice low. "Wanna have a party instead?"

For a quick moment, she envisioned hordes of scantily clad girls wiggling their butts for his enjoyment, and shuddered at the thought. "We'll dance some other time," she replied, her lips close to his ear, almost touching it. "Let's make tonight about you and me."

TWENTY-SIX

DIARY

"You agree?" Surprised, Elliot stood and shoved his hands in his pockets. Under the brim of his hat, his eyes searched Kay's, expecting answers.

Kay stood and grabbed her keys. "Let's go. I'll fill you in on the way."

"Where are we going?"

"Jenna's," she replied, leading the way out of the office. In the parking lot, she hesitated between the two Interceptors, but Elliot pressed his remote and unlocked his. She climbed onto the passenger seat. The sun had heated the inside of the black vehicle to almost unbearable levels.

Elliot started the engine and turned the AC knob to the maximum, a flow of icy air coming out of the vents as he pulled out of the parking lot. He seemed preoccupied with something. She waited for him to bring it up.

"You have so much more experience than I do," he eventually said, "especially when it comes to murder cases of the twisted, psycho kind." He turned onto the highway leading to the interstate, then continued. "But shouldn't we focus on

Kendra first? Until we know otherwise, she's still alive. She's only been missing for fifteen hours or less."

Kay shifted in her seat to look at Elliot without turning her head too much. "That's exactly what we're doing. If you believe these cases are related, you'll understand that we might find more evidence in Jenna's universe than Kendra's."

"Why is that? Kendra's disappearance is fresh, new, and we might find more about her state of mind from interviewing her friends and searching her social media."

"That's one way to go about it," she replied. "Just like traveling from here to New York City has dozens of possible route options, based on choices made at each juncture, an investigation can follow a number of paths. If conducted properly, they'll all lead to the same conclusion."

"Only one of these routes is the fastest," he replied. "To New York, I mean, and to Kendra's whereabouts too. I don't—"

"Don't you think I'm painfully aware of every single minute that passes while we don't know where Kendra is?" She'd raised her voice, the stress of the past few hours taking its toll. "Whenever we make a decision whether to interview one witness or another, we gamble with people's lives. That's the invisible burden of a cop's life, to have to do that, do your very best, and always second-guessing yourself. To blame yourself if the outcome is less than ideal." She breathed, willing herself to lower her voice. Elliot wasn't responsible for anything that was wrong in her life. "But we can't afford to hesitate; that's worse than anything. We make these decisions based on our skills, experience, and instinct." She paused for a beat, absently looking at the landscape dashing by. The rich hues of summer green grasses met the deeper shades of teal and viridian borne by distant evergreens, tall and proud, reaching for the perfectly azure sky. She turned her attention to Elliot. "My gut tells me there's more to learn from Jenna's world than Kendra's."

The brim of Elliot's hat moved down then up in an almost imperceptible nod. "Why?"

"Mostly because Jenna's recent life had been filled with unusual events. Whatever happened to her last April, we still don't know, and it might've set events in motion. The man she was seeing, the older guy from San Fra—"

"Yeah, him. What am I missing?" He shot her a quick glance.

There was a beat of loaded silence, the only sound the rhythmic thumping of tires against asphalt seal joints. "Well, his name is Gavin Sharp," Kay replied, letting out a long breath of air.

Elliot glanced at her again. "What? Is that anyone you know?"

She chuckled with sadness. "That's my father's name." She paused for a second, weighing the words before speaking them. "What you probably don't know is that my father disappeared eighteen years ago after nearly killing my mother."

She swallowed with difficulty, her throat constricted, refusing to articulate the name out loud and hoping Elliot couldn't read her body language to see through her lies.

Elliot whistled. "Whoa... are you saying?—"

"No. Jenna wasn't dating my father," she replied, instilling as much calm as she could into her brittle voice. "But you can understand why I needed some time to sort through this mess."

Silence filled the space between them for a long moment. "You didn't feel you could trust me?" He sounded hurt, and he had every reason to feel that way.

"No, it's not that, Elliot. It was just the shock, that's all. In eighteen years, I haven't heard his name, except when people were asking me if we knew anything about him. He has outstanding warrants. My father is a wanted fugitive."

A beat. "I take it the vending machine sandwiches aren't that bad after all?"

She smiled weakly. He was quick to piece together what had happened. "I wouldn't recommend them, though."

"So, who is this guy? Any relation to you whatsoever?"

"None that I know of." Another sigh broke free from her chest. "But this will dredge up ancient history again."

"How old were you when it happened?"

She glanced at him quickly, not realizing she'd lowered her eyes. "Thirteen. But the abuse had been going on for years. I just... I never knew any other way until he was gone."

Elliot's hand left the steering wheel and found hers. He squeezed it gently, instilling strength into her heart. "What do we know about this Gavin Sharp?"

"Well, he's got a record." She was glad to change the subject.

"Make my day and tell me it's for rape."

"Nope, sorry. Just simple assault and battery, a sports game brawl gone bad. Served his half-year, then nada. I'm guessing he picked up some new skills on the inside, learned how to lay down low."

Elliot brought the SUV to a stop in front of the Jerrell residence. "What are you expecting to find here?"

"Answers," Kay replied, before climbing out of the Ford.

It took a while for Brenda Jerrell to open the door. Kay kept insisting, seeing that her car was in the driveway. Several oak leaves had fallen onto the windshield; that car hadn't been driven in a couple of days.

Mrs. Jerrell was as pale as a sheet, with a haunted, empty look in her eyes. After a moment's hesitation, she recognized them and stepped to the side, letting them in.

The living room was shrouded in darkness, the curtains still closed although it was two in the afternoon. The air was stale, dust swirling in the air in visible particles wherever a ray of light broke through the curtains. The door to the bedroom, where Mr. Jerrell had killed himself, was gaping open, a bloodstain dried a deep shade of maroon on the carpet at the foot of the bed. A blanket and a pillow were set on the couch; she must have been sleeping in the living room.

"Please tell me you have help," Kay whispered, clasping the woman's hands in hers. They were cold to the touch, lifeless.

She stared at Kay with an empty gaze as if not understanding. After a moment, she said, "M—my sister is coming over from Detroit. Tonight."

"Good," Kay replied softly. "Don't be alone at a time like this. Please call me if you need help," she added, putting her card into her hand.

She nodded. "I don't know how to live without them. I just don't," she whispered, her voice frail, brittle. "Did you find who took my baby's life?"

"We're still investigating," Kay replied gently. "Actually, we need your help."

She nodded, gathering her robe around her body as if fighting off a chill.

"Do you remember anything else about Jenna's change in behavior from last spring?"

No answer, as if Mrs. Jerrell hadn't heard the question.

"Maybe she met someone, or lost someone?" Still no answer. "Was she being bullied at school?" During the last interview with Jenna's mother, both parents had mentioned bullying. Kay hoped if she got Mrs. Jerrell to a point where she remembered something, it would be easier to get her to talk.

"Yes," she whispered. "But we don't know who it was."

"Did she tell you anything about it?"

She shook her head while her gaze found the floor. "She didn't tell us. We would've done something, talked to someone. She just... closed up, buried everything inside," she patted her chest with her fist a couple of times, hard, punishing, "because I wasn't here. I was gone."

"It's not your fault, Mrs. Jerrell," Kay said, speaking firmly yet gently. "You were putting food on the table for your family. You know who does that?" She didn't reply. "Heroes do that, Mrs. Jerrell. Heroes like you."

The woman raised her eyes and looked at Kay, her face still expressionless. A tear streaked her cheek. "It's too late now."

There wasn't much she could do, not while Kendra was still missing. Her life could be hanging by a thread, and time was running out. Hating herself for rushing, she asked, "May we see Jenna's room?"

Mrs. Jerrell led the way and opened the door. Kay stepped inside, studying every detail of what she was seeing and the picture it painted of whom Jenna used to be.

Her bed was tucked in the corner. Above it, on the side wall, a large poster celebrating the release of Gavin DeGraw's new single, "Soldier." The artist, wearing a brown fedora, played the piano in the rain.

Kay stared at the real DeGraw's face, seeing a vague resemblance with the San Francisco Gavin Sharp, so vague it could've only been in her imagination. Hers, and a young girl's in love, a girl who'd struggled with bullying and was looking for a protector, someone to defend her and ease her pain. Her very own soldier.

A familiar refrain came to Kay's mind. She mumbled some lyrics from memory, a little out of tune.

"What?" Elliot asked.

"This," Kay replied, pointing at DeGraw's poster. "It's why she fell for him, and she was dying to tell someone about it."

"Fell for whom?" Mrs. Jerrell asked. A flicker of interest lit her eyes.

Kay turned to face the pale woman, wishing there was some way she could avoid giving her an answer. "We have reasons to believe she was dating an older man from San Francisco."

"Dating?" She looked away as if to search her memory. "My

daughter was depressed and rarely ever left the house. She spent most her time on her computer."

"Where she met this man," Kay added.

Mrs. Jerrell licked her dry, cracked lips. "Is he, um, did he kill her?" Her voice turned hoarse, brittle.

Kay nodded. "Seems that way, yes."

"Do you know who he is?"

"Yes, we do, and a warrant is being issued for his arrest."

"Who is he?" she pressed on, clasping Kay's arm with her trembling hands.

Kay hesitated, wondering what Mrs. Jerrell would think upon hearing the suspect's name.

"Unfortunately, we can't disclose this information," Elliot replied. "This is an ongoing investigation."

"I see," Mrs. Jerrell replied, letting go of Kay's arm and pulling away.

"Did your daughter have a diary?" Kay asked. Like most teenagers in love, Jenna must've been dying to chat with someone about her new romance, only she didn't have anyone to talk to. A diary would've been the next best thing.

"Not that I know of," Mrs. Jerrell replied.

"Do you mind if I—"

Kay stopped mid-question, noticing Mrs. Jerrell's gesture of invitation. She looked around the small bedroom, wondering where Jenna would've hidden a diary. Not the desk drawers; too obvious. Nevertheless, she pulled them open and ran her hands underneath, searching for an object that might've been taped out of sight.

Nothing.

Elliot started looking inside the closet, opening shoeboxes and running his hands through the larger pockets of winter coats, while Kay stared at the bed. She kneeled beside it and looked underneath. The mattress platform was a wooden frame with three-inch-wide beams running across. Shining her flashlight, she checked the underside of the mattress one inch at a time. About halfway down, she noticed a darker area, rectangular, with irregular edges.

Jenna had cut a hole into the mattress.

"I got something." Kay put on fresh gloves and reached under the bed, trying to get to the hole. Elliot grabbed the mattress by the edges and lifted it up, exposing the cut. The edges of a small notebook were visible inside the mattress, together with the end of a red bookmark ribbon. Careful not to injure herself against the edges of the springs or damage the diary, Kay extracted the small notebook one inch at a time. Maybe it contained the answers she'd been looking for. Or, at least, a lead—something to point them in the right direction to uncover what had happened to Jenna last April.

The diary was green, with an intricate gold-foil floral design embossed on the hardcover, and a magnetic clasp that held it closed. Based on the discoloration of the page edges, Jenna had filled about half of it. Kay released the clasp, and the diary opened where a dry rose, the petals now a weathered, faded pink, had been pressed between the pages.

A rose, trapped between neatly written pages in endless cursive, the quintessence of teenage love. For a moment, Kay was tempted to take a seat on the worn-out carpet and start reading, but it had to wait.

Mrs. Jerrell stared at the little object as if it was from another world. "May I, um, please?—it's from my daughter." A stifled sob shattered her breath.

Kay took her hand and squeezed it. "I promise I'll return this to you. It's evidence, and we have to study it as quickly as possible. That can't happen until it has been dusted for prints."

Elliot opened an evidence pouch, and she slid the diary in there, then folded the flap and sealed it.

Seemingly resigned, Mrs. Jerrell stood in the bedroom's doorway, desolate, speechless, watching them walk away. From the living room, Kay stopped and asked, raising the evidence-sealed diary in the air, "Who would've known about this?"

Mrs. Jerrell wiped a tear from her eye. "*I* didn't even know about it. I—I wouldn't know." She shook her head and clasped her hands together tightly. "Maybe Mackenzie or Alana, her best friends. They were close... before April, at least, they used to be."

TWENTY-SEVEN

FLAWED

They didn't drive more than a mile or so toward Mackenzie Trenton's home, when a text message from Doc Whitmore made Elliot hit the brakes and flip a U-turn with the sirens on to keep oncoming traffic out of the way. Weaving quickly through the afternoon rush, he didn't leave Kay too much time to think about the diary. She'd planned to read a few pages before interviewing Mackenzie Trenton, to have some idea where Jenna's mind was at, maybe get some insight into her relationships with her best friends.

"Thanks for saving me in there," she said as soon as Elliot turned off the siren, her cheeks flushed. She'd never needed rescuing before; the feeling was new to her and a bit overwhelming. She'd frozen when Mrs. Jerrell had asked about the suspect's name. Frozen, her, with all her experience. Unbelievable.

Elliot didn't reply immediately. He just flashed a quick smile, a kind and supportive one. "Working this case is gonna feel like trying to bag flies, if you're thinking of containing people's reactions when they hear the perp's name. You can't. They're gonna shoot their mouths off so much they'll make you wonder if they ate bullets for breakfast. But that's people, and you know it. They gossip."

She chuckled, lowering her gaze, feeling vulnerable. She was the psychology PhD, yet she needed some sense talked into her by her down-to-earth partner. He was right, even if he didn't know the entire story. She couldn't let herself be intimidated by her own fears again. Before the dust was to settle on the Gavin Sharp name again, there was bound to be some rough-water sailing, questions she wouldn't expect, idle gossip, speculation, and misdirection.

She could handle it. She had to.

"Thanks, partner," she replied. "Now, let's see how the ME reacts to it, shall we? Call it a test run."

"Yes, ma'am," Elliot replied, pulling in front of the medical examiner's building.

Inside, the stainless-steel exam tables were empty, and the powerful ceiling lights were off. Dr. Whitmore and one of his assistants worked quietly, a well-oiled machine swapping samples and operating lab equipment smoothly. The ME was taking the slides lined up on the tray without lifting his eyes from the microscope's ocular, while his assistant prepared them skillfully and quickly, taking dictation notes on a clipboard with the results.

Kay stopped by the ME and smiled in lieu of a greeting, then handed the evidence pouch holding Jenna's diary to the doctor. "Could you have this dusted for prints really quickly, please? We're in a rush."

Doc Whitmore beckoned his assistant, a young brunette wearing a faded pink lab coat. She abandoned the clipboard on the table and took the pouch with visible curiosity, unsealed it, then extracted the content carefully, setting it on a clean lab table on wheels. Kay watched her hands as they moved quickly, spinning the fingerprint powder brush with precise gestures of her long, thin fingers clad in blue latex gloves. In its wake, black powder settled on the diary's covers and spine, revealing swirls, arches, and loops she then lifted with clear adhesive tape.

Kay turned to look at Doc Whitmore. "Any DNA results yet?"

The ME gestured toward a computer that searched through records silently, only the faint whirring noise of its hard drive giving it away. "I just loaded the first sample into the system. The other DNA samples are still grinding in the sequencer. It will take a while."

"What if I tell you whom to run it against? Would that speed things up?"

"Yes," he replied enthusiastically, "but only the CODIS search part, not the sequencing. If I have them identified in CODIS, it will take a minute or two."

"Yeah, he's in CODIS all right," she replied. Elliot looked at her encouragingly. "His name is Gavin Sharp."

"Who?" Doc Whitmore asked, looking at Kay above his thick-rimmed glasses with a stern expression on his face.

"Gavin Sharp," she repeated, still reeling at the sound of his name spoken out loud by her own voice. "Not the one from Mount Chester, who's missing... not my father. There's another one, in San Francisco."

Doc Whitmore's gaze lingered on her for a moment more, scrutinizing, impenetrable. "Isn't that an odd coincidence?... I'll say." He stood and peeled off his gloves, then rinsed his hands at a small sink by the end of the long lab table. Patting them dry, he glanced at Kay quickly as if to see if she really meant what she'd said. Then he walked over to the computer that was running the CODIS database, and started typing on its plastic-covered keyboard. "Gavin Sharp, you said?"

"Yes," Kay replied, holding her breath. All evidence pointed to the San Francisco man who'd lured Jenna into meeting with him.

Doc Whitmore typed the name in the search field, then

waited for a brief moment. The system returned two results. "Selecting the one in San Francisco," he said, highlighting the second database entry, then hitting enter. The system beeped quietly, and a message framed in a red box appeared on the screen.

"Not a match," Doc Whitmore said, looking at her for a moment as she struggled to contain her disappointment.

If not Gavin Sharp, then whom? What were they missing? She shot Elliot a glance; he looked just as dismayed as she was feeling.

"It's only one unsub, right?" she asked, unwilling to believe Gavin Sharp was in the clear.

"The same fingerprints were found on both condom wrappers, and they're not in AFIS. They're not a match with this man's prints."

They had nothing... and Kendra's time was running out.

"If you don't mind me asking," Doc Whitmore said, "how sure are you of this man's identity? This name coincidence... that's strange, to say the least."

Pressing her lips tightly together, she nodded. Of course, he was suspicious. Everyone with half a brain would be, and Doc Whitmore was smart as a whip. "It's how we got to him, Doc. He's the man Jenna was chatting with online, and dating at times, when he drove over from the city."

The ME leaned closer to the computer screen and squinted a little. "This man is fifty-six years old! Dating? That's not dating, that's—" He'd raised his voice, but then stopped abruptly, lowering his fiery glance. "I guess I've seen worse. We all have. I was just wondering if you'd mind if I run the other Gavin Sharp, that's all."

She shrugged, already knowing the answer. "Go right ahead, Doc. You were going to run the sample against the entire CODIS anyway, right?"

The ME ran the name search again, and selected Kay's

father, then hit enter. A moment, and the disappointing beep warned no match was found. "Oh, well. I'll continue running it and, hopefully, we'll get a match soon. But it could take a while."

"Why did you call us, Doc?" Elliot asked. He'd held his distance, observing. He was quiet, but his keen attention caught things she sometimes missed.

"Ah, yes," Doc Whitmore, replied, straightening his back and sliding his hands into his lab coat pockets. "I have a few interesting results to share." He walked over to the table and grabbed the remote. The wall-mounted TV came to life. He clicked the buttons a few times, then stopped on a side-by-side view of hair fibers. "The two hair fibers we found on Jenna's clothing were not hers. I suspected that, considering the length and color; I believe I'd already shared that with you."

Kay had almost forgotten about the hair fibers... her initial mental image of the unsub was that of a male with longer hair, possibly bleached. When she'd come across the Gavin Sharp from San Francisco, she'd been so shocked she'd forgotten all about those two hair fibers.

Damn... this was sloppy work, unforgivable. Her logic had been flawed, warped by emotion. Screw all the Gavin Sharps of the world.

"Was it bleached, Doc?" Her voice was tentative, not her usual assertive tone.

"Yes, it was. I thought I'd... well, I'm sorry. Yes, it's bleached. Here," he pointed with his index finger at the screen, "this is the natural color of the hair, um, caramel brown. Too bad we don't have root follicles."

"Got it," she said, ready to go. Doc Whitmore's assistant, Cheryl per her name tag, deposited Jenna's diary in Kay's hands, and vanished. She'd sealed it in a new evidence pouch, signed and dated it.

"Thanks, Cheryl. Please let me know when you have a match."

"It's all Jenna's," she replied. "I didn't dust all the pages, but—"

Kay shook her head. "There's no need, thank you." She turned to the doc, but he held his hand in the air to stop her.

"I'm not done yet; there's more." The image shown on the TV screen shifted to a photo of two purple condom wrappers taken at the scene. "I believe I told you the prints found on these wrappers belong to the same man, but he's not in AFIS."

Kay felt a pang of anxiety coursing through her veins. Another thing she'd missed... Gavin Sharp's fingerprints would've been in AFIS; he was an ex-con. She'd wasted precious time chasing this man, when evidence was telling her he wasn't Jenna's rapist.

Oblivious to her internal turmoil, Doc Whitmore continued. "I was able to match the lubricant found in these wrappers to the traces lifted off Jenna's body. It's a perfect match; you'll be happy to hear that, because these wrappers were found in a public place, and defense could have them thrown them out during trial. However, the match was done at an enzymatic level, taking in consideration the duration the lubricant had been exposed to air once the seal was broken. You see, its chemical composition slightly alters in the presence of oxygen. Both samples, the wrappers and the trace lifted off Jenna's body, had been exposed to oxygen for approximately the same period of time. It's a solid match that will hold in court."

Court.

The word resonated in her mind, echoing strangely as if it were a notion eons away.

Before court, they needed a suspect, a lead that would take them to Kendra, and they needed it quickly, if there was any hope to find that girl alive. She shuddered at a thought; every minute Kendra spent in captivity was on her and her flawed thinking. If she died, her blood would be on Kay's hands.

"All right, Doc," she said, touching the doctor's shoulder. "What else? Give me something I can use right now to—"

"She was drugged." His voice was stern, contradicting the understanding Kay read in his forgiving glance. "She had GHB in her system. She would've been sedated, malleable, hardly able to fight her assailant but still awake. She would've felt a bit dizzy, maybe nauseated. Had she survived the attack, the next day she would've probably not been able to recall any of it."

"Someone slipped her a roofie?" Elliot asked.

"Yes," Doc Whitmore replied. "Seeing that, I prioritized the stomach contents analysis. You'll have something definitive by tomorrow morning at the latest."

She checked the digital clock on the wall. It was almost five. A smile blossomed on Kay's lips. "Thanks, Doc."

"Do you think this case has anything to do with the missing girl, Kendra Flannagan? I know her parents; I've known them for years. They're good people."

"It might be the same unsub, Doc," Kay replied, slightly frowning. "I'm thinking Jenna was his first rape, maybe unplanned, perhaps opportunistic. Messy... disorganized. But he discovered how much he likes it, so much, that he needs more time... he used two condoms, right?"

Doc Whitmore nodded, staring at her with a somber gaze through his black-rimmed glasses.

"Perhaps he took Kendra because he'd like to have more time with his victim, in a place where he can discover who he really is and can contain her better." She shuddered as the thought was starting to take shape. "A place she can't escape from... someplace where no one can hear her scream."

TWENTY-EIGHT
SHARDS

Natalie Gaskell watched the digits change, obsessively, unable to focus on anything else, although an open bestseller was placed face down in her lap. Her eyes darted nervously between the clock and the empty driveway, both symbols of her irrelevance.

Neither husband nor son took her seriously enough to come home.

She hated herself for making idle threats... how could she turn off Richard's cell service, when that phone was her last link to him? It was her lifeline, her only hope of speaking with her son again. It seemed that, whenever she made a threat, it only made things worse between them. She could feel his hatred as if it were a physical presence between them. Raw, unforgiving, searing, a place she couldn't walk back from.

Remembering their last fight brought a knot to her throat. She closed the book and abandoned it on the sofa, then stood and walked over to the bar, her eyes still fixed on the empty driveway sprawling in front of the picture window. Shadows were growing longer on the perfectly manicured lawn, soon to make room for nightfall.

If Richard had any plans to come home after school, he would've been here already.

Hand frozen in midair for a second or two, she considered calling Renaldo's house, where Richard seemed to enjoy spending most of his time. But her call wouldn't be welcome. It would have him shouting at her, making threats, accusing her of following him, of damaging his relationships with his friends. No good would come out of that.

Instead, she chose the cut crystal bottle filled with twelve-year-old Scotch, and poured herself a triple in one of the matching glasses. A few ice cubes followed, plopped unceremoniously into the glass after she'd fished them from the dispenser tray with her fingers. A couple of droplets landed on the lacquered bar, a few others on her silk blouse, but she didn't notice.

For the fifteenth time at least since that morning, she picked up her phone and speed-dialed her son's number. It went straight to voicemail. Her son, her own flesh and blood, was driving her crazy. It was the entitlement, the rebellious nature, but also the arrogance he exuded. He'd grown into that from a sweet little boy whose mind was way ahead of his age and who soon realized he was smarter than most. After that realization, came the aloofness, the disaffected behavior that drove her insane.

One thing was certain. If he didn't want to come home, there was no way she could make him. The same went for having a conversation with him. It seemed that everything had to happen on his terms.

The sound of tires crunching the pavement drew her attention. It wasn't Richard's Jeep. Edward's Maybach pulled into the driveway slowly, then entered the garage. She listened as the garage door rumbled to a close, then took a final sip of Scotch before abandoning the empty glass on the coffee table by the sofa.

Hearing his footfalls approaching, light taps of leather soles against luscious marble tiles, rage swelled inside her chest. It was his fault that Richard was gone. The boy idolized his father, the lying, cheating bastard that he was, and hated her because of that.

"So, you finally made it," she said the moment Edward walked into the living room.

He threw her a tired glance and loosened his tie. Then he took off his jacket and left it on a chair together with his briefcase, on his way to the same bar she'd visited minutes earlier.

The architect who'd designed their cottage had placed the bar in the corner of the room, right next to the picture window overlooking Mount Chester's barren rock peaks. It was complete with four-legged stools, a stone countertop nesting a small sink, a wine cooler, a minifridge with an ice dispenser, and several glass shelves on the back wall to hold bottles that didn't need to be chilled.

Edward went behind the counter and opened the fridge. "Want anything?"

She was just about to make another comment about Bambi or whatever the hell her name was, but his question seeded an urgent thirst in her throat. "Yeah." She collected her empty glass from the coffee table and walked over to the bar, realizing she was swaying her hips. She wore bleached, stretch denim with black heels and a blue silk blouse that shimmered in the electric light. "I'll stick to Scotch, if you don't mind."

Without looking at her or saying anything, he took her glass and drained whatever was left in it into the sink. Then he filled it about halfway, adding a few ice cubes. Putting it in front of her, he said, "I don't mind."

Of course, he didn't mind. To mind, one has to care first.

"Where's Richard?" he asked, after taking a long sip of vodka, straight from the freezer.

"Oh, you realized he's not home?" she asked, her voice

dipped in venom. "It's interesting to see the things you notice if you can be bothered to be here."

He shot her a quick glance, and undid the top two shirt buttons. "Forget I asked."

"No," she shouted, slamming down the glass so hard the translucent, gold liquid sloshed out, landing in a small puddle on the counter. "You don't get to tell me what to do, on the rare occasions when Miss Bambi lets you off leash."

"Jeez, woman," he said, running his hands through his hair. "And you're wondering why the hell I don't want to come home anymore?" She stared at him, defiantly, inviting him to continue if he dared. "This is not a home; this is pure hell! I'd rather spend my evenings with my murderous clients, waiting for their bail to be posted. Yeah... I'd rather spend time in jail than here with you," he added, his voice back to his normal pitch reserved for the courtroom. Cold, factual, uncompromising, every word a stab into her heart.

Without another word, Natalie crossed the large oriental rug to the chair where Edward had abandoned his jacket and briefcase. She unlocked the latches with a loud pop, opening the briefcase and rummaging through it.

"Hey," Edward shouted. "What the hell do you think you're doing?"

Frantic, she searched under the stack of papers and inside the pocket, but didn't find the condoms she knew he used to have with him. "Where are they, Edward?" she asked, turning to face him when she sensed he was near.

He looked at her with a strange expression in his eyes. It was surprise, disgust, but also pity. No trace of the love that used to be... nothing. "They're gone, Natalie. I don't use them anymore."

A million things wanted to be spoken, choking her. Rage demanded she asked whether Bambi—or whatever her name was this time—was using an IUD now. Logic wanted her to probe and find where else he would stash his condoms, out of her reach, so she couldn't keep track of how many he used.

The hurt wife who'd been cheated on and still loved him won the battle.

"I don't believe you," she eventually said, leaning against the wall for support. Her knees felt weak, shaky.

"What do you want from me, Natalie?" he calmly asked again, stopping in front of her with his hands on his hips. "No matter what I say, I make you mad. If you want me gone, just say the word."

The thought of spending endless days wandering alone through the cottage, drink in hand, made the bile rise in her throat. Tears threatened to break open the floodgates, turning her voice brittle. "I want my son back. And I want you to stay."

Edward sighed and turned away, staring out the window for a moment. It was getting dark outside. "You pushed him away," he said factually. "You need to stop with the shouting matches. He's just a kid. Our fights are too much for him to take."

Of course, it was all on her. Typical Edward... damn narcissists, it was never their fault, even when it was.

"You cheated on me," she said, the words hissed with undertones of rage. "And he still blames me. This isn't fair."

He drew closer to her, reaching out with both hands to touch her shoulders. "Life isn't fair, Nat. Never was, never will be." Feeling his hands through the thin fabric of her blouse sent a wave of irritation through her bloodstream. She wasn't ready for closeness yet. Not when every time she closed her eyes, she saw him fucking that skinny bimbo hard and fast, just the way he liked it.

She pulled away and looked at him intently. "Make him come home or I'll report him as a missing person. I'll get the cops involved if you can't handle your own son."

Slack-jawed, Edward stared at her for a long moment. She turned on her heel and walked away. As she reached the stairs, she heard an object crashing into the bar's glass shelves, bringing everything down in a thunderous explosion of shards.

She didn't look back.

It must've been Edward's glass, thrown at the wall in a fit of rage. He had very poor impulse control, just like Richard.

TWENTY-NINE
MACKENZIE

The setting sun's colors were starting to lay colors on Wildfire Ridge, threatening darkness the moment it would disappear behind the hills. Nightfall was quick in mountain regions.

Elliot drove to Mackenzie Trenton's place fast, making her queasy, but she didn't lift her eyes from the pages of Jenna's diary.

April 20

My name is whore.

Tramp. Slut. Floozy. Harlot.

That's what they call me, wherever I go. Whatever I do.

Not to my face, because that would take courage, and they're nothing but cowards. I know that, but it still hurts. I thought they were my friends.

Some of them still pretend they are, but when I walk into the room, they all stop talking, and change the subject to something like sports or schoolwork.

What hurts the most is no one bothers to ask me, is it true? And give me a chance to explain.

They just call me names behind my back, and whisper lies about me.

April 23

Dad asked me if I'm being bullied at school. Oh, Daddy... I could never tell you what's going on. It would break your heart. Mom's too. I wish I could tell you, though. I wish I could tell someone that I don't understand why the world's gone insane and they're taking it out on me.

Alana came by today. I'm ashamed to look her in the eye. I'm sure she's heard what everyone calls me, but she's never said a word. Not to me. She's so sweet... I can't look at her without wondering what she knows and isn't telling me.

Wish she'd stop coming. It's only making it worse. I'd rather be left alone. Two more months until summer vacation, then one more year in this hell.

I'm not gonna make it. I can't.

April 27

I entered the chem lab today and everyone stopped talking, except for Rennie and Richard. Then someone whispered, "Shush, the slut's here."

This will never end. I don't know what they were saying. I stopped wanting to find out. Why can't they just say it to my face? Why can't I get the right to defend myself?

Slut. That's all I am now to everyone who used to be my friend.

I can't stand it anymore.

Wish I was dead. Then it would be over.

The SUV stopped abruptly, and Kay raised her eyes from the tear-stained, cream-colored pages filled with neat cursive handwriting. She closed the diary and tucked it into the unsealed evidence bag.

"Why would these kids call Jenna a whore behind her back?" Kay asked, a frown wrinkling her brow as she looked at Elliot. Tapping on the closed diary in her lap with an accusing finger, she added, "She was a seventeen-year-old schoolgirl, for crying out loud."

Elliot cut the engine, then pointed at the small house with petunia flowerbeds on both sides of the entrance. "We'll find out soon enough."

They were almost on the porch when the door swung open, and a teenage girl stepped outside. She wore a sleeveless shirt with a floral pattern and white shorts. Her long blonde hair was tucked behind her ears. She was smiling at them, a shy hand raised in a tentative greeting.

"I was wondering when you'd come," she said. "Kids are texting, saying cops are talking to people who knew Jenna. I was her best friend," she announced, undertones of sadness in her voice.

Where were those texting kids getting their information from? Kay wondered. They'd only just started with Mackenzie. Some smartass kid might've given himself airs stating the logical and obvious. Of course, cops were going to talk to people who knew Jenna.

They stopped on the concrete path, and Elliot showed his badge. "We have a few questions, yes."

The girl continued to grin nervously, twisting a strand of her hair with long nervous fingers, annoying Kay just a little bit with her indecisiveness. Mackenzie didn't budge from the porch; she didn't seem to want to invite them in. The color of her hair might've matched the two fibers Doc Whitmore had found on Jenna's body, but Mackenzie's hair fell in loose curls almost to her waist. Too long to be a match.

Kay smiled encouragingly. "May we come inside?"

A flicker of a frown clouded her eyes. "Um, sure," she said, still hesitant, shifting her weight from one foot to the other. "It's messy, you know."

A battle seemed to take place inside Mackenzie's mind. Eventually, she opened the door, holding the knob as they walked through, and closing it behind them. Then she led them to her bedroom.

"My folks aren't at home, and they said people shouldn't come when they're out." Her smile turned into an anxious giggle. "But I guess you're all right."

"I'd like to think so," Elliot replied, smiling and touching the brim of his hat.

Mackenzie's bedroom was all about vampire romance, mainly *Twilight*, represented generously with large-size movie pictures for all the installments. A bookcase flanked a small desk, filled with vampire books.

Kay looked around, taking a quick inventory of the items and how they portrayed her witness. The furniture was inexpensive, but neat and clean. Just like the house, this room spoke of a family life with simple values, lived in harmony, and frugally. "You prefer books to movies?"

"I like both," she replied, standing uncomfortably, stepping with one foot over the other. She was instinctively minimizing her footprint, indicative of deep-set insecurity and shyness. "But with books, you can spend more time with the stories," she chuckled, letting go of the hair strand she was twisting and proceeding to torture her long, thin fingers, kneading them together.

Mackenzie Trenton was a ball of nerves.

Except for the bed and the desk chair, there was no other place to sit in the small room, so Kay decided to stand. "Were you and Jenna close?"

"Uh-huh, yes, we were," she replied quickly. "The two of us and Alana. Did you speak with Alana yet?"

"Not yet, no," Kay replied, wondering why Mackenzie wanted to know. Had the two girls rehearsed their stories? "How often did you guys hang out?"

"At least a few times a week," Mackenzie replied, her eyes darting all over the room. "But since spring, she didn't want to go out with us anymore. Not that often." She shifted her weight from one foot to the other, staring briefly at the ceiling. "Not recently."

"Were you on the day trip Jenna took on April seventeenth?"

She shook her head. "Mom wouldn't let me go. I woke up with a cough that day."

Elliot leaned against the bedroom door. "What was different about Jenna? What had changed?" With a quick head gesture, he drew Kay's attention to a collage of small photos on the wall. It was Mackenzie with Alana and Jenna in various locations. At the mall, at Katse Coffee Shop having bagels, on Mount Chester, hiking. Always smiling, happy, carefree.

Mackenzie chewed briefly on the tip of her finger, a gesture familiar to Kay. She did the same when feeling unsure of herself, thinking hard about what to say or do.

"I don't want to say anything, um—she's dead now, and only good things..." Her voice faltered, while her eyes looked at Kay, pleading for understanding.

"It's all right," Kay said. "I'm sure she wouldn't mind, as long as it's the truth. We're trying to catch the man who killed her."

"I heard she was raped too," Mackenzie whispered. "I can't think of anyone who, um—you know, would've done this."

"Tell us about Jenna, and what changed in April," Kay insisted.

Mackenzie looked at the door, as if seeing if anyone could come and save her from the answers she had to give. "Um, she turned into a different person. She was becoming cold, paranoid, and moody." Another bite on her finger. "A bit trashy." The word was whispered, while her eyes darted all over the room as if afraid she'd be overheard. "Way too eager to get out there and live her life." The statement seemed to pain her, make her uncomfortable.

But what was she talking about? Jenna's parents had said that she'd stopped leaving the house in April, while Mackenzie was saying the opposite.

"Tell me more," Kay encouraged her. "It will help us catch her killer. You're doing your friend a favor."

Mackenzie's eyes brimmed with tears. "I miss her, I do." She sniffled and cleared her throat, staring at the floor the entire time as if embarrassed by her moment of weakness. "She stopped being honest with me. With both of us, Alana and me."

"How? What do you mean?"

Her chest heaved as she sighed, her eyes now searching for answers in the pattern of the rug beneath her feet. "She was telling me she's at home, studying, and didn't want to hang out with us, but the following day there were always stories. Who she went out with. What she did."

"You mean, she was sleeping around?" Kay asked.

"Yes," Mackenzie replied, sounding relieved she didn't have to say it first. "But I don't know for sure. It's just what I kept hearing, you know, kids talking, texting, that kind of stuff." She paused for a moment, looking at Kay, hoping what she'd said was enough.

It wasn't. Kay held her gaze, encouraging her to say more.

She bit her finger again and stepped in place, repeatedly glancing at the door. "Um, like when everyone was saying she'd slept with Renaldo. I asked her if that was true, and she just stared at me. She didn't say a word. I tried to talk with her, but she was insulted I'd even asked her."

Kay exchanged a quick look with Elliot. Even if the girl had been sleeping around, that wouldn't've been the first time it had happened. They were teenagers; reckless, impulsive, driven by raging hormones and not a lot of common sense. There had to be something else that had got her assaulted and killed.

"Then what happened?" Kay asked patiently, taking a seat on the desk chair, in an unspoken message to Mackenzie that she wasn't leaving until she got to the bottom of whatever had been going on.

Mackenzie's shoulders dropped but her eyes darted once more toward the door before she spoke again. "Then the website happened," she whispered, "that came out in May, I believe, right before summer break. That's what drove Tim away."

"Who's Tim?" Elliot asked.

"Tim Carter, he was Jenna's boyfriend. He's a nice guy, a bit shy, loyal like a dog." Her smile widened for a split second, then waned. "All the gossip, he didn't believe it. He didn't want to. But when he saw the website, he dumped her. I was there, with her, when they broke up. He showed her the website, and she didn't say anything... she just stared at the screen. I didn't know what he was talking about when he showed her... I found out later, and, oh my gosh." She covered her mouth with her hand. "It was horrible."

"What website?" Kay asked, wondering why the more she heard, the less she understood. Those kids seemed to coexist in a parallel universe.

Mackenzie's cheeks caught fire. She bit her lip nervously, then the tip of her finger. "I don't remember exactly." Seeing Kay's expression, she added quickly, "But I can bring it up on my phone. It was something like, I-put-out-dot-whatever, this part I don't remember." She extracted her phone from her pocket and typed incredibly fast. Then, not daring more than a quick glance at Kay, she showed her the phone screen.

Kay took the phone from Mackenzie's trembling hand and stared at the screen in disbelief. The website was dubbed Jenna

Puts Out. Jenna's face, smiling innocently, reminded Kay of the photo Mrs. Jerrell had showed them, from before April, the one she used for Jenna's college applications. It could've been the same photo, slightly tilted and cropped. A few well-chosen words were next, in a brief paragraph highlighting the girl's willingness to meet up and have sex "with one or more partners in an exploration of everything teen sexuality had to offer." Then a series of photos followed, artistic closeups and various angles of naked breasts, waxed pubic area, and lower back with gluteal cleft.

Speechless, she handed the phone to Elliot. The same consternation landed on his features, accompanying a deep frown that marred his brow under the brim of his hat.

"This was Jenna's site?" Kay asked.

Mackenzie shrugged. "She didn't say anything about it for a while. Then, in July sometime, after she'd cut her hair shorter, she told me it wasn't her in those, um, body photos, and she didn't know who made the site and why. She was heartbroken we all believed it was hers." Mackenzie was still flushed, avoiding Kay's gaze, probably from embarrassment. "By fourth of July, everyone had seen it and was making her life hell. But I guess some kids had known about it for months... that would explain why they kept calling her those awful names."

"What names?" Elliot asked.

"You know," Mackenzie said, wringing her hands together. "Like whore and slut. Stuff like that. I didn't know at first. They were hiding from Alana and me, knowing we were her friends."

Kay stared at Mackenzie, thinking. It seemed Jenna had been the victim of a smear campaign worthy of a presidential candidate, not some high school kid from Small Town, California. Who would have the knowledge and malice to do that, and why?

Facing such adversity at her young age would explain Jenna's depression, her visible change from a self-confident and happy teenager to someone who looked as despondent as she did in her most recent photos. Her falling in love with Gavin Sharp, a father figure, a man who probably knew nothing of that dreadful website.

But how did any of this smearing and cyberbullying connect with Kendra?

"Tell me about Kendra Flannagan," Kay asked, handing Mackenzie back her phone.

A quick, fleeting frown clouded the girl's relieved gaze. "Kendra? She's a junior. I don't know that much about her. She started hanging out with Alana and me last month or so, after Jenna stopped."

"Is Kendra being cyberbullied too?" Elliot asked.

"What?" Mackenzie reacted. "I never thought of it that way, but yeah, I guess it's cyberbullying." She thought for a minute, biting her lip. "No, I haven't heard a peep about Kendra."

"Did Kendra know Jenna?" Kay asked, throwing a shot in the dark.

A shrug. "I don't know... maybe. It's not such a big school, you know. Everyone knows everyone."

"When's the last time you saw her?"

"Kendra? Yesterday, she was at school. Afterward, I don't remember. We went out, a larger group, and hung out at the mall. But I don't remember if she was there... she could've been. Alana and I were raising money for Jenna's memorial fund."

"Does she have a boyfriend? Who does she go out with?" Kay asked.

Mackenzie's lips pressed together in a line. "I don't know. Honest." She held her arms out in an apologetic gesture. "My parents won't let me hang out at her place because of the wine and the drunks." She laughed. "As if we'd go there to drink wine."

Kay looked at Elliot briefly, then thanked Mackenzie for her help. The girl led them out, visibly relieved the interview was over.

"One more thing," Kay said, from the doorstep. "What we talked about is strictly confidential. You can't tell anyone or text anyone about it. It's against the law."

Suddenly pale, Mackenzie nodded. "I got it. I watch a lot of TV. I know how this works."

Kay repressed a sigh. Everyone did.

THIRTY
CABIN

The cabin had been deserted a long time.

It was a single room, built out of stacked logs, blackened by smoke and dirt. The gaps between the logs had been sealed with chinking at some point in the cabin's history, but in places, that chinking was long gone, and the wind whistled through the narrow spaces, bringing the evening chill inside.

Thick dust covered the sparse wooden furniture. A small table and two small chairs, nothing but slices of tree logs with four legs screwed under them. In a corner, a stove with a fallen-apart chimney was good for nothing but providing another hole through which the wind could blow leaves and dust inside. On the wall next to the stove was the door, rattling with every strong wind gust but remaining closed. Kendra could see the fading daylight through the gap underneath it.

On the opposite wall, several pieces of chain with hooks had been nailed to the logs, probably used in the past to hang game for skinning or gutting. Kendra's hands were bound together tightly with a rope that had been hung from one of those hooks. It was high enough to not let her sit down on the dirt-covered floor, and her entire body ached, screaming for some warmth and rest.

She didn't remember much or how she got there. She'd awakened to find herself like that a few hours ago, feeling nauseated and dizzy, thirsty, and weak, frightened out of her mind. But at least she'd been warm for a while, for as long as the sun had been shining. With the vanishing remnants of the day came the night chill, cutting into her flesh with every wind gust that made it through the cracks in the walls. Terrified, she'd watched the shadows grow longer and the insidious, horrifying darkness creep in, engulfing her until she couldn't see anything.

She'd tried to free herself, tugging at the restraints, hoping she'd dislodge the rusty hardware from the walls and break out of there, but it hadn't happened. Instead, her wrists had pulled against the rope until her skin was burned raw and now throbbed with searing pain.

Every now and then she screamed, hoping someone would hear her, but no one did. Only the howling wind replied with strong gusts and the smell of rain in the air. In the distance, thunder rolled, and the occasional lightning lit up the cabin for a fleeting moment, before allowing darkness to return.

Her teeth clattered and her breath shattered with sobs. Who had brought her there? Why couldn't she remember? She was still wearing the same clothes as when she'd left the house; she remembered that much, sneaking out dressed in a V-neck T-shirt and some frayed jeans, and a new pair of sneakers she had in her bedroom closet, in a box, unopened. Otherwise, she would've had to go to the door to get her shoes and risk getting caught.

She wished she'd been caught instead of being here, even if her mother would've grounded her for a year. Sobbing bitterly, she called out for her mother, although she knew she couldn't answer.

No one was there but her, alone in the dark, chained to the wall in a dilapidated cabin about to fall apart in the storm.

Still standing, she almost dozed off, but woke with a start when her head tilted to the side, leaning on her arm. Darkness was complete, not a single shred of light coming from anywhere. Lightning, now farther away, barely flickered, unable to tear the shroud of blackness that surrounded everything. Gusts of wind still came inside through the crevices between the logs, chilling her blood.

Then the sounds changed. The way the wind fell on her skin was different. A strong gust engulfed her entire body as a squeak made her hair stand on end. The door had opened. She could see the faintest trace of light in the gray clouds masking the moon through its opening. Then the squeak was heard again as the wind died, and with it, that trace of light coming from the moonlit clouds.

The door had been closed again.

She was no longer alone.

Panic rushed through her body in myriad needles poking her skin, urging her to run, to escape. Shrieking, she tugged against her restraints as hard as she could, but nothing happened. The chain didn't budge, only clinked and grated in a muted protest of rusted iron.

Frozen in place, she listened intently, hoping to hear something, and she did. Someone was breathing next to her, close. Terrifyingly close. She pulled away until she backed herself against the wall, whimpering. That breath was drawing closer and closer, until she could feel it, heated and smelling of cigarettes, searing her skin. A bolt of lightning lit the room enough for her to see a man's silhouette.

"Please," she whimpered, "please, no." She sobbed, unable to control herself, gasping for air.

His hands brushed against her, slowly, taking their time contouring her body, sending icicles through her blood. When he reached the neck seam of her T-shirt, he grabbed it with both hands and ripped it effortlessly.

She screamed, kicking and writhing against the restraints, but only the wind answered her call.

The wind, and his laughter.

THIRTY-ONE
ALANA

Sometimes Kay felt she didn't belong in Mount Chester anymore. Not professionally, anyway. The town was growing quickly, becoming a distant Silicon Valley suburb, but it still very much worked as a small town.

It seemed the tricks of the trade that had made her successful as a profiler for the FBI didn't necessarily apply here, in a small town. Victimology, for example. She'd examined closely the backgrounds of the two girls, Jenna and Kendra, looking for places where their lives had intersected. Chances were the unsub had seen them somewhere, and that was a sure-fire way to identify where that could've happened.

But in Mount Chester, the two girls' lives overlapped almost entirely. They went to the same school, hung out at the same mall, visited the same coffee shop, and went to the same movie theater, a small one nested inside the Winter Lodge. Why? Because Mount Chester only had one of each of those places.

Her tried and tested methodologies were failing to identify the unsub, and Kendra was still missing. She'd been gone almost twenty-four hours. Kay knew well what that meant.

She'd looked at phone records, and examined Kendra's social media streams, splitting the task with Elliot. This time, nothing of any importance was revealed. Meanwhile, the BOLO was still out on Gavin Sharp, but he seemed less and less likely to have had anything to do with Jenna's death or Kendra's disappearance. Did he belong in jail? Absolutely. However, she'd had to withdraw the existing arrest warrant and replace it with another, charges reduced from aggravated sexual assault and murder to a banal statutory rape. A misdemeanor.

He'd probably never be caught. Overworked and understaffed SFPD would always deprioritize the execution of his new warrant in favor of other, more serious ones. Dangerous criminals were a priority, and Gavin Sharp was no longer listed as one. If he'd got away with it for a year, he'd get away with it for good. The statute of limitations would apply.

Earlier that day, she'd spent two hours buried in data while Elliot had interviewed Tim Carter. He'd returned with little useful information; just validation of what they already knew. Jenna had started sleeping around sometime last April, and then the website appeared. Kay had asked her old FBI analyst to lend a hand and track down the money trail leading to that website. Someone must've paid to have it up online; that didn't come for free for a reason.

Frustrated, she turned her attention on victimology again, while Elliot drove them to Alana Keaney's residence.

What did the two girls have in common, other than everything pertaining to their environment?

Both were brunettes with blonde highlights in their hair. For Jenna, that was the old look she used to have in her college application photo; then that had changed to a more rugged look, an uneven cut without the highlights. Jenna came from a struggling family; her mom was a nurse, her father a veteran on disability. Kendra's family was well-off, her parents were successful winemaking entrepreneurs. Yet, no ransom call had been received, confirming Kay's suspicion it was the same unsub.

The K-9 unit had tracked Kendra to the nearby winery guest parking lot, where she must've climbed into a car and vanished. There was no camera surveillance covering that area. They had no license plates, and no idea who the unsub could be. Deputies had been interviewing potential witnesses all day: winery customers, delivery people, the postal worker who delivered their mail. No one had seen a thing.

Both girls were unattached, not dating anyone at the time the unsub came into their lives. Both of them had abandoned behaviors—Jenna's self-imposed isolation, and Kendra's peaceful routine—to go out with the unsub. That person must've been someone they both knew, someone with enough pull, enough appeal to make them leave their homes without talking to anyone about it.

There was no way of knowing who that could've been, not when she couldn't narrow down the suspect list. Everyone knew everyone and met with everyone everywhere; that was the reality of rural communities. However, kidnapping people and holding them hostage was still difficult. The unsub needed space and privacy. A budding sexual predator would be younger, maybe in his early-to-mid-twenties, not the typical mid-twenties to mid-thirties she used in her serial killer profiling based on the highest probability of suspect age. That probability was founded on thousands of cases studied and analyzed. The career span of a serial killer usually encompassed several years of activity, making age analysis somewhat irrelevant in her present case. As for the age they usually started killing, statistics pinpointed that at about twenty-seven.

But was he a killer already? Or just a rapist, continuing to evolve? If Jenna had fallen into the ravine trying to flee from the unsub in a haze of Rohypnol, he might've not matured yet to the statistically probable age of twenty-seven.

How old, then?

Definitely old enough to have access to a place where he could hold Kendra and sexually assault her undisturbed. Where no one would see anything or hear her screams.

Old enough to know how to lure these young girls out of their homes. Both girls lived a clean, low-risk life, although Jenna, at least for someone who didn't know her personally, might've appeared an easy target living a life of promiscuity. Maybe that was the appeal.

And he'd been wrong about that, it seemed.

Not only he'd been wrong, but she might've fled to her death, leaving him unsatisfied. He'd spent enough time with her on Wildfire Ridge to leave two condom wrappers behind, but it wasn't enough, not for him.

It was all about containment.

After Jenna, he might've realized how many mistakes he'd made in the heat of the moment. The condom wrappers left at the scene with his fingerprints on them. The semen he might've realized he'd smeared on the victim. The fact that she got away —potentially—before he was done with her.

What had appeared as a disorganized, impulsive rapist/killer, might've been just someone who was quickly learning how to be organized, methodical, and effective.

Kay smiled, pulling her phone and checking her messages. She knew exactly how to catch an unsub like that. First step was to make him feel safe and buy Kendra some more time.

There was no message nor callback from the TV reporter she'd been trying to reach. Maybe Barb Foster didn't want to speak with her. She dialed the number on handsfree and sighed, prepared to leave a more detailed message. A deeply unsettling one.

Ride the wave, don't try to stop the wave, Kay told herself as encouragement, thinking of what she was about to say.

Surprisingly, the reporter picked up. "This is Barb Foster."

"Hey, Barb, it's Detective Kay Sharp, FCSO."

A beat. "Oh, I'm so sorry I didn't get back to you." Kay could discern the deception in her voice. She wondered what Barb was hiding. "The day got away from me. So, tell me, what's that exclusive you were threatening me with?"

Kay chuckled. Elliot gave her a long glance, then pulled to a stop in front of the Keaney residence. "We have a suspect in Jenna's murder," she said, lowering her voice just a little, to pretend she was doing this discreetly. Elliot stared at her, bewildered. "I wanted you to hear it from me first, and to be the first to run with it, because, um, of the unsub's name." Her throat dried up, constricted. She was about to open the mother of all cans of worms, but Kendra needed it to stay alive.

"I'm all ears. Shoot."

"The unsub is one Gavin Sharp from San Francisco."

Elliot grinned. He'd probably figured out what she was doing. Killing two birds with one stone.

"Come again?"

Kay held her breath. "Gavin Sharp, fifty-six years old, from San Fran."

"He's not your—I mean, he's—"

"No, it's a different Gavin Sharp, just a coincidence, but still. This man lured Jenna on several dates."

"And I can quote you on this?"

She hesitated. "You can understand my reluctance, Barb, because of the coincidence and all." She held her breath for a moment, then exhaled slowly. "But yeah, okay. Keep it to an absolute minimum, please."

The reporter whistled her appreciation. "This is good stuff! How did they meet? Where did this Sharp character find Jenna?"

"Online. He stalked her for months. Oh, and Barb? I need a favor from you, a big one."

Barb laughed quietly. Kay could feel the sarcasm in the air. "Of course, you do. Tell me."

"The perp might've set up a fake website for Jenna; you might've found it already. We believe it was part of his strategy to throw the scent off himself. I don't think anyone has anything to gain if the part about the website comes out." Jenna's memory deserved a little decency, and so did her mother.

"Oh, come on, Detective," she reacted, putting the phone on speaker on her end. She was probably having her editor listening in. "Freedom of the press and all. We knew about Jenna's website. It's coming out in the ten o'clock news. It's already loaded on the teleprompter."

A wave of anger swelled Kay's chest. She darted one glance at Elliot to see if he was on her side. His eyes glinted with frustration. "Barb, let me make this abundantly clear: as far as law enforcement is concerned, that site is considered child pornography. Mention it on the ten o'clock news, and you're going down for distribution of kiddie porn. Ask your legal department if you don't believe me. I'll be coming for you myself."

Silence fell so heavy Kay thought she might've muted the line on her end. "You drive a hard bargain, Detective," the reporter eventually said. All sarcasm and giggles were gone. "We'll remove it. Can we at least say there's a warrant out for Gavin Sharp?"

"BOLO too, Barb. Run with it. As of this morning, when I called you the first time, he's a wanted fugitive, and the search for Kendra Flannagan still continues. Got to go now, thanks," she added, before ending the call with one tap on the media center screen. She'd barely remembered the old landline phones from her childhood, but she missed the cathartic effect of slamming down the hell out of a receiver.

Elliot laughed. "You got a few tricks in your saddlebag, partner. Whew... ha!" He made the gesture of cracking a whip, a gesture that seemed natural to him; he might've had his days in the rodeo circuit, although he didn't seem the type to seek the limelight. Maybe he used to work on a cattle farm. "You drove that point right across, I'd say, louder than Grandpa's Sunday tie. Got Logan off your back too."

She nodded in thanks for the compliment, hiding her amusement with his choice of words.

A few moments later, she rang the doorbell to the Keaney residence.

Distant voices came through the door, pitches raised in a passionate argument. Then the door was opened by a teenager dressed in a miniskirt that barely covered her butt, a lacy top, and four-inch heels. She was wearing heavy makeup and jingled at every move, both her wrists weighed down by layers of bangles and charm bracelets. Long earrings mixed several strands of fine silver chain with her blonde hair.

"I told you already, better leave *something* to a man's imagination. Do you really want to come across as desperate?" A frustrated, shouting voice came from inside the house, but the girl holding the door impatiently and chewing gum with her mouth open didn't seem to care.

"Yeah," she said, tapping the heel of her shoe impatiently. "What?"

"Alana Keaney? Detective Sharp with the FCSO, this is my partner, Detective Young," Kay said, flashing her badge. "We have a few questions, if you don't mind."

"Who is it?" the voice inside the house asked.

Alana glared at Kay and propped her hands on her hips. "Really? I don't have time for this right now. I have a date. It's almost eight already."

"I understand," Kay replied. "You either answer the questions here or at the precinct. Your call."

Footsteps approached quickly from inside the house, clacking loudly on the hardwood. A woman appeared in the doorframe. She could've been Alana's older sister. Slightly older.

"I'm Alexandria Keaney, Alana's mother," the woman said.

Kay stared at the two women, at a loss for words. They were almost identical, the mother's youthful appearance replicated to perfection by the daughter in hairstyle, skin tone and complexion, eye color, makeup. Even their gestures matched, and they spoke with similar tonality and choice of words.

"What is this about?" Alana asked. "And how long will it take?"

"This is about your friends, Jenna Jerrell and Kendra Flannagan," she replied. "You knew them both, didn't you?"

A shadow clouded Alana's eyes. Kay thought she saw the glimmer of a tear, but the girl breathed that away, shielding her eyes for a while until the sorrow was gone. Probably remembering she had a tough persona she had to uphold, she glared at the detectives again, although her gaze softened a bit when she looked at Elliot.

Like mother, like daughter.

The mother's eyes had landed on her partner's body and had not moved away since, browsing up and down from head to toe, then landing on his face, so intently Elliot was becoming uncomfortable.

"How long, again?" Alana asked, taking out her phone and texting something quickly. Her thin fingers tapped sideways because of her long nails. "Twenty minutes or so?"

"As long as it takes," Kay replied quickly, her voice stern, impervious to the display of hostility.

"There's an Alexandria in Tennessee," Elliot said calmly, his eyes on Mrs. Keaney. "Nothing much but farmland and cows, but beautiful. Is that where you're from?"

Kay had to bite her lip to keep a straight face. *Way to go, partner.*

Livid, Alexandria crossed her arms at her chest and stopped

undressing him with her eyes. "No, that's not where I'm from. I'm named after the one in Egypt. Doubt you'd know about that one."

He grinned. "The one with the library and the lighthouse? No, I don't know anything about that one."

Humiliated, Alexandria lowered her gaze and decided to shut up.

Alana's phone chimed. Reading her screen upside down, Kay could see she'd texted Nick about being late. That was a name she'd grown familiar with during the investigation, Alana's boyfriend by everyone's account. He'd replied simply with a thumbs-up emoji.

"When's the last time you spoke to or interacted with Kendra Flannagan?" Kay asked.

Reluctant, as if she'd been asked to lift fifty-pound boulders, Alana sighed and looked through her messages. "Last night. She said she was going out on a date. She was all excited about it. Here," she said, holding the screen in front of Kay's face, a little too close for comfort. "See for yourself."

Kay didn't flinch. "Did she say with whom?"

"No. She doesn't have a boyfriend." She scoffed, then looked sideways as if trying to remember. "Not one that I know of. We aren't all that close. She's new to our group. And a junior." She said the word as if it were an insult.

"You don't like juniors?"

Alana shrugged, and all her jewelry jingled in protest. "All they want from us is our old homework." Her lip curled in disgust. "As if I'd keep any of that shit."

"Language, Alana," her mother quickly intervened.

"Was Kendra close to Jenna?" Kay asked, still looking for things the two girls might've had in common other than the obvious.

"No," Alana said with a sad chuckle. "Jenna... had become, um, easy, if you know what I mean." Her eyes darted at Kay's face, then away from it. "Kendra's a nice girl. I'm willing to bet she's still a virgin."

"Alana," her mother reacted. Her voice was loaded with frustration and embarrassment.

Her daughter turned to face her ostentatiously. "Yes, Mom. What?"

"She hates it when I call her name without saying anything else," the mother explained, sounding apologetic yet contrived. "We're both heartbroken about Jenna, you know. My daughter isn't that good at sharing her real feelings and prefers to act up." A shrug, followed by an eye roll that was intended to draw Kay's sympathy. "She's a teenager," she added, mouthing the words, as if Alana wasn't standing right next to her.

"Do you know about Jenna's website?" Kay asked, staring at Alana intently. The girl's pupils dilated when she heard the question.

"What website?" Alexandria asked.

Alana looked at her mother then at Kay as if weighing her options.

"Don't even think of lying," Elliot said. "My partner charged someone with obstruction of justice for far less than this."

Alana rolled her eyes and blew air into a chewing gum balloon until it popped.

"What website, missy?" Alexandria asked, getting in Alana's face.

Alana pushed her mother away with a hand gesture and a quick, fiery glare. "Jenna's. Leave me alone," she said, sliding past her mother and leaning against the open door. "She had this call girl website put up, if you have to know. There. Now I won't hear the end of it as if it were mine or something."

Alexandria's hand covered her agape mouth as she gasped. "Goodness... what is wrong with kids today? It's not enough I'm insane with worry every time she's late or she doesn't call, but...

adult websites too?" Shaking her head, she wrapped her arms around herself, staring at the floor where the tip of her shoe tapped nervously against the hardwood.

Yet Kay didn't feel her display of concern and surprise was entirely genuine. She couldn't put her finger on it. It wasn't something the woman had said or done; more like a gut feeling telling Kay she didn't have all the information. Their emotions were all wrong.

"Anything else you two would like to share regarding Jenna or Kendra?"

"Oh, that poor girl, she's still missing, isn't she?" Alexandria said, earning herself a quick, sideways glance from Alana. "You think the same man has her?"

Kay didn't reply. Turning to Alana, she asked, "Anything at all that could help us find Kendra?"

Alana seemed to hesitate for a while, then said, lowering her voice, "Um, not sure if this matters, but Jenna had started seeing an older guy."

"How much older?" Kay asked, a little surprised Alexandria had no reaction. She must've known about that son of a bitch and had done nothing about it.

"Not sure. Just... older. Jenna used to call him DeGraw, but that was a nickname... she's crazy about Gavin DeGraw and his music. She keeps—kept—playing him on loop. I wonder if this older guy killed her."

"Since when did Jenna know about the website?" Kay asked, changing direction quickly, a strategy meant to throw people off their lies.

Alana didn't flinch. "Poor Jenna... she had no idea until Tim broke up with her because of it. She was stunned."

"Why do you think she didn't say anything to anyone, if the website wasn't hers? To Tim, especially?"

Alana's eyes shifted around as if to figure out what lie to tell. "She said if Tim believed that website could've been hers, then he deserved to go." She thrust her chin forward. "I was proud of her that day."

"Did she love Tim?"

Alana nodded, her earrings bouncing in sync with her hair. "She did. She told me many times. Tim is a nice guy."

"How about this older guy? Did Jenna love him?"

Alana frowned. "More like she was obsessed with him." She threw her mother a quick glance, then added, a little louder than a whisper, "I don't think Tim and Jenna had sex. It was the older guy who did it with her."

"Alana!" her mother called out in an outraged voice. "You have to pardon her manners, Detectives," Alexandria said, looking at Kay then, more lingering, at Elliot. "It's not like I don't try to teach her to behave better. She doesn't know what she's talking about."

Kay watched the two, wondering what they were hiding. Had Alana been at odds with Jenna in some way? No one she'd spoken with seemed to think that, and she wasn't getting that vibe.

"One more thing," Kay said, "what happened to Jenna on that day trip in April?"

A fleeting microexpression of panic washed over Alana's face. "Um, she overheard the guys calling her a whore. Renaldo was bragging about doing it with her. Everyone was laughing, some guys were drawing straws as to who was going to, um, do her next."

"*Do her next?*" Alexandria said, visibly appalled. "How can you talk about your best friend like that?"

"I'm not talking about her, Mom. I'm telling the cops about those assholes in their own words," Alana replied, her voice subdued, saddened.

The two women had stopped talking. Alana watched the time with increasing anxiety; the twenty minutes she'd told her boyfriend about had since passed.

Kay handed them each her card and said, "If either of you remembers anything at all, please call me, day or night. My cell is on the back."

"Is that it? We're done?" Alana asked, visibly relieved.

"Yes, unless you're hiding something, in which case you and I will *never* be done," Kay said, lowering her voice just enough to make it sound threatening. "Don't let me slap an obstruction charge on you."

Instead of intimidating her, Kay's words had the opposite effect on Alana. Her eyes turned to steel. "Go right ahead. I don't know anything more than I've already said. You'd make a fool of yourself."

Alexandria gasped. Leaving the mother and daughter to sort things out between themselves, Kay climbed into the SUV, reflecting on how the two looked almost identical. Mrs. Keaney must've had Alana at a very young age.

Elliot was about to peel off when a red Beemer pulled up in the driveway, driven fast by a young man with dark hair and stunning good looks. Alana squealed and climbed into the Beemer, then spent a long moment in the young man's embrace. Alexandria watched them from the doorway, pale and immobile with her arms crossed at her chest and an indecipherable expression on her face. Her hair, slightly longer than Alana's, blew in the wind, occasionally whipping across her face while she watched her daughter melting in her boyfriend's arms.

Mother and daughter looked like sisters.

THIRTY-TWO

LATE

After Alana and the cops were finally gone, her knees had felt so weak, she had to lay down on the sofa for a while. Eyes wide open, she stared at the ceiling, listening to the strong thump of her panicked heart against her ribs.

Why were the cops circling her daughter like vultures? And what was she thinking, allowing her to be interviewed without an attorney present? She must've been out of her mind... cops were sneaky like that. They'd said something about that missing girl, Kendra, and she'd instantly felt like a harpy for wasting even one minute of that girl's life on her own daughter's legal rights.

She was insane.

Since Alana had left, it felt as if she'd held her breath the entire time, her chest tired of seizing air inside her lungs. Slowly, she exhaled, feeling part of her angst drain away with the air leaving her weary body.

Some of her anxiety still clung to her, becoming a part of her, painful and inextricable. Should she call a lawyer? It was Friday night, almost ten at night. She'd blinked, and an entire hour had coursed by since Alana had left with Nick.

Squeezing her eyelids shut, she willed her mind clear of any obsessive thoughts about her daughter and her boyfriend. Alana had a right to live her life to the fullest, to fall in love, and she could've done far worse than Nick.

And yet, for hours, while darkness had crept into the living room where she lay still on the sofa staring into emptiness, she could think of nothing else.

Her daughter's curfew was midnight, and at two in the morning, still alone and restless, Alexandria stood on shaky legs, looking for a bottle of wine to uncork for comfort. She'd tried to call her, but Alana's phone went straight to voicemail.

Maybe Alana had fallen asleep in Nick's arms and that's why she was late, or she was up for seconds. Perhaps she was losing her mind, one minute of obsession at a time, while her daughter did little else but lived her life like any other teenager out there.

Once Alexandria had started looking at the green digits on the clock's display, minutes started to drag, slower and slower as her anxiety rose.

Where was she?

Was she okay? Had something happened to her? Was she upset after being interrogated by cops? Was she worried? She'd said nothing to her, just rushed into the arms of that—

She just wished she'd be back home already, so she could put the wine glass down and get some rest. Tomorrow, she'd start figuring things out. Speak to an attorney about Alana. Find out what she had to do to protect her daughter. Jails were littered with innocent people who either didn't have the brains to shut up or didn't have the money for a good legal defense. Cops couldn't care less if they ruined innocent lives. She wasn't going to let Alana fall prey to whatever the hell had been going on in that school of hers. Adult websites? And what else, for crying out loud?

She'd dozed off when a squeak in the floorboards startled

her awake. Alana was taking off her shoes by the door, attempting to sneak in without waking her. The sound of a revved engine was fading away.

"That was some party, wasn't it? Did you sleep with him?" she asked, forgetting everything else she'd planned to say to her daughter. The living room light switched on, blinding her. She raised her hand to her eyes, shielding them.

"And what if I did?" Alana asked, standing in front of her with her hands on her hips, ready to fight.

She didn't want to argue. She wanted to have some peace again, the two of them close like girlfriends, like sisters. The way they used to be.

She stood, a little unsure of herself, and wobbled over to the window to pull the curtains closed, while Alana watched with a cold, merciless stare.

"Not again, Mom," she whispered, staring at the half-empty bottle of wine. "You've been drinking. You're turning into a regular wino."

Alexandria turned to Alana, her cheeks burning with humiliation. "I've been worried about you!" she said, raising her voice and slurring her words a little bit. "You were supposed to be here before midnight. It's almost five."

Mother and daughter looked at each other for a beat, breathing fast, ready to jump at each other's throats. Slowly, their gazes softened. Alexandria opened her arms, and her daughter rushed into them, hiding her face at her mother's chest the way she used to when she was younger.

"I'm sorry, Mom."

"Oh, baby," Alexandria whispered, caressing her daughter's hair. "Those cops... I—I was scared. But don't worry, we'll start preparing right now."

Her daughter pulled away enough to look at her with a puzzled expression. "Preparing for what? I didn't do anything wrong. You're overthinking this, Mom. They just wanted to know if I knew anything useful about Jenna, and I told them what I knew."

Alexandria stared at her daughter, scrutinizing her, wondering if she was telling her the truth. All kids told lies, especially to their parents. Why should Alana be any different, as much as she liked to believe it could be true?

"Go to bed, Alana," she said calmly, pulling away. "It's very late, and we need rest."

THIRTY-THREE
MIRANDA

Kay had been up most of the night, glad Jacob was out, probably spending the night with his girlfriend. She couldn't sleep; after a couple of hours of failed attempts at some shut-eye her body badly needed, she went back into the kitchen and started the coffee maker.

It wasn't even three in the morning, but she couldn't sleep when Kendra was out there fighting for her life, going through hell.

The kitchen smelled clean, of putty and primer, and Kay had to watch her step all the time. The floor was covered with old newspapers, littered with pieces of dried putty, and snowed with a fine white dust from sanding. She didn't mind the mess; she gave the walls a quick look and decided that this morning she was going to skip the renovation day starter.

Her mind was on Kendra. Was she still alive? Where was she? How much time did she have left?

Kay fired up her laptop, while her weary mind spun and ground the same bits of information she'd been obsessing over the entire day yesterday.

What did she know about this unsub?

What if he'd taken Jenna up on Wildfire Ridge, thinking she was easy, the way that website was describing her? Then why give her a roofie? Because she wasn't willing to have sex with him that easily? Not all the pieces of that puzzle fit.

Kay pulled a chair out and sat in front of her computer, leaning her chin into her clasped hands. Closing her eyes, she tried to visualize the meeting between the two. Jenna had been a depressed girl who'd been cyberbullied recently and had withdrawn from the world, yet she'd decided to go out with this man. The unsub, a younger, budding predator, someone who had probably chosen Jenna because of her website, her reputation. But why? If he was slick enough to get Jenna to leave her home and meet him, he was probably someone who could easily get dates.

Kay sifted through behavioral models in her mind, quickly discarding everything that didn't fit. Why Jenna? Why the girl whose reputation was in shreds?

Because he wanted someone who couldn't cry rape. Someone compromised, someone no cop would believe. He was itching to get rough, but didn't know how to get started. He was a power-assertive predator; to him, it was all about overpowering his victims.

Budding sexual predators weren't exactly models of clear and articulate thinking. They had urges they sometimes failed to comprehend but followed nevertheless, unable to stop themselves, even if they understood those urges could be the end of them.

What if he'd been trying to get to Jenna for a while? Her phone records were still pending; only Kendra's had been processed already, and that was because her parents had cooperated with the police, handing them the printouts themselves and authorizing the carrier to download all the data and share it with the detectives.

Kay checked to see if there was any news as to Jenna's

phone records, but nothing had been filed yet. She typed a quick note to Deputy Farrell, asking her to expedite the records and get Mrs. Jerrell involved in obtaining them as soon as possible.

The unsub must've reached Jenna somehow, and that wasn't by singing a serenade under her windows. The answer had to be in her phone. The actual device, crushed in the fall, was still with the ME. Last time she'd checked, they hadn't been able to get the device to start.

Satisfied, she pushed the laptop aside and went back to visualizing the meeting between the unsub and Jenna. The girl must've been less than willing to have sex, much less than the unsub had anticipated. But he'd come to meet her already aroused, his urges screaming for release. So, he drugged her and took her up the mountain, a long hike for someone who's drowsy from the Rohypnol. Maybe he drugged her up on the ridge, because she fought back, but had climbed the ridge voluntarily?

Maybe he wasn't very strong, physically, to subdue Jenna, and needed the roofie to make her compliant.

Or maybe he'd discovered something while she fought him as hard as she could. He discovered who he really was. A sociopath, aroused by Jenna's resistance and her screams. Someone who found that overpowering her was the one sensation he'd been looking for his entire life. And he couldn't get enough. But she couldn't fight too much or too hard; she was already drugged.

That's why he took Kendra.

How?

She browsed Kendra's phone records quickly, looking for a message or a phone call that might've suggested who he was.

Prior to Kendra leaving the winery, there hadn't been any text message on her phone reading like an invitation or a date.

But there was a call from a phone number with a San Francisco area code.

Kay typed another message to Deputy Farrell, asking her to identify who that caller was. She almost sent it, but something held her back. She wondered if she wasn't missing something in the messages and phone calls going back and forth between those kids, like a web of secrets and lies bouncing around in their group. How did Jenna's reputation get tarnished? Who had initiated the cyberbullying?

She typed another short paragraph to the deputy, asking her to get phone records for all the players in the twisted game that had cost Jenna her life, maybe Kendra's too. "Expedite it, please," she wrote, cringing at the thought of how long it was going to take.

She needed a faster way to find the unsub, if she was going to find Kendra alive.

It was almost five in the morning, too early to do anything, but she couldn't sit still and waste two more hours of Kendra's life. She got dressed quickly in jeans and a white cotton shirt, and grabbed her keys on the way out.

This morning, she was reversing the roles. She would pick Elliot up and start tracing the path of the destructive smear campaign that had been cast over Jenna's existence.

She'd never visited Elliot, but she knew where he lived. He'd showed her the place in passing; it was an older farmhouse on about two acres of grassy land. When she arrived, the house was veiled in darkness, lit only by the pale light coming from the moon through thick live oak foliage.

She walked around the back, at first to see if one of the rooms were lit, but it was still very early. At the rear of the house, the strong moonlight, unobstructed by trees, landed on the windows and an open sliding glass door, dimly lit from the inside.

Feeling like a stalker yet curious nevertheless, she drew

close, pussyfooting through the grasses until she reached the open sliding door.

Elliot was asleep on a large bed, a sheet covering only parts of his naked body. The light from a night table lamp on the other side of the bed cast pale shades of yellow on his taut muscles and tousled hair. She looked at him sleeping, her eyes lingering on his body, knowing just how wrong it was what she was doing and yet unable to stop. Things could be different for Elliot and her, so much different, if she could take the chance. If he would say something for once.

She turned away from the unsettling view, leaning against the glass and looking at the waning moon. Toward the east, the sky was starting to change color. A sigh left her lungs... she was being ridiculous; if she'd been in his place, she would've been appalled by this behavior. There was no excuse.

She knocked against the glass, loudly, refusing to look inside again until the light changed.

"You decent in there?" Kay asked. "May I come in?"

Elliot sat on the bed, gathering the sheet around his body with a rushed gesture, looking confused. "What happened?" He locked eyes with her, turning flush. She hid a smile. "I overslept? I'm sorry. What time is it?"

"You didn't oversleep," Kay said, beginning to regret her impulse to visit. "I'm early."

"Oh," he said, wrapping the sheet tightly around his waist before leaving the bed. Still perplexed by her unexpected visit, he seemed uncertain of what to do next. "Take a seat," he said, gesturing toward the bed. "I need to get dressed. Did anything happen?"

She remained standing. "No. I just... couldn't sleep, that's all, and I thought it would be okay if I picked you up today instead."

"Sure, that's fine," he said, turning around and looking for something. "I was up late. Miranda kept me up half the night.

She was sick... her belly ached." He found his slippers under the bed and put them on, then rushed into the bathroom.

Her heart sank. Miranda? Dashed, she started noticing things. The bed, a king-size, looked as if it had been slept in on both sides. The other side lamp had been on before she'd arrived. There was a woman in Elliot's life, and Kay stood there like an idiot in another woman's bedroom. Her blood froze at the thought Miranda could walk in at any moment and catch her standing by Elliot's bed.

"I'm going to go," she said, her voice trembling slightly. "Pick me up when you're ready, okay?" She stepped outside in the cool air of the early dawn and breathed. *Stupid. What did you expect? That he'd wait for you forever, to make up your damn mind?*

He caught up with her, barefoot in the dew-covered grass, wearing a pair of jeans with the belt still undone and fussing with a golf shirt. "Where are you going? You're here already, and I'll be ready in less than no time," He slid the golf shirt over his head and buckled up his belt. "Let me introduce you to Miranda."

Breath caught in her throat. *Oh, hell, no*, she thought. "Maybe some other time, all right?" She was dying to get out of there. "We need to go to work. I know what we've been missing. We've been looking at this entire thing wrong."

THIRTY-FOUR
ESCAPE

A jay shrieked loudly somewhere near the cabin, startling Kendra awake. She was lying naked on the cold, musty floor, the smell of dirt and rotting leaves pungent and sticky, filling her nostrils with the threat of death.

Sunrise was drawing near, but there wasn't enough light yet to dissipate the shadows in the small cabin. Still, she knew she wasn't alone. As memories of what had happened filled her awakened mind, she started crying silently, covering her mouth with her hand, desperate to keep perfectly quiet. Her body ached, bruised and bloodied and too weak to put up too much of a fight.

Shivering, she sat up and stared into the darkness, slowly starting to perceive her surroundings. A couple of feet away, a man slept on the floor, his breathing heavy, sometimes interrupted by bouts of snoring. His breath touched her leg at times, and she withdrew, moving slowly, quietly, putting as much distance between them as possible. Folding her knees at her chest and wrapping her arms around them she waited, holding her breath whenever his snores stopped abruptly, or another bird's morning cry risked awakening him.

As soon as blackness turned into dim shades of gray, she stood, unsure on her legs, holding on to the walls for balance. She had to get away, now, while the man was still asleep. That was her only chance; there wasn't going to be another. She couldn't survive another night like the one that was just ending.

She was backed into a corner, the man sleeping on the floor barring her path toward the door. She waited another minute or two for more light to pierce the darkness, anticipating her moves one at a time, knowing she'd have to be fast.

Holding her breath, she stood and stepped close to his torso, then over it, terrified that the rotting floor might squeak. It didn't, and he slept on, undisturbed. Three more steps and she reached the door, held closed with a chain on a nail.

Staring at the rusted hinges and recalling the grating creak they put out when the door opened, she built the courage and released the chain. The door opened a couple of inches, groaning, and a gust of wind brought fresh, damp chillness inside. The man shifted and moaned, but continued his sleep. Quickly, she tiptoed outside and closed the door behind her, locking it with a gate latch that barely hung from two rusty screws.

Then she started running downhill, her bare feet aching and bleeding against sharp rocks and fallen tree branches. She had no idea where she was, but knew she had to get off the mountain as quickly as possible.

Out of breath, she turned her head for a moment just as she was entering the woods, to catch a glimpse of the cabin. The sight froze the blood in her veins. The door swung open, battered by the wind against the frame with rhythmic thuds. He had to be awake by now. No one could sleep through that.

Whimpering, she rushed downhill, hiding at times behind a thicket or large tree trunks to peek behind her, then darting away, rushing downhill as fast as she could. She'd just stopped behind a large fir when she heard a twig snap somewhere close, and she froze in place, holding her breath. Birds were singing in the distance, but the near ones had fallen silent, fearing the approach of a predator. Just like her.

Pressing her hand against her chest as if to steady her thumping heart, she listened but couldn't hear anything, any other sound beyond the panicked whooshing in her ears. She was ready to bolt again when he reached her.

Without warning, he grabbed a fistful of her hair and started pulling, dragging her with him uphill. Shrieking and crying, she scratched at his hand, but he didn't seem to care. He just looked at her with a strange smile.

"Please, let me go," she cried, when she realized they were almost back at the cabin. "My parents have money, they'll pay you whatever you want, I swear."

"Shut the hell up," he muttered, grabbing her arm and shoving her ahead. His gait was strong and steady, not stopping nor slowing down.

"No cops, I promise you," she continued, realizing she wasn't reaching him. "A million dollars, I know my parents have it. You can take that and go wherever you want, be free of—"

He squeezed and twisted her arm until she screamed, his hand merciless and cold when it touched her flesh. Glaring, he drew close to her face until she felt his breath on her skin.

"Shut the fuck up already!"

He shoved her inside the cabin, then slammed the door shut and latched it with the chain. She faltered backward until she reached the wall and stood, frozen, shivering, wrapping her arms around her trembling body and losing her mind with fear.

"No, no," she whimpered, seeing him approach. She held her hands out in front of her as if to stop him. He grinned and grabbed her wrists tightly, then bound them with a piece of rope he recovered from the floor. Then he hung the knot against the hook above her head, pinning her in place.

She was going to die there, like Jenna. There was no escape.

A sob swelled her chest, releasing a stream of tears that

smarted where her face and lips were swollen and bruised by his blows. There was no end to the nightmare. No one was going to find her there, in the middle of the woods. Tugging against the hook with the last ounce of strength she had, she raised her tear-blurred gaze to him and saw him standing inches away, staring at her, smiling.

The look in his eyes froze her blood. Breathless, she watched him inch closer, looking at her body with hateful eyes. He touched her swollen lip and she whimpered, pulling away as far as the restraints allowed. Chuckling, he tasted her blood off his finger, a sparkle darkening his eyes as he did.

"Anything else you want to say now?" he whispered. His voice, loaded with the unspoken threat of pain to come, trailed off into silence.

Then she screamed, the jays outside falling silent.

THIRTY-FIVE

CAPERS

Out of all the things Elliot had thought possible on a Saturday morning before sunrise, finding Kay Sharp standing by his bed wasn't one of them. He didn't dare to imagine what might've fueled her intention to show up on his doorstep like that, but he minded it less than an old dog would a juicy cow bone.

"What do you mean, we've been looking at this wrong?" he asked, sprinting to catch up with her on the way to her SUV, after falling behind to slip on a pair of boots. He put his hat on right before climbing into the passenger seat, proud to uphold the rather uncomfortable and uniquely Texan tradition of wearing wide-brimmed Stetsons while inside vehicles.

Tense and tight-lipped, Kay shifted into gear and peeled off as if a raging bull were chasing them, thirsty for blood. "Someone started a fire that burned through Jenna's life. I believe the primordial motive lies with that original perp."

"What, a school bully? That's who you think raped and killed Jenna?"

"This was no ordinary cyberbullying," she replied, seeming a little more relaxed with every mile she drove. Her breakneck speed had slowed to slightly above legal limits. "We're talking about someone who had the motive and knowledge to work a smear campaign that started slowly, inconspicuously, and ended with that website, the final blow."

"Where are we going?" Elliot asked, wishing he'd had time for a bite to eat before leaving.

The SUV sped by Katse, but he didn't ask her to stop for the usual order of coffee and croissants to go. The place was still closed. It wasn't six yet.

"Office. I asked Farrell to pull all the phone records for this bunch. Somewhere, in the timing of innuendo and shreds of gossip, we'll find the perpetrator of the smear campaign."

"This could take weeks! Kendra—"

"Doesn't have much time, I know," she cut him off, her voice brimming with frustration.

"When did you request the phone records?"

She muttered an oath. "Today, at three in the morning, by email."

"Hate to break the news to you, but you're not in Kansas anymore."

"Huh?"

"We're not the FBI. We're a small county sheriff's office. Those records will take a week. More, if we need subpoenas that aren't filed yet."

She pulled over and stopped on the side of the road slamming her foot down on the brake pedal, tires throwing pebbles and dust in the air. "We ain't got a week!"

"Kay," he said her name calmly, searching her eyes, "look at me."

Keeping her hands on the wheel, white-knuckled as they'd been since they left his house, she turned her head toward him, staring down, hiding angry tears. "She doesn't have much time, Elliot. This kind of unsub, he's... exploring. Trying new things, to find out who he is. Any of those new things could kill Kendra. All of them are making her life a living hell she'll never forget for the rest of her life. And we're stuck here, on the side of the road, with nowhere to go?" She turned her tearful eyes away and let go of the steering wheel to clasp her hands together in her lap.

"Kay, you know this. You know it better than anyone else. Use what you have and let's find this son of a bitch. Work this like you did for all the scum you caught before." He paused, but she didn't reply. "I haven't heard of a single scumbag who got on your radar and walked away a free man."

She breathed deeply a couple of times. "It all goes back to Jenna, to how the unsub chose her, and I believe it was because of the website. We still don't know who paid for that. We used K-9 to track Jenna up the mountain, we found the primary murder scene, and still, we don't know much. The only thing we didn't consider is why Wildfire Ridge out of all places."

He grinned, seeing how she'd started to work her magic. Soon she'd have that perp by the throat, reeling him in like a twenty-pound bass on a Sunday morning fishing competition, nice and slow.

"He must be comfortable on that mountain. Perps like him usually go where they're feeling safe, be it a garage or a basement, a hunting lodge—" She stopped talking, her eyes fixed on the still dark Mount Chester slopes, the rising sun hiding behind its peak. "She's on that mountain somewhere," she said excitedly, turning to look at him. "Kendra must be up there. Let's get K-9 units—"

"It's a big mountain, Kay," he replied. "It would take weeks to search it, even with dogs."

Her hands found the steering wheel again and squeezed. "You're right. We know he's younger, twenty-something, maybe twenty-five. He's fit; he chose to climb a long hike. Yet he roofied Jenna... why?" She shook her head. "It makes no sense. He was someone she knew... maybe another online predator she met, like she did Gavin Sharp?"

"We found Gavin based on her text messages," Elliot replied. "There was no evidence of another man in any of her messages, emails, or social media. None in her phone records either. She barely talked with anyone."

"I've been digging into Gavin Sharp's background," she said, changing the subject abruptly like only women did. "I found the cop who locked him up last time. His shift isn't starting until eight. There are things detectives don't bother to put in reports, the little things only they know about their collars. He might still remember something useful."

Elliot frowned, resisting the urge to lift his hat and scratch the roots of his hair. "Didn't DNA clear that creep?"

She closed her fists and slammed them against the wheel. Gently, he reached out and touched her hand. "Kay, you'll find—"

She pulled away as if his touch burned her skin. "You should save this for Miranda," she snapped. Then she started the engine and drove off, most likely to hide a flurry of emotions he could read on her face.

Kay Sharp was jealous.

Of Miranda.

Well, throw your hat over the windmill, cowboy. He looked away to hide a smile. Then that smile withered when he remembered Laurie Ann Sealy and the reason he'd left Texas. His commitment to never get involved with a coworker again.

"We'll find him," he said, keeping his hands on his knees. "You and I will nail this bastard and we'll get Kendra."

She breathed out forcefully. "How do we do that, huh? We can't map Jenna's last twenty-four hours. Can't figure out how these girls were lured out of their homes. We don't know where they went—"

Kay's phone chimed. She had a new text message. Without looking at it, she handed Elliot the phone, careful not to touch his hand in passing.

"It's from Doc Whitmore. 'Call me when you wake up,' he says. He knows the hours you keep, huh?" He made the call on the vehicle's media center, and it was picked up almost instantly by the medical examiner.

"Good morning, Kay," he said.

"We're both here," Kay replied. "Good morning, Doc. You spent the night working again?"

"I had the second DNA profile running. I just dozed off on the sofa. I couldn't go home, you see, with that poor girl still out there."

"Tell me what you got," Kay demanded, visibly impatient like she always was.

"Ah, yes. Remember we found two DNA samples on Jenna's body. Considering we found the same fingerprints on the condom wrappers, we assumed there was only one rapist, but the second semen sample belongs to a different donor."

"What?" Kay asked. "There are two unsubs?"

"Precisely. The second sample isn't a match to Gavin Sharp either. There's no match for the first one in CODIS, and the second is still running."

"All right," she replied, sounding defeated. "That's something, I suppose. Maybe we'll get lucky with the second perp."

"I got more," he announced, a hint of pride coloring his voice. "I finished analyzing Jenna's stomach contents. About four hours before her death, she had a tuna sandwich with mayo and capers."

She grinned, slowing the SUV slightly before making a screeching-wheel U-turn on the deserted highway. "You just made my day. There's only one place in town that serves that. And it opens in about twenty minutes."

"I know." He could hear the smile in Dr. Whitmore's voice.

"Thanks, Doc. Get some rest," Kay said.

The doctor laughed. "I'll follow the doctor's orders." Then he ended the call, leaving a brief silence to fill the space.

"Who makes them? Are you thinking Katse?" Elliot asked.

"No," Kay replied, sounding very sure of herself over something he didn't quite know what it was. She shot him a quick look and smiled for a brief moment, then the smile waned, and her jaws clenched as if she'd remembered something bothersome. "Capers are small, pickled fruits of a Mediterranean bush."

How did she know what he was thinking before he had a chance to think it? If she did that so damn well, how could she not know how he felt about her?

The road curved around a hilltop and soon Mount Chester came into view with its sharp peaks and dark evergreens. Kay pointed at the mountain with an accusatory finger. "Katse doesn't add capers to their sandwiches, but those guys do, up at the Winter Lodge."

THIRTY-SIX
LEADS

Alpine Subs opened at six thirty, probably catering more to the hotel employees than tourists at that early morning hour. It was built as an annex to the Winter Lodge restaurant, with a small storefront facing the hotel parking lot, and direct access from inside the lobby.

A single, beat-up black Hyundai was parked in front of it, probably belonging to the sandwich shop staff. The light was on inside. Even if the "OPEN" sign was still off, Kay didn't want to wait. She climbed out of the SUV and walked briskly to the door, a step behind Elliot.

The air was crisp and cold, slightly warmer where the rising sun's rays hit the valley. Her breath turned briefly into mist before vanishing. Dawn's early colors were fading away, leaving the rocky peaks a silver gray serrate against the azure. In the distance, a hawk cried, circling above ground near the chairlift's lower terminal. A mouse must've been out looking for food in the frost-touched grass, grabbing the hawk's attention just as Jenna and Kendra had grabbed the unsub's.

The psychology behind TV and print media advertising applied to criminal investigations equally well. One has to *see* something to want it. They have to know it exists, to put their eyes on an appealing visual, and, as desire blooms, to decide if they're going to pursue what they want.

The unsub must've seen Jenna somewhere, maybe in person before the website told him she might be a good choice for exploring his dark urges with. That's what Kay had believed until the earlier call with the medical examiner, and part of that still held true.

A second hawk joined the first in circling aboveground, stalking its prey. They took turns crying, flying lower and lower, getting ready to strike. Kay wondered if the mouse saw them coming, if it realized the danger they posed from a distance.

Two instead of one changed everything. The dynamic of the kill, of the sexual assault itself, of the initial choice of Jenna as a target. But two instead of one matched what she'd found at the crime scene. Two recent male shoeprints. Two condom wrappers. One unidentified partial print on one of the wrappers that wasn't found on the other.

Elliot knocked on the sandwich place door and waited, peeking through the glass.

"It's not open yet," a young man shouted from inside. "Come back in ten!"

Elliot opened his wallet and stuck his badge against the glass. The seven-point star clinked loudly.

"All right," the young man said, dropping a case of shredded lettuce on the counter with a frustrated expression on his face. He walked quickly to the door, wiping his hands on his apron, then unlocked the door. "What can I do for you?" He wore a black T-shirt with a colorful print, a familiar rock star's face, but someone Kay couldn't name. Or maybe an actor's. A black, knitted cap embroidered with the *Star Wars* script in yellow covered his forehead almost entirely. Military dog tags on a chain jingled when he moved. "Come on in."

Kay showed him Jenna's photo on her phone. "This girl was

here on Tuesday afternoon and had a tuna sandwich with capers. Do you remember her?"

The man hesitated, tilting his head to get a better view. "I—um, it gets busy here in the afternoon. I'm not sure."

Kay realized she was showing him the old photo, the one taken for Jenna's college applications, where she was a smiling, happy girl with blonde highlights in her hair, before her entire life had fallen apart. She swiped and displayed the more recent one. "How about this one?"

"Yes, I remember her now, she sat over there, by the window," he pointed. "Over there, with two guys." He frowned, lining his forehead with several parallel lines under the brim of his *Star Wars* hat. "Is this the girl they found by Wildfire Ridge the other day?"

"Yes, that's her." Kay looked at the ceiling but didn't see what she was looking for. "There's no video surveillance here?"

"No, ma'am. They said they're bringing cameras next year. But tourists don't really like it, especially out there, on the patio." He grinned, showing two rows of perfectly white teeth. "Especially after closing time, if you know what I mean."

Kay glanced quickly toward the restaurant patio, deserted at that hour. The lounge chairs lined up with a view of Mount Chester's peak were a local attraction, especially on warmer evenings lit by the moon. Restaurant patrons stayed well after closing, sometimes wrapped in sleeping bags or blankets taken from their hotel rooms, and enjoyed the fresh air and stunning view. Or, as Kay remembered, occasionally listened to a young tourist playing his guitar and crooning in the moonlight. She wondered if the three students who'd found Jenna's body might've seen her earlier, when they were having dinner on the restaurant patio. Maybe they'd taken a photo of the landscape, catching something in the foreground; people, faces, car tags.

"What's your name? I'm Detective Kay Sharp, this is my partner, Elliot Young." She extended her hand.

The young man hesitated before squeezing it, wiping his hand quickly against the starched apron. "Dwayne," he replied, all serious, a little tense. "Dwayne Goodrow."

Elliot shook his hand, looking at the tattoo on the man's arm. "Where did you serve?"

The grin returned. "Marines."

"Rangers," Elliot replied, taking two fingers to the brim of his hat.

"Cool," Dwayne replied, holding his fist in the air. Elliot bumped it.

It was amazing to see just how easily males bonded over a shared interest.

"Dwayne, what can you remember about the two men who were here with the girl in the photo?" Kay asked.

"Um, not much." His hands found the apron pockets and dove in. "It gets busy, and this week, it's just me, pulling doubles. Carrie is sick. She's my boss, the store manager. She's been out since Sunday." His gaze shifted to Elliot. "I have to ask the patrons for a break to take a leak, if you know what I mean." Elliot smiled with understanding. "Those guys, they were white. Dark-haired. Slender but muscular, like youths who are into sports."

"How old?" Kay asked.

"Um, I'd say about the same age as the girl, maybe a year or two older; not more."

"Did you happen to see what car they drove?" Elliot looked behind him toward the parking lot.

Dwayne shrugged. "I can't see much past the counter, especially if I have people waiting in line."

"Tell me more," Kay asked. "We'll send a sketch artist to sit with you, but I need whatever you can give me right now."

He scratched his forearm, stopping short of the bulldog tattooed there and stared at the ceiling briefly. "Um, I'm not really sure. Both were clean-shaven, wearing clean clothes, jeans and shirts, but new. Kind of looked like each other; maybe they were brothers."

"How tall?"

He scoffed quietly. "They were sitting down, but I noticed their legs were kind of long for that small table. Say, about six-two one of them, an even six feet the other?" He looked down for a moment, then at Kay with a bit of worry in his eyes. "Don't hold my feet to the fire over this, all right? I can't be sure."

"Anything else you remember?"

Dwayne shrugged, seeming a little embarrassed. "They tipped well, and seemed to be in a good mood."

"Can you pull the credit card receipt?"

"There wasn't one. I broke a crisp new hundred-dollar bill for them, that's why I remember. They let me keep the change to fifty. No one does that here."

"How about the girl?" Kay asked. "Was she in a good mood?"

He frowned for a moment, looking in the direction of the table where they'd sat. "Y—yes, she was, but not at first. She seemed tense, a tad grim or maybe shy, but they cheered her up quickly. They seemed to know each other well."

They knew her well. They were younger than she'd profiled. Those were rock solid leads she could use to narrow down a list of suspects.

"Did anyone sit at that table after them?" Elliot asked.

Dwayne pressed his lips together and nodded. "I wipe it clean every night, with disinfectant. I'm sorry, but if you're looking for prints, they're long gone."

A moment's silence, while Kay gave her next steps some thought. A sketch artist should probably be able to generate some composites within an hour at the most. Then she could show the composites to Jenna's mother and Kendra's parents, teachers at school, anyone who could've met the two young men and could identify them. Maybe they picked Jenna up from school a couple of times. Or Kendra.

Perhaps they were seniors at that school themselves. Or recent grads.

She checked the time; it was still early, not even seven. Then she remembered it was Saturday. Otherwise, she would've taken Dwayne and had him stand in front of the school as kids came in, asking him to pick the two young men out of a very long and unsuspecting lineup.

But a yearbook might do the trick.

"One of them said something about the chairlift that got my attention," Dwayne said, looking out the window with concern as cars were starting to fill the first line. Soon he'd have customers. "The taller one, he said he knew someone at lift maintenance who would take the three of them up on the mountain, free of charge. It sounded weird to me, because the chairlift doesn't run in the summer. Only after the first serious snow covers the slopes."

Kay gave him her card. "You've been very helpful, Dwayne. If you remember anything, please call us. I'll have the sketch artist here in about thirty minutes."

THIRTY-SEVEN
URGES

Alexandria tossed and turned for a while, unable to fall asleep. The sheets felt hot to the touch, unbearably so. Sweat beaded on her forehead and her chest, urging her to rid herself of the silk nightgown she was wearing. The threat of a migraine circled above her head like a vulture, unrelenting. At about five thirty, she opened the window and let the chilly morning air fill her room, welcoming the breeze.

The phone chimed and woke her up, seemingly seconds after she'd dozed off, but she'd been asleep for about an hour. It was daylight outside; a narrow sunbeam pierced through the curtains, dancing on the pattern of the thick Oriental rug.

She sat on the side of the bed, easily ridding herself of any slumber remnants when she saw the sender of the message.

I'm naked on the bed, the message read, *ready for you. C'mon, babe, have mercy on me.*

A photo followed the message. It was an explicit closeup of a rather imposing erection. The sight of him, hard and lusting for her, sent shivers through her blood; the arousal was instantaneous and unbearably intense. A whimper rose from her constricted throat.

Your place? she typed, not bothering to pretend her sensibilities were shocked by the photo. Their relationship was as basic and as primal as they came; there was no need for lies.

ASAP, baby, the reply came immediately. *The things I'd do to you right now...*

Energized, she sprung from the bed, immediately realizing she was a bit unsteady on her feet. Remnants of last night's wine were still coursing through her veins. Regardless, she didn't hesitate; a cold shower would scatter all that and reinvigorate her mind and body.

She stepped into the shower wincing, anticipating the pain of the cold water. When the first jets sprayed against her heated skin, she gasped, breath caught in her lungs for a long moment, then leaving her chest in a pained groan. Regardless, she gave her hair a thorough shampoo, then rinsed it with a few drops of jasmine conditioner so it would run silky smooth against her lover's skin.

She didn't feel the cold anymore; her imagination was running wild, her desire lighting a fire in her blood that couldn't be extinguished. The thought of Alana crossed her mind as she left the shower, bringing a brief frown to her face. Making quick work of blow-drying her hair, she felt confident Alana wouldn't even know she'd gone. Her daughter had just come home an hour ago; she'd be asleep like a log until lunchtime at least. There wouldn't be any difficult questions to be answered.

Standing naked in the middle of the closet, she didn't hesitate. She knew exactly what she'd wear. A black, strappy, lacy teddy by Cosabella, a shimmering blue satin shirt that matched her eyes, and a black pencil skirt that hugged her hips tightly. Strappy sandals on three-inch heels completed the attire. As a last thought, she grabbed her swimsuit and slid it in her purse. Maybe later they could stop by the beach and take a dip into the cold Pacific waters to soothe the raging fire that burned inside, before it consumed whatever was left of her sanity and common sense.

Less than fifteen minutes later, she rang the doorbell, looking at the imposing residence with a touch of envy. She could tell an architect lived there and had designed the place for himself. Modern lines throughout and a flat roof over a cubist structure with panoramic windows and perspective games in the way walls aligned, luring the viewer inside through a massive pivot door in oak with horizontal accent lines. Nervously biting her lip, she noticed how those lines barred the visitor's entry if the door was closed, but invited entry when open, aligning with the wide hallway she'd seen before.

The parallel lines shifted as the door opened without making a sound. He stood there naked, hard, grinning at her as she became unexpectedly flustered, hesitant to come in. He reached and grabbed her forearm, pulling her inside, then into a fiery embrace that swept her off her feet. Behind her, the door whooshed to a silent close.

THIRTY-EIGHT
CALLS

With Elliot behind the wheel, driving toward the chairlift terminal, Kay took to phone duty. Seemed that more and more of their work involved making or receiving calls. Things changed, in the way people thought and acted, in the landscape of their town, in the way criminal minds wove their plans of action.

It was an evolution.

The age of remote work had brought along a major migration from high-density, urban centers to distant suburbia, small towns like Mount Chester suddenly becoming attractive destinations for Silicon Valley people who wanted to get out of the daily grind. Affordable real estate, especially for undeveloped land, the proximity of the Mount Chester ski resort, and the direct connection to San Francisco via the interstate that passed a mile west of Mount Chester's town hall, made her hometown a prime-time destination for San Franciscans seeking a better life.

That in itself had changed the way they policed the county. Within a year, the town's population had doubled in size. There were rumors of land speculators starting to acquire local acreage as soon as it hit the market. Later this year, one of the biggest residential builders was set to break ground just north of the town for a multiunit housing development like Mount Chester had never seen. Every day she ran into people she'd never met before, strangers, not folks she remembered seeing at church growing up or going to school with.

But the culture of Mount Chester was still that of a small town. Everyone was watching everyone, not out of malice, but out of habit and lack of better things to do. Veteran residents, wary of newcomers, had tightened their ranks watchfully, yet none had stepped forward after Barb's newscast call for information into the disappearance of Kendra Flannagan.

Dwayne Goodrow, the sandwich shop attendant, seemed to be new to the resort, yet had noticed a lot more about the unsubs than she'd hoped for. Being how famously unreliable witness testimonies were, Kay could only hope Dwayne's military background had taught him how to notice relevant details and retain them for a while longer than the average Joe.

Five years ago, an investigation like that would've probably taken her on a different path. The hypothetical sandwich maker would've recognized the two men who had met with Jenna at Alpine Subs. He would've probably given names, not descriptions. Would've said something like, "It was so-and-so's older kid and that tall, skinny friend of his, you know, the one who plays basketball at—"

Those days were gone.

Mount Chester, soon to become a former small town, was growing and evolving into a hybrid settlement, where permanent and part-time new residents shared a shapeshifting culture with the traditionalists who had been born there. The rural, bedroom community culture was morphing under the influence of distant suburbia with all its good, bad, and just plain different.

Kay's first call was to Jimmy Bugarin, the chairlift operator, who'd offered his help last Wednesday. At almost seven, her call found him up and ready to meet them at the base of the mountain as soon as he could get there.

The second call was a formal request for a sketch artist. Deputy Hobbs took that one; he was going to wake the artist up and drive him over to the sandwich place. Then, another call had Kay speaking with Deputy Farrell; her assignment was to get yearbooks for the last four years of senior high graduates and show them to Dwayne Goodrow at the earliest. There was no news on the phone records yet, but she was going to follow up.

Elliot reached the chairlift terminal by the time she'd finished making the calls. It was a little after seven, under a bright sun, and the air was warming up quickly, raising mist from the meadows. Yet Kay hesitated before leaving the SUV.

There was something else she wanted to do. Shooting a quick glance at Elliot, she realized she would've been more comfortable by herself for the call she was about to make.

Quick to read her mind, as always, Elliot asked, "What's up?"

She stared at the phone she was holding, weighing her options. Sooner or later, she'd have to make that call. Might as well be sooner.

"I want to speak to the cop who collared Gavin Sharp," she said, feeling choked for some reason. "Maybe he remembers something, anything—"

"From more than thirty years ago?"

She lowered her eyes to the phone's screen. Him putting things like that, she felt like an idiot. He was right. And still, she couldn't let go of the phone, of the idea she could find out more about that man. About her father.

Elliot turned in his seat to face her. "Is that cop still alive?"

"Yes," she replied. "He was a rookie when he busted Sharp. He's still on the force, a captain."

She avoided Elliot's gaze. Since she'd stood in his bedroom, staring at the bed where he'd slept with someone else, she hadn't looked straight at him for a single moment, afraid he'd see the anguish inside her heart. Elliot didn't belong to her; she had no stake, no right to be jealous. Still, when she recalled the wrinkled sheets on the left side of the bed, she couldn't breathe right, and her eyes blurred up.

"What's your obsession with this man?" Elliot asked. His voice was gentle, understanding. He had no right to be like that... he was nothing but a coworker who belonged to another woman. "The sex was consensual, and Jenna was underage, all right, but barely. In other states, age of consent is seventeen or sixteen, even."

"We're not in Texas here," she muttered. "In California, age of consent is eighteen, and—" She stopped talking, choking on her own anger. None of what she was feeling was rational.

"He's not the unsub, right?" Elliot pressed on, keeping his voice calm and soothing.

"Yes, DNA cleared him. All we can nail him for is statutory rape, and only if he cops to it. Otherwise, we have nothing."

"But you're in a horn-tossing mood over this perp."

She flashed an angry glare at him, quick to look away afterward. "He's an online predator, Elliot. Someone who lurks out there and hunts for vulnerable young girls. This time, Jenna happened to be seventeen. What if she were younger? Do you think he would've backed away? What if the next one will be fourteen?" She raised her voice with every question, shouting at him in the enclosed space of the SUV.

Elliot didn't fight back. "Make the call, then. You've got plenty of notches on your gun to call the shots here."

"It's not about the case, Elliot," she admitted, feeling ashamed. "It's about my father. There are a lot of similarities between this man and my father, not just the name." She raised her gaze from the phone screen turned dark and saw him frowning.

"Such as?"

She shrugged. "Pretty much... everything. Place of birth, schools attended, that kind of thing."

"So, it's not just a coincidence, this name thing, with your father, is it?" He took off his hat and ran his fingers through his hair a couple of times before putting it back on. "Anything else I should know, before I start wondering why a conversation with my partner sounds so damn close to a suspect interrogation, chock-full of lies?"

"No, there's nothing else," She swallowed hard, feeling her throat still constricted. "I think my father stole this man's identity, and I'd like to confirm that if I can."

Elliot crossed his arms at his chest. "Make the call and get a load off your mind, then. It won't tell you who your father is, though."

"Maybe it will."

She dialed the number quickly, as if afraid she'd change her mind. A man picked up the call after a second or two. "Captain Bracero? This is Detective Kay Sharp, Franklin County Sheriff's Office," she said in one quick breath.

"Franklin? That's north of Marin, right? What can I do for you, Detective?"

"Way north of Marin, Captain. About three more counties or so. I'm calling about an old case, a Gavin Sharp. You collared him for—"

"A slobberknocker in a bar? Yeah, I remember him," he replied. "What do you need to know?"

"That's some memory," Kay chuckled. "How come you remember him?"

A poorly disguised groan came from the other end of the conversation. "There was something slimy about this perp. It's like when you know, in your gut, that they're hiding something, right? Well, this guy wasn't hiding anything that I could find, but I was willing to bet a dime or two he'd be back behind bars pronto. Good thing I'm not a betting man... I would've lost. I suspected him of breaking and entering at some point, five years later, but it fell apart. I had no evidence and he lawyered up."

"Was there anything about him that caught your attention? Something he did or said?"

A moment of silence. "Um, he was blabbering something about having his identity stolen. Kept saying that there's another man pretending to be him out there, or something like that. I didn't pay no mind to it. I had about half a dozen witnesses who put him in that bar, throwing punches. He sent a man to the hospital with a concussion and a deep gash across the forehead that needed a few stitches."

"Had he filed a report prior to his arrest, about this identity issue?"

"My thoughts exactly." Kay could hear the smile in his raspy, well-smoked voice. "I asked, and he had the nerve to say he hadn't filed because he didn't want to deal with no cops."

Kay held her breath. "Did you investigate the identity fraud accusation?"

"Nah... there was no point. He was flat broke, this douche, didn't have a penny to his name. Awaited trial in the pen 'cause he couldn't scare up two hundred bucks for bail. Why would someone steal his identity? And do what with it, exactly?"

Kay didn't answer. Thoughts and memories rushed from the deepest recesses of her mind to the present, clamoring and whirling, eager to come out.

"Um, some old cop I am," the man added, his voice a lower tone, embarrassed. "I just realized, your name is Sharp also, isn't it? Are you related?"

Kay managed to laugh and make it sound genuine. "Just a coincidence, Captain, nothing else. It's a common name in California. Thank you for your help."

"Anytime." The call ended, leaving silence in the car for a while. In the distance, an older model truck had turned onto the road leading to the chairlift terminal. It was probably the owner, coming to meet them.

"There," Elliot said. "Now you know. Does it make you feel any better?" He reached out to squeeze her hand, but she pulled away before his fingers touched her skin.

Why didn't he understand, once and for all, that things had changed between them if he was sleeping with someone else? Why was it so damn hard?

She didn't say anything, afraid her voice would betray her. Instead, she focused on the entire Gavin Sharp situation.

Precisely thirty-two years ago, when Gavin Sharp from San Francisco had been arrested for beating a man in a sports bar, he'd said something about another man using his identity.

That year, Kay's father had met her mother. Months later, he'd proposed and married her in a small, modest ceremony of which only a couple of photographs remained.

About a year later, Kay had been born into a hellish childhood with an abusive, violent stranger for a father.

THIRTY-NINE
PASS

The old Chevy Silverado rattled to a stop by the chairlift terminal entrance, where Kay and Elliot waited. Jimmy Bugarin, wearing a black T-shirt with frayed hems and visible holes here and there, and a pair of khaki cargo shorts, hopped down and grinned widely, showing two rows of misaligned teeth stained by tobacco use. A tuft of hair still clung to his scalp at the top of his head, surrounded by shiny baldness. A whiff of stale cigarette smoke engulfed him like his own personal cloud.

"What can I do for you, Detectives? You want me to start up this rust bucket and get you on the mountain real quick?"

"No need for that," Elliot replied, shaking the man's hand. "We just need some information from you, that's all."

The man rubbed his hands together, seemingly excited for some reason. "Shoot."

"We're looking for two young men, under twenty-five," Kay said, forgetting for a moment that Jimmy Bugarin was more comfortable speaking with Elliot than her. His frown and hands shoved quickly into his pants pockets reminded her. "My partner will give you all the details."

He instantly relaxed and turned his attention to Elliot,

almost smiling with relief. Kay refrained from shaking her head. Some men had issues dealing with women, set so deeply within their psyche it was beyond logic or redemption.

Elliot shot her a quick look, then said, "We don't have a sketch yet, but we should have one soon. For now, I can tell you one's six feet tall, the other's six-two. They're Caucasian and dark-haired, with 'hair that needs a trim,' in the exact words of our witness." He made air quotes with his fingers as he spoke.

The frown returned on Jimmy's forehead, and his stained, stubby fingers found the brow creases and scratched them thoroughly. "Um, no disrespect, but why are you asking me about these two characters? I believe I done tellin' you I wasn't here on Tuesday, when that poor girl died. My kid was sick with the flu. I was here Wednesday, when I took the other cop up on the mountain with his dog."

"Yes, I remember you mentioned it," Elliot said. He spoke calmly, unrushed, as if they had all the time in the world. But his strategy worked. Jimmy tilted his head a little and raised an eyebrow.

"Then what do you need, folks?"

"One of these guys mentioned you."

"Huh?"

"The same witness who gave the descriptions said one of the men was saying they knew someone at lift maintenance who would give them a ride up the mountain, free of charge."

The man shrugged. "I wasn't here. I didn't give no one no bloody ride up the mountain."

"We know you didn't," Kay chimed in, seeing how defensive Jimmy was becoming. "We had the K-9 unit track their footsteps up to the ridge. We know they hiked."

"Who would say that about you?" Elliot asked. "Do you have friends or anyone who could claim you'd do that for them? Run them up there for free?"

Jimmy scratched the roots of the unruly tuft of hair that

marked the top of his head. "I don't do that for anyone." He pulled out a pack of smokes from his side pocket and lit up, sending a whirl of blue smoke in the air. "I mean, yeah, for cops or any other officials, I won't charge. Mountain rescue? Sure. But the rest gotta pay or I go broke. I don't run the lift in the summer. Told y'all that."

Kay groaned silently and looked at Elliot, urging him to end the conversation. They were wasting time. The man had nothing. "Thank you, Mr. Bugarin."

Jimmy turned to leave, but changed his mind. "Um, I'd make an exception for one my regulars, you know. For season pass holders."

Kay's eyes lit up. "Do you have many of those?"

"A few. These mountains are filled with San Francisco weekenders with more money than they can figure out what to do with. Season passes ain't cheap. For one person, that's eleven hundred, nine hundred if they're a student or ex-military. For a family pass, that's north of two grand for the winter, and I don't care if it thaws early."

Elliot whistled. "And that's just for the lift?"

"Uh-huh." Jimmy took another drag and blew it out slowly, savoring it. "Lift, parking, and ski storage in one of them lockers out back."

"We need to see your records," Kay said. A flicker of sheer panic lit up Jimmy's eyes. "Just to see if we can identify who these men are, based on your credit card receipts."

He bit his lip, while his eyes darted all over, panicked. "There's not much credit card receipts, ma'am. I give discounts for cash business, and I write the receipts by hand. No real way to track anyone. If they lose their pass, they have to pay for another one."

Kay looked at him intently. Maybe the IRS would have a field day with him, or maybe he was honestly paying his taxes as he should have. Either way, that wasn't her business.

"But you'd recognize one of your seasonal pass holders if you saw him?"

"Yes, I bet I would, 'cause they're on the slopes a whole lot, getting their money's worth."

"Thank you, Mr. Bugarin, we'll be in touch later today when we have the composite."

"I'll be here, tinkering with this hunk o' junk," he mumbled, heading toward the terminal.

Elliot looked at Kay. She quickly looked away. "I know how to handle this," she said, rushing toward the SUV. She climbed behind the wheel and started the engine. Elliot took the passenger seat and immediately fired up the laptop. "I have an idea too. Who uses the ski lift a lot? A passionate skier, right?"

"Yes," she replied, not sure where he was going with that statement.

"What else are they going to do if they're so crazy about their time on the slopes?"

She grinned widely. "Post their pics on social media. One of the kids in Jenna's entourage that predates April is a skier. Have at it, partner."

She peeled off, throwing small pebbles in the air, heading toward the precinct. If the phone records she'd requested weren't there yet, she was going to take the matter into her own hands and get those records pronto.

"Got him," Elliot announced as she was taking the right turn onto the highway. "Richard William Gaskell is the name. He fits the description to a T. Six-feet-two, dark hair, needs a haircut badly. He's a senior year student. There's a bunch of photos from last winter when he went skiing, including a selfie he took with Jimmy Bugarin."

Kay beamed. "Let's go grab him."

"Not so fast, partner. His parents are hotshot criminal attorneys from San Francisco."

"Don't tell me he's Edward Gaskell's kid. The man is the

fiercest defender of organized crime scum on this side of the contiguous states." Her fist found the edge of the wheel slamming hard. "Damn it to bloody hell. We're not catching a break on this one, are we?"

"We need real probable cause and a watertight warrant. 'He likes to ski' isn't going to cut it with attorneys for parents. Probably we can get Bugarin and our friend Dwayne to pick him out of a photo array, and that would be good enough for a solid warrant." Elliot looked at the screen, still scrolling through social media posts. "He's got pictures with several other boys who fit the description."

Kay shook her head. One wrong move, and Edward Gaskell could ask one of the pieces of organized scum he'd kept out of jail for a small favor. Regardless, she wasn't going to let his precious son off the hook. "Let the witnesses help with the second unsub. If they can't, just make a short list and we'll nab him during questioning." She ground her teeth, furious at her own powerlessness. "It will take time Kendra doesn't have."

"He's going to Harvard, so I'm going to assume he's smart, but I got a big hole in the fence. Why would a smart attorney's kid leave fingerprints and semen at the scene? Does it make any sense?"

Kay let her mind wander as she drove, and almost missed the exit for the precinct. Only one scenario could justify the blatant disorganization of an apparently intelligent and educated unsub.

"Yes, it makes sense, if he thought this was going to be a rape while the vic was on Rohypnol. She wouldn't remember a thing the next morning, and her tarnished reputation would invalidate any claim she would make about the assault. He must've been aroused at the thought of seeing his victim in school every day, defenseless, fearful, forever defeated and shamed. It's the ultimate power trip." She slowed her speed and turned onto the precinct's street. "Something must've happened. Not only Tuesday, on the ridge, but in April."

"What do you mean?"

"I'm saying, why did all these kids start bullying Jenna all of a sudden? We still don't know."

FORTY
GONE

"Well, if it isn't my trusted Detective Sharp," Sheriff Logan greeted her the moment she stepped inside the precinct. He must've had someone notify him the moment she came in.

His words were a bitter déjà vu of Friday morning. Unlike the day before, now he was fuming. He'd crossed his arms at his chest, blocking the way with his massive build and glared at Kay. When he spoke her name, his voice was loaded with undertones of frustration and disappointment. She froze in place so abruptly Elliot nearly bumped into her.

"Good morning, Sheriff," she said, calmly holding his gaze. "We have some news."

"Ah, we'll get to that," he replied, turning around and walking briskly to his office. They followed.

As soon as he took his chair behind the old, scratched desk littered with case files and reports, he looked at her again. "You stood right there, yesterday morning, and somehow omitted telling me the unsub, as you like to call them, has your father's name."

"Sheriff, I—"

He held his hand up in the air, silencing her. "Spare me.

You must think I'm the biggest idiot who ever wore a badge, if you didn't so much as bother to tell me before I heard it on the news last night."

She deserved the roasting; she'd lied to people who didn't deserved to be lied to, and she had to own that. She took a deep breath slowly, reminding herself the only blame was hers. "Sir, as soon as I pulled up the perp's profile from the DMV, it became apparent he's not my father, as I had feared for about ten seconds. Then I proceeded the way I would've with any other unsub; his name didn't matter to me. I now realize I was wrong, and I apologize; you should've been informed."

His glare softened. She clenched her jaw but managed to let the uncomfortable silence fill the room. After a moment that seemed to drag on forever, the sheriff clasped his hands on the pile of reports placed in front of him and let out a frustrated sigh.

"At least you spoke with that reporter and got her off our backs." He sighed and leaned against the back rest of his worn-out leather chair. "You said you had news?"

"We have the first unsub identified; we need to ask two witnesses to pick him out of a photo array before we say one word about it to anyone." She lowered her voice as she said the last part of the phrase.

"Who the hell is he? No one gets special treatment here."

"Edward Gaskell's son, Richard."

"Mother—" he stopped in time, but the expression on his face said the rest. "I don't need to say this, but be very careful when handling this suspect."

"Copy that," she replied, shooting a quick glance toward Elliot. As usual, he'd remained standing, leaning against the doorframe. "We're waiting for some other evidence. DNA on the second unsub, phone records—"

"Gaskell's kid isn't in CODIS, is he?" The sheriff ended his question with a bitter chuckle.

"Of course, he isn't. Getting his DNA has to be handled by the book," Kay added, stating what was on everyone's mind. "His father has a knack for getting evidence thrown out of court on minute matters of procedure. He and I have crossed paths in court in the past." She looked at the time and a frown creased her brow. "If there isn't anything else—"

Logan dismissed them with a hand wave, and she was quick to rush out of there. She stopped at her desk to drop her keys, then rushed to the evidence locker. Moments later, she was holding Jenna's diary in her hands.

"Here," Elliot said, putting a tall paper cup filled with steaming coffee in front of her. "It's strong enough to hang your washing on it."

She smiled for a brief moment. He always made her laugh, but that didn't mean anything. Maybe he made Miranda laugh just as much. Or more. Her smile vanished. "Thanks." The chair she pulled grated loudly against the floor.

Elliot shot her a quick look that seemed lit by something she couldn't name, maybe the beginning of a smile, but her partner's face was dead serious as he fired up his laptop and took a seat.

"What?" she asked, her voice sounding a bit annoyed.

He shrugged. "I didn't say anything." He looked at her the same way as before, as if he knew something amusing about her he wasn't going to share. As if she had food stuck in her teeth or something. "I'll pull all the photos on Gaskell's social media with other kids who fit the description, and start identifying them for the second photo array."

She abandoned the diary on the desk for a moment and gathered her thoughts. The last time she'd read Jenna's notes seemed like ages ago. They still believed Gavin Sharp was the rapist, and that he'd acted alone.

Opening the diary, she turned the pages quickly to the last entry she'd read, and continued on. As she read through, she noticed tearstains, now dry, discoloring the paper.

May 2

I heard it myself, in camp, how they talk about me. Otherwise, I'd think I'm going crazy. It's whispers, mainly, that stop when I walk by. Laughter too, giggles, snorts, comments. I wanna scream at them and scratch their faces, do something, anything, to end this silence.

Alana still comes by, but I can barely take it. She's nice to me, and treats me like she's always done, but I know she knows, and it's killing me she's not bringing it up. How long will we play this charade? Yesterday I sat with her and Nick over lunch. No one else sat with us, and Nick always draws a crowd.

I was the crowd repellent. Maybe I should sell my services.

Alana is lucky to have Nick for a boyfriend. They seem so in love, just like Tim and me. Maybe they'll last longer that we do.

May 5

Tim and I were supposed to go to the movies, but he canceled. He said he wasn't feeling well. I offered to go there and spend time with him watching TV, but he didn't want me visiting.

I knew this would eventually happen. I just hoped that Tim, out of all people, would know it's all lies. Why doesn't he believe me? Why did he pretend to have food poisoning, instead of asking me what's going on?

This will never end. I'm alone in this world. No one will talk about it with me. My own parents feel like a burden to me. If it weren't for my dad and what it would do to him, I'd jump off a cliff. We got plenty of those here.

May 8

Mackenzie and Alana went to the movies on Friday with Nick and some of his friends. They didn't ask me. I felt left behind at first, then I remembered everyone knew Tim was supposed to take me. It's not their fault.

Then today someone called me a name after first period.

Jenna Whorell.

They twisted my name... my father's name. I'm no longer Jenna Jerrell. I no longer know who I am. Maybe they're all right, and I'm wrong, and losing my mind at the same time. Maybe it's one of those senseless, endless nightmares, Matrix-style, from which there's no awakening.

I decided to ask Mac about it, if she knew why people were saying these things about me. She got all flustered, turned red as a beet, and didn't say anything but kids being mean and telling lies, and that I shouldn't listen to any of it. I shouldn't care.

Alana said the same. I didn't see it at first, but she's a good person. She seemed a little harsh and a bit arrogant, but she's kind, loving, and a good friend. Doesn't matter what day of the week it is or what time, I can call her. She doesn't judge and doesn't ask, but if I want to, I can talk about it with her. She's there for me, ready to hang out like we used to do.

Before all this.

Today, after class, someone groped me in the hallway. Hard. It hurt.

Alana came by after school and I told her about it, then I cried in her arms until my tears ran dry. At least I have her and Mac. To them, I'm the same person I always was.

Even them, I'm ashamed to look in the eye.

May 10

It's over.

Tim left me. I'm numb with pain.

And yet, I can barely think of him after what he showed me. There's a website out there, with pictures of my naked body for everyone to see. They're not real, but how would they know, when they don't even bother to ask?

Tim didn't ask. He just showed me the website, pale and shaking like a leaf. He had tears in his eyes, but he was glaring at me as if I'd done something wrong. He believes I did. He thinks I've slept with everyone but him.

He's gone now.

But that horrible thing is still out there for anyone who wants to look.

Who could've done this to me? And why? Why me?

As I was leaving school today, someone asked me how much I charged for an hour.

An hour of what?

I didn't dare to ask.

Kay's phone came to life, startling her. She checked the screen and immediately picked up. It was Deputy Farrell.

"Talk to me," she said, putting the phone on speaker and placing it on the desk.

"You're not going to like this, Kay. Goodrow's not here."

"What do you mean he's not there?" She sprung from her chair as if getting ready to storm out the door, and slammed her hands against the desk. "He was there!"

"I arrived at Alpine Subs at about eight thirty. The door was locked, the sign was off. No one knows where Dwayne Goodrow went. I asked hotel management, called his boss... she had no idea he was gone. Going to his address on record next. He lives on the other side of the mountain."

"Do you have the yearbook?"

"Yeah, got that with me. I'll show it to the chairlift operator before I head out to track Goodrow. I have a BOLO on his car already."

"How about phone records for the entire list of names I gave you?"

"We should have them by noon, at the earliest."

Kay scrunched her eyelids shut. "Keep me posted," she said, slowly sitting down and ending the call.

This wasn't happening.

The only man who could put Richard Gaskell with Jenna right before she was killed was now gone. Without his positive ID, there were not enough grounds for a warrant.

FORTY-ONE
GOODBYE

They didn't make it to the bed at first. Littering the place with Alexandria's clothes, he peeled them off ravenously, while she moaned and panted into his kisses. Her self-control was gone, vanished the moment she'd laid eyes on his firmly toned abs and the hardness resting against them.

With one sweep of his forearm, he cleared a section of the kitchen island countertop and lifted her there. The granite felt cold under her heated skin. Leaning her head backward and abandoning herself to him, she laughed, secretly aroused at the thought of having passionate sex on another woman's granite countertop. Would she know? Would she feel it?

Later, they made it to the bed. She dozed off, satisfied and spent, in his strong arms. She woke up under a barrage of hungry kisses and exploring hands, and the fire she'd thought was out for a while rekindled to a blaze within seconds. This time, he took it slowly, playing with her until she begged for it.

When she startled from her faint-like slumber in his arms, it was almost eleven, and he was sound asleep still. She studied his face, wondering why she couldn't resist his touch. He was handsome in a breathtaking kind of way, but so were others. It was him... their chemistry, the way their bodies fit together like perfectly matched pieces of a puzzle. And still, there was at least one other woman in his life, and she hated him for it. Hated herself too, for letting herself be used like that. For needing it so badly.

She shifted, pulling away from him, and tugged at the sheet. He mumbled something in his sleep, but then awakened and reached for her breast. She held her breath for a moment, the decision to leave still lingering in her brain, but then gave in under his touch.

"It's strange for someone like you to be so skilled with women," she said, her voice starting to tremble as his hand moved in small circles on her skin.

He chuckled. "Someone like me? Really? You can't even say it?"

"How do you do it?"

A hint of a vain smile tugged at his lips. "While other guys watch porn, I read about pleasuring women. It's, um, much more instructive," he added in a low whisper, placing a kiss on her neck. "Don't you agree?"

She closed her eyes, trying to steady herself. "You mean, like *Fifty Shades* or stuff like that?"

His grin widened and his eyes sparkled as he shot her a quick glance. "Maybe. Whatever the lady wants, the lady gets," he added, whispering close to her neck. Her skin reacted when his breath touched it, but her mind was turning ice cold.

"Who else's been in this bed tonight?" she asked, her voice chilly.

He sighed and turned on his back. His hand left her body barren, aching for more. "We're back to this again?"

She bit her lip, but decided to continue. Maybe it was time to have a real conversation with him. "I feel used. One of the many who rush over whenever you want sex and leave when you're satisfied."

He folded his arms under his head and looked straight at her. The smile was gone. A flicker of impatience darkened his eyes. "We use each other, all right? Don't tell me it's something else, 'cause I'm not buying it."

She shook her head and rose, leaning into her elbow, ready to get out of bed but still not wanting to. "How many times have I offered to speak with Alana about you? Then we could stop hiding."

His jaws clenched. "I'm not ready for that. Honestly, neither are you. This is a small town, not somewhere you can lose yourself. Everyone would turn on you and make your life a living hell."

"I don't care." As she spoke the words, she looked away from him, wondering. Maybe he was right, and she was insane, wanting what was never hers to begin with. "The question is, are you able to commit to a real relationship?"

He sat on the side of the bed, looking at her with pity. He touched her face with his fingers, caressing her cheek gently, then playing with a strand of her silky hair. "Why mess up a good thing?"

She breathed away the molten rush that mellowed her resolve under his touch. "I'm not one of the girls you have lined up, dying for you to call. I'm special, and I deserve someone special. If you haven't figured that out by now, I guess you never will."

He nodded a few times, staying silent for a moment. "This is who I am, Alexandria, and I'm fine with it. We can make each other happy every now and then, or we can go our separate ways. It's up to you entirely."

Tears of humiliation stung her eyes. She'd gambled and lost, her hand not strong enough. He was a much better player than she was, mostly because she was not a player at all. Somewhere in the past several months, she'd fallen for him. Against all common sense, and knowing it could never be, she was deeply in love with the indifferent, callous bastard who could light her blood on fire with one touch.

He could never know it.

She stood, wrapping the sheet around her body and hiding her face. Feeling weaker by the second, she started looking for her clothes, backtracking the path that led to the front door. The memory of their embrace when she'd first arrived brought a sob to her chest. Breathing deeply, she managed to gather her things under his impenetrable gaze and keep the threat of tears at bay.

She was leaving, and he didn't care. He wasn't saying anything or doing anything to stop her.

When she was almost at the door, he asked, "How will I know what you decide?"

She looked at him for a long moment, letting her eyes burn into her memory the sight of his naked body leaning casually against the wall. "You'll know when I don't take your calls anymore."

She opened the door to leave, hoping he'd stop her, but he didn't budge. Almost running to her car, she didn't look back, but heard the door close behind her.

Barely seeing the road through her tears, Alexandria drove straight to the coast, sobbing hard. Pain ripped through her chest as she repeatedly told herself this was it, the final goodbye, the moment where sanity returned to her ravaged mind. And perhaps she could still save herself somehow.

About an hour later, she ran across a deserted and sunny stretch of beach, heading toward the water. Without bothering to get undressed, she rushed into the frozen waves of the Pacific, welcoming the awakening shock of the freezing brine and the merciless strength of the powerful surf hitting her body until it was numb.

"Oh, God, what have I done?" she cried, despairing and brokenhearted. "What the hell was I thinking?" She sobbed still, her breath shattered by the shaking of her body, her teeth clattering from the cold.

When she crawled back to the beach, she could barely walk. She let herself fall onto the sand and wailed until she was out of breath, her tears lost in the salty water dripping from her hair.

"I wasn't myself," she whispered, when the tears had finally stopped. "I still am not."

FORTY-TWO
RENALDO

"I swear to God, Elliot, when we find out who put that website out there, I'll throw the book at them." Kay was fuming, staring at the diary she'd abandoned on her desk. "Let's go over this and make sure we've covered all possible bases. We're tracking down the money trail behind the website's hosting, that's one," she counted on her fingers. "We have subpoenas for all that, so we're rock solid. That will give us the IP address of the person who uploaded the content, their credit card info, everything we need. Then, we have subpoenas for all those phone records, and two deputies following up with the respective carriers. Are we forgetting something?"

"I have six possible kids who could be the second unsub, shortlisted. None of them have records. I was counting on Dwayne Goodrow to pick out the perp from the photo array, but—"

"Yeah." She clenched her jaw for a moment, powerless and frustrated. "What's up with that? Do you think Dwayne's a part of it?" She gave the thought a moment, but it didn't gel. If she knew anything about people, Dwyane wasn't mixed up in what had happened with Jenna. He'd been forthcoming and helpful, holding her gaze with steady, honest eyes and without a flinch. Then why the hell did he run before he could make the ID? Had Gaskell reached out, or maybe used his father's interloping clients to scare him off?

It was possible.

Nevertheless, they'd find him. BOLO was out and everyone was looking for him. A material witness warrant would be next, if he didn't show up before the end of the day. Either way, Kendra had been missing for more than thirty-six hours, and, without Dwayne, they couldn't arrest Richard Gaskell and interrogate him. Time was flying by, and time was the one thing Kendra didn't have.

"Maybe he got scared, thinking the crime had started from his sandwich place and he might be somehow held responsible. Some people don't like dealing with cops. Or maybe he's got a record." Elliot didn't sound convinced.

Without sitting down, she typed Goodrow's name into AFIS and didn't find an entry. "He's clean. That's not it." For the tenth time since she'd been back at her desk, she checked her email for the phone records she'd been waiting for. Still nothing. "Show me those names again," she asked Elliot. "And their faces."

All were dark-haired high school seniors matching the rather vague description offered by Dwayne. One name stood out.

"Let's go see him first." Her fingertip tapped against one of the faces. "Renaldo Cristobal. I've heard his name before."

"You got it." Elliot grabbed his hat and stood, stomping his feet silently to arrange his jeans. They had ridden up his boots. "Mackenzie Trenton mentioned him."

"Yes, he was one of the first people who was spreading rumors about Jenna. I wonder what he has to say about that."

Elliot drove faster than she would have to Renaldo's address, cutting the commute short to only a few minutes. He braked hard in front of the house, while Kay stared at the front porch with a raised eyebrow. The house was modest and old, clean but falling into disrepair. The front porch, poured in a thin layer of cement, had cracked in multiple places, and weeds were growing in the cracks.

"Why would Gaskell's kid hang out with someone like Renaldo?" she asked, hurrying to the front door. She lowered her voice as she rang the doorbell. "Rich kids usually flock together."

"Maybe they share a common interest," Elliot replied as the door swung open.

"Yeah, I'm sure they do."

Renaldo stood in the doorway, turning pale as he looked at the badge Elliot held in front of his eyes. He took a step back at first as if to invite them in, then changed his mind and stepped outside, closing the door behind him.

His face was delicate, almost feminine, and his hair raven black and shiny, parted in the middle and about an inch short of touching his shoulders. The black circles under his eyes didn't match his visibly fake casual demeanor. He was definitely hiding something, fidgety and scared to be standing a few feet away from the detectives.

"We have a few questions about Jenna Jerrell," Kay said. "Do you mind if we come in?"

He threw the door an uncomfortable look, then stared at the cracked cement at his feet. "I'd rather we talked out here, if that's okay. I'm not, um, I'm—" He stuttered, looking pitiful as he wrung his hands together.

"It's all right," Kay replied. The livid kid barely managing to stand straight in front of her didn't have the intestinal fortitude to be a killer. "We can talk out here. It won't take long."

Renaldo breathed, but still didn't look at her.

"Tell me about the rumors that were started about Jenna last April." She watched his reactions carefully. If anything, he seemed slightly relieved; still scared, but he breathed deeply and lifted his eyes for a brief second, while his face was turning flush.

"I don't know, um, who started it. I had nothing to do with it."

"We have a witness who testified you were bragging about sleeping with Jenna. Is that true?"

He took a step back until he hit the closed door. "Sort of, I mean, no. I didn't sleep with Jenna. No, I didn't."

"Why the hesitation?" He didn't reply. "Didn't you actually say you slept with her?" Still no response. "Did you just brag about it?" Elliot asked, lowering his voice to a friendly, conspiratorial tone. "Just between guys?"

Sweat broke in tiny beads on the boy's forehead. He was constantly fidgeting, shifting his weight, pacing in place. His hands found the depths of his pockets, stretching the thin fabric of the slacks he was wearing. "I didn't sleep with her," he finally said.

"Who's lying? You or our witness?" Kay asked, her voice cutting into his resistance like a hot knife through butter.

He seemed ready to collapse. Looking around as if afraid someone could overhear him, he whispered, "I'm not lying, I swear. I didn't sleep with her, but yeah, I said I did." His voice broke into an embarrassed whisper. "I'm ashamed of what I said, and I'm so sorry."

"Why did you say you slept with her if it wasn't true?"

His spine bent a little, the oversized green shirt fluttering in the gentle breeze against his thin body. On his chest, the logo of a local hardware store Kay recognized was embroidered in bright yellow.

"Listen, kid, we ain't got all day," Elliot said gently. He squeezed his thin shoulder with a reassuring gesture. "You have nothing to be afraid of. But there's another young girl missing,

one of your classmates, and that means you have to tell us everything you know and quickly, so we can help her."

Kay caught a quick glance filled with terror when Elliot had
mentioned Kendra, but didn't intervene.

Renaldo nodded and swallowed with difficulty. "One day I
went to school, and everyone was different with me. Girls were
smiling and giggling when I walked by. Guys were winking,
patting me on the back like we were pals, and we'd never been
pals. That's how it started. Everyone was saying I'd slept with
Jenna, out of the blue, and, um, I didn't deny it."

"Why?"

"It was cool to feel like one of those guys who get the beautiful girls, you know? I didn't think it would matter."

"So, you did brag about it, didn't you?"

Terrified, he threw a couple of side glances as if seeing if
anyone could rescue him from Kay's merciless questions. "Only
if anyone asked, but I was just trying to be cool."

"Did you think of Jenna for a second?" Kay whispered,
barely refraining to grab the young man by the shirt and slam
him against the wall.

He shook his head quickly. "I didn't think it mattered. It
wasn't the first time there were rumors about Jenna sleeping
around with others in our school, many others. I thought it was
cool that they thought I could, um, sleep with a girl like that."

"So, you were okay to be just one of the many who'd slept
with her?" Elliot asked casually.

His cheeks blushed darker. "I didn't know at first, that there
were others... that many. Then I stopped saying anything, and
let people believe what they wanted."

Kay took a step closer to Renaldo, staring at him intently. "I
want you to think hard about what I'm about to ask." He
nodded. "Before that day, when suddenly everyone was saying
you'd slept with Jenna, did you hear any rumors about her
sleeping around?"

He scrunched his eyelids shut, but a tear still found its way between lashes and rolled down his cheek. He wiped quickly with the back of his hand. "N—no, I don't think so."

Kay's eyes darted quickly toward Elliot. They hadn't uncovered the author of the cyberbullying attack; just another victim of it, although Renaldo didn't even know it. The bully had picked him because he was weak, an easy-to-manipulate young man who'd grown tired of being marginalized in his rather small social circle. The perfect target, Renaldo had grabbed the opportunity and had become the spreader of rumors, confirming them.

"Who do you think started those rumors about Jenna and you?" she asked, although she already knew the answer.

"I—I don't know," he replied. "I'm really sorry... it happened quickly."

"Before that day, did you hear anything at all gossiped about Jenna?" He didn't respond, just looked at Kay with a vacant stare. "Anything at all?"

He bit his lip for a moment, probably thinking whether to say what he remembered or not. "Just minor stuff, you know, girl stuff."

"Like what?"

He lowered his eyes again and ran his hand quickly against his nostrils, sniffling. "Just... like the color of her panties."

Kay waited, making the silence increasingly uncomfortable for Renaldo.

"And, um, that she shaved down there." Redness had reached the tip of his ears. The young man was a nervous wreck.

"That's it?"

Renaldo breathed. "I swear, that's all I remember."

"Where is Kendra Flannagan?" she asked out of the blue, ready to catch his reactions.

His pupils dilated and his eyes shifted away from her. A

deathly pallor washed over his face. "I don't know." His reply was calmer than she'd expected. Reassured. Rehearsed.

Kay gave the boy another look, head to toe, wondering if his apparent calm meant he didn't have anything to do with Kendra's disappearance, or was about something else. A slimebag like Richard Gaskell would teach his partners in crime about lawyering up. "Where were you on Tuesday evening, between eight and ten in the evening?"

The boy's skin turned a whiter shade of pale. His right hand touched his chest where the embroidered logo of Harry's Hardware Store shone in bright yellow. "At work. I work almost all weekdays," he added quickly with an uneasy, fearful smile. "I have to. I come home from school, change, and work evenings at the cash register."

Words poured out of his mind in a rushed rhythm she knew well. Liars did that, trying to build evidence in support of their deception, offering unnecessary details while losing themselves deeper and deeper in a web of lies with every word they spoke.

A manipulated pushover or not, Renaldo was hiding something.

FORTY-THREE
U-TURN

"Why isn't Renaldo in cuffs right now?" Elliot asked. "I'm willing to bet the farm he knows something about Kendra. That kid is a ball of fraught nerves."

Kay looked at him for a quick moment, second-guessing herself. She'd almost slapped the cuffs on him moments ago.

"If he's in on any of the Gaskell stuff, he'll lawyer up in a second and we'll only be wasting time. Let's visit the second name on the list." Elliot started driving. "Meanwhile," Kay continued, "I have to remind you we have absolutely nothing against Gaskell except he likes to ski, and he knows Bugarin, the chairlift operator. We can't be one hundred percent sure he's the one, although my gut is telling me he is."

"Yeah, all right, I'll cool my jets a little, but Kendra's still gone, and that little twerp is hiding something."

"The little twerp is taller than me," Kay replied with a faint chuckle, wondering why she also thought of him as small and insignificant at his six-feet stature. Must've been his demeanor. "And he might just be anxious, nothing more. Some people live their entire lives feeling like frauds and fearing that one day they'll be exposed, when in fact they've done nothing wrong.

Renaldo behaves like a chronic anxiety sufferer, but, on the flip side, that doesn't make him innocent either. It just makes it difficult to tell."

"I'll check his alibi," he said, dialing dispatch. "Hey, it's Elliot," he said, the moment the call was connected.

"Hey, Detectives, I was just about to call. I have the sheriff for you."

The line went dead for a moment, then after a click, Logan's low voice filled the silence in the SUV. "Sharp?"

"And Young too," Kay replied, entertained by how their last names sounded together. "What's up, Sheriff?"

"A new missing person report was filed just now. I took the report myself. Would you like to venture a guess who's gone missing now?"

Kay's heart skipped a beat. If the unsub had taken another girl, that meant Kendra was gone. "Mackenzie Trenton or Alana Keaney," she said, holding her breath, wishing it wasn't true.

"Nope," the sheriff replied. "Richard Gaskell is gone, out of all people. His mother filed it in person."

"What?"

"I almost had that reaction myself. He was last seen Thursday night, at about eight p.m."

"But that's the time Kendra was—"

"Exactly," the sheriff replied. "It confirms your suspicions, but it still isn't enough for a warrant. Still circumstantial." The line disconnected without warning, in typical Sheriff Logan style.

"Son of a bitch," Kay muttered. "Gaskell isn't missing... he's holed up somewhere, torturing that sweet girl. We should interview the mother, see if they have other properties. The unsub would go where he knows the environment."

"Roger that," Elliot said, taking the next turn right.

She ran a quick search in the SUV's system, and selected

the Gaskell residence address. Navigation displayed the directions on a map without voice assistance. It wasn't far. "Do you think she knows?"

"That her son might be a rapist and a killer? I seriously doubt that. Not many mothers can face reality about their children. That's my two cents' worth, but I'm no shrink."

She gave a wry laugh. "You're doing just fine. I'll call for Renaldo's alibi. Logan's news threw us off that trail." She was about to touch the screen, when another call came through, this time on her cell. It was from Dr. Whitmore.

"Hey, Doc," she greeted him. "What's up?"

"The second DNA sample wasn't in CODIS either, but there's a familial match to a convicted felon now deceased. He was shivved in prison ten years ago. He's your suspect's father. His name was Pedro Cristobal. Does that ring a bell?"

"Son of a bitch," Elliot said, flipping a U-turn that nearly tipped the SUV over. "He lied to us, played us like a friggin' fiddle."

"I take it that's a yes," Dr. Whitmore said, a smile clearly audible in his voice.

"A definite yes, Doc," Kay replied, still trying to connect the dots in her mind. What would someone as frail as Renaldo be doing raping and killing a young girl?

Homicidal teams existed, well-documented in criminology statistics; they weren't unheard of. In such killing partnerships, there were usually two different personalities, a leader and a weaker, more obedient follower, but it still didn't feel right to her. "One more thing, Doc. What was Pedro Cristobal convicted of?"

"Aggravated sexual assault."

"Thanks, Doc."

The call disconnected, leaving Kay to her thoughts for another minute until they reached Renaldo's house.

Renaldo was too weak; he'd be a liability to any strong, organized unsub, especially one who was discovering who he was through experimentation. No one likes to experiment with witnesses present.

Maybe that's why Renaldo had been left behind with Kendra. Perhaps Renaldo was himself an experiment, a failed and discarded one. Even if he had the right genes for it.

From less than ten yards away, Kay watched Renaldo zipping up a large duffel bag with a hasty move, then swearing under his breath when the zipper caught the edge of a garment and became stuck. He threw the half-zipped bag onto the back seat of his old Honda Accord, and dialed a number on his cell, while rushing back inside the house. In his frenzy, he didn't notice them, although the Ford Interceptor was stopped two cars behind the old gray sedan.

"Damn it to hell," he shouted seconds later when he came out of the house, carrying a few things he'd gathered. A jacket, a pair of running shoes, the charger for his phone. Then he threw everything in the back seat of the Honda and hopped behind the wheel, still holding the phone to his ear.

"Where the hell are you, man?" Kay heard him whisper breathlessly into the phone as she approached. "Cops were here today, asking me all kinds of questions. You know, about Jenna. Call me already 'cause I'm freaking out."

He was about to start the engine when Kay knocked against the half rolled-down window of his car.

"In a rush, aren't we?"

Startled, he stared at her with his mouth agape in disbelief, then lowered his head, defeated.

She grabbed his arm, and he offered no resistance. Opening the door, she pulled him out of the vehicle and slapped a pair of handcuffs on him. The contact with the cold metal made him twitch, but he didn't say anything.

"Rennie?" a woman called from the house. She was tall and slim, with dark hair loose on her shoulders. She wore a simple white shirt that had seen better days and a pair of sweatpants. Seeing Renaldo hauled away by Kay, she rushed to them, sobbing, holding her hand at her open mouth.

"Don't take my son! He hasn't done anything," she pleaded, grasping at Kay's arm. Elliot pushed her gently away.

"Step aside, ma'am." Then he grabbed Renaldo from Kay's grip and loaded him onto the back seat of the Interceptor.

Kay turned to the woman. Her thin lips were quivering. "You're his mother, I'm assuming."

"Yes," she replied, sniffling and wiping her tears with her fingers.

"You'll need to come with us too."

She took an instinctive step back. "Me?"

"Your son is underage, right?"

"He's only seventeen. He'll be eighteen next year in March."

"Legally, that makes him a minor, and you should be present during his questioning."

Her chin trembled badly. "What is this about?"

Kay looked at her with compassion. Her life was about to change, and not for the better. "The rape and murder of Jenna Jerrell."

As if scalded, the mother turned on her heel and rushed to the SUV, shouting angrily. "Did you do this?" She pounded with her fists against the back window of the Ford, then opened the door and slapped Renaldo over the head until Elliot clasped her wrists and held her arms still.

"Ma'am, you're not helping your son right now. Please follow us to the precinct in your own vehicle, and have some ID with you."

She wrapped her arms around her body, running her hands up and down as if freezing to the bone, although the sun was high and the air was warm, loaded with the scents of summer. Standing in place for a long moment, she watched them getting ready to leave.

Elliot had started the engine when Kay's cell rang. She didn't recognize the number, but it was local. Because of Renaldo's presence in the back seat, she got out of the SUV and took the call, holding the phone tightly against her ear.

"Detective Sharp? Hi, it's Mackenzie Trenton, Jenna's best friend. You said I should call if I think of anything."

Kay walked briskly away from the vehicle until she was out of earshot. "Yes, hi, Mackenzie. What do you have?"

"I just thought of something I didn't realize sooner or I didn't pay attention to. Kendra had recently become the subject of gossip too, but minor things, nothing serious. Not like Jenna."

"What kind of minor things? Do you remember some examples?" Kay rubbed her aching forehead with the tips of her fingers. Sometime in the past hour, the threatening cloud of a migraine had engulfed her head.

Mackenzie hesitated for a moment. "Like dating two guys at the same time," she laughed nervously. "This is high school, you know. It's not unheard of. And wearing her pants commando-style." Another moment of silence. "Um, there were whispers she'd had a complete Brazilian done. You know, waxing," she blurted in an uncomfortable whisper. "I didn't know if this means anything, but I remember now that's how it started with Jenna too. Innocent stuff at first, almost just for laughs... of course, if you're not the target of it. Then, I guess, it's not that funny." Her voice had turned somber, heavy under the threat of grief.

"Tell me about Richard Gaskell," Kay asked. "What kind of person is he?"

"He's okay, I guess. No one likes everyone, right?" Another nervous snicker. "He's the team quarterback, which makes him sort of a superstar, but he's a little harsh for my taste. Always hitting on girls, not always in a good way. Well, all the boys kinda hit on us all the time, but he's too serious about it. He doesn't have much of a sense of humor, I guess. He's too intense." She breathed loudly into the microphone as if tired after speaking so quickly.

"Could he have started the rumors about Jenna?"

"Who, Richard?" She scoffed. "No... he's too butch for that. The way the rumors were worded when I heard them first, and now that I know they weren't true, I promise you they were started by a girl, not a boy."

"What makes you so sure?"

"Boys are... simple." A snicker.

Kay couldn't refrain from smiling, amazed how Mackenzie had already discovered the secret to men's psychology, and she wasn't even of age yet. If she managed to remember her discovery throughout her life, she stood a great chance to find the elusive happiness in relationships that most women chased but never found.

Men *are* simple. Even the smartest of men would not bother with the intricacies of thought and speculation women enjoyed so much.

If a man would've wanted Jenna discredited, he would've probably whispered rumors to other men about blow jobs and hand jobs, about how many times she came during sex, and other such obscenities.

She thanked Mackenzie and ended the call, then joined Elliot in the SUV, wondering again who could've started the gossip attack on Jenna, and why. A girl made a lot more sense; the thought had crossed her mind before. But whom? There were several girls in Jenna's class she hadn't interviewed yet, and who might've been great candidates. Once the phone records came back, she'd know exactly whom to question.

The why, that was simple. Jealousy rose to the top of the list as motive for a slew of petty crimes committed by women. Statistically, jealousy ruled. It was at the top of the list, unchallenged, followed at a distance by more mundane reasons like money, drugs, anger, and so on.

Soon, they'd know, when the money trail behind that website was exposed.

FORTY-FIVE

INTERVIEW

Jealousy. A powerful motive.

But jealousy over whom? Jenna had a boyfriend at the time the smear attack had started. Tim Carter. Elliot had interviewed him and found him to be heartbroken over Jenna's death, blaming himself for abandoning her when she'd been cyberbullied, for believing those lies. The fact that Tim had been honest as a boyfriend albeit a misguided one, didn't mean some girl wasn't jealous over him.

Kay didn't remember high school fondly, although there had been good times too. It seemed that technology had warped the way kids interacted with one another. A bully no longer shoved someone against a wall or tripped them to take a fall and scrape a knee in a roar of merciless laughter. Bullies could be lethal, armed with social media, the internet, and the most dangerous of all words: "forward." Before social media, the wildfire of gossip took weeks to spread, because people actually had to meet with one another to talk about things. Rumors took longer to spread, and died after a while, forever forgotten, run out of fuel. These days, a rumor that landed on someone's social media page could be forwarded to thousands of others in a matter of seconds, and the digital footprint it left in cyberspace was permanent. All it took was one image, one link, or one comment to ruin a life forever.

Social media had empowered the bullies.

However, all cyberbullies left traces online, and she would find this one even if she had to peel away every layer of chitchat that filled these kids' lives with meaningless garbage, to get to the bottom if it.

That had to wait, though.

Kendra was still out there, and the second unsub was seated only a few feet away, in the interview room, looking like he was about to burst into tears under the unrelenting glare of his mother.

Standing behind the two-way mirror, Kay studied Renaldo in detail. He was pale and seemed to shiver every now and then. Following her instructions, the deputies had left the handcuffs on and chained them to the table. Every now and then, his shoulders heaved, burdened by long, shattered breaths. She would've loved to let him stew for a few hours, but Kendra didn't have the luxury of time.

She entered the interview room and sat across from Renaldo, placing the case file she'd brought on the scratched stainless-steel table with slow, deliberate moves. Mrs. Cristobal looked at her with terror in her swollen eyes. Her eyelids and nose were red, irritated by tears and frequent wiping. She held a tissue crumpled tightly in her hand and probably needed a fresh one.

Renaldo looked at her in passing, then away, toward the door, avoiding his mother just as he was avoiding Kay. His ink-stained fingers were steepled in front of him, a sign of self-confidence that didn't jibe with anything else in his demeanor.

Kay opened the case file slowly, pacing herself although she felt like rushing over to Renaldo and grabbing him by the shirt to shake him until he told her where Kendra was being held.

That would've gotten her nowhere in no time flat.

Instead, she pulled his ten card from the file and a photo of a condom wrapper, covered in black fingerprint dust, printed on letter-size paper with a glossy finish.

"I'm not asking you if you had sex with Jenna Jerrell right before she was killed," she said, speaking softly. "You see, we already have the evidence that puts you at the scene. Your right index print, taking the condom out of its wrapper. Your semen, which means your DNA, on the victim's cheek."

"She wanted it," Renaldo said. "She was cool with it."

His mother was holding her breath, covering her mouth with trembling fingers.

"Cool with it?" Kay asked calmly. "Was that before or after the Rohypnol one of you slipped in her drink?"

Mrs. Cristobal gasped and sprung to her feet, leaning over the table corner to smack her son over his head. "You're no son of mine! How many times did I tell you about consent and how to treat a girl? I bet it's that creep, Richard. That boy is trouble, I've always—"

"Shut up, Mom. You're ruining everything." He squeezed his eyelids shut, then lowered his head until he was able to bury his face into his shackled hands.

"Where is he now, huh? Do you think his posh parents will let him be chained to a table, like you?"

"Please sit down, ma'am." Kay pointed at the empty chair as sharply as she'd spoken. Mrs. Cristobal obeyed after throwing a quick apologetic glance. Kay turned her attention to Renaldo. "Do you really think she was cool with it, Renaldo?"

"I don't care what any of this says—" he gestured with his bound hands, cuffs and chain rattling against the table, trying to point at the photo, "she was willing."

"Are you sure?"

He scoffed and shrugged, staring at the door. Kay sat across from him, his mother at his right. The door at his left was the only direction he didn't seem afraid to look toward. "Everyone knew Jenna was a bit of a slut."

Mrs. Cristobal just glared at him, speechless. Kay opened the case file and went through several pages, pretending she was reading them carefully. "Was she?"

Renaldo's brow furrowed. "Look, I'm sorry she's dead, but she was just fine when we left."

Kay looked straight at him. "We?"

Flustered, he started to stutter. "I—I mean, me, I left, after we, um, yeah, and she was fine."

She picked up the photo of the condom wrapper. "It was a 'we,' Mr. Cristobal, not an 'I.' Someone you are so close with that he actually opens your condoms for you. See here?" She tapped the photo with her fingernail. Renaldo held his breath. "These are his fingerprints, not yours."

He lowered his head closer to his chained hands and ran them nervously across his face. "So what?"

A crooked smile fluttered on Kay's lips. "That's nice, to have friends like that. I mean, so close, you share everything. Even your girl. Did he bother to tell you he'd given her a roofie? Or you didn't know?"

His gaze darted at his mother for a brief moment, then at Kay, probably wondering if she could be trusted. "I didn't know she'd been roofied, I swear to God."

"Don't you dare," his mother whispered, pinning him under her fuming stare.

"I didn't know, I swear," he repeated, shaking his head.

"Yet he's close enough of a friend to open your condoms for you." She raised an eyebrow. "I don't know what I'd feel about a friend like that. You see, because Jenna had Rohypnol in her blood, legally she was raped. Even if she'd said yes, it's still rape. That's the law," she added, shrugging with mock indifference.

"But—but wait a minute, I didn't know! I really didn't." He tried to stand, but his chained hands forced him back on his seat. "Mom," he called, turning his pleading gaze toward her. The woman's lips were pressed tightly into a thin, uncompromising line. A tear found its way down her pale cheek, but she didn't say a word.

"As far as I'm concerned, I'm okay with you going to jail for fifteen years for Jenna's rape. And you know, cops will do anything to close their cases quickly, so I'll pin her murder on you too, because, legally, I have that right." Kay smiled, pretending to examine her fingernail.

Mrs. Cristobal started sobbing, pressing the tissue in her hand against her mouth as if to smother her wails.

"What? No," Renaldo said, trying again to stand and having to sit back down. "I didn't kill her. I told you, she was alive when I left."

"That doesn't matter, really. You see, let's say she took her own life after you left. She jumped off a cliff, and it was her own decision."

Renaldo nodded vigorously. "Yes, that's exactly what must've happened. She was depressed lately. Ask anyone."

Son of a bitch, Kay thought, the kid's words pissing her off to no end. The speed with which he'd say anything about Jenna, only to protect that piece of scum, Richard. "It still doesn't matter, because it was closely tied to the commission of a crime, her rape. The Rohypnol too, which is poisoning. So, essentially, the person who drugged her is legally her killer. Was that you?"

He shook his head so forcefully his hair bounced around his head. "No, that wasn't me, I told you." His dilated pupils were staring right into Kay's eyes. "I didn't know she'd been drugged until you told me."

"Then who should be cuffed here instead of you? If you didn't do it, you could walk out of here a free man."

A look of hope washed over Mrs. Cristobal's face. "Please, tell her."

He lowered his gaze for a moment, then looked up. The

expression on his face had morphed into something Kay hadn't seen before. "I want a lawyer," he said calmly, resting his cuffed hands one on top of the other.

Kay stood, struggling to contain her frustration. The weakling had an iron core buried deeply inside the deceptive appearances. "Where is Kendra?" she asked, looking away from them, standing three feet away from the door, about to leave.

"I asked for a lawyer," he replied coolly. "You're not supposed to ask me any more questions."

"I wasn't talking to you." Kay turned toward his mother. "Where would Richard have taken Kendra? You must know... something, anything that could lead us to her. If she dies before we get to her, it's on your son's head."

The woman squeezed her eyes shut, sniffling, her breaths shattered and raspy. "I heard them talking about the old Somerset hunting cabin, the one that's been locked in estate battles for years after John Somerset died."

Renaldo's fists found the table surface. "Shut up, Mom. You don't know what you're doing."

But Kay had already left. In the observation room, Elliot was waiting with a big grin on his face.

"We caught a break, partner. Deputy Farrell found Dwayne."

"Where the heck was he? Why did he run?"

"He didn't. He got a call that his four-year-old daughter had collapsed in daycare. He was at the hospital with her. She's going to be fine."

"Did he look at the photo arrays?"

Elliot's smile widened. "He picked Richard Gaskell without a moment's hesitation. Warrants are forthcoming."

FORTY-SIX

FOUND

Wildfire Ridge wore its stunning auburns and orange hues as the sun was rushing to meet the Pacific. First in a convoy of vehicles rushing toward the mountain with flashers off, Elliot's SUV headed straight for the chairlift terminal, while other units took various positions around the mountain.

"If Richard Gaskell is up there," Kay had instructed all available deputies, "I don't want him sneaking off that mountain and disappearing. He's got money, he's intelligent, resourceful, and he will attempt to flee. In ten hours, he could start living large in the Dominican Republic if we don't pay attention. He's to be considered extremely dangerous; he's killed before and will not hesitate to do so again if cornered." She looked at them, one by one, inviting questions. "All right. Deputy Farrell, take the Winter Lodge. Deputy Pickett, you drive around the mountain and take the foot of the trail to Blackwater River Falls. Deputy Leach, take the trail to Wildfire, where we found Jenna's body. If I were running off that mountain, that's the path I'd take." She'd turned to leave, but then remembered something. "No flashers, no sirens. If he sees us coming, he might kill Kendra."

Jimmy Bugarin was waiting for them at the terminal, smoking a stogie. The bluish, acrid smoke stung her nostrils as she approached in a rushed step.

"I've kept the lights off just like you said. You sure you want to ride this up in the dark? It's creepy."

"Yeah, we're sure, and once we're up there, shut it down," Elliot replied, shaking the man's hand. "Let's get going."

Bugarin went inside the terminal. Through the open door, Kay saw him turn a lever clockwise with a grunt. Rumbling and creaking as if it was about to fall apart, the chairlift was set in motion.

"Come on over here," Bugarin said, pointing at a section under the chairlift's bull wheel. Kay looked at the whirring guiding wheel above her head with suspicion. "Stand right there, by that sign, and let the chair come to you. When you feel it hit your legs, let yourself fall back onto it."

Elliot took her hand and she held on tightly, welcoming the strength steadying her as she took a seat on the moving chairlift. The moment her feet lost contact with the ground she felt dizzy for an instant and squeezed his hand tighter. Then she pulled away, instantly regretting it, but there was no turning back. He wasn't hers to hold hands with; he'd never been, and never would be. He belonged to someone else. Remembering that felt like a punch in the gut. He should've told her, long ago, before he'd started taking her out for dinner, mowing her lawn, or showing up on her doorstep in the morning to pick her up for work. That Miranda sure didn't know anything about any of that, or he would've been dead by now.

"Don't forget to lower the safety bar," Bugarin shouted behind them.

Elliot reached above their heads and lowered the safety bar. She grabbed it with both hands, holding on to it for dear life as the chairlift whirred into the deepening darkness. It felt surreal, dizzying, as if flying, wind whooshing though her hair. In the distance, the serrated cliffs of Wildfire still clung to the deep purples of the late dusk.

The safety bar moved under her hands, but she still held on.

"We're almost there," Elliot said. Reluctant, she let go. He pushed the bar above their heads, then his hand found hers and clasped it. "The ground will rise to meet your feet. When it does, jump ahead then move quickly to the left, to get out of the chair's way. I won't let go." She could hear the smile in his voice. "Never."

Still, when the ground pushed against her feet she startled, but his grip was firm, and she let him guide her to the side. "Whew," she said quietly, once they were out of the way. "I have to try this sometime, when I can see what's around."

Elliot typed a text quickly and the chairlift stopped whirring. From there, it was a ten-minute hike to the Somerset cabin. Kay remembered the place from when she was a kid about Kendra's age, and she hiked up there with Jacob. The old man Somerset hadn't been up there in a while, and some kids knew about it. She couldn't imagine why someone would want to spend any amount of time there. The cabin was barely standing. John Somerset was a trapper, rumored to have Native blood. He'd never taken to any of the local tribes; instead, he'd chosen to live a life of seclusion, hunting and trapping the old Pomoan way. When he died, his heirs were shocked to find several million dollars in the old man's accounts, and so the battle had begun over the inheritance.

It was completely dark when the cabin came into sight, a dark shadow against a dimly lit sky. A setting crescent moon barely contoured the cabin's shape. No sound came from inside, and the air didn't carry the smell of recent fire.

Weapon drawn, Kay approached the cabin slowly, carefully listening for any sound. On the other side of the small clearing, Elliot tiptoed through the tall grasses, keeping an eye on the back of the cabin.

She took out her flashlight, ready to shed some light on the interior. She remembered the cabin had a latch. Feeling her way along the door's edge with her fingers, she found it, locked. Pulling it slowly, she held the door with her foot, then released it quickly. It bounced open, creaking loudly, just as she remembered it would.

She turned on the flashlight and gasped at the harrowing sight.

Chained from the wall, Kendra had collapsed to her knees. Her head hung and her hair flowed over her bloodied, naked body. Bruises and dried blood covered every inch of her skin. She wasn't moving.

Kay cleared the room with precise and hurried movements, pointing her flashlight and gun at every corner, then shouted, "In here."

Holstering her weapon, she rushed by Kendra's side and felt for a pulse. It was there, barely noticeable and thready. Elliot came inside and lifted her body off the ground, so that Kay could release her wrists from the chain they'd been bound to. He set her gently on the small table, and took off his jacket to cover her body with. Kay cut the rope tied around her wrists and started massaging her hands, rubbing some heat into them.

"Call for EMS air," she said, feeling for her pulse again. She was frozen, still unconscious. "She won't last long; she's in shock. We need to warm her up." Kay wrapped her legs in her own jacket, shivering under the cold breeze after she took it off. It was barely forty-five degrees at night, up on Wildfire, even in the summer.

Then she started blowing warm air against the side of Kendra's neck, where the carotid arteries were close to the skin. Rubbing her hands together quickly to heat them up, she placed them on the other side of the girl's neck and on her chest, and kept blowing.

After a few minutes, Kendra moaned and opened her eyes.

The look in them was one of sheer panic, until Kay squeezed her hand and said, "I'm a cop. You're safe. We're taking you to the hospital."

Kendra closed her eyes. A tear escaped the corner of her eye and disappeared under Kay's fingers.

"Who did this to you?" Kay asked, continuing to warm up her neck as best she could.

Kendra moaned again, then whispered, "Richard Gaskell. He's a senior at my school."

"How about Renaldo? Was he here too?"

"N—no." She drifted away into unconsciousness. Kay feared she wouldn't last until help arrived. All she could do was keep fighting to warm her weakened body.

"We need an emergency airlift on Wildfire Ridge, at the old Somerset cabin," Elliot said into the phone, standing in front of the cabin. Then he listened intently, while his jaws clenched. "If you're not here faster than greased lightning, I'll make it my mission in life to see you writing parking tickets in Crooked Creek, Alaska, for the rest of your career," he said coldly, the tone of his voice matching the harshness of his words. "I don't care if he says he can't land here. Figure it out. Pilots are supposed to be smart, aren't they? Then he better not have me show him how it's done. Any half-decent Texas hog hunter would know how to land that chopper here. They should have a basket on a rope just in case." Another pause. "He better make it faster than that."

Elliot ended the call and rushed back inside. "They'll be here in ten minutes or so." Then he crouched by the old fireplace and started a fire, using old, dusty kindling he'd found in the cabin and some dry pine tree branches he'd picked up nearby. Within minutes, the fire warmed up the dreary cabin, and Kendra's face started to get some color.

About thirty minutes later, they watched the EMS chopper

taking off with Kendra onboard, lifting a whirl of leaves and dust in the air.

"Gaskell's gone, isn't he?" Kay said, as soon as her voice could cover the sound of the departing chopper.

"Damn right." Elliot kicked a small rock, sending it tumbling across the clearing. "He's been gone for a while. Left this girl here to die."

Kay's eyes stung under the threat of tears, maybe from frustration or powerlessness, or perhaps relief that they'd found Kendra alive. She couldn't tell, but it didn't matter, because they instantly dried once the glimmer of a new plan took shape in her mind. "I know just how to get that bastard to come out of the woodwork."

Elliot picked a long grass straw and bit on the tip of it with a wide grin. "Never had a doubt in my mind."

Smiling, she fished her phone out of her pocket and looked at the bars. Only two, but it would have to work. She retrieved a number from the phone's memory and called it on speaker.

"Barb? How would you like another exclusive?"

"Are you kidding me? Shoot," the reporter replied, not bothering to conceal her excitement. The sound of shuffled papers came across clearly. She was probably getting ready to take notes.

"Don't bother jotting things down. Record this call instead, because I need you to quote me word for word, and use my name as your source."

The shuffling stopped. "Whenever you're ready."

"In the death of Jenna Jerrell, we have one suspect in custody, Renaldo Cristobal, one of her schoolmates. The second suspect is still at large. As you well know, when there are multiple perpetrators, the one who collaborates with law enforcement first is the one who gets the deal. Mr. Cristobal is forthcoming and eager to help with the investigation. We are confident we'll bring this case to a close in the next twenty-four hours." She paused for a second. "Got that?"

"Sure did. I'll get it out in tonight's news. How about Kendra? Did you find her yet? People want to know."

Kay stared at the EMS helicopter's strobes disappearing in the night. "Not yet, but we're close. When we do, you'll be the first to know."

FORTY-SEVEN
MR. SHARP

Kay had fallen into a deep sleep that felt like a coma the moment her head had touched the pillow the night before. She woke with the first light of dawn, numb, wishing she'd pulled the curtains shut before going to bed. The sun shone through the sheers, its rays landing playfully on her face, luring her out of bed with the promise of a good day.

Stretching between the sheets with the deliberate moves of a lazy feline, she delayed the moment her feet would touch the cold floor, feeling around for her slippers. For a moment, she weighed her options, but then stood on the side of the bed and yawned.

She'd dreamed about something, the dream now a fuzzy and nonsensical memory about her flying weightlessly over Wildfire Ridge like Superwoman, her only propulsion the power of her thought and the strength in Elliot's grip.

Elliot.

Nope.

She wasn't going to think about him. Not today. Instead, she'd finish prepping the kitchen for the paint job she'd scheduled for Tuesday afternoon.

Stepping carefully over the paint-stained newspaper laid on the floors, she went into the kitchen and started the coffee maker, then ran through the motions of brewing a strong one. Within seconds, the mouthwatering aroma of French Vanilla filled the room, scaring away the last remnants of slumber.

Brushing her teeth and a quick, refreshing shower took her all of ten minutes while the coffee sat a little to darken. She filled her cup to the brim and proceeded to inspect the kitchen walls carefully, one patched hole at a time, coffee in hand like a professional contractor. She felt good about the job she'd done. Maybe it wasn't as perfect as it would've been if Jacob had held the putty knife, but with every patched hole she found healing.

Running her hand over an uneven section of the wall, she let out a long sigh; she'd grown dangerously close to finding peace. Her eyes veered toward the window, where the two willow trees stood tall, their leaves immobile in the still morning air. Maybe, for a while, Elliot could keep on mowing the back-yard if he wanted. For both Jacob and her, running the tractor over that stretch of grass between the willows was still a trigger, a painful reminder of the truths that should stay buried forever. And some lies she wished didn't, like her father's real identity.

She took a piece of sandpaper and ran it back and forth over the lumpy patch job she'd worked on the week before, stopping every few seconds to check if it was smooth enough. She loved the simplicity of the work, and how immersive it was. Her hands moved quickly, finishing the wall, while her mind roamed freely, wondering what secrets her father had taken with him to his grave, then asking herself whether Richard Gaskell would take the bait she'd laid out for him. What if he didn't? What if he was gone already?

A quick rap against the door, and Elliot's beaming face appeared in the window. Startled out of her wandering thoughts, she smiled, rubbing her hands together to shake off some of the putty dust. Her heart still swelled when she saw him; the discoveries of the past week had done little to change that, regardless of how illogical that was.

"Guess what the Marin County cops dragged in?" He paused for effect, while she tilted her head, still smiling, curious. "One Gavin Sharp. He's waiting for you at the precinct."

Her smile vanished, replaced immediately by a tension she felt in her shoulders and the back of her neck, stiffening her weary muscles in aching rigidity. Within minutes, she was dressed for work and ready to go.

The entire drive she was silent, and Elliot respected her choice, although he occasionally looked at her as if waiting for her to say something. She couldn't think of anything to say. Her past and present collided in her mind, thinking of all the questions she had for the real Gavin Sharp.

She was still silent when they arrived at the precinct and as he followed her to the observation room. Standing by the two-way mirror, she looked at Gavin Sharp with undisguised curiosity. Her father had chosen that particular man to steal an identity from. Understanding why would bring her closer to figuring out who her father really was.

The real Gavin Sharp was charismatic, just as she'd noticed looking at his DMV photo. He seemed familiar in a weird, sickening way, because he looked like her father, only better. Younger. Healthier. The man seated at the scratched metallic table with his arms crossed wasn't the boozer her father had been. He was fit, and took good care of himself. No saggy abdomen running over the line of his belt. No bloodshot eyes that barely stayed open. No bulldog jowls stained with liver spots and raspy from an overgrown stubble. No; this man's eyes were clear, his hair neatly trimmed, his demeanor one of slightly worried self-confidence.

She threw Elliot a quick glance. "You can watch if you'd like," she said, seeing how he wasn't going to follow her into the room. "It's not personal; he's just another perp." The brim of

Elliot's hat moved down a little, then back up in a silent nod. "Fact is, we can't prove the statutory rape charge; Jenna did a number on us when she used a nickname for him. I have to get a confession."

She entered the room and Gavin Sharp quickly stood, bowing his head in a greeting accompanied by a welcoming smile as if they were meeting at some fancy restaurant, not a police interrogation room with stained walls and stale air that stunk of sweat and fear.

"I'm Detective Kay Sharp," she said, waiting for the effect her last name was sure to have on the man.

"Oh." His smile widened. "Are we related?"

She shook her head, looking him straight in the eye. "It's a common name in California."

"Would've been nice."

"What?"

"To have a relative with the police, when there's a warrant out for my arrest."

"No such luck, Mr. Sharp. Have you been read your rights?"

"Yes."

"And you're waiving your right to counsel?"

He shrugged. "This is a big misunderstanding, really. I'm sure we'll work this out, you and me. Why get the lawyers involved?"

She opened the file she'd brought with her, a simple folder filled with several blank sheets of paper she'd snatched from the printer outside the room. "Statutory rape, in the case of Jenna Jerrell. You think you can work this charge out real quick?" The sarcasm in her voice seemed to wash past him like water over goose feathers.

He looked at her sheepishly and clasped his hands together on the table's dented surface. "You probably hear this a lot, but I had no idea she wasn't eighteen." His smile held steadily, maybe a little tense, and so did his gaze. "Someone as stunningly beautiful as you can understand this, I'm sure. I'm willing to bet a pretty penny that the men around you are willing to bend a rule or two just to steal a moment of your time."

Unbelievable. He was flirting with her, and he was good at it.

She flipped a page of the nonexistent case file. "I have in here that some years ago, someone stole your identity. Is that true, Mr. Sharp?"

He leaned back against the back of his chair and sighed. "Wow, this happened a long, long time ago. Why do you ask, after all these years?"

"Who was the man who stole your identity? Do you remember?"

He didn't reply; instead, he studied her with increased curiosity as if he was about to put two and two together.

"Let me tell you what this is about, Mr. Sharp," Kay continued. "There are several crimes that were committed in the past three decades, cases still open that have your name listed as a suspect. An aggravated assault," she pretended to read, "a couple of B&Es, a few robberies." She closed the file and set her hands on top. "A couple of those were investigated and it was proven you weren't the one responsible. We'd like to catch the man who is. For others, we don't know that you weren't the actual perpetrator. You might remember being questioned in some of these cases?"

His eyes widened and filled with worry. "No, I don't recall. Like you said, it's a very common name. Maybe it's a coincidence?"

"Or maybe the man who stole your identity committed these crimes. We'd like to interview him. Are you sure you don't recall who he is?"

He looked straight at her. "No, I never knew his real name. I just had things starting to happen around me, like these crimes you're talking about, but it wasn't me. Like taking a job and being told someone with my name had just quit the same job, but it wasn't a coincidence, because he'd given the same place of birth as mine. One time, someone had changed the address on my driver's license. Stuff like that, uncanny."

"All right," she said, frustrated she couldn't get anything out of him. He was telling the truth, though; she believed him. "One more thing left to discuss then, Mr. Sharp, and that's the statutory rape charge."

He nodded, tight-lipped.

"You see, I believe my colleagues were in a rush when they wrote the warrant. It should've been for soliciting a minor, which is by far a lesser charge, one that can be pleaded down to nothing, really."

He nodded again, interlacing his fingers and rubbing his thumbs nervously. "Jenna is so beautiful and smart and sensitive. I couldn't not talk to her. She's going through a very difficult time, and all she needed was a friend, someone who'd listen to her and try to make her smile. She's a wonderful young woman."

"Was."

"What?"

"Jenna was killed last week, on Tuesday."

He sprung to his feet and started to pace the room restlessly. "Oh, my goodness... I swear to you, I had nothing to do with that. I was wondering why she—" He cupped his mouth in his hand for a brief moment, then turned to face Kay. "I swear. On Tuesday, I was—"

"Don't care, Mr. Sharp. I know you didn't kill her. I know who did. Sit down, and let's finish this."

Visibly relieved, he pulled the chair and sat.

"During this investigation, we uncovered her relationship with you, and we know you two met in person on several occasions."

"Yes, we did."

"How old are you, Mr. Sharp?"

He cleared his voice before speaking and lowered his gaze. "I'm fifty-six. I'm sure you already knew that, and I know what you're going to say, but—"

"Do you?" Kay snapped. "Do you really know what I'm going to say?"

He shook his head and looked at her imploringly. "No, I don't. I'm so sorry, I shouldn't've said that. Please continue."

Kay sighed and stood, feeling the urge to put more distance between her and the pervert seated across from her. The thought of that man's hands touching Jenna revolted her, stirring up memories she didn't want fresh in her mind ever again.

Yet, just a few more months, and the relationship would've been legal, and modern society would've thought of the fifty-six-year-old man as a player and a lucky bastard instead of a pervert, for dating an eighteen-year-old girl. What difference a few months made. Or a few miles... other states had a lower age of consent, of seventeen or even sixteen in some. Was he really that unlucky? Or would he have had sex with Jenna even if she were fourteen years old, or twelve? Thankfully for the sake of her own peace of mind, she only had to enforce the law, not make such difficult judgment calls. That was a job for the courts.

"During said investigation, we have uncovered that you did far more than soliciting a minor over the internet. You actually had sex with a minor on several occasions." He started to shift in his seat as if bursting with the need to speak, but she stopped him with a raised hand. He froze in place with his mouth slightly agape. "We have uncovered a diary, in which Jenna wrote that she had told you she was of age, so you're off the hook if you had sex with her. Because you didn't know she was seventeen, did you, Mr. Sharp?"

"No, I didn't, I swear. And we only had sex four or five

times, not more. She wanted to come live with me in the city, but I didn't want that, not before she finished school, so people wouldn't come looking for her."

And with those few rushed words, he'd confessed to statutory rape. It felt good, knowing he'd pay for what he'd done, and he'd be registered as a sex offender. And yet, a thought kept bothering Kay as she wrapped up the interview.

The man seated in front of her was the only one who'd offered Jenna a bit of warmth in the past few months. In a predatory kind of way, but still. The ones who'd made her life a living hell were still out there, free to go about their business, undisturbed.

"Mr. Sharp, we're charging you with statutory rape and soliciting a minor. I strongly suggest you get a lawyer before saying anything else."

Stunned, he watched her leave the room, then started pounding on the door that closed behind her. "You fucking bitch! You had no right... I trusted you. Damn lyin' cops. Get me a lawyer!"

She listened for a moment, happy to know he wouldn't be out there looking for another underage girl to seduce, at least not for a while.

Elliot appeared from the observation room while Gavin Sharp was still yelling invectives through the closed door. "Should I go in there and teach him some manners?"

"Nah, partner, it's all good."

Except one thing she didn't want to talk about, not even with him.

Her father... who was he? And what had he done that had made him steal the identity of a slick city pervert like that? Did she have the courage to stare into that particular abyss?

FORTY-EIGHT
CONSCIENCE

The precinct was almost empty. Most deputies working on Sundays were out enforcing speed limits as waves of tourists moved up and down the coast to make the most of their week-end. Regardless, someone had just heated up Mexican food in the microwave, filling the air with the mouthwatering smell of fresh quesadilla de pollo.

Kay ignored the growling in her stomach and grabbed her keys from her desk. "Wanna visit with Doc Whitmore? I have a few questions, but they're not all case related. Then I'll have to stop for a bite to eat."

Elliot looked at her for a moment as if trying to figure out if she wanted him to tag along or she was just being polite. She didn't know either. "Sure." He held the door open and seemingly waited for her to remember they'd driven down to the precinct in his SUV, because she'd obviously forgotten. She couldn't hide a smile as she slid her keys into her pocket.

"You drive, partner."

She climbed into the SUV, wondering if what she was about to do could be a costly mistake. Maybe sleeping dogs were meant to let lie, and it was only a matter of strong willpower to

let the entire thing go. Who cared about her father's real identity, when it made no difference whatsoever? Or perhaps that's
why she couldn't think of anything else to do with her life than
being a cop. She needed to know.

A blue Lexus pulled in next to them, and the woman
behind the wheel waved at them. It was Kendra's mother. Elliot
walked over to the driver's side and shook her hand through the
rolled-down window, but she got out of the car and hugged him.
Kay walked over quickly, her heart pounding with fear that they
might've been too late.

"Is Kendra...?"

"Yes," Mrs. Flannagan said, letting Elliot go and crushing
her in a hug. "Thank you, Detective, you saved my little girl. I
wanted you to know just how grateful we both are. My
husband's still with her, in Redding, where they took her." She
pulled away just as Kay was getting uncomfortable. People
rarely hugged her; she didn't really enjoy physical closeness like
other women did.

Mrs. Flannagan took a step back and looked at Kay, then at
Elliot, with her hands clasped together in a pleading gesture.
"Please, find the bastard who did that to my little girl and make
him pay. Promise me, you will. She'll never be the same again,
my poor baby." She sniffled and ran her hand quickly over her
eyes. "But at least she's alive. We'll get her a therapist, anything
she needs. They're saying she'll make a full recovery, but she
was—" A sob rose in her chest, choking her. "Another hour, and
my baby would've been gone." She bit her lip, possibly in an
attempt to control her tears. "Promise me he'll pay."

"He will," Kay replied. "We won't stop until he's caught."

"What's that I'm hearing on the news, about poor Jenna.
There were two of them?"

"Not with Kendra, no." Kay squeezed the woman's hand. "I
promise you that."

On the short drive to the morgue, Kay wondered if they

could keep their word. Where was Richard Gaskell, and why wasn't he taking the bait?

"I would've expected Gaskell senior to land on our doorstep by now, with some stack of papers or another. A gag order, a planned surrender, anything to help with his son's situation. He should know a wanted fugitive is at risk of getting shot."

"The day's still young," Elliot replied, pulling into the morgue parking lot. "The news just hit the air last night. Not everyone is as fast as you are. Any faster, and you'd catch up to yesterday and go at it all over again."

She chuckled, entering the somber building. As always, Elliot's enthusiasm visibly waned as he walked through the glass doors.

The reception desk was empty, and the morgue was eerily silent. The light was on in the autopsy room, and Kay pushed the stainless-steel door and walked right through. Doc Whitmore looked up from a printout he was reading, holding it too close to his eyes, a sure indication the doctor needed to see the optometrist soon.

"Good morning, Doc." She walked over and gave the man a quick hug. Something from Mrs. Flannagan's intense emotion still tugged at her heart, or maybe the fear of what she was about to discover.

"What brings you here so early on a Sunday?" Doc Whitmore asked. "Not that I don't appreciate the company, because it gets lonely in here talking to myself."

"I need a favor, off the record," she asked, just as Elliot was coming into the autopsy room, probably relieved to see both exam tables were empty.

"Sure, anything I can help with, I'd be happy to." Doc Whitmore looked at her above the rim of his glasses.

"My DNA is in your database, for crime scene exclusions and such."

"That's correct."

"Well, I'd like you to run it through CODIS, and look for familial matches."

"Oh." The doctor stood and stared at her through the lenses this time. "What am I looking for?" He tilted his head a little and scratched his hair right above the left ear. "I believe I already know, but I can't assume. Better said, I shouldn't."

"My father. Maybe I can find out who he really was," she scoffed bitterly. "He wasn't Gavin Sharp, that's for damn sure."

"All right," he said, and started typing into his CODIS computer. Moments later, the search was running. "I don't believe it will take that long. You might remember from your days in the FBI, that these databases search by county, then by state. Since he was local, I'd estimate a couple of hours, not more."

"Thank you, Doc, I appreciate it. And you'll keep this on the down low?"

"I see no reason why not."

She placed a quick kiss on his cheek and turned to leave, but he said, "Not so fast, young lady. I got some more results for you two."

Kay's mood shifted, leaving the darkness of her troubled past behind. Elliot drew closer, his interest piqued. Doc Whitmore grabbed the remote and clicked it. The TV came to life, displaying a photo of Jenna's face. A laceration ran across her cheek, from her right temple to almost the tip of her nose.

The medical examiner pointed at the laceration with the tip of his finger. "The trace substance in the laceration on Jenna's face, that was pink nail polish with glitter. It was the glitter that caught my attention, but then the mass spectrograph found traces of resin, ethyl acetate, benzophenone, and mica. That last one was the glitter. The color was pink, CL two forty-three, that matched the fingernail found at the scene, but didn't match Jenna's shade."

A moment of deep silence engulfed the room. The case

wasn't over yet, and it still wouldn't be, even if they found and arrested Richard Gaskell. Something else had happened to Jenna while she was up there on Wildfire Ridge.

Kay looked at Elliot, then at Doc Whitmore. "The hair fibers too, and the pink hair clip, those point to a female unsub, and now the nail polish in her wounds. There was a shoeprint too that didn't match our narrative."

Doc Whitmore flipped through some images on the screen, until he found the crime scene photo he was looking for. "There, the athletic shoeprint that came after Jenna's Converse." The easily recognizable Converse pattern was slightly obscured by another shoeprint, a woman's size. "It's a Nike, by the way, a Streetgato, to be exact."

"It was right there, in front of us, but we wouldn't see it, because of the rape and the semen," Kay muttered. Turning to Elliot, she said, "Come on, partner, we have a killer to catch. Any news of those phone records?"

He checked his email quickly. "Nothing yet."

"Then we have to do this the old-fashioned way. Beat the pavement."

They were almost at the stainless-steel doors when the CODIS computer chimed. Kay froze in her tracks for a moment, then walked back to the screen.

"We have a match," Doc Whitmore asked, turning to face her and blocking the screen with his back. His voice was gentle and riddled with concern, like a parent's. His hand squeezed her shoulder while a frown ridged his forehead. "Are you sure you want to know this?"

Her breath caught. "Yes, Doc, I'm sure. I have to know who he is."

He stepped aside, allowing her to read the screen. A few feet away, Elliot's expression was one of steeled support.

She read the information quickly, her eyes rushing across

the familiar database fields. "Jonas Solomon Castigan," she whispered, "that's who my father really is."

But the name didn't tell her the whole story. Reading about him, she realized she'd already known who her father was. A brute. A killer.

Three years before Kay had been born, Jonas Solomon Castigan had been arrested for the fourth time, for the murder of his battered wife and two small children, two little girls ages four and seven. The dates of death were several days after the incident report; at the time of the arrest, he'd been charged with domestic abuse, assault, and battery. Somehow, he'd managed to post bail and had since vanished. The warrants had been changed to murder in all three counts, after his wife and little girls succumbed to their injuries. And no one had seen him since.

Heart pounding in her chest, she stared at the screen, speechless, lost in a trance, until she felt Doc Whitmore's hand squeezing her shoulder.

She'd learned nothing new, except a name that didn't mean anything to her. If she hadn't pulled that trigger eighteen years ago, another woman and her two children would've probably shared that same fate.

With a quick, lopsided smile, she looked at Doc Whitmore before deleting the search. He nodded. She clicked the mouse button, and the screen cleared.

And with it, whatever remained of her guilty conscience.

FORTY-NINE
SPILLED

Kay had spent the entire day on Sunday pressing telecom providers to send the records she'd requested. It being a day off for most people, she didn't achieve anything but to have left several messages in an uncompromising tone of voice, and aggravate a few others. The best she could hope for was tomorrow, by lunch at the latest. She'd heard that before, through Denise Farrell, and they'd already broken that promise.

Frustrated and exhausted after what had proven to be an emotional rollercoaster of a week, she declined Elliot's invitation to dinner, wondering how come his Miranda was putting up with those kind of absences from home. But it wasn't any of her business what that woman did or didn't do; the simple fact that she existed had thrown everything off track.

Had it really been on a track? She and Elliot? Or was it all in her imagination? How could she have gotten her signals crossed so badly? Wishful thinking, that must've been it. The way she felt when he touched her hand. The way he looked at her and smiled. The heart-swelling closeness she'd felt whenever he was near.

"Motivated perception," she mumbled, kicking off her shoes

in her deserted kitchen and turning on the lights. *That's what it was, nothing else*, she told herself, thinking she'd lost nothing, because she'd had nothing to begin with, just misinterpreted friendship from her partner. Then why did she feel an unbearable burden of sadness that weighed on her chest until she couldn't breathe?

Jacob was out on one of his regular dates with his girlfriend, a young woman who was going to become his wife if he knew what was good for him. He was head over heels for her, but, in typical macho fashion, didn't stop to acknowledge it and count his blessings. He'd probably be gone for the rest of the evening, a good opportunity to get something done in that kitchen. Like painting it.

Eyeing the patched walls with the fixed stare of a predator ready to pounce, she wondered if she had it in her to finish it by herself, instead of waiting for Jacob. He'd taken the afternoon off on Tuesday to help her, but what was she supposed to do? Watch TV?

She changed into the painter's outfit, the stained T-shirt and matching shorts, then brought the paint roller kit she'd picked up at the hardware store where Renaldo used to work. After laying everything out neatly on the kitchen table, she grabbed the gallon of lemon meringue yellow latex with a matte finish, and struggled a little to get the lid open with the putty knife. Then she stirred the paint thoroughly, per the precise instructions of Renaldo's former boss, old Mr. Harry's Hardware Store himself.

Careful not to drop the heavy paint bucket, she tilted it slightly and poured some paint into the tray. Then she wiped the bucket rim and put the lid back on. Next she rotated the paint roller thoroughly, and tried her hand on a section of wall that would soon be covered by the fridge. Just in case she got it wrong.

The door swung open behind her, but she didn't react,

thinking it was Jacob. "Just in time to get dirty," she quipped, admiring her handiwork.

"Just in time to get something straight, bitch. No way Rennie's snitching on me."

The paint roller dropped from her hand, clattering on the floor and sending droplets of lemon meringue yellow on her legs.

Startled, she turned on her heel to find herself staring down the barrel of a gun. Richard Gaskell grinned at her with a lascivious yet hate-filled look in his eyes. She could feel his lewd, sticky stare traveling up and down her body, her bare legs, her cleavage.

Instinctively, she felt her side for her weapon, but it wasn't there. She'd put it in the drawer as she always did when she got home.

"Yeah, nice try. Don't you think you and I should have a talk?" He gestured with the gun toward a chair. Kay continued to stand, calculating her moves. "Sit," he shouted.

Kay thrust her chin forward in a gesture of open defiance she was sure the emerging power rapist wouldn't tolerate. "Are you ready for the chair, Richard? Because that's what you're getting for killing a cop. No lawyer in the world can save you from that. Not even your daddy."

A glimmer of fear dilated his pupils. The hand holding the gun hesitated a little. Kay seized the opportunity and lunged, grabbing his right arm with both her hands and pushing it up, to get the gun pointed at the ceiling instead of her chest.

A football player, Richard was much stronger and taller than her. He grabbed her hair with his left hand and at the same time his knee found her stomach. Her arms flailed as she fell, taking down the putty knife and bucket of paint, sending them clattering to the floor. The lid came off and lemon meringue yellow spilled in a gushing river of latex, covering the newspapers she'd set down.

She landed hard on her side and curled in a ball with pain, gasping for air. Inches away from her face, Richard's feet almost touched the fallen putty knife. Coughing, she wriggled closer to the knife and grabbed it, holding it tight and hiding it under her body.

He grabbed her arm and pulled up. She let herself weigh heavy, inert. "Get up," he commanded.

When she didn't obey, he raised his right foot to step aside or kick her into compliance, but she was ready. Lightning fast, she drove the putty knife straight into the Achilles tendon of his left foot.

He screamed and fell to the ground splashing and slipping in the spilled paint, shouting disarticulated oaths in a broken, raspy voice and holding his ankle with both his hands. His fingers quickly took the color of the blood dripping from his wound. Near where he writhed in pain, lemon meringue yellow borrowed shades of crimson red.

The gun had slid under the table, and Kay didn't hesitate. She crawled under there and grabbed the weapon, then pointed it at Richard, pushing herself farther away from him with her feet. When she could finally stand, she walked over to him, careful not to slip and fall on the slick surface.

The pain in her stomach had ebbed to a dull throb, and she held her arm over her belly as if that could soothe it somehow. Looking at Richard, at the size of his biceps, she was astonished she'd managed to bring him down.

I must've been crazy, or something, she thought, realizing that it could've gone entirely differently if he'd been a fraction of a second faster in his reactions.

She weighed her options. If she pulled the trigger, no one would ever doubt her call. She would be cleared in the shooting of a wanted fugitive and murder suspect who'd broken into her home without anyone giving it a moment's thought. Only she'd know differently.

"Shoot me," he said, his voice broken with tears and throaty from his earlier pained screams. "What the hell are you waiting for?"

She grinned. "You'll do fine in jail, Richard, don't worry. It will take you a year or twenty, but you'll get the hang of it. They love quarterbacks in there."

Taking a step closer, she pistol-whipped Richard hard. He fell unconscious in the puddle of bloodstained latex at her feet. "And that's for spilling my paint, you son of a bitch."

FIFTY

TRACE

Richard Gaskell wore a charcoal suit with a white shirt and a blue tie. His left foot was bandaged and elevated on a chair, immobilized in an air cast that caught his pant leg. His hair fell in disarray on his ridged forehead, while his thick eyebrows converged above his nose at an angle, reminding Kay of bird wings in flight drawn by a preschooler.

By his side was another man in a high-priced suit, this one older, shorter, and bulkier, with a menacing look in his beady eyes and an expensive leather briefcase laid out in front of him.

As usual, Kay studied the suspect's demeanor before entering the interview room, preparing her strategy, trying to get a read on the suspect's state of mind. There would be tension in that room. Hard feelings. She'd wounded him the night before, the cut to his Achilles tendon requiring surgery that had lasted well into the hours of the morning.

Yet they were there, most probably against medical advice, eager to answer whatever questions Kay had and make the "misunderstanding go away," in Gaskell's own words. Kay shook her head; another one of those misunderstandings that would be easy to clear, at least in the suspect's opinion.

Not so fast.

She took a fresh cup of coffee from Elliot's hand and thanked him. "Could you please follow up on the website money trail and those phone records, while I wrestle with them for a while?"

"You got it," he replied, then disappeared. He'd been increasingly unreadable lately, quieter, his usual smile a rare sight. It wasn't her fault if things got a little awkward between them after her visit to his place. She wasn't the one hiding a relationship.

She grabbed the two case files she'd placed on the printer table and walked into the interview room with a spring in her step. The air, usually stale and stenchy, now reeked of expensive aftershave in an amalgam of smells that didn't go well together. The lawyer's forehead was covered in tiny beads of sweat. For a moment, she thought of lowering the temperature setting in there. On second thoughts, she just took a seat across from the two men and clasped her hands together on top of the two thick manila folders.

"Mr. Gaskell, thank you for coming in today."

"Abraham Ackerman representing Mr. Gaskell," the lawyer said, extending a chubby hand and half-standing from his seat. She pretended not to notice it, fearing it might've been just as sweaty as the rest of the defense attorney.

The attorney sat with a quick sigh. "My client wishes to clarify several things."

"Does he wish to make a formal statement?"

One moment of hesitation. "Not at this time."

"Then, why don't you let me ask your client a few questions?"

Ackerman pressed his thin lips together for a moment, making them disappear. "Please proceed."

"Mr. Gaskell, witnesses place you with Jenna Jerrell on the

evening she was killed. Specifically, at the Alpine Subs restaurant." She paused.

Gaskell looked straight at her, unperturbed.

"Is there a question you'd like to ask?" Ackerman touched the knot of his tie briefly, probably wishing he could loosen it a bit.

Kay swallowed an oath. Fourteen hours after breaking into her house, Gaskell was an entirely different person. Reassured, calm, empowered by the thousand-an-hour attorney by his side, probably the best legal defense Daddy's money and relationships could buy.

"We found two condom wrappers bearing your fingerprints up on Wildfire Ridge. Your semen was found on the victim. Please provide an account of what happened last Tuesday, starting with when you called Jenna and asked her out."

The attorney whispered something in Gaskell's ear. The young man nodded, the frown on his forehead deepening. Then he crossed his arms at his chest and waited silently.

"My client is only willing to answer questions regarding the condom wrappers found on Wildfire Ridge."

Kay nodded. "Please, answer this question, then. Were you up on Wildfire Ridge with Jenna Jerrell and Renaldo Cristobal?"

Ackerman touched Gaskell's arm, just as he spoke. "Yes, we were up there, and yes, we had sex. Consensual sex, to be clear. Your witness can confirm we had sandwiches together before that, and she was there willingly, having a good time."

"Was it at Alpine Subs where you drugged Jenna with Rohypnol?"

The two men brought their heads together for a brief moment, whispering something Kay couldn't decipher. "I wasn't aware that Jenna had been drugged with Rohypnol or any other drug," Richard replied.

"What happened after you had sex with Jenna?"

"I left. She was very much alive and wanted to stay some more up on the mountain. I can't be held accountable for what other people did after I left."

"Actually, you can. Forensics has determined beyond any reasonable doubt that the so-called consensual sex was, in fact, rape. The law stipulates that consent cannot be obtained or implied when the victim had been drugged with a date-rape drug. Furthermore, the sex was violent, causing bruising and lacerations, as documented by the medical examiner in his report."

Gaskell snickered and shrugged. "Some girls like it rough."

Kay clenched her jaw for a brief moment. "As such, her death is considered to have happened during the commission of a crime, inculpating you, her rapist, for her murder. Ask your lawyer."

There was worry in Gaskell's eyes as he leaned toward Ackerman and the whispering resumed.

"Detective, you know very well all this sexual assault business is circumstantial at best and won't hold in court. This particular victim's compromised reputation will make that job really easy for me. No jury will believe the rape allegation on which you're basing your murder charge."

Kay felt dizzy for a brief moment, seeing her entire case fall to shreds right before her eyes. She needed solid evidence, like traces of Rohypnol on Gaskell's clothing. The search warrant had been filed for the Gaskell residence and Richard's vehicle. Until then, she had Kendra.

"Your client also kidnapped, raped, and tortured another one of his schoolmates."

"I resent the implication," the attorney said.

"What implication?"

"When you said, another. You're implying he kidnapped, raped, and tortured Jenna Jerrell. My client did no such thing."

"Well, your client will be charged with it, nevertheless.

We'll let the jury decide. I've been told that if the victim was given Rohypnol, and she went with the two boys on the mountain while being drugged, that could be construed as kidnapping. You know, the issue of consent and all that."

"You can't prove my client was in possession of Rohypnol or slipped the victim the drug."

Gaskell touched his lawyer's arm. Some more whispering, while the lawyer's jowls moved quickly, partly hidden behind the hand he'd raised to cover his mouth. When he straightened his back, he seemed a little less confident.

"Then, there's the issue of assaulting a police officer in her own home," Kay said softly, a flicker of a smile touching her eyes.

"There was no such assault," the lawyer replied coldly. "My client was invited into the home, when he reached out to the lead detective in the case to discuss his surrender. The weapon he carried is registered to his name and wasn't used in said assault. There's no evidence of forced entry."

Stunned for a moment, Kay gasped. It was preposterous. The nerve of that man, of Richard Gaskell himself. He stood there, staring straight at her, playing with his keychain. After the interview was over, he'd walk out of there and he'd have the time to destroy whatever evidence still remained of the night on Wildfire Ridge. Within hours, he'd be arraigned, and bail already posted, while her search warrant could still take a while.

The attorney smiled and closed his briefcase. "If there isn't anything else, we're leaving."

She laughed, staring Gaskell straight in the eye. He flinched. "No, you're not," Kay replied. "I'm not putting your client up for arraignment yet; we have the right to hold him for forty-eight hours before arraigning him, and we're doing just that. He's staying put."

"Detective," the lawyer shouted, springing to his feet, out of breath and turning a dark shade of purple foreboding of future cardiovascular problems.

"You decided to play this like we're in the twilight zone. Well, now we are. Enjoy your stay."

A knock from behind the two-way mirror got her attention. She stood and took her case files with her, then tuned halfway toward Ackerman. "A rape charge can be pleaded down to a year or two, Counselor, but a murder charge can't. Your client is looking at hard time in a maximum-security prison. I suggest you tell him it's in his best interest to collaborate before Renaldo Cristobal does." She grinned. "Something to think of over the next forty-eight hours. That boy might be the smartest of the two after all."

There was no response, just the same arrogant demeanor on Gaskell, although his façade was starting to crack at the seams.

She left the interview room and closed the door behind her gently, although she would've wanted to slam that door hard enough to rattle the walls and with them, Gaskell's arrogance.

The moment she walked into the observation room, her gaze locked with Logan's. He wasn't pleased.

"I told you, Detective, kid gloves with this perp."

"Sheriff, I don't believe we have much of a choice here. He's a lying sack of—"

He scoffed. "Of course, he is. How different would our jobs be if perps only told the truth?" A quick bout of sarcastic laughter followed his comment.

"Boss, if we can't get Renaldo to cop to the rape, and we can't find any evidence of Rohypnol on Gaskell's clothes, we can't charge him with anything on Jenna Jerrell. That girl won't get the justice she deserves."

"Twenty-four hours," Logan said, checking his watch, "starting now. Not a minute more. And stop using the media as you see fit, without running it by me first. Is it true you promised Barb Foster you'd notify her when you found Kendra?"

She bit her lip. "I completely forgot, but yes, I did promise her that. I'll fix it."

"I think you fixed enough for one day, Sharp. An entire team can't mop the shards you leave in your wake. Get me the evidence we're missing and close this murder case already. People are starting to wonder what the heck we're doing here. I've been getting calls from the district attorney every day, and he's not asking about my health."

"Yes, sir," she replied, standing to the side so that Logan could leave the small observation room without brushing against her. The air smelled of stale cigars in his wake.

Of stale cigars and defeat.

She wished she could wipe the arrogant little smirk off Gaskell's lips, but knew she couldn't. Not with so many questions unanswered, most of which pointed to a woman being involved in this mess somehow. A woman with long blonde hair, pink nail polish, and a size eight athletic shoe.

Leaving the observation room with a spring in her step, she bumped into Elliot. "Sorry," she mumbled, hiding the fire that lit her cheeks. "We're done here... let these two stew for a while."

"How did it go?" A flicker of the same secret amusement lit Elliot's eyes, but his face remained serious.

"Ugh," she groaned, "it drives me crazy he's going to skate the rape charge for Jenna, and with it, the murder charge too. We're still not sure what happened up there on Wildfire, and who the woman was—"

"What woman?"

"The one who left the hair strands and the pink nail polish on Jenna's body. The footprints that came after Jenna's Converse."

"This might help," he said, handing her the report he was holding.

She read it quickly in the dim light. It was issued by the Northern California Computer Crimes Task Force (NC3TF). They had traced the money behind the website that had ruined Jenna's life. Tracing a series of maneuvers worthy of a mobster involving PayPal and prepaid credit cards, they had identified the email address behind the originating source of funds, and that email was registered to Alana Keaney.

FIFTY-ONE
JEALOUSY

Alana Keaney, Jenna's friend, the one in whose arms poor Jenna had found solace.

Seated in Elliot's SUV as it sped toward the Keaney residence, Kay was fuming. The crime in itself, the cyberbullying, was bad enough as it was. But still pretending she was Jenna's friend and taking in her pain, her tears, that was pathological. Sadism, pure and simple. That girl got off on Jenna's suffering and came back for more of it, over and over, not getting enough.

NC3TF had confirmed that the nude images used for Jenna's site were stock photos, but Kay didn't care. She was still going to throw the book at that sadistic little bitch.

And still she believed there was more about Jenna's death than she'd been able to uncover. That's why she'd refused Logan's offer to take backup and arrest Alana. Instead, she wanted to go at it a different way.

"What if there's more to this?" Kay asked, shooting Elliot a quick look. He was focused on the road ahead, weaving through traffic quickly with the flashers on. "And why did she do it? They both had boyfriends, right? So, that means jealousy is out as motive..." Kay bit the tip of her finger, thinking. The pieces of the puzzle weren't lining up as neatly as she would've liked.

"Maybe," Elliot replied. "Sometimes people become jealous over things that don't matter or don't really exist. Over assumptions, let's say."

"What do you mean?"

"I mean, things are rarely what they seem. People imagine things and start believing them. Then motive builds off of that."

"Okay, that speaks to motive, perhaps. But I'm afraid there's more."

Elliot shot her a quick glance. "Like what?"

"Like rape by proxy," Kay sighed and grabbed the door handle as Elliot took a turn fast onto Alana's street. "I'm thinking what if Alana instigated Gaskell to rape Jenna? You've seen him... all you have to do is point him in the right direction and pull the trigger. He'd go, especially if he believed all that gossip about Jenna."

Surprised, Elliot looked at her again as he pulled by the curb.

"Just imagine, Jenna's saying no to him, and he believes she's sleeping with everyone but won't sleep with him. That must've set him off big time." She grabbed the door handle, ready to get out of the car. "We need those phone records like we need air."

"The carriers said it's going to happen today," Elliot said in a lower voice, catching up with her on the Keaney driveway. "With text messaging and all that."

"I sure hope so," Kay whispered, ringing the doorbell. "It's five already. Keep your eyes on that inbox please, maybe we get lucky. I need an ace or two up my sleeve to prove she set Jenna up to be raped."

Alana opened the door widely and froze when she recognized them. She wore a black leather miniskirt with a zipper in the front, and a white lacy see-through T-shirt over a sleeveless top barely larger than a sports bra. Countless thin silver chains hung from her neck, and bangles adorned both her wrists. She seemed ready to go out, wearing strappy sandals on three-inch heels and clutching a small matching purse.

"May we come inside?" Kay asked, showing her badge with a quick move.

"I've got to go, don't have time for this," Alana said.

"And I'm afraid this can't wait, and it would be better for everyone involved to have this conversation inside." Kay took a step forward, but she didn't budge.

"It's either here, on your own couch, or back at the station, in cuffs," Elliot said coldly.

She rolled her eyes, chewing gum loudly. "Jeez... you need to chill some. Okay, come in."

"Who is it?" Alexandria called in a weak voice.

As they entered, the woman came into Kay's sight, lounged on the sofa in a white terry bathrobe by a coffee table where an empty glass and an almost empty bottle of Cabernet told her story. The curtains were almost completely closed, keeping the living room immersed in a filtered light, probably the only kind her hangover could handle.

Merciless, Kay reached for the light switch and turned it on. Alexandria stood, blinking and shielding her squinting eyes with her hand. There was a slight tremble in her fingers.

Alana stood by the sofa with her hands propped on her hips. "Can we be through with it, already?"

Elliot moved closer to the door, probably in case she wanted to bolt, although on those heels she probably wouldn't get too far.

"Your daughter is underage, correct?" Kay asked.

"Yes." Alexandria licked her dry, cracked lips, looking around the room for something. She tightened the robe sash around her waist, then walked over to the fridge barefoot and got herself a can of Coke. She popped the top and drank a good portion of it thirstily, then returned to the sofa and sat, leaning her forehead into the palm of her hand. "What's this about?"

"We have made two arrests in Jenna Jerrell's rape and murder case."

"Yes, we heard it on the news," Alexandria said, deciding to stand after all. She walked into the bathroom quickly. "Excuse me for a moment, I'll be right back."

Behind the closed door, Kay heard the water running.

"Okay, ask me what you wanna ask me so I can go," Alana said, pacing the living room like a caged animal.

"Let's wait for your mom." Last thing Kay needed was some smartass attorney to claim she'd interrogated a minor suspect without a parent present.

When Alexandria came out of the bathroom, her face was red as if it had been wiped energetically with a towel. Strands of her disheveled hair were still moist where they'd touched her face.

"You were saying you made some arrests, that's great," Alexandria said, smiling politely. "What's that have to do with my daughter?"

"Both Renaldo Cristobal and Richard Gaskell are attempting to plead their charges down. In that process, they're making sworn statements, and some pertain to your daughter's involvement in this case."

Alana clacked her heels against the hardwood, walking over to Kay. She stopped a couple of feet in front of her with her hands propped on her hips. "What involvement? I didn't do anything."

Kay ignored her and stepped to the side, so she'd have a direct line of sight with her mother. "Seems that Alana has been instigating them, dropping words in Richard Gaskell's ear about how approachable Jenna was and how much she liked sex."

The woman's jaw dropped as she turned to glare at her daughter. "Alana?"

"I didn't do this, Mom," the girl said, her voice a few notes higher than her usual pitch. "I was an idiot, okay, and just repeated what I heard, you know, other people were saying about her. But I *never* told those guys to rape her. You have to believe me," she said, her pitch climbing even higher as she looked at Elliot, then at Kay.

Elliot was scrolling through something on his phone and seemed completely absorbed by what he was doing.

"I find that very hard to believe, but that doesn't matter." Kay shrugged and feigned indifference. "It's the evidence that really matters, not any given cop's opinion. And we traced the IP of the computer where those messages originated from. They came from here," she bluffed, holding her gaze steady and hoping it would stick.

Panic washed over Alana's face, leaving behind it a trail of deathly pallor that surfaced through her makeup.

"Why?" Kay asked gently. She had her confirmation. Somewhere, buried in mountains of data, was the proof that Alana had set Jenna up to be raped.

Alana started crying, her sobs lacking sincerity. "I was stupid, that's why. She was eyeing my boyfriend, and I didn't want to lose him."

"We also traced the website you so generously built for Jenna. The money came from your account," Kay continued calmly.

Alexandria's eyebrows shot up. "The, um, adult one with Jenna's naked photos? That website?"

Kay smiled and turned to Alana. "How about Kendra's website? When's that coming out?"

Alexandria approached and stared Kay down. "My daughter won't be answering any more questions without a lawyer present." In a gesture of defiance, Alexandria threw her long hair over her shoulder. It flew in wavy, silky strands, about the same length as the hair fibers found on Jenna's body, and exposed a pale blue hair clip shaped like a butterfly.

Kay's breath caught in her chest. Her eyes found Alexandria's fingernails. They were painted in pink, glittery nail polish, the type she would've expected a teenager to wear. Alana's nails were done a deep shade of purple.

In a split second, she took inventory of the remaining pieces of evidence, until then unexplained. But it was all there, and it had been, right in front of her eyes, since she'd questioned Alana the first time. Only it made absolutely no sense at all. Why would Alana's mother have climbed on Wildfire Ridge to kill Jenna after she'd been assaulted?

"Well, I'll be damned," Elliot muttered, staring at the screen of his phone. "You can't beat this with a stick, no matter how long."

Kay looked at him and saw he was turning beet red under her gaze. "What's wrong?"

He stared at her wide-eyed, in a visible impasse, his cheeks flushing even more. She walked over and reached for the phone. He hesitated a little, but she gestured her impatience with her fingers, and he caved.

The phone records had been delivered to Elliot's email, neatly highlighted where the content had investigative relevance. NC3TF had done one hell of a job screening through and synthesizing hundreds of pages of content. Their notes included common location histories for the subpoenaed phone numbers.

Leaning against the wall for a moment, she scrolled quickly through a few pages, then returned to the one Elliot was reviewing, still open in the background. The photos attached to the chat transcript put a faint, furtive smirk on her face. She placed the phone back into Elliot's hand with a straight face and a glimmer of amusement in her eyes.

"Nothing to worry about," she said to the two women who

had drawn closer together. Alexandria had wrapped her arm around Alana's shoulders. "Your daughter will be charged with some minor felonies. Distribution of child porn, to start."

"Those photos aren't Jenna's," Alana shouted. "You can't do this to me."

Kay grinned. "Sure, I can. On the website you built, you're stating that they are. Until we sort this out, you're coming with us. Then there are two counts of instigating a violent act. Ooh, I have to remember to mention that to the boys' defense teams. It's called discovery, you know. I *have* to do that."

"Don't worry, sweetie." Alexandria squeezed her daughter tightly. "We'll get you a good lawyer. It's just misguided thinking, a childish prank, nothing else," she added, looking at Kay pleadingly.

Alana turned and buried her face in her mother's shoulder, sobbing hard, this time for real.

Elliot took out the handcuffs he carried at the back of his belt and approached Alana. "It's time to go, come on."

"There's also the matter of a pesky little murder charge," Kay added.

Alana turned as if she'd been bit by a snake. "I didn't kill Jenna! I was with—"

"She was here, with me," Alexandria said.

"No, she wasn't. She was with her boyfriend, Nick, at the time of the murder."

"Then? Why are you charging my daughter with murder?"

Kay chuckled. "We're charging you, not Alana."

Alexandria let go of her daughter's shoulders and took a step back. Her hand rushed to her chest. "Me? What reason could I possibly have to kill that girl?"

"One of the oldest in the book," Kay replied. "Jealousy. How long have you been sleeping with your daughter's boyfriend?"

Alana stopped crying instantly, her eyes filling with tear-drying rage. "What? Is that true?" She didn't wait for her answer, just pounced, trying to pull at her mother's hair with both her hands. "I hate you!"

Alexandria pushed her back, placing her hands against Alana's throat and squeezing until the girl choked.

Elliot grabbed Alana, holding her flailing arms and leading her away from her mother. Kay reached for Alexandria, but before she could grab her arm, the woman lunged at Kay, trying to slap her across the face. Kay dodged the blow and caught Alexandria's wrist, then slapped the handcuffs on it.

"That's exactly what's putting you in jail for life, Mrs. Keaney, this kind of blow you were just aiming at me," Kay said, taking the woman outside. "That's how Jenna landed at the bottom of Wildfire Ridge, isn't it? Was it because the boys didn't finish her off like you'd hoped?"

"Lawyer," Alexandria hissed at her, trying to free herself from Kay's grip.

"Yeah, you'll get one, don't worry. I think you knew from your daughter's messages that Nick was starting to like Jenna. I believe you read Alana's notes to Nick, where she was telling him he couldn't date anyone else but her, with specific reference to Jenna and a certain time when they chatted at school a little longer than your daughter would've liked. That was last March, right before the smear campaign against Jenna started."

Kay paused for a moment. Alana was staring at her slack-jawed, perplexed, but her focus was on Alexandria, who had turned deathly pale. "I guess, in your warped mind, it was okay for Nick to be with your daughter, but no one else, huh? I also believe you found out that Alana was instigating those boys to go after her, and you went up there on the ridge to make sure they did a good, thorough job."

"You went through my messages?" Alana shouted. "You read my stuff? You fucking bitch! Dad was right, you're a whore. I never want to see you again," she spat between sobs. "How could you do this to me?"

"Any responsible parent follows their kid's online activities," Elliot said, a tinge of humor coloring his voice. "Very few take matters as far as your mother has. That's a first for me." He opened the door and led Alana to the deputies waiting in the driveway. "I have to meet this Nick fellow. He seems to know how to get to a lady's heart."

Kay swallowed a chuckle, then looked at her partner. He'd just turned over Alana to Deputy Hobbs, who was reading her rights before loading her into his vehicle. Her partner's face was back to normal, but when their eyes locked, he blushed again. It would be a while before he'd forget he had showed her another man's dick pic.

Deputy Farrell took Alexandria from Kay. She was still struggling to break free.

"Separate vehicles," Kay instructed. "Separate cells too." Then she looked at Alexandria's feet, wondering. "What size shoes do you wear?"

"Lawyer," Alexandria snapped. "That's all I'm saying."

"She's about a size eight," Farrell replied. "Why?"

"After you load her, see if you can find an athletic pair of shoes size eight in their house. Pack them and tag them, and bring them in. I bet they match the footprints we found at the scene."

"Will do," Denise Farrell replied, putting her hand on Alexandria's head as she loaded her into her SUV.

Kay looked at Alexandria with curiosity. She'd had it all. A perfect house, a beautiful daughter, no worries about making ends meet financially. Good health and good looks. Still, she'd thrown everything away with both hands the moment she'd slept with her daughter's boyfriend.

Then her thoughts went to Jenna. Probably she hadn't even been looking in Nick's direction. She'd loved Tim. There was no mention of Nick in her diary. She'd been bullied, raped, and killed for nothing, for a figment of Alana's imagination. And everyone around Jenna had ganged up on her, quick to rip her to shreds.

Kay straightened her back and filled her lungs with fresh air loaded with the scent of Monterey cypress. Elliot came to her, rubbing his hands together, satisfied.

"Guess what? They found traces of Rohypnol on a jacket Gaskell left behind in his Jeep. We nailed him for Jenna's rape."

She grinned widely. "When did you call for backup?" she asked.

"After I saw the phone transcripts. I replied to Farrell's email and asked for two units. I knew it was gonna be like herding cats, collaring those two." He shifted his weight from one foot to another, seeming undecided about something. "Hey, I need your help," he eventually said. "I'm having a hard time with someone."

FIFTY-TWO
RIGHTS

"What's going on?" Kay asked, as soon as Elliot set the SUV in motion.

Elliot didn't speak at once. He looked into the distance, seemingly lost in thought as if trying to figure out what he should share. "For a few days, now, I've been distrusted and treated as if I'm a liar." He flashed a quick glance in her direction, then focused on the road. He took the ramp to the highway slower than he usually did. "I lie to perps during interrogations like we all do, but that's not it. The stuff I'm talking about is personal."

Kay frowned. "What are you talking about?"

"I'm talking about when people no longer look me in the eye, as if my word isn't worth a tin can of buzzard bait. It's people I trust and appreciate, whose opinion matters to me, and they don't find it in their hearts to tell me what's wrong. I might be dumber than a cart of river boulders and maybe I'm missing something, but I sure as hell don't lie."

He drove past the exit for her house, but she didn't say anything, preoccupied with his words. "Who's giving you a hard time? Is it someone we work with?"

He shot her another quick glance. "It's you."

Her breath caught. "Oh." She barely whispered the word, more like mouthed it. He was right, though. He was an intelligent cop with great instincts, and he was bound to figure it out at some point. She should've seen it coming. He deserved better than what she'd dished lately. Much better. But being open with him meant showing her feelings, and she wasn't ready for that.

"I don't know what to say. I'm sorry. I should've—"

"Will you help me with my problem?" he asked, a smile fluttering on his lips and tingeing his voice.

There was only one thing she could do, although she was dreading it already, seeing he was slowing down, ready to take the exit for his place. "Sure, partner, why not?"

They drove the rest of the way to his place in a loaded, tense silence as Kay braced herself for what was about to happen. He'd insisted she meet Miranda before, and that was probably what he was planning to do, although she couldn't think of a reason why that would help.

When they arrived, the house seemed empty. No lights were on, although the sun had passed over the tree line and was about to set. Shadows were long, as long as the seconds that dragged on forever, fraying Kay's nerves.

He got out of the SUV and beckoned her to follow him. She did, struggling to keep her heart steady and her face relaxed, when she was cringing inside. If she were that woman, and her partner dragged some thirty-year-old blonde from work to meet her after staying late every day? She'd be at her throat in no time flat.

Surprisingly, Elliot walked around the house and headed toward the fenced acreage he called a backyard. He lived in a small farmhouse, placed on a couple of acres of lush pasture. The house was just as dark in the back, but he kept on walking until he left it behind, heading for the barn.

"Wait here," he said, "it's dark inside."

He unlocked the barn and walked in. Moments later, he came out, holding a horse by the reins.

"Kay, this is Miranda." He patted the horse's neck, then whispered next to the animal's ear. "Miranda, this is Kay."

Relief flushed over her, bringing tears in her eyes. She laughed out loud. "Miranda is a horse? I thought—"

"Yeah, I know." He looked at her with a hint of that secret amusement in his eyes.

All this time she'd been fuming over his secret woman, and he knew exactly what was going on. She wanted to strangle him, but it wasn't his fault. He'd offered to introduce her to Miranda the first time she'd visited.

"May I?" she gestured toward the horse. She was beautiful, his Miranda, a reddish-brown color with a white star on her head. She was snorting and sniffing the air toward her, then she nodded once, slowly, as if saying hello.

"Let me read you your Miranda rights," he said, smiling widely. "You have the right to visit her whenever you'd like. You have the right to ride her, and feed her an apple a day, to keep the horse doctor away. You have the right to bring her baby carrots, she loves those.".

Kay laughed again, approaching the horse. She held her hand out, letting the fine animal sniff her, then touched the side of her neck, scratching gently. The horse drew near and looked at her without blinking.

"May I ride her? Really?" She couldn't stop laughing at herself, at how foolish she'd been.

"Yes, really, if you're up to it." He put Miranda's reins in her hand and went inside the barn, then returned with a saddle. He put it on the horse's back and tightened the girths. Then he looked at her for a long moment. "And you have the right to always tell me what's wrong."

She lowered her head, ashamed, feeling her cheeks on fire,

afraid he'd see right through her. Probably that moment had passed already, or she wouldn't be there. For a beat, she wished he would sweep her off her feet and melt her heart with a kiss.

He didn't move, and she was left waiting, wanting, until she finally pulled away, then resumed scratching Miranda's neck. "I thought, because the night lamp was on the other side of the bed, and the sheets were, um, never mind," she laughed.

"You assumed, when there was no real evidence." He patted the saddle. "Here, hop on. Have you done this before?"

"When I was eight, my mom took me for a pony ride for my birthday," she admitted humbly. "I might fall. She's tall."

"She's also very gentle, she won't throw you off. Hold the reins, yes, like that. Grab this, it's called the horn." He pointed at the front of the saddle at something that looked like a vertical handle. "Right hand on the back of the saddle. Left foot here."

She slipped her left foot into the stirrup, hopping in place on one foot as the horse moved and feeling ridiculous. She wasn't going to make it. "I—let's not—"

"Now pull yourself up as if jumping over a big hurdle. Shift your weight over to your left foot, then straighten it and throw your right leg over her rump."

Too embarrassed to back down, she did as instructed and felt his strong hands on her waist helping her, his touch setting her blood on fire. She settled into the saddle and grinned widely, taking the reins and gently pulling them. The world looked different from the back of a horse, and she loved every moment of it.

"Remember, she's very gentle," Elliot added, giving her a head-to-toe look with unspoken pride in his eyes. "Now, hold the reins like this, between the pinkie and the ring finger, and then put your thumbs up top. You get excellent control like that. Don't pull the reins, or she'll walk backward. Just straighten your back, nice and tall, and squeeze her with your legs a little when you're ready to go."

She did, and Miranda set off in motion slowly. After a few steps, she pulled the reins just a little, and she stopped. Thrilled, she beamed at Elliot. "Do I get to say yeehaw?"

He walked over and stopped by her side.

She leaned forward slightly, patting the side of Miranda's neck and getting familiar with how it felt to be in the saddle. "What?" she asked, seeing how he was looking at her. There was an intensity in his gaze, something she'd never seen before.

"You're missing something," he said, then took off his hat and put it on her head.

A LETTER FROM LESLIE

A big, heartfelt ***thank you*** for choosing to read *The Girl on Wildfire Ridge*. If you did enjoy it and want to keep up to date with all my latest releases, just sign up at the following link. Your email address will never be shared, and you can unsubscribe at any time.

www.bookouture.com/leslie-wolfe

When I write a new book I think of you, the reader, what you'd like to read next, how you'd like to spend your leisure time, and what you most appreciate from the time spent in the company of the characters I create, vicariously experiencing the challenges I lay in front of them. That's why I'd love to hear from you! Did you enjoy *The Girl on Wildfire Ridge*? Would you like to see Detective Kay Sharp and her partner, Elliot Young, return in another story? Your feedback is incredibly valuable to me, and I appreciate hearing your thoughts. Please contact me directly through one of the channels listed below. Email works best: LW@WolfeNovels.com. I will never share your email with anyone, and I promise you'll receive an answer from me!

If you enjoyed my book and if it's not too much to ask, please take a moment and leave me a review, and maybe recommend *The Girl on Wildfire Ridge* to other readers. Reviews and personal recommendations help readers discover new titles or new authors for the first time; it makes a huge difference and it means the world to me. Thank you for your support, and I hope to keep you entertained with my next story. See you soon!

Thank you,

Leslie

www.LeslieWolfe.com

facebook.com/wolfenovels
bookbub.com/authors/leslie-wolfe

Made in the USA
Monee, IL
30 September 2022